TRAIN'S CLASH

TRAIN'S CLASH

THE LAST RIDERS, #9

JAMIE BEGLEY

Train's Clash

Young Ink Press Publication
YoungInkPress.com

Copyright © 2016 by Jamie Begley

Edited by C&D Editing &
Diamond in the Rough Editing
Cover Art by Young Ink Press
Map by C&D Editing

All rights reserved.

Connect with Jamie,
JamieBegley@ymail.com
www.facebook.com/AuthorJamieBegley
www.JamieBegley.net

ISBN: 1946067024
ISBN-13: 9781946067029

Map of
Treepoint, Kentucky

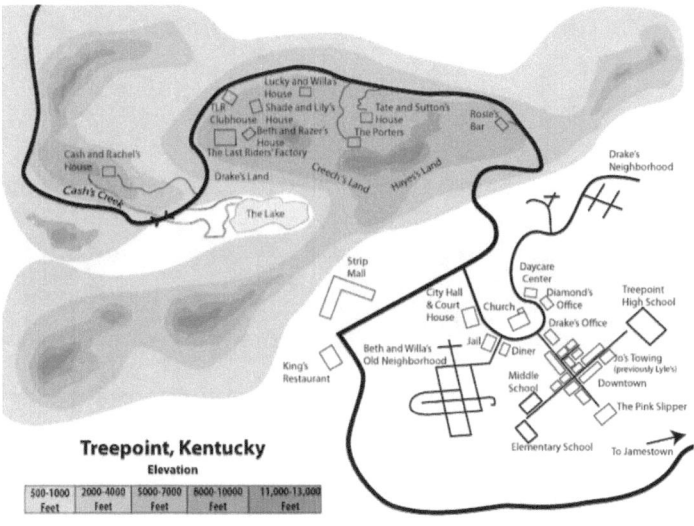

Treepoint, Kentucky
Elevation

500-1000 Feet	2000-4000 Feet	5000-7000 Feet	8000-10000 Feet	11,000-13,000 Feet

PROLOGUE

Killyama juggled the grocery bag in one hand and a six-pack of beer in the other as she unlocked the door. Swinging it inward, she walked inside then slammed it shut with her foot.

"Don't bother helping," she snapped at the man lounging on the couch.

He clicked the remote, turning off the television, and then stood indolently, his tall body only hinting at the muscles underneath the faded denim and T-shirt. He walked toward her as she set the groceries and beer on the counter.

Turning back toward him, she was met with a hard smack across the face that sent her back against the counter.

As her fingers went to the corner of her mouth, coming away with blood, he taunted, "You're getting slow."

At that, Killyama swung her fist out, trying to nail him in the gut, but he sidestepped and caught her fist. Then she jerked her other hand up, nailing him under the chin. However, he didn't release her.

They began to struggle against each other. He knocked her against the round table next to the kitchen table, causing his dirty breakfast plate to fall to the floor as she found herself lying back across the table. Taking her shot, she lifted her booted foot to kick him in the balls as he tried to pin her hands to the table.

"Son of a fucking bitch! You always go for the balls."

"Hammer, if you know that, you should watch them better." Killyama snickered, sitting up on the table as he bent over, trying to catch his breath from the pain.

When he regained himself, he hobbled to the counter, taking a beer out of the carton and twisting off the top. "Want one?"

"What do you think?"

Hammer tossed one to her then watched as she opened the bottle.

"Getting bored already?" she asked.

He took a long drink of his own beer before answering, "Yes. I don't know why you have to live in this small-ass town."

"I like it, and my friends are all here. You don't have to stay. You could stay anywhere you want."

"That's true, but who would watch your back?"

Killyama snorted. "Who would watch yours?"

Hammer set his beer down on the counter. "I got called up for an assignment."

"How bad?" She kept her expression neutral, knowing he would mock any concern she had.

"If they call me in, it's bad." He began picking up the broken dishes from the floor, tossing them into the trash. "Do you know where my paperwork is, in case I don't come back?"

Her hand tightened on the beer as she took another sip. It wasn't strong enough to numb the fear she felt over him leaving.

"They say Fiji is nice this time of year," she joked past the lump in her throat, knowing that was what he expected of her.

"I can pick my own crew," he told her, ignoring her attempt at humor.

She narrowed her eyes at him, seeing the impassivity on his face, before he quickly lowered his eyes.

"Don't—"

"I need him. He's the best chopper pilot in hot areas. If I'm going to bring my men out of there alive, I need him."

"Or none of you will come out alive; is that what you're trying to say?"

Hammer crossed his arms over his chest. "Yeah, I guess it is."

Finishing her beer, Killyama scooted off the table and placed the empty bottle next to his. "I guess it doesn't matter what I say. I've begged you to quit taking these assignments, yet you still do. Now you're going to take—"

"Dammit, Rae, I don't want to leave with you pissed off at me!"

"Then you're shit out of luck!" she snapped, picking up her car keys.

"Where are you going? I need to leave in an hour."

"Drive your own damn self to the airport, or get Jonas to drive you."

"I was kinda hoping you would tell Jonas for me."

She scoffed. "I guess you're really super fucked, then." Angrily, she went to the door where she paused, her hand on the doorknob. She tried to control the tremble in her voice, not wanting to expose the turmoil that had her wanting to beg him to stay, as she told him without looking back, "Be careful."

"I will."

Killyama nodded, opening the door, and then paused again. "Do me a favor?"

"What?"

"Make sure you bring Train back. If anyone's going to kill that fucker, it's going to be me."

&0 CR

"Tell me again, exactly, why the hell we're sitting in the parking lot of Sex Piston's beauty shop?"

Train ignored Rider's aggravated complaining, watching for the woman who drove him crazy. Any other time, Killyama would be hanging out at Sex Piston's shop. However, they had been sitting there for the last couple of hours with a no-show from her.

"You're going to miss your flight."

Train ignored Rider's reminder for the third time, but he did glance down at his watch, seeing Rider was right; whether she showed up or not, he was going to have to leave.

Just then, an ugly green car pulled into the parking lot, coming to a stop. His dick went hard before she even stepped out of the car.

"Sex Piston's clients don't have dicks," she smarted off at his door before he could even step out.

Train kept his mouth shut, determined not to get into an argument with her this time. He had already anticipated her friends tipping her off that he had been hanging out.

He put up his guard before telling her, "I'm not here for Sex Piston. I wanted to see you."

"Fucker, we don't have a word to say to one another." Placing her hands on her hips, she cocked a hip out.

"That's where you're wrong." He took a step toward her. "I'm going out of town, and I plan to settle this between us before I leave."

Killyama shot him a killing glance. "Spit it out, then."

Train was surprised she had given in so easily until he realized Sex Piston and her crew were watching from inside the shop.

"The day we went for a ride and ended up fucking each other—"

"Asshole, I don't need you to remind me."

"Hear me just one damn time, Killyama!" he yelled.

Her mouth snapped closed.

Taking a deep breath, he continued, "When I told you I wouldn't fuck you again, I didn't mean it the way it sounded."

"So, you're saying what?" She slid her hands into the back pockets of her leather pants, rocking her feet back and forth. "You would have done me again?"

"Maybe. What I was trying to tell you was that I don't fuck women more than once who don't belong to The Last Riders."

"So, the only way you would do me again is if I became a Last Rider?"

"Yes."

Killyama stared at him in silence, something Train didn't take as a good sign, thinking she would rather chop her left tit off than become a Last Rider. Then she broke eye contact as Rider rolled down the window.

"Train, we've gotta go."

She angrily jerked the truck door open. "Yeah, you don't want to miss your flight. We don't have a damn thing to talk about, anyway."

"Killy—"

"Don't call me that! We're done talking."

Train felt his hands clench into fists. Just like every other time he tried to talk to her, it had ended up in an argument. Just once, he wished the funny, sexy woman who had gone for a ride with him would show again. He wanted to see the woman who had brazenly tried to ride his bike, who didn't have a shy bone in her body, and who was the one who had made the first move between them, igniting a fire that hadn't been put out since that day.

"Yes, we are," he growled.

Before he could change his mind, Train pinned her to the hood, thinking, *Damn! It couldn't feel as good as the last time I kissed her.* However, when his tongue entered her mouth, he had to admit he had been mistaken. It was even better.

"You have exactly two seconds to get your hands off my bitch," Sex Piston snarled at the exact moment he felt cold steel pressed against the back of his head.

Lingering, he released her lips, yet whispered against them, "We're not done." He then held a soft kiss against her lips for an infinite second.

She pushed him away. "Yes, we are."

In another second, he was surrounded by women who could make any dick shrivel. That's when Train noticed Rider, who was a scared little bitch, hadn't volunteered to have his back.

Train stepped up to the truck. "I'll see you in three months. Don't forget me."

"Dude, you're already a memory," Killyama said as she turned away.

After shutting the door, Train rolled down the window. "Don't worry; I'll remind you when I see you again."

Before she or any one of the other bitches could say anything else, he hit the door as Rider drove away, the wind blowing strands of hair into his face.

"You do know that was a loaded pistol pointed at you, right?"

"Killyama wouldn't have let her kill me."

Rider shook his head at him.

"Don't worry," Train assured. "I'm not stupid enough to under-estimate her or those friends of hers."

"Really?" Rider spared him a glance as he drove onto the inter-state. "Then tell me something."

"What?" Train pulled a rubber band out of his pocket before dragging his hair behind his head.

"How did Killyama know you were going on a flight?"

CHAPTER ONE

"Are you out of your fucking mind?"

"Are you going to help me or not?" Killyama swung her legs off the side of the hospital bed. Swaying, she grabbed the handrail to keep herself from taking a nose dive toward the floor.

"Lay your ass back down." Sex Piston lifted her feet back onto the bed.

"I want to go home," Killyama complained, laying her head down on the pillow and closing her eyes. She had to fight back the dizziness, taking deep breaths to calm the nausea that had her gut in a vice grip.

"What's the damn hurry?" Sex Piston slid the handrail up, preventing her from trying to get out of bed again. "You only got out of surgery five hours ago; the doctor won't release you for another couple of days."

"I'm not asking for his permission. I want to get out here before…" Killyama looked toward the doorway as the door opened after a brief knock.

The reason she had been trying to get away walked through the door behind Lucky.

Crowding into the small room, the two men ignored the women huddled around her bed. Her friends hadn't left her side since they had met the ambulance at the Jamestown Hospital after she had been shot trying to save The Last Riders' president's wife.

Winter had gone into labor during a home invasion that had only one objective: to kill Winter and Viper. Anyone else who had thwarted that goal was simply collateral damage. Raul Silva had a

1

score to settle with The Last Riders and the Destructors after putting an end to his cartel's tyranny in a small town over the Mexican border.

Lucky came to stand at the foot of her bed as Train leaned against the wall underneath the small television set mounted high on the wall.

"How are you doing?"

"I'm still breathing." Killyama focused on Lucky, ignoring Train as if he weren't even in the room.

It wasn't easy ignoring him since the biker was tall, even with his frame leaning against the wall. His black hair was pulled back in a ponytail, legs braced apart, and his muscular forearms showed under the black jacket he had pushed up to his elbows. His skin was dark, hinting a Native-American heritage, with high cheekbones and a sensual mouth. He had a sex appeal that could hit a woman any time he entered a room, and the fucker knew it.

"I can see that." Lucky's lips twisted in humor. "Stud called when you came out of surgery and said the doctor didn't think there wouldn't be any lasting damage."

"I heard that Viper's kid isn't doing well."

Lucky's humor vanished. "No, she isn't. That's why I'm here and not Viper. He wants me, as vice president, to extend our gratitude to you and Sex Piston on his behalf."

"Well, aren't you being all fancy talking." She looked away from the two men's gazes, not wanting them to see how concerned she was for Winter and the baby's condition.

Everyone who knew her thought she didn't have a soft bone in her body. She hated soft-spoken bitches who could cry at the drop of a hat. Killyama prided herself on holding her own, no matter what she was up against. She had no intention of dropping her heartless façade in front of these two men.

"It's a serious topic. The Last Riders don't take what you both did lightly. Anything you want, if it is within our power, we'll take care of it."

Sex Piston swung her head toward Lucky. "We'll call it even. You don't owe me shit. If Raul had lived, everyone knows that fucker would have come after Stud, Cade, and Fat Louise. Besides, I only held Winter's hand. Killyama is the reason we got out alive."

Killyama averted her eyes from Sex Piston. If the bitch got mushy in front of the men, she would bitch slap her, right after she hugged her.

Lucky nodded at Sex Piston, and then turned toward Killyama. "How about you? You need a new ride? That car you drive is a piece of crap. The muffler is held on with a zip-tie."

"Don't need a car," Killyama refused. She could tell from Train's stiffening stance he had expected her to jump on the chance of getting rid of the car. "It's a classic. Just because it's old doesn't mean I need to get rid of it."

"Take your time. Let me know when you decide—"

"Believe me; I will." Killyama sat up straight, almost laughing at the trepidation on both of their faces. "Scared, Train? Afraid I'll ask for another ride?"

"You want another ride, then all you have to do is ask." His indifferent shrug took all the fun out of baiting him. "I think saving Winter's life is worth more than a bike ride."

Unable to bite back the hateful words spilling out of her mouth, she caustically replied, "I agree, especially not one from you. From what I remember, a ride from you wasn't that great."

Red stole up from the neck of his T-shirt.

Sex Piston had a soft spot for the wives of The Last Riders. Many of them had become friends. Her best friend was just grateful that everyone had lived. However, sentiment didn't figure into Killyama's conscience when she needed to keep someone away from her. If she had to portray herself as a self-serving bitch in front of Train, so be it. It was better than him realizing the truth.

Bikers were notorious for living a free and easy lifestyle, yet The Last Riders took that lifestyle to new heights. The Destructors might screw the same women, but at least they fucked behind closed doors and didn't put on a show for everyone else to see. You couldn't say the same for The Last Riders, which was one of the reasons Killyama kept her guard up around him.

Lucky raised an eyebrow. "Is there someone else you would rather ride with?"

"Hell no. I bought my own bike. You can go back and tell Viper that when I decide what The Last Riders owe me, he'll be the first to know. Shade didn't have a problem calling in the IOU for getting Fat Louise out of Mexico, did he?"

Killyama felt Train's stare boring a hole through her. Thank God Sex Piston had talked Killyama into letting her fix her hair. The thought of Train seeing her hair filled with blood and matted against her head had the feminine side of her cringing. She fought hard to repress that side of her, but every now and then, it slipped out where he was concerned.

"No, he didn't." Lucky didn't let the sparks that were flying back and forth between her and Train faze him.

Killyama wanted Train gone, because whatever pain medicine they had given her was wearing off. However, neither man made a move to leave.

"Anything else?"

"Train, give me a minute."

Train didn't move from his position against the wall until Lucky turned to give him a look that Killyama couldn't see. When he straightened from his relaxed stance, she kept her eyes glued to Lucky, not wanting her expression to give her away.

Train was like a magnet that kept pulling her toward him, despite her mind telling her that she just needed to get laid. He lived in Treepoint, and she lived in Jamestown. They didn't run into each other that often, unless Sex Piston talked her into going to their town, so it would be a while before she would see him again.

When the door didn't open, Killyama lifted her eyes to meet his. He made sure she saw the ominous look promising retribution before he opened the door to leave.

After the door shut quietly behind him, Lucky gave his own warning. "Don't let Train fool you. He's not going to keep taking the disrespect you keep throwing at him."

"Train wants my respect, then he has to earn it. Just because I fuck a man once doesn't mean he's automatically getting it. He knows exactly what I think about him. If he has a problem with that, he can take it up with me. I don't need you or anyone else playing interference."

Lucky lost his affable expression. "I bet you played with matches when you were a kid."

"I still do. Train's the one you should be warning. I keep a fire extinguisher if I need it." If Train ever tried to lay a hand on her, he would find a forty-five shoved up his ass.

"I'll pass that on to him." Lucky nodded to the women raptly watching the exchange. "I better get going. I don't want to tire you out." More like she was tiring him out.

She lost her bitchy attitude when Lucky moved to the side of her bed, placing his hand on the arm that was covered in bandages and hanging in a sling.

"Thank you, from all of The Last Riders. May God bless you for being there when Winter and the baby needed you."

Killyama remained silent as Lucky prayed for her recovery and then left them when he finished with the somber reality that a child was still fighting for her life.

"I feel so bad for Winter and the baby." Fat Louise's lip trembled.

"We all do. I only wish I had been the one to put the bullet in Raul."

"Jackal may have pulled the trigger, but you made it possible." Crazy Bitch sat down on the bottom of her bed. "I nearly pissed myself from laughing when Sex Piston told us about you swatting the gun toward Jackal with your flip-flop."

"Best dollar and ninety-nine cents I ever spent." Killyama laughed with her friends.

"You're really going to ask them for payback?" T.A.'s question had the laughter coming to a sudden stop.

"Do I look stupid? It's not every day that I can have The Last Riders at my beck and call."

Fat Louise shook her head, giving her a reproachful look. "That's not why you saved her."

Fat Louise had always been the softest-hearted in their crew who had formed a bond during high school. However, her marriage and the birth of her now three-month old son had turned her into a tender-hearted sap.

"No, I did it to save Sex Piston and my own life. Winter was just a bonus."

"Bullshit." Sex Piston pinned her with a steely gaze. "I saw you jumping Raul, blocking Winter with your own body. You were ready to martyr yourself to save her, just like when you saved me from those six bitches who jumped me on the school bus."

Killyama picked up the television remote, turning up the volume, and Sex Piston took it away from her, turning it off.

"You want to hold it over Train's head, don't you? When are you going to get over him? He damn sure isn't pining over you."

"No, he isn't." Killyama dropped her lashes, shielding her eyes. Damn, she felt like crap, and Sex Piston telling her what she already knew didn't help.

Her probing gaze had Killyama trying to sidetrack her friend. "Don't think I forgot you didn't run when I told you to."

"We made a pact in high school to always be there when we need each other. I wasn't leaving you alone."

"The fierce five are still standing strong, aren't we?" Killyama reached out, and Sex Piston took her hand, linking her other hand to Fat Louise's, who reached for Crazy Bitch's, who turned to T.A., who got off the bed to take her hand. "Bitches rule. Boys drool." Killyama spoke the silly chant they promised to keep. "From fat to slim, from bad hair days and bad tatts, we swear never to steal each other's boyfriends, or never talk about each other behind our backs—"

"I might have broken that one," Sex Piston interrupted.

Killyama saw Crazy Bitch elbow her without releasing her hand.

"Or stop driving the green cherry breaker we all lost our virginity in—"

"Didn't Sex Piston lie about that one? Ouch!" Fat Louise complained when T.A pinched her with her free hand.

"Despite husbands with big bikes and bratty kids, we'll be friends, side by side to the end of fucking time."

"Technically, Sex Piston moved away," Crazy Bitch reminded them.

"Bitch, cut me some slack. I drive to town every day just to be with you all." Sex Piston tried to drop her hands, but they didn't let her.

"Um...You never said...Just how big is Stud's bike?" T.A. sniggered. "How do we know you didn't break that rule, too?"

"I told you about Cade. You all didn't stop hounding me about the bitch's code until I did," Fat Louise voiced.

Killyama fought sleep to hear Sex Piston's answer.

"Shut up. Stud didn't get his nickname by driving a moped."

CHAPTER TWO

When Train heard footsteps coming down the hall, his hand instinctively tightened in Sasha's hair as she sucked on his cock. Even though he knew it was one of the brothers heading toward their room, the sound of heavy footfalls always brought back memories from his childhood that were better left forgotten. He had learned before entering the military that evil uses darkness to strike their unwary victims.

He could tell from the footfalls that it was Rider, and when he heard the door across the hall from his open yet not close, he loosened his hold, letting Sasha slide his dick farther down her tight throat.

"What's wrong?" Jewell lifted her head from the mattress, tightening her thighs over his shoulder as she pulled him back down to her glistening pussy.

"Nothing." Train lowered his mouth, obeying her silent demand. Pressing his lips on the eager pussy, he created a suction around Jewell's opening that had both of her thighs gripping his shoulders even tighter.

"Damn...that feels *so* damn good," she said on a moan, twisting the covers.

Train didn't break the hold he had created. Using his tongue, he delved between the lips of her pussy, exploring her as if he had never tasted her before. He could feel her thighs shaking as he built her toward an orgasm.

"More..."

Train lifted his head, leaving her pussy with a swipe of his tongue across her clit. "I can't give you more unless Sasha is willing to give up my dick."

Sasha shook her head, unable to talk with his dick in her mouth.

Train moved his hips to give her more, burying his cock to the root. Then he reached out, touching her throat where he could see the outline of his cock.

"That's sexy as fuck." His praise had Sasha doubling her efforts to please him.

"Then yell for Rider..." Jewell panted.

Train lifted himself on his elbow to stare down at her humorlessly. "You think I need another man to handle two women?"

Jewell's face went white. "No...No, I-I only meant..." Jewell stuttered to a stop. The woman knew if she pissed him off, it would be a while before she worked herself back into his bed.

"You want my dick more than Sasha does?" Train combed his fingers through Sasha's hair, slipping his cock from her airway long enough for her to take a deep breath before plunging back in again.

"I want to come!" Jewell pleaded, dropping her legs to the mattress and turning so she could scoot down his body, making room for herself between his legs.

She moved her mouth below Sasha's, finding his balls, where she sucked one into her mouth then alternated to the other one until he broke out in a cold sweat. He barely managed to keep himself from coming.

Train stared down at the two women diligently working on his cock. "Stop, Sasha."

Her sultry face dropped in disappointment as she moved to his side.

"Ride me, Jewell."

He didn't have to ask her twice. She slung one leg over his hip, grabbed a rubber and quickly put it on him before poising her pussy over his dick and dropping down on him with a groan.

"You needed that bad, didn't you?"

Jewell licked her bottom lip as she nodded.

"Come here." He held out his hand to Sasha, and she took it, moving closer to his shoulder. Train raised himself up to lean back against the headboard and ordered, "Stand up." Then he maneuvered her so she was standing, straddled over him, making him eye-level with her pussy. "Now, isn't that a pretty sight?"

He gently licked her, building her desire until her clit quivered under his tongue. He used his hand to part her fleshy lips, seeing the throbbing center of her desire.

Jewell was pounding herself down on him as he licked Sasha to an orgasm, while Sasha stood over him, holding on to the headboard.

"I wish I had my phone. I'd take a picture of this," Sasha told him. "The women at the Ohio clubhouse would be jealous as fuck if they saw. They all want you to come back to stay again."

He used one of his fingers to enter her opening, spreading her juices to make his entry easier. Sasha might fuck a lot, but she was one of the tightest women he had ever had.

"Am I hurting you?" he asked when he added another finger.

"No!" She shoved her pussy further into his face, demanding more.

Train cupped her ass cheek to hold her steady. His balls tightened as Jewell's pussy clenched around him like a vice.

He slapped at Sasha's clit with his tongue as he felt her come on his fingers. Taking her by the waist, he then lowered her to his side before she dropped down on him.

"That was fun. Can we do it again? This time, I want your dick." Sasha leaned over to plant a kiss on his mouth.

He licked her bottom lip before plunging his tongue inside, giving her the taste of herself.

When he pulled away, he told her, "It might take me a couple of minutes, but I'm game." He looked down at Jewell. "How about you?"

Jewell pulled herself off his limp dick to lie down on his other side. "You know me; there isn't much I'm not up for."

Train scooted himself down between the two women. He lazily played with Jewell's nipple with one hand, and with the other, he kept Sasha's orgasm on a slow burn by rubbing her throbbing clit.

Sasha shifted to her side, moving her arm to his waist and making his cock accessible to her searching hand. "You're already getting hard again. Moon is quick on the draw, but I think you have him beat." She playfully bit down on his shoulder.

Train turned his head to give her a warning glare. "Don't leave a mark. I don't like that shit."

She stopped immediately. "Sorry."

He twined a hand around her neck before pulling her down to kiss her pouty lips, taking the sting away from his words.

Train had fucked long enough to know that, when a woman left a mark, they considered it a mark of possession. He didn't belong to any one woman, and he never would. Monogamy was for a man who worked from nine to five.

He believed playing to his strengths. He was the man to call when someone needed something done. He could fly his chopper through war-torn areas and never break a sweat, but the thought of putting a ring on a woman's finger gave him nightmares.

Jewell stirred next to him, wanting her own share of his attention.

Train squeezed her tit, plumping it up. Then he tore his mouth from Sasha's ravenous lips to pluck the tip between his teeth, giving her the bite of pain he knew she craved. He took his time rebuilding the women's desires and his own.

They were all going to be tired as fuck in the morning after the night's excessiveness. Him and Jewell were used to working with little to no sleep, but Sasha was going to be miserable when he had to drag her ass out of bed in the morning.

Moving Sasha's hand away to fix another condom on his dick, he then pulled her underneath him without releasing Jewell's breast. Train slid his dick into her slippery pussy, thrusting hard enough that both women bounced on the bed. He had deliberately worked her desire high enough that she could take him in her tight cunt.

"You okay?" Train watched the myriad of expressions cross her face as he fucked her while moving his hand down to Jewell's pussy.

"Oh...yes!"

Train fucked her, never losing the control that had Sasha screaming out her orgasm in the lighted bedroom. Then, when he would have moved off her, Sasha's grip around his waist tightened.

Train stiffened. "Let go."

He didn't miss the fleeting, mutinous expression she tried to hide. Sasha might not know it yet, but it would be the last time she was invited to share his bed.

Twisting his hips to the side, he removed the condom, tossing it into the trashcan next to his bed before taking another off his nightstand.

"Get on your knees, Jewell."

The woman eagerly got into position, turning her ass up toward him. Jewell was a constant bed partner of his, so he didn't have to exercise the same control he had to with Sasha.

He rode her long and hard with Sasha watching. He didn't touch her again, when usually, Train made sure all participants received their own portion of attentiveness. However, she had broken his cardinal rule by letting her possessiveness show.

It was the reason he had joined The Last Riders—the women had to share them. Anyone unable to follow that rule wasn't made a member. It was a rule that kept everyone happy. It took the jealously out of the relationships they shared, not only from the women, but with the men as well. They were all on equal footing, which kept the men from the fights that plagued other MCs.

The men who belonged to The Last Riders were dangerous and deadly. Most, if not all, had served in the military and had firsthand experience of losing friends in the heat of anger.

Feeling Jewell coming on his dick, Train allowed himself to orgasm, relaxing his control long enough to enjoy the sensations coursing through his body.

Jewell dropped down to the mattress. "I can't move."

Train slid out of bed, giving her an affectionate pat on her ass. "Go to sleep. I'll wake you in time to get ready for work." Then, naked, he went out into the hallway to the bathroom next door to his room.

Most of the bedrooms had bathrooms; his didn't. Viper had offered him the bedroom that used to be his before he had built his own house on the opposite side of the factory, but Train had refused. He was content in his small room, just as he was about being a soldier in the club.

Rider's door was open, so Train casually looked inside, seeing him fucking Stori. He didn't interrupt, ignoring the silent invitation that the open door meant.

When any of the brothers wanted privacy, they kept their doors closed. An open door indicted that, if anyone wanted to participate, all they had to do was go inside. Whoever's room it was would tell them just how far they would be allowed to play. Some of the brothers liked to put on a show, while others had a no holds barred, figuratively.

As Train showered, he adjusted the height of the nozzle so his hair wouldn't get wet. He washed every inch of his body, the sexual satisfaction already disappearing, leaving the ache of longing that was never far away to return.

His dark eyes stared back him in mirror as he shaved after showering. Sasha and Jewell weren't going to be the only ones who were going to be tired in the morning. In fact, the weariness in his soul was becoming visible more and more as each day passed.

He wasn't a kid anymore. The late nights and fuck fests were beginning to take a toll on him. The pussy and the pot might keep his memories at bay, but they came back as soon as the party was over.

When he left the bathroom, he saw that Stori was already asleep on Rider's bed, and Crash and Rider were sitting on the floor in front of the television set, playing video games.

"Train!"

He stopped before entering his own door at Crash's call, moving toward Rider's door. "Yeah?"

"I found the info you wanted. It's on Rider's desk."

Train moved from Rider's doorway, going to his desk. He picked up the plain folder sitting on top. "Why didn't you just email it to me?"

Crash laughed. "Emails can be hacked."

Crash was a hacker with a gift. There wasn't a computer he couldn't get into. It might take time, but he would find some way to breach the defenses. The harder the job, the more he took it as a challenge.

"It's a big file."

"You wanted everything I could find on Killyama. It's in there. Viper also asked for a copy. Guess he's worried about the IOU he promised."

"I asked for her information before, and you couldn't get it; how'd you get it now?"

"Emails are the windows to the soul, my friend. Remember that."

Crash maneuvered his joystick with a dexterity that Rider couldn't keep up with. Rider slammed his own controller down on the floor when his spacecraft erupted into a ball of flames.

"Besides, I don't know what you're bitchin' about. I gave the folder to Shade a year ago and told him to pass it on to you. I just updated it when Shade gave it back to me last week."

"Thanks."

Irritated, Train left the bedroom, anxious to read what was contained in the folder. If it weren't so late, he would call Shade. The brother had promised to pass any information he had found on Killyama.

When he returned to his room, he found both Sasha and Jewell fast asleep.

Turning off the light on the nightstand, he then turned on the one at his desk before opening the folder and starting to read.

He was dead tired. By just the first page, it was hard to keep sleep at bay. By the end of the folder, two hours later, though, any desire for sleep had disappeared.

Closing the folder, he locked it in his drawer, wishing the women weren't sleeping in his bed so he could take his frustration out by punching a hole in a wall.

He had always known that convincing Killyama to join The Last Riders was a forlorn hope. What he had just read proved it.

His cell phone ringing had Train lifting it to his ear, even before he saw it was Viper calling.

"Did you read it?"

"I just finished. I'm going to kick Shade's ass in the morning."

"I know. He's not answering his phone." Not trying to hide his own fury, Viper's voice cracked like a whip through the cell phone.

"What are you going to do?" Train asked.

"What am *I* going to do? What are *you* going to do? You're the one with the hard-on for the bitch. I told you the brothers aren't

15

going to open their arms to her, anyway. It's not like you were serious about her, or are you?"

"I told you that I thought she would make a good Last Rider…if she could tone down her aggressiveness toward the other women… and men," Train added as an afterthought. "The problem is, from Crash's report, Killyama is not only business partners with them, they've been in her life since she was a little girl." Train brought his fingers to his eyes, pressing hard until he saw spots as he tried to figure a way out of the box he found himself trapped in. "If Hammer and Jonas find out I'm trying to convince her to join the club, they'll talk her out of it."

"Crash is sure they aren't related?"

"Crash doesn't make mistakes. There isn't a way of knowing for sure until he, or I, can find out who her father is. No father is listed, and her mother still lives in Jamestown." He sighed. "It couldn't have been easy growing up without a father. He thinks either Jonas or Hammer dated Killyama's mother at one time and drew close to her, stepping in as father figures."

"They did a hell of a job training her to take care of herself."

Viper's compliment was well deserved. The skills they had taught her had earned the respect of The Last Riders on more than one occasion.

"It explains how she took Raul down. She made a pretty penny when she collected the bounty on him."

"She shared the reward with Jackal and Fade's family. She makes good money working with Hammer and Jonas. Now I can understand why she didn't jump on the chance of me buying her a new car for saving Winter's life. I wish I had read Crash's report before I gave her my IOU. Money, I can come up with. What's making me nervous is her possibly asking me to track down any felons she's searching for. I need some breathing room after looking over my shoulder for Raul."

"What about the promise you made to me? The only reason I took the shit she was throwing at me was because of Raul. I didn't want to hurt her in the crossfire. When Shade called in the IOU when we saved Fat Louise, Shade cashed it in. You told me the club wouldn't interfere again between her and me." The members had agreed that, if he could talk Killyama into joining the club, they would give it a trial run to see if she could earn any votes.

Train held his phone away from his ear. The loud laughter had Sasha turning over in her sleep.

"Don't blame me. I put her IOU in the pot to be fair to everyone who helped. If you hadn't been drunk off your ass, you would have seen Shade was bluffing. You lost that pot because you wanted to."

Train clenched his jaw. "Are you saying I sabotaged myself?"

"I'm saying, don't bet more than you're willing to lose."

"I was already drunk when you threw it in the pot," Train reminded him. "I was the one who was sabotaged."

"Looks like you're going to have to get that woman the old-fashioned way."

"How? She won't talk to me."

"I don't know. That's your problem to deal with. I caught my woman."

"Not without some help. Who was the one who helped Rider carry that fucking big tub into your new house?"

"Brother, I didn't say I wasn't grateful. I don't know why you're bitching at me. I'm not the one cock-blocking you."

Viper was right. Train had fought wars that were easier than trying to seduce Killyama into his bed. She had been the one to walk away from the brief sexual encounter without a mark. He swore, if he thought hard enough, he could still feel her lips on his neck as she told him to fuck her harder.

His hand shook as he held the phone. He had to have her again. This time, in his bed. Whether it was just the two of them or others, he would leave that up to her to decide, but he had to get her there first.

"Shade says I'm wasting my time."

"Maybe you are. It's not like you don't have enough pussy to keep you busy."

"I want her." Train wasn't afraid to admit he had a fascination for the woman. He just wanted her on his own terms.

"I don't know what to tell you. Have you thought about asking Shade for his advice? They seemed to have gotten along when she paid off her debt."

"Son of bitch didn't even tell us that Killyama is a bounty hunter, and I know he knew. He kept telling me she could kick my ass. I should have known he wasn't joking around. The fucker doesn't have a funny bone in his body."

"Raul didn't know what he stepped into when he decided to attack Aunt Shay's house. Crash sent a couple of Killyama's arrest records; Raul didn't stand a chance against her. Killyama is used to trapping deadly felons."

"I read them." Train began massaging his temples. He was getting a headache just thinking about the reports he had read.

"You should still ask Shade. But I'm going to give you a piece of my own advice…From one brother to another, watch your balls."

CHAPTER THREE

"Wait...Killyama!" Jonas swung his arm out, blocking her from following the bail jumper down the dark alleyway.

Killyama skidded to a stop. "He'll get away!"

"He's not going anywhere. Hammer is moving the car to head him off. He's already called the cops. Let them flush Crawford out."

Damn, Killyama knew Jonas was right, but she had been looking forward to taking Crawford down. The scared pussy was determined not to go back to jail.

She saw the blue lights nearing them as they waited at the front of the alley. Putting her Glock into the holster at her hip, she pulled out the required paperwork she would have to show to the officer responding to Hammer's call.

Holding her hands up in the air when she saw two cops getting out of their car, she told them, "I'm Rae Stokes with No Escape Bail Bonds. I have an armed jumper who ran down the alley. I have another bondsman blocking the end."

The two police officers cautiously entered the alleyway, followed by others who had just arrived, while one stayed behind to check out her paperwork and their identifications.

Killyama bit back her irritation. She had wanted to be the one to flush Crawford out and have the pleasure of handcuffing him.

The officer had just handed back her paperwork when the other officers came out of the alley with Crawford, whose cooperation disappeared when he saw her.

Trying to struggle out of their restraining hold, he snapped, "Fucking bitch!"

"*I'm* the bitch? I paid fifty thousand to bail your sorry ass out of jail." Her professionalism slipped a notch at his foul language. If she didn't have so many eyes on her, she would punch his fucking lights out.

Jonas moved in front of her so Crawford wasn't near her as he was loaded into the squad car, telling her, "Hammer is here with the car." He then nodded toward the SUV parked on the street behind her.

Killyama angrily spun on her boots. "I don't need anyone trying to protect me from the jumpers."

"I wasn't protecting you. I was protecting him." He strode next to her, his long legs easily beating her to the vehicle.

Killyama opened the car door and jumped inside. It had been a long day of pursuing Crawford, and it wasn't over yet. In fact, it was after midnight before she left the jail where the jumper had been booked in. When the paperwork was done, she called dibs on the backseat, stretching out her legs to relax.

"You want me to find a hotel, or am I driving you home?" Hammer asked before they exited the parking garage.

"Let's go home. I can drive if you're too tired." Killyama scrolled down the text messages she had been too busy to answer during the day.

Hammer didn't answer as he pulled out onto the street.

"Everything okay in the office?" Jonas turned to look over his shoulder, watching as she read her messages.

Her lips tightened as she dropped her phone into her lap. "Yes, Venny said it was a slow day."

"Thank fuck. I need a day off. It's good to have you back." Hammer didn't take his eyes off the road as he gave the compliment.

"What? Did you hear that, Jonas? Aw, I knew you liked working with me."

"What choice do I have?" Hammer flicked the blinker as he accelerated to merge onto the interstate. "It was hire you, or attend your funeral when you got your ass killed. Besides, you can run faster than me and Jonas."

"A turtle can run faster than you two," she good-naturedly insulted the men in the front seat.

Jonas passed her a bottled water. "You have anything planned this weekend?"

"I have to go to a party that The Last Riders and Destructors are throwing."

Killyama didn't miss the look the men shared.

"The two clubs are having a party together?" Jonas was the one to ask the question they were both curious about.

"It's not like you're thinking. Jesus, I tell you one little secret about The Last Riders and you think all MCs are like them. The only thing the Destructors have in common with The Last Riders are motorcycles."

"You think so?" Hammer shook his head, disbelieving.

"I know so. What else could we have in common?"

"You seriously don't think the Destructors are doing some of the same women in their club?"

"Maybe, but at least they don't let others fucking watch." Killyama crushed the water bottle in her hand. "If you're so damn interested in The Last Riders, I'm surprised you two didn't join when you got out of the service."

"Neither Jonas nor I needed a club. We had families to go back home to."

"That one-room cabin isn't a home."

"It is to me. Besides, me and Jonas wouldn't fit in with The Last Riders. Most of them were in the Navy; we're Rangers. We lead the way."

She made sure Hammer and Jonas heard her mock gagging noises as they fist bumped in the front seat.

"You were probably worried they would see the needle dicks you two are packing."

"They would have been jealous."

Killyama held on to the armrest as Hammer's boasting had him swerving from taking the lane that was an exit. She needed to make sure her living will was up to date.

"Now I really want to throw up. Talking about your dicks is creeping me out."

"You were the one who brought it up."

"It's not like we're related," Jonas spoke up. Killyama could see his grin in the dark.

"Yes, you are. You're like honorary uncles."

"It's an honor?" Jonas's grin grew wider.

"Hell yes. Well, you are. Hammer's more like a distant cousin."

"That's cute, kid. Hear that, Hammer?"

"You only like him more because he bought that motorcycle for you on your sixteenth birthday and taught you how to shoot a gun. I gave you a car. I never hear you thanking me for that."

"Believe me; I have thanked you several times, and so have my friends." Killyama's mind went back to the numerous times the car's spacious back seat had been used instead of a motel room.

Hammer turned on the music, and Killyama relaxed back in her seat. She was growing tired of the drive from Knoxville to Jamestown. It would be easier to live there, but she couldn't bring herself to cut ties with her friends. Hammer grouched about it constantly. Even Jonas was getting fed up with her excuses.

When Hammer had opened his business in Knoxville after he had left the service, he had expected her to move there, too, but she had nixed that idea. Killyama couldn't leave her bitches behind for the job she had begged him to train her for. They needed her to watch their backs. Two of them might have husbands now, but they still needed her. Or, that was what she told herself. She refused to name the real reason she remained in Kentucky.

She hated herself for the two hours she had spent alone with Train. It had the side effect of not being able to get him out of her system.

The Last Riders should tattoo a warning label on their backs: *once is not enough*. Every time she was near him, he could make her body quiver in need as if she were an addict begging for a fix.

Closing her eyes, she thought back to the day she had shown up at The Last Riders for her ride. She remembered being so cocky as she leaned against her car with her arms folded, glaring at Rider as he made yet another excuse on why he couldn't take her out on a ride that Shade had promised for saving Lily's life.

Train had been working on one of the bikes, watching the argument with an amused expression. Inwardly, she had begun to feel humiliated that Rider obviously didn't want to take her out. Men were intimidated by her, yet she had hoped The Last Riders were different.

Seeing Shade and Lily show up to witness Rider standing her up had made it even more embarrassing.

"Hey, girl," Killyama had greeted Lily, not removing her glare from Rider.

Folding her arms even closer against her chest, she had decided to turn the tables on Rider. She wasn't about to let even more people see her humiliation if she could help it.

"What's going on?" Shade asked.

"I was supposed to give her a ride today"—Rider nodded his head sharply at Killyama—"but my bike won't start. She thinks I'm fucking with her."

"Babe, if you were fucking with me, I'd hope I would know it." She grinned evilly at the furious Rider.

Rider's face turned red. It took everything she had to keep from laughing at him. It was like taking candy from a baby.

"I meant that I wasn't trying to get out from giving you a ride."

"I know what you meant. Do I look stupid?"

Silence met her question.

She was dressed in leather pants and a black T-shirt that had a skull with a dagger in the eye. It read: "Come and get me." Her makeup was dark and smoky, and her biker boots had metal spokes sticking out. She was willing to admit she was dressed like a ball buster, something that worked to her advantage. No one was stupid enough to insult her directly.

She could see Rider was becoming flustered.

Better him than me, Killyama thought to herself.

"We'll have to make it another day. I have to order a part," Rider hedged.

"You've already put me off three times. I'm tired of this shit. Forget it." She turned around, opening her car door as she gave Shade a smirk. "The Last Riders don't know how to keep their word. Good to know for future reference."

"I'll give you a ride myself," Shade stated.

Killyama made a mental note that Shade didn't like anyone calling out The Last Riders' inability to keep their word.

"No offense, but I don't ride with a man who's got a woman at his back."

Shade was grinding his teeth so hard it had his wife looking at him worriedly.

"I'll give you a ride," Train offered, setting down the tool he was holding.

This time, Killyama remained quiet, tilting her head to the side as she studied the man. The fucker knew she was trying to get them all pissed off.

Since becoming friends with Beth, she had talked to the men intermittently, so Killyama had gotten a feel for their personalities. Beth had described Rider as being funny and easygoing, which was why she had wanted to get to know him better. Beth had never mentioned Train. If she had, Killyama must have missed it, being more interested in Rider.

She took a deeper look at Train, seeing he had a dangerous edge to him. He was the kind of man you would jump off a cliff with, not caring if you were going to hit rocks or seep into a beautiful ocean of blue.

Rider's flirtatious demeanor and good looks drew in women like a lure, whereas Train's dark looks were somber. He didn't need to bait the trap; he was a shark who would grab you and unwillingly pull you under. Train wasn't like Rider. He wasn't frightened of her, and his dark eyes gave no insight into his true personality. However, she had never run from the unknown, and she didn't plan to start now.

"Deal." Killyama shut the car door.

Train led the way to his bike, where she swung one leg over the seat after he did the same, snuggling close him. He shot her a look over his shoulder before turning on the motor, and then she hung on as he shot out onto the road.

Killyama was willing to admit she might have bitten off more than she could chew. When he had offered the ride, he hadn't appeared mad. However, the look he had given her from over his shoulder showed how angry he was about the insult she had thrown down. Her mama hadn't raised an idiot, but her pride wouldn't let her back down. Instead, she held him tighter.

The trepidation vanished within half a mile. She loved riding on a motorcycle. She had her own, but when she rode by herself, she had to be careful, watching the road and the assholes who didn't want to share it. With Train driving, all she had to do was enjoy.

Loosening her hold when everyone was out of sight, she held him by his belt. Killyama had ridden motorcycles long enough to know that he was good. Better than good. He handled the curvy roads like a pro, slowing down for the curves then accelerating as they turned a corner. The bike glided over the pavement smoothly.

His motorcycle was sick. It made hers feel like a bicycle.

Her adrenaline pumping, she tightened her thighs around Train's waist before lowering her mouth to his ear so he could hear her over the sound of the motor. "Let me drive!"

She couldn't hear his answer, but the shaking of his head wasn't hard to understand.

Seeing a straight stretch of road, she loosened her thighs to raise herself off the seat. Using her long legs, she tried to slide around to the front of him.

"Are you trying to get us killed!"

Train's shout didn't stop her. She found herself sitting in front of him, but it wasn't in the position she had wanted. He had taken one of his hands off the handlebars, jerking her so she straddled him, her breasts pressing against his chest.

Unable to prevent his gaze from catching hers, she looked down at his tanned throat. His neck muscles were clenched in anger as he slowed the bike down, pulling the motorcycle to a stop on the side of the road.

"Are you fucking crazy?" His eyes burned with fury, his voice deadly low.

She obstinately shouted at him, "You could have let me drive!"

"No one drives my bike but me. Get off. Now."

She got off the bike. Then, instead of giving her time to get behind him again, he began pushing his motorcycle backward so he could make a U-turn.

"You're going to leave me here?"

Train didn't reply. He simply pulled back onto the road to leave her choking on his dust.

Gaping after him, she couldn't believe he had left her. Even as she started walking, she kept thinking he would be waiting around the corner. When he wasn't there, she then thought he would be around the next one. When her high-heeled boots were beginning to rub her heels raw, she was forced to admit the son of a bitch was forcing her to walk back to The Last Riders' clubhouse.

"You son of a bitch! I'm going to kick your ass when I get there!" She began screaming every profanity she could think of to take her mind off the pain in her feet. "Your fucking bike better not be where can I get my hands on it!" she threatened in the silence of the empty mountainside.

She had no idea how far she had walked before she saw him on the side of the road, waiting.

"You fucking bastard!" Killyama yelled as she drew closer.

With that comment, she was left eating his dust again.

She tried to run after him but was forced to stop when she fell on the roadside gravel, where it took several minutes to choke back the fury and tears clogging her throat. Then, firming her lips, she shakily got to her feet. There wasn't a man alive who could make her cry.

It took five minutes of agony before she saw him again. She wanted to stubbornly walk past him, yet her pride had taken enough of a beating. Therefore, she gingerly climbed on behind him, not trusting him not to leave her sitting in the dirt again. She promised herself she would kill him when he dropped her off at her car.

As soon as her ass was on the motorcycle seat, he took off. Angry, she wanted to rip his head off. The carefree abandonment that she had begun the ride with was gone. Now she had no problem keeping her hands to herself until he brought them to a stop in the parking lot where her nightmare ride had begun.

Fuming, she didn't spare him a glance as she got of his bike before limping toward her car. Instead of opening the driver's side door, she opened the back one, reaching inside for the bat she always kept there.

Her hand was around the handle when she was pushed from behind, falling forward, her face planted into the backseat. She turned her head to see Train standing over her in the door, one arm braced on the car door, the other one on the roof, blocking her exit.

"Settle down before you hurt yourself."

His calm voice had the opposite effect he had intended, fueling her temper higher.

"The only one who is going to get hurt is you! You left me with a sprained ankle in the fucking mountains!" She flipped onto her back, lifting her foot to wave it in his face.

"Let me see." Train's frown of concern was too little, too late.

When he leaned down to see her ankle, she used her good foot to kick out at him, nailing him in the balls. With a hiss, he fell forward, pinning her underneath him.

Killyama took advantage, slamming her hands into his back and using her teeth to bite his shoulder.

"Bitch, let go."

When she didn't, she felt his teeth sink into her own shoulder.

Releasing his flesh, she stopped struggling so he would stop biting her.

Train looked up at her. "You've got a hell of a temper."

"Get off me!"

"You going to hit me again?"

"I'm going to wrap that bat around your fucking head!"

"Why are you so mad at me? I'm the one you practically made roadkill. Besides, you could have called Beth or one of your friends to come and pick you up."

"Beth was having dinner, and so were my friends when I called."

"You told them you were stranded and none of them wanted to leave to pick you up?"

Surprised, she lifted her brows in confusion. His voice had never risen when she had almost made him crash, or when she had cussed him out. He hadn't even lost his cool when she had nailed him in the balls. Yet, it had taken him to think her friends had ignored a plea for help to get a rise out of him?

"I didn't tell them I was stranded. When they told me what they were doing, I told them I would call them later."

"That was a dumbass move."

"Why? Because I didn't want to disturb their dinner? I can take care of myself."

The fight had left her. Exhausted from the long walk and the fight with Train, she sank into the seat. That was when she noticed he had been stroking the pounding pulse at the base of her throat.

The sensuous touch of his fingers against her flesh had her sucking in a deep breath. His eyes grew even darker, and the shadow of his beard on his chiseled jaw gave the appearance of an outlaw who took what he wanted.

She reached out to twine her arms around his shoulders, her lips twisting up into a sardonic smile when he flinched.

"Scared?" she taunted.

"Of you? I don't get scared."

Killyama raised her lips to press them against his. Train remained still, not stopping her, but not participating, either.

She pulled back a fraction of an inch to whisper, "Prove it."

Slowly, he opened his mouth. It was a kiss she wouldn't ever forget. It was like being reborn in a burst of desire that was almost painful because it wasn't enough. She needed more from him. She needed him to kiss her harder, to taste her the way she was tasting him.

Her control withered when he took the reins, tilting his face to the side so he could widen her mouth, turning the tables on her as she found herself being kissed by a man who could kiss as expertly as he could ride a motorcycle.

Train's weight settled more intimately against her. She could feel the bulge of his dick through his denim jeans. The slick leather leggings she wore allowed him to notch himself in a way that made her wonder if he had pulled them down. She surreptitiously slid her hand down to make sure her pants were still on.

"What are you doing?"

There were a few things a woman hated to admit. The fact that she couldn't tell him just when she had lost control of the situation was one of them.

Killyama moved her hand from the slick material of her pants to his T-shirt, showing no rhyme or reason, other than she wanted to make a lame excuse to herself for more breathing room.

When she tugged his T-shirt up, Train lifted himself, making it easier for her. Then his shirt slipped from her fingers, falling to the floorboard.

"Damn." She stared up at the magnificent chest she could see when the parking lot lights came on.

Train stared down at her, his face a mask of seriousness. The two were frozen, neither one making a move, time standing still.

Her thoughts were a jumble of emotions. She wanted to push him out of her car and hightail it out of there as if the demons of hell were after her. The parts of her below the waist, though, wanted to jerk him down and fuck his brains out. From his expression, Train was just as undecided as she was.

When he started backing out of the car, she pulled him back down.

"Fuck me."

Bracing his hands on the seat, he resisted her efforts. "You sure?"

"Dude, you want to fuck or not?"

Train started backing out of the car again. "I'll pass."

Perversely, his hesitation had her wanting him more. She wasn't a slut, but when she usually asked men to have sex, they couldn't get it out of their jeans fast enough.

Raising herself up, she pulled up her shirt, showing him the black lace bra that cupped her tits. "You sure?" she mocked, softening her voice into a seductive murmur as she trailed her fingertips down the tattoo on his bicep, losing the bitchy expression she usually wore.

Her body wanted him.

Train moved back inside the car, and Killyama gasped at his expression as he sensuously slid between her thighs, catching her mouth with his.

She combed her fingers into his long hair. She usually hated dudes with long hair, but on Train, the clean, masculine scent of it put her pussy in overdrive.

Train reached behind her to unfasten her bra, leaving her breasts free to brush his chest. She could feel the pounding of his heart against hers as their mouths dueled passionately.

Killyama scooted down so she could lay under him full-length. The old car had a big seat, and they took every spare inch of it, both of their feet hanging out of the open car door.

The close confines made it hard to struggle out of her tight pants, yet she managed while Train raised himself enough to unbuckle his belt and unzip his jeans to slide on a condom. Then, using his hips, he brushed the tip of his cock across the lips of her pussy.

Having sex with him was like riding a motorcycle at high speeds—you didn't know if you were going to reach the end or crash and burn. The searing heat of his entry scored her to her soul. She had expected him to fuck her in a heated rush. Instead, he started pinching and kneading her breasts. The pleasure had her squirming as he continued to thrust into her.

Killyama wasn't a small woman, but he made her feel petite as she was overwhelmed by the strength of the muscular body surrounding her. She was torn between fear and excitement. The sex she had initiated wasn't supposed to feel this good. It hadn't ever before. Then she realized that it was Train who was making the difference.

He wasn't only taking; he was giving her the pleasure that many were incapable of. He wanted her to enjoy it as much him. He was taking her on a ride that she never wanted to end.

Dropping the last of her guards, she rocked her hips back and forth, fucking him back as she sucked in a deep breath to inhale the musky scent they had created in the confines of the car.

When Train lifted her hips up to drive higher, her slick pussy gripped his cock, trying to keep up the furious pace he had set. Then, when he stroked his tongue on the tip of her nipple, she dug her fingernails into his back, unconsciously raking deep scratches into his flesh.

"Easy, firecracker."

Killyama pushed his mouth away from her nipple. "Don't call me no fucking nickname you've called another woman."

Train stopped moving. "I've never called anyone that before. If you want me to call you something else, then tell me your real name. I'm not calling you Killyama when I fuck you."

She almost told him to get off her right then, but the snug fit of his cock inside of her stopped her. Her mama hadn't raised no idiot. The second lesson every woman needed to learn was when to give in.

"You can call me Killy."

"I can deal with that." Train started moving again.

Her pussy gripped his cock tighter, trying to prolong the ecstasy that was rapidly building into the orgasm that he was so damn determined to give her.

Killyama shuddered as she came, and Train grimaced as she felt him throbbing inside of her. The shared orgasm made her self-conscious, especially when he moved to the side and hooked an arm under her neck.

"We're supposed to be all cozy now?" Her usual sting was missing from her words.

Train's lips twitched. "I take it you're not feeling a post-orgasmic glow?"

She laughed. "I need a cigarette for that."

"Sorry, but I don't have one handy."

"Damn, I need it. I haven't had sex since I stopped smoking."

"How long since you stopped?"

"A year ago."

Train sat up, folding her legs over his lap. Then he reached into his jeans pocket and pulled out a joint. "Will this do?"

"You have a lighter?"

He handed it to her.

"How did you join The Last Riders?" Killyama asked as they sat, smoking the joint.

"I was friends with Viper's brother Gavin in the Navy. We trained as pilots together. It was his dream to form an MC when we got out."

"I'm sorry. Beth told me about Gavin when her and Razer broke up. She told us that another club member killed him."

"Memphis."

"I'd kill someone who betrayed a friend of mine like that." She stared at his cold expression through the smoky haze.

Train took the joint away from her, taking a hit. "How'd you meet Sex Piston and your other friends?"

"Middle school. We've been friends ever since."

"They the ones who came up with Killyama?"

"What? You don't like it?"

He shrugged. "It's different."

She laughed, shaking her head. "My mother did."

"Your mother?" Train laughed.

"Yep. Every time I got in trouble, she always said I was killing her."

"Jesus, you're killing me."

"See? It's contagious."

"I can imagine you driving her crazy. I bet you turned her grey trying to keep up with you and your friends."

"Nope. She had me when she was seventeen. My mama doesn't have a grey hair yet. If she does, Sex Piston would have told me."

"Your mother is living?"

"Yes. Yours?"

"No, both of my parents are dead." Train licked his fingertips before putting out the joint. "I better get going before Rider comes out looking for me."

She didn't want to see him go. Hoping to convince him to stay a little longer, she trailed a finger down his chest to the V of his jeans, which he had zipped up but hadn't buttoned. "You sure you don't want another round? I'm better the second time around."

Train placed his hand over her teasing finger. "No, I don't want to fuck you…"

His blunt reply had her jerking her legs down. She picked up his T-shirt and tossed it at him as she maneuvered herself out of the car.

"Get out."

"Wait. Listen to me—"

"There's nothing to explain."

As soon as Train stepped out of the car, Killyama slammed the door closed then opened the front door to slide in front of the steering wheel.

He tried to hold the door open to keep her from driving away, but she reached inside the glove box and took out the gun she kept there.

"Dude, either step back, or I'm going to shoot the first target I see." She aimed her gun at his dick.

He hastily stepped back, dropping his hand from the door. "Just wait a minute. I wanted to—"

"Looks like neither one of us are going to get what we want." She shut the door then started the motor, making sure to keeping the gun trained on him.

Her car jerked as she backed out then turned the wheel, making him leap out of the way.

∞ ∞

"You fall asleep back there?" Hammer asked.

"No, I was remembering the other reason I like Jonas better. He doesn't talk as much as you on the way back to Jamestown."

"I don't think you should go to the party tomorrow night. I'd feel better if you put some distance between you and The Last Riders." Hammer sped up to pass a car that was going too slow to suit him.

"Why?" she asked cautiously. Had he found out what she had done with Train?

"For years, you told us to keep our mouths shut about our connection. Me and Jonas are going to hear shit from The Last Riders that we know you. Ever since they became buddies with the Destructors, they've been meeting Stud at the clubhouse in Jamestown. Jonas nearly pissed himself when he saw Rider and Train riding through town, and they almost saw him. Hell, how are we supposed to explain why we were in Kentucky?"

"Tell them it's none of their damn business. Besides, you don't have anything to worry about. Those two shitheads couldn't find their ass with their own two hands."

"Are you listening to this?" Hammer asked Jonas. "I just spent three weeks with Train in a shithole. I may have even made a few jokes about him calling Treepoint a hellhole, and he would have done better picking Ohio to live in."

"Why? Kentucky isn't that bad."

The men shook their heads at her. "When's the last time you tried to buy beer on a Sunday? They have more churches than schools."

Killyama leaned her head back on the seat. "So? Do what I do—buy it on a Saturday."

"All I'm saying is, don't blame me when they find out about our connection to you."

"Like I said, they couldn't find their ass with their own two hands. Let's change the subject; your bitching is ruining my good mood."

"You're in a good mood?"

"Yeah, I am. Crawford is gonna be sitting in court tomorrow, and I'm gonna get my money back. So hell ya, I'm in a fucking great mood."

"I'm glad you're in a good mood. My ass is killing me." Jonas leaned his seat back.

"I told you I'm not moving. You both can move back to Tennessee. I told you I wouldn't leave Jamestown when we went into business together. When you moved to Knoxville, I did fine without you. It made no sense why you two moved back. I don't need you both watching out for me anymore."

"That's not going to happen until you stop chasing after runners. We promised your dad we'd take care of you, so you're stuck with us until you find someone else for the job, or you get married." Hammer started laughing, and Jonas joined in.

Killyama bristled, straightening up in her seat. "I don't know what's so fucking funny."

"I don't know. Maybe it's because you haven't had a date in over a year. Or maybe because I can't think of one man who's willing to put up with your mouth. Or that you've sworn to slam any man's head with a meat mallet if he tried to put a ring on your finger."

Jonas unsuccessfully tried to dodge the punch she landed on his shoulder.

"What are you hitting me for? Hammer's the one who said it, not me."

"He's driving, and you were laughing, too," she snarled. "It's not like you two are dating anyone, either."

"That's because we can't find anyone to date in Jamestown." Jonas shifted his seat back to a sitting position to make it harder for her to punch him again. "Most of the women are either married or trying to get a ring on their finger. I have to go to Lexington to get laid."

"I can hook you up with…T.A. and Crazy Bitch."

Both men shuddered.

"No thanks. I'd rather drive for three hours before I hook up with one of those scatterbrained bitches."

"Me, too," Jonas agreed.

"You'd be lucky if they would have you," she protested. "T.A. is just like the women you like, Hammer. She has big boobs and—"

"Yes, she does. But she has a bad habit of being friends with you and Sex Piston. I don't need her talking about my junk when she gets mad at me."

"T.A. only talked about Pike's little pecker when she broke up with him."

"Once is enough. I can't even drink a beer with him now because I keep hearing her call him dicklet in my mind. Then she compared him to Rabbit. Once a man hears a woman make fun of a man's equipment, it fucks with his head. Doesn't it?" Hammer looked at Jonas for confirmation.

"Don't bring me into this conversation."

"Pussy." Killyama sat forward, placing her elbows on each of their seats. "Come on, Jonas; you're perfect for Crazy Bitch."

"No."

"Why?"

"Because she scares him." Hammer reached for the pack of gum he kept on the dashboard without taking his eyes off the road.

"Crazy Bitch is the sweetest woman I know."

"That's not saying much. Besides, I asked her out last year. She turned me down."

"Really? She never told me. Did she say why?"

"She said I acted too nice. I even tried to give her flowers. She said she'd never trust a man who gave her flowers again."

"I'll talk to her."

"Don't bother. She said she wouldn't date another man who couldn't pass a lie detector when asked if they would ever hit her. By that point, I wanted to strangle her, so I knew I wouldn't pass."

"She didn't mean it."

"Yes, she did. I was only asking her on a date, not asking her to shack up with me."

She shrugged. "It's your loss."

"Yes, it is…Thank God."

"I'll keep my eye out. You both are going to end up old and lonely if you don't stop being so damn picky."

"I'll make a deal with you. I'll go out with someone you want me to if I can pick someone to go out with you."

"Who? I'm open to suggestions." Then she thought better of her acceptance, needing to clarify her terms. "As long as he doesn't have a little dick."

She saw Hammer roll his eyes in the rearview mirror. "I'm not going to ask them how big their dick is!"

"Why not? I'll ask the women what bra size they're wearing before I decide who to fix you up with."

"A woman's tits aren't the only things I'm interested in. They have to have a brain, too."

"Shasta didn't have a PHD after her name." Killyama rolled her eyes back at him. "She could barely add two and two when you were married to her."

"You're never going to let me live that down, are you?"

"No. But I have to admit, I miss her. I liked her better than some of your other girlfriends."

"I divorced her, because you told me she was letting you party with the Destructors."

"I didn't party with the Destructors. At least, not back then. I was just hanging out with them."

"Biggest mistake I ever made was trusting Shasta with you…and not convincing your mom not to let you hang out with Sex Piston. I listened to Shasta when she lied and said you were just hanging out at my apartment. I didn't know you had made it party central for you and your friends. She left me with two months' back rent when she left me for T.A.'s cousin. The fucking whore even took my car."

"Shasta wasn't the reason I made friends with them. She couldn't handle me any better than you could."

"Your mama blamed me for you running wild."

"I wasn't running wild. Sex Piston just liked hanging out there. She needed—"

"Every time one of those bitches needed you, you took off running. Still do."

"Don't blame them. They've never asked me to do anything I didn't want to do."

"No?"

"No!"

"I'm not even going there with you. You've broken me. I'd rather do another tour of duty than argue with you. I stand a better chance of winning a whole fucking war than winning an argument with you."

"I'm not that bad."

"Yes. You. Are."

Killyama sat back huffily. "I'm going to pick the meanest bitch I can find for you to go out with."

"Then I have nothing to worry about."

"Why?"

"Think about it."

If Hammer weren't driving, she would backhand him on the back of his laughing head.

Chapter Four

"Want another beer?"

Rosie's bar was crowded to overflowing with Last Riders and Destructors, but Train had sat at the end of the bar facing the door so he could see anyone entering.

It was only when Rider shoved him to get his attention that Train took his eyes off the doorway.

"No thanks. I'm still working on the one I have."

"Taking it slow tonight, aren't you?"

Train shrugged. He had to keep his wits for when Killyama showed up...if she did. He was growing increasingly more frustrated. He had expected her to be there with bells on for the party the two clubs had planned. Leave it to her not to show. The woman never did what he expected of her.

"I'm still recovering from last night," Train lied. It was bad enough that he was sitting on his stool like a lovesick puppy. He didn't need to give Rider even more ammunition to make fun of him. From the sideway glance Rider shot him, his lie hadn't worked.

Rider took a drink of his beer before slamming it down. "I'm going to go dance with Ember. She misses Raci. Want to help me so she won't feel so lonely?"

"Go ahead. I'll be there in a minute."

"Sure you will." Rider gave him a mocking look before heading toward the dance floor.

Train tightened his grip on his beer. He could handle the brothers knowing he wanted Killyama, having never cared what other people thought of his actions. He had learned at a young age that expectations came with chains that you couldn't break from. Train would be damned if he would let anyone keep him from accomplishing anything he wanted to.

With a father who was too lazy to work, the entire neighborhood had shown their judgmental attitudes every time he had walked out his door. The fights that had taken place between his parents had just added more gossip to feed the gossipmongers. The whispers about his parents had grown to include him as he grew older, following him down the school's halls or when he tried to date one of their daughters.

When he was younger, he had received sympathetic looks. As he grew older, though, they had grown warier, assuming he had inherited his father's violent temperament. Train had quickly learned to meet his date somewhere rather than have a judgmental father slam a door in his face.

Train eyed the rowdy crowd. Viper and Stud were sitting at a table to his left. The presidents of the two clubs were talking as they watched their men become increasingly boisterous, each club member claiming bragging rights as to who had settled the score with Raul.

When their attention went to the door, Train stiffened as Sex Piston, Fat Louise, T.A., Crazy Bitch, and Killyama filed inside.

His gut twisted in need, fighting the urge to get off his stool and carry her outside to her ugly green car she refused to get rid of. If she hadn't driven, he wasn't picky; he could fuck her against the side of the building or spring for a room at the local hotel.

His eyes stalked her as she followed her friends to the table Fat Louise's husband was sitting at.

Biding his time now that she was here, Train motioned to Mick to hand him another beer.

"Thanks." Train started to reach for his wallet, but Mick stopped him.

"It's on the house for fixing my car. It hasn't run so well since I bought it."

"I enjoyed working on it. I usually only have the men's bikes to work on."

As Mick talked, Train made sure that Killyama didn't slip out of sight. He knew none of the brothers would ask her to dance, but he was interested to see if any of the Destructors would. From the file Crash had given him, he knew no men were sleeping over at her apartment, but that didn't mean she wasn't sleeping over at someone else's.

She was wearing blue jeans and a black top that rose up the front, showing her flat waistline, then rode to her hip, accenting her ass. The plunging neckline showed the gleaming V of skin between her breasts. Her pert breasts were so firm Train thought he could bounce a quarter off them. The thin straps crossed at her shoulders, lacing down the long length of her arms.

Killyama had the best body he had ever seen on a woman. She moved like a lioness, confident in her ability to handle anything or anyone who dared to think they could tame her.

Train took a drink of his beer. He should have asked for something stronger. Usually, beer was all he had, but he was sure he was going to need something stronger tonight.

The women were joking and laughing among themselves, all except Killyama, who every now and then would respond to one of them. She seemed a part of their group, yet curiously detached, always keeping her eyes on what was going on around them.

"She's a nice-looking woman. She yours?"

Train's lips twisted. "No. I don't have a woman."

Mick raised a brow. "Then why are you staring at the redhead like a rare steak?"

"I didn't say I didn't want her."

Mick chuckled as he stepped out from behind the bar, going to Killyama's table to take their drink orders. He came back a few minutes later to fill several beer mugs, placing them on a tray on the bar. Taking a bottle of tequila off a shelf, he then poured out just as many shot glasses before loading the round tray then carrying them to the table.

Train wished he could hear what he was saying to them, because the whole table turned to stare at Train. He felt like a six-year-old under their scrutiny. What the hell was Mick saying?

Before Train could ask, Mick held out his hand when he returned. "That'll be thirty bucks."

Train gaped at him. "I thought my beer was free?"

"It is. The round of beer I gave them…" Mick nodded his head toward Killyama's table. "That costs you the thirty."

Train closed his mouth as he reached for his wallet. Flicking the bills, he pulled out three tens.

"You're not going to tip me? Don't you want to know what she said?"

Train tightened his lips, taking out three ones before hastily putting his wallet out of sight before Mick could ask for more.

"Jeez, thanks." Mick's sarcastic comment didn't keep him from shoving the cash into the cash register.

"I didn't offer to buy their drinks," Train reminded the bar owner. "Besides, Viper is footing the bill for the Destructors."

"Viper's not the one trying to get into that redhead's panties. If you weren't such a skinflint, you would have thought of that yourself. Didn't your daddy teach you how to court a woman?"

"No, he must have missed that lesson." The only lesson his father had taught him was to show him how to open a beer bottle with his teeth. Despite himself, Train couldn't help asking, "So, what did Killyama say?"

Mick almost dropped the beer he was opening. Expertly managing to catch it before it could spill, he set it down on the bar.

"I didn't know that was her nickname. She's been in the bar a couple of times with Beth, but I never heard it before. You're jonesing after a woman called that?"

"Why not? I love to live dangerously."

"You sure you're not related to Greer Porter? That's something he would say when he's chasing after a woman out of his league."

"A gerbil is out of Greer's league. You going to tell me what she said or not?"

Mick reached into the cash register and took out three dollars, setting it down in front of him.

"Why are you giving the tip back?"

"I might own a bar, but I still have a conscience. I won't try my hand at matchmaking anyone called Killyama. Love is hard enough without trying to fuck a woman prone to violence."

Train slid the tip across the bar toward him. "I'm not looking for a relationship. I want her to join The Last Riders."

"You're trying to get her to join? You stand a better chance of getting shot in the dick than getting that woman to become a member. Here she comes. Slip out the back exit while I distract her."

Train remained sitting as she approached, feeling his dick getting hard. He felt like he was drinking tequila with the way he felt when she sauntered toward him, imagining touching that satiny flesh she was exposing with his lips.

"I'm tired of waiting. I'm thirsty." Killyama's curt voice yanked him out of his fantasy.

Confused, he stared back at her stupidly. "Then drink your beer." Train stared over her shoulder to see her beer and tequila shot were still full.

"I asked him whose cash you were using when he said you were buying us a round."

"Really?" Train gave Mick a penetrating stare. "What did he say?"

"He said to ask you. You were supposed to come over and answer my fucking question."

Train looked at the table again. "I see who was paying didn't bother anyone else at the table."

"I have standards. Unfortunately, they don't. So...?"

"Viper paid."

"That's what I thought."

He snaked his hand out to catch her arm as she was about to turn away. "What the fuck does that mean?"

Mick abruptly left, moving to the other side of the bar as he rolled his eyes toward the exit.

Train tightened his grip on her arm when she tried to pull away.

"I figured, if you couldn't even take a woman out to dinner after you fucked her, you're certainly too cheap to buy her and her friends a drink."

Train clenched his jaw in frustration, his boots hitting the floor. Maneuvering through the crowd, he dragged her to a small table at the back of the bar.

"Sit down."

"Make me."

Train dropped her arm, staring at her coldly. "Let's get this straight between us right now. I don't like playing games. I would like to talk to you and get some shit settled between us, so we can at least be civil when others are around. But if you're too immature to listen, then I guess we don't have anything to talk about anyway."

He expected her to storm off; therefore, it took him a moment to realize that she had taken the chair he had pulled out for her.

Sitting down across from her gave him a view of the bar as he gathered his thoughts to begin the conversation that would either end in another argument or a cease-fire.

"I'm not a man who enjoys conflict. I'm also not one who will run from it, either. I have tried to talk to you about the day we spent together, and every time, we just get in a fight. I'm tired of you making me feel like shit, or that I took advantage of you. We both know that isn't true."

"I never said you took advantage—"

"You implied it to everyone who would listen." Train carefully monitored the range of emotions flickering in her hazel eyes. "I have never been dishonest with a woman. Ever. I like to keep everything on the up and up. That way, no one gets hurt. Unfortunately, I hurt you, which was not my intention. I really like spending time with you when you drop that attitude you carry around."

"What's wrong WITH my fucking attitude?" she snarled.

Masking his own emotions from her caustic words, he still sought to soothe her hurt feelings. "When a man is attracted to a sexy woman, he doesn't appreciate being nearly run down by a car or nearly shot by one of her friends."

Killyama's voice dropped to a seductive murmur. "Would you prefer me to bend over and kiss your ass?"

"That's not what I'm saying. You're twisting my words again." Train tried to cool himself down, getting fed up with her attitude toward him.

The afternoon they had spent in the back seat of her car was good, but if that was going to be the first and last they had been destined for, then he was just going to have to suck it up and come to terms with it.

"You have mad skills protecting those around you, you're loyal as hell to your friends, and having sex with you nearly blew my mind. So much so that I got ahead of myself and was trying to see if you would be willing to consider becoming a Last Rider. I have had some sexual relationships in the past where the women resented my involvement with The Last Riders. I have no intention of leaving the club ever, or entering a serious relationship. I like you, and I think we can have some good times together, but I want to be up front so we can avoid more of the misunderstandings going on between us."

Her eyes were narrowed on him the whole time he talked. It was the longest time she had let him speak without interrupting him since he had met her. When she did speak, it was only to say, "I need a drink." She stood up, leaving him to go to the bar.

Train stared down at the table, running over the spiel he had just given her. Maybe he should have taken a different tack. However, he didn't want any lies to come back to haunt him.

The image of her the day he had gone to Winter's aunt's house was burned into his memory. Killyama and her friends had been skinny-dipping in the pool. He hadn't been able to take his eyes off her. Even T.A., who had breasts that would make any man drool, hadn't been able to draw his gaze beyond a cursory look. He had to have her again.

He hid his shock when she sat back down in the chair in front of him, chugging her beer before she sat it down on the table.

"So, because some bitches couldn't take you fucking around on them, you decided it was easier to only fuck bitches who are Last Riders?"

"Yes." He would rather come out as a jerk now than when their hookup was over.

"I'm not going to join The Last Riders. I'm going to nip that in the bud right now. You're not the only one who has a club they're loyal to. Seems like we're at a stalemate. Later." Killyama pushed back her chair and started to rise.

"Wait."

He was used to women trying to get him to give in to their demands, and Killyama was plainly saying she wouldn't regret it if she never fucked him again. Unfortunately, he couldn't say the same, and he knew that if she left the table, he would never have her again.

She paused, tilting her head to the side. Train racked his brain, trying to come up with another way to have her one more time. Or two.

"Dude, I'm not giving up the Destructors any more than you would give up The Last Riders. You might have been a good fuck, but it wasn't that good."

Her haughty sniff had him wanting to pin her against the wall beside them and remind her just how good it had been.

He pushed his own chair back. He'd had enough. Train never lost his cool with a woman, but he was damn close to losing it with her.

Killyama stuck one long leg out to keep him from walking away. "Chill."

Train sank back down onto his chair as she took her time to finish her beer.

"Maybe we need to give a *little* to get a *little*."

"What in the hell does that mean?" Train asked in confusion.

"We could hook up occasionally when we want a little something-something. No strings attached. You'll have to give up the rule of not banging a woman who doesn't belong to The Last Riders."

"What will you have to give up?" he asked suspiciously.

"That you'll be doing other women."

"That won't work for me."

"Why not?"

Train rolled his eyes. "You've been giving me shit ever since we were together, and you think you won't pull out a gun if you think I've been with another woman? And there will be other women."

She shrugged. "Who says you would be the only man in my life?"

"You're seeing someone?" His jaw clenched. "Is it serious?"

"If it were, would I be thinking of doing you?"

"Men get killed when they think their woman is cheating."

"Women do, too. Looks like we'll both have to take our chances that we'll be open and honest, not only with each other, but others, too. I don't do relationships, so I don't have a problem telling them they aren't the only one keeping my tits warm."

He bet she didn't.

Train nodded. "I can do that." He wanted her badly enough that he was going to take the chance. He drowned out the voice at the back of his mind that told him he was the one to fall for his own spiel.

"I can, too."

Train started to get up again. "Let's go."

"Whoa. Slow down, sailor. We need to settle the ground rules."

"Rules?" Train's brow furrowed. He knew it was too good to be true. Killyama never did anything easy.

"Rules. You shouldn't have a problem with that. The Last Riders are big on rules, remember?"

"Tell me what they are, and I'll decide." He wasn't about to let his dick and Killyama talk him into anything else that he would regret later.

"Protection. You use it with everyone."

"That's a given."

"Even if they are giving you a blowjob," she clarified.

"Have you lost your mind? I'm not putting a condom over my dick when a woman gives me a blowjob." Shaking his head vehemently, he made himself stop when she gave him an unblinking stare.

"Then don't expect me to go down on you without one."

Train gritted his teeth. "It's not like I would go to you right after being with another woman—"

"I'm giving you a choice. Either you can get all your blowjobs from other women, or my mouth is the only one that's going to be sucking you off." She shoved aside the bowl of nuts he had been nibbling on to push the nearly empty bowl of pretzels she had been eating toward him.

Train stood up without a word, going to the bar. "Give me a whiskey."

"You never drink whiskey," Mick commented, reaching for the bottle.

"Give me a double." Train took out his wallet, paying for his drink before going back to the table where Killyama was leaning back in her chair, legs crossed at her ankles.

Train sat down, downing his shot. "Any of the women in the club will give a blowjob anytime I want, so you can scratch that."

"Fine. I'm better. But if that's what you want, it's no skin off my nose."

Reminding himself he didn't hit women, he started to get up again, but Mick beat him to the punch, setting a bottle of whiskey on the table.

"You looked like you needed it."

When he started to reach for his wallet, Mick shook his head. "Shade said it was on him."

Shade was at Viper's table. The brothers were amusing themselves by watching the show.

"Tell you what," Killyama continued when Mick left. "I'll give you one, and then you can decide. How's that?"

Train reluctantly nodded. "You're not going to go all psycho when I choose other women instead?"

"You won't," she replied confidently. "But no, I won't go psycho."

"Okay."

"Cool. Now to my next rule."

"There's another one?"

"Yeah. I'm not going to fuck you at my apartment."

"Why not? Are you living with someone?" he asked suspiciously.

"No. I only invite men into my bed who are special. This is sex. Stud keeps a spare bedroom; we can use that."

"What's wrong with my room at my club?" She was taking the wind out of his sails. He had hoped he could gradually convince her to join The Last Riders. If she didn't come to the clubhouse, how was he going to show her what she was missing?

"I can be fair. We'll take turns on which club we use, but don't expect me to take any part in that swapping crap."

"All right." Train lowered his gaze to refill his glass. Nowhere in the rules she was sprouting off did she say he couldn't try to change her mind. "Anything else?"

"No."

"I have one of my own. I said before I won't ever lie to you. I expect the same from you. Don't ever lie to me. If you do, I'll walk away without looking back."

She stared at him for several minutes before nodding. "I agree." She held her hand for him to shake.

Train stood up so fast he had to catch his chair from falling. Taking the hand she held out, he rushed them from the bar. She didn't have trouble keeping up with his long strides.

"Where in the hell are we going?"

"We're going to my room. It's closer." He stopped at his motorcycle. Getting on, he turned his head to see she hadn't gotten on. "We going to do this or not?"

Train thought he saw a vulnerable expression on her face when he had turned around, but when he looked again after starting his bike, it was gone. He assumed it was just a trick of the light in the dark parking lot. Killyama didn't have a vulnerable bone in her body.

She got on behind him, twining her arms around his waist. "You sure you won't let me drive your bike?"

"I'm sure." He peeled out of the parking lot like the hounds of hell were after them. He wanted her in his bed and under him before she could change her mind...or add more demands.

The cool night surrounded them as they rode. Train didn't even feel it, too excited at having her again. He won a battle against Killyama, and she didn't even know it. He was going to make sure she would crave him every second she was away. It wouldn't take long for her to realize The Last Riders could give her something the Destructors couldn't. Him.

Train almost laughed out loud. She would be begging to become a Last Rider.

Chapter Five

Killyama stared around the small room as Train removed his shirt. The room was smaller than she had expected, the majority of the space taken over by the large bed and a nightstand that seemed to be an afterthought. Besides that, there was a small desk on one wall. Its surface was clear and neat.

When she had gotten off his bike and climbed the long flight of steps to The Last Riders' clubhouse, she had told herself she would turn around. Instead, she had meekly followed him inside and up the stairs to his room.

She had expected the main room to have a few of The Last Riders that hadn't attended the party at Rosie's, but it was empty as the sounds of their steps echoed hollowly in the silence.

"It's a small room," she noted. "You sure no one's going to come in?"

"No one comes in without knocking unless the door is open."

"It's quiet."

Train sat down on the edge of his bed to take off his boots. Then he unbuttoned his jeans. "Everyone's at the party or watching TV in the back room."

"Cool." She looked around the room again, trying to decide what to do next.

Train reached out and used the bottom of her top to tug her toward him, solving her indecision.

He pushed her midriff top higher. "Do you know how bad I want you?"

Not answering him, Killyama took out the leather band that held his hair back. It fell to his shoulders, giving him a pagan appearance.

She had lied to him when she had told him that sex with him wasn't that great. She had wanted him again before he had even pulled out of her, and she had spent months reliving the experience.

He would never convince her to leave the Destructors. The Last Riders didn't have Sex Piston, T.A., Crazy Bitch, and Fat Louise. They also didn't have Stud. She didn't know what kind of president Viper was, but Stud had earned her respect, and she liked him. There weren't too many men she could say that about.

The feel of his mouth on her stomach curled a fissure of awareness between them. Killyama kicked off her boots so she could then kick her clothes away, wanting nothing separating her from the heat of his touch.

Train fell back on the bed sideways, gripping her waist until her pussy was poised over his mouth. He held her easily, dancing his tongue over the lips of her weeping slit. Slowly, he sat her down so he could part her thighs wider.

"Damn, you're not wasting any time." She could appreciate a man who knew what he wanted and wasn't shy taking it.

Unbuttoning her top and taking it off, she tried to catch her breath as her bare breasts heaved. Leaning back, she then placed her hands on the mattress so he could delve his tongue deeper inside of her.

He tongue-fucked her like there was no tomorrow. In her mind, there wouldn't be. She had promised herself she would take it one day at a time, telling herself she could do him and keep her shit together. However, she hated to admit that him calling her psycho had actually scored a hit.

When he began using his teeth to graze her swollen clit, she trembled, unable to hold the tremors that rocked her body.

"Poor baby, how long have you been holding that in? I was just getting started," Train crooned as he used his body to roll her over, positioning them until their heads were at the top of the bed and he was on top of her.

"Maybe I was faking it." Killyama tried to keep her face impassive as he loomed over her.

"What did I tell you about lying to me?"

"You said you would walk away, but I don't think you'll be going anywhere with that stick poking me."

Train laughed, burying his face in her neck. "I never know what you're going to say next."

His laughter brought back the time they had spent in her car. At first, she had blamed the joint for making her feel carefree and relaxed with him. Now she realized it was him. He wasn't hard to talk to, and he was tender in how he touched her. It made her feel special.

Killyama shook the thought away. She wasn't special to Train. No woman was, not unless she was a Last Rider. Then she would become one of many. She didn't get in line for any man. She didn't care how big of a stick he was carrying.

She licked her bottom lip. "Is that a good or a bad thing?"

Train tangled his hand in her hair, lifting her mouth to his lips. "It can be a little frightening. Most of the brothers are afraid of you. You can rip a man to shreds with your mouth. I can get used to it as long as it stops at the bedroom door." He tugged her bottom lip into his mouth, nibbling on it, almost making her forget what they were talking about. Oh, yeah, she remembered; the pussies in his club were afraid of her.

"I like to keep men on their toes."

"You definitely do that. I wanted to strangle you when you told me that you had 'Fuck You' tatted on your ass." As he said that, he rose up then flipped her over onto her stomach, brushing his lips over the curve of lower back. "Another lie?"

"Technically, it wasn't a lie. I was thinking about getting a tattoo there, but I hate tramp stamps. I might be a tramp, but I don't need to advertise it."

"My name would be perfect tatted there."

"I don't tatt men's names on my body."

"Why?" Train whispered into her ear, making goose bumps rise on her arms.

"Same reason I don't see any woman's name on you."

"I used to have one. I had it covered."

"Where?"

"On my arm."

"Why get it covered?"

"She lied to me."

Train reached into his nightstand, taking out a condom. She felt him lift away as he opened it and put it on before she felt his weight drop down on her again.

"That feels good," she moaned.

"I haven't done anything yet."

She bunched up the pillow beneath her cheek to lay more comfortably. "I like the way you fit against me."

Killyama felt him pause, then his cock dipped between her thighs. She was so aroused he easily slipped inside of her with a hard thrust.

She was surrounded by Train's body, his thick cock taking her an inch at a time as she quivered under him. She stayed still, letting him do all the work. Truthfully, she was worried she would come again too soon.

She liked everything he was doing to her—his groans, the way he wasn't too rough yet forceful, the overwhelming buildup of giving herself to him. This was the only time she let her feminine side come out, a time when she could be all sweet and girly. She always had to look out for herself, but in bed with Train, she felt safe and protected, when usually she was the one who had everyone else's back.

When she felt Train's cock throbbing inside of her, she allowed herself to come again, holding the pillow and burying her face in it to keep from screaming out loud. She was not going to let any of the other Last Riders hear her. A woman had to have some pride.

Train heaved himself off her, settling down beside of her. She turned to her side so she could stare at him. She couldn't see his dark eyes under his lashes, but she could see that he was breathing heavily. Killyama reached out, smoothing her hand over his corded waist.

"Poor baby, how long have you been holding that in?" Killyama mocked his words back at him.

From the look on his face, he had enjoyed the sex as much she had.

Giving him a small pat on his waist, she raised up, slipping her legs off the bed.

"Where are you going?" Train grunted out, trying to grab her and pull her back to the bed.

Evading him, she bent down for her top, and then slipped it over her head. "Going back to the party," she answered, running her hand through her tumbled curls.

"Why? I thought you would stay the night?"

"Some other time. Where's the bathroom?"

Train wasn't happy with her answer. The satisfaction on his face evaporated and was replaced with injured male pride.

"In the hall. It's the one next to mine on the left," he answered abruptly.

"You don't have your own bathroom?"

"No. Don't worry about it; no one else is upstairs. I would have heard them come up the steps."

Grabbing her pants and boots, she heard him get out of the bed as she left to go to the bathroom. She took her time washing up, giving him enough time to get dressed, and not returning until she had redressed.

Tersely, he grabbed his keys off the nightstand. "Ready?"

"Whenever you are." She kept herself calm and measured, offhandedly making herself seem unmoved by what had happened between them on the bed.

Train nodded, going for the door, but then he stopped in front of her. "Why don't you want to stay?"

"Dude, you think I don't know the difference between asking me out on a date and asking me to be a Last Rider? You're the one who decided to draw a line in the sand. Don't blame me if I'm not going to tiptoe over it when you want more."

She hadn't been looking for a relationship the day in the car when she had tried to entice him into another round, but she also hadn't been looking to feel like a slut when he was ready to leave. When he had told her no and then mentioned The Last Riders, she knew exactly what he thought of her.

"Do you bitch this much when one of the women in the club don't stay with you?"

His jaw tightened. "Never mind."

She couldn't read his expression, but his eyes were dark and stormy as they made their way from the club to his bike. Jumping on behind him, she grabbed his belt as Train started his bike. The night had grown cold and damp. Shivering, she pressed her breasts against his back.

He stopped the motorcycle before he pulled out of the parking lot. "I have a jacket in my saddlebag."

Killyama twisted sideways, opening the bag to take out a leather jacket. Seeing the patches on the back of it, she started to put it back.

"What are you doing? Put it on." Confusion clouded his features.

"It's a Last Riders' jacket; I'd rather freeze." She put it back in the saddlebag.

Train turned off the motorcycle and got off.

"What in the hell are you doing?" Turning, she saw him going to a truck that was parked at the end of the lot. A minute later, he came back with a tan jacket.

"Put it on," he demanded.

Taking it from him, she slipped it on and then grabbed his belt again when he got back on the bike.

Pressing her breasts to his back, she softly whispered into his ear, "Thank you."

"You're welcome. Killyama?"

"What?"

"I'm a pretty easy-going guy, but I will only take so much."

"You warning me?"

"Yes."

"Then I guess we'll find out which of us has the biggest set of balls."

"I don't lose." Starting the motorcycle, he pulled out onto the road.

"Neither do I." She raised her voice, determined that he would hear her own warning above the sound of the motor. "Neither do I."

CHAPTER SIX

"Have you lost your ever-loving fucking mind?" Sex Piston snarled when Killyama rejoined her friends at Rosie's bar.

Killyama took the chair that faced away from Train as Fat Louise tilted her chair forward so she could hear Sex Piston's furious tirade.

"Chill out. I know what I'm doing."

Sex Piston's anger didn't faze Killyama. She did know what she was doing.

"No, you don't. For months, I've watched you eating your heart out over that man—"

"That's an exaggeration."

"No, it's not. Does he not have enough pussy warming his back that he needs you, too?"

"You know me better than that."

"I thought I did." Sex Piston sniffed, turning her angry face away from her.

Killyama sighed. "Cade, will you get me a beer?"

She didn't know if it was the polite tone she had used, or if Fat Louise's husband just wanted to escape, but he left the women alone.

"Train said he thought I was a psycho."

"You're not a psycho."

Sex Piston and her had been friends for long enough that Sex Piston instantly knew how his words had hurt her. They all did.

"You're not the psycho. Crazy Bitch is," T.A. interrupted.

"I know, right?" Killyama lifted her hands up helplessly. "I told him I could handle hooking up every now and then, and I can."

"Since when do you give a fuck what he thinks?" Crazy Bitch had been listening quietly, her eyes watching the party behind Killyama.

"I don't." She shrugged. "I've had hook-ups with other men. It's no big deal. What makes me mad is Train thinking I'm so into him that I'm acting like a psycho."

"So you're going to teach him a lesson?" Sex Piston asked suspiciously.

"Yes."

"How long is this lesson going to take?"

"I don't know. One or two times. As good as he was tonight, maybe three."

"That's the bitch I know and love."

The whole table broke out laughing as Cade set a mug of beer down in front of her.

"Is it safe to come back?"

"Can we dance?" Fat Louise tugged on Cade's arm before he could sit down again.

"Sure."

Killyama watched as they left, skirting the crowd to find a spot on the dance floor. When she saw Train dancing with Jewell, she turned back around, keeping her expression nonchalant, to meet Crazy Bitch's eyes.

"It's not going to be as easy as you think."

"If not, then I won't see him again."

"Men are poison."

"They have their uses," T.A. said as she swayed in her chair before turning to flirt with Rider, who was sitting at the next table with Bliss and Drake.

"Name one thing that a vibrator can't do better," Crazy Bitch said caustically.

"A vibrator won't miss you when you're gone," Sex Piston spoke up, smiling toward Stud as he pulled a chair up to sit down next to her.

"It's also there when you need it, which is more than I can say about any man I've been with."

"Then you've been with the wrong men," Calder said as he came up and leaned a hand on the back of Crazy Bitch's chair.

"I've been with enough to know they're all the same."

"You haven't been out with me."

"That's because you were so high you stood me up, which makes my point valid."

Calder's face turned red. "I told you I was sorry when I got out of rehab. I'm clean. Give me another chance. We could dance or go for a ride—whatever you want."

"No thanks. I'm good."

"I'll dance with you." T.A. hastily stood at Calder's suggestion.

"Can you handle two?" Killyama asked.

"Always." Calder nodded, and Killyama rose to her feet.

She had talked to him a few times since he had been out of rehab. She had expected him to slide back into the addiction that had him doing prison time, but so far, he had remained clean.

Killyama and T.A. let Calder dance between them as the music rose loud enough that she expected the old building to collapse. Calder would focus on T.A. for a minute, and then he would give Killyama a share of his attention. He kept his hands to himself until the music turned seductive. Then it wasn't Calder who was doing the touching; it was T.A. and Killyama. It was hard not to.

Calder was as handsome as his brother. Maybe more so. He had a rougher, tougher attitude than Stud did, though. That was like catnip to women. Even The Last Riders' women were giving him the once-over as he easily kept up with the two women who were having fun teasing the man.

"Need some help?"

Before Calder could answer, Train snagged Killyama around the waist, lifting her off her feet until she was plastered to his body.

When Calder would have reached out to take her out of his arms, Killyama stopped him.

"It's cool."

"You sure?"

Calder and Train stared at each other, daring the other to instigate the fight brewing between them.

"I'm sure." She nodded. "Without me, you can teach T.A. how to dance. She broke two of my toes."

"I know how to dance. It's not my fault my breasts get in the way so I can't see my feet."

"I should be so lucky," Killyama wisecracked despite becoming aggravated by Train's arrogance of carrying her to a dark corner of the dance floor.

"I knew you were a smart woman," Train said as he set her down on her feet.

"Why? Because I didn't let Calder beat the crap out of you?"

"No, because you stopped me from beating the crap out of him."

"Who's being a psycho now? You couldn't take Calder if he had both his hands and feet tied behind his back."

"Stay here. I'll be back in a minute." Train grimly started toward Calder.

Killyama grabbed the back of his T-shirt, jerking him to a stop. "Is this a joke? Beth and Lily both say you never fight."

Train gaped at her. He looked like she had just called him a pussy. "When did they say that?"

"I don't remember. Does it matter?"

"I fight all the time. Go ask Rider or Moon."

"You're drunk."

"No, I've only had a couple of drinks tonight, and that was a couple of hours ago."

"Then I don't understand…"

Train released a ragged sigh. "I didn't like seeing you dancing with him."

"Tough titty. I don't have to put up with this bullshit…The Last Riders share women all the time. You think I'm buying this He-Man attitude because I danced with another man?"

"I wanted you to stay the night."

His reluctant admission had Killyama wanting to give in to him and give him everything he wanted, but she wasn't going to do it. They weren't in a normal relationship, and the sooner he figured that out, the better it would be for both of them. She would never be happy as a Last Rider, and Train didn't want a woman who wasn't one.

"Maybe next time…if you're good." She gave him a brazen smile as she started dancing.

"Better than I was tonight? So you know, I was pretty damn good tonight."

Her head fell back with laughter.

Train stepped into her, letting her feel the bulge behind his jeans.

"I've had better."

Train laughed back, bringing his arms around her waist as they swayed to the music. "I haven't."

"See? What did I tell you?"

Lucky and Willa were dancing next to them, smiling at their laughter. That made Killyama bite back her laughter.

"The problem is, The Last Riders are used to having their cake and eating it, too."

He dropped his hands from her waist to cup her ass, pulling her tighter. "I'm not biting into that one. Can we just enjoy the music without getting into a fight?"

"Yes," she conceded.

Relaxing into him, she let the music take her away from the other women who would go home with him and from the club members who would eventually tear them apart. It was inevitable.

Like all men, Train thought their fate rested in his hands. What he didn't realize was that it rested in hers. He believed the end would come when she couldn't take him betraying her with other women. He was wrong. She would betray him.

CHAPTER SEVEN

"Need a hand?" Viper squatted down next to Train worked on Rider's motorcycle.

"No thanks. I got it."

When Viper didn't move away, Train knew he was there to have a talk. Viper wasn't like the other brothers who would stop by to chat. The Last Riders' president was too busy taking care of the business side of their club. If Viper was there, he was there because he had something on his mind.

"I saw you hanging out with Killyama last night."

"So did all the other brothers."

"What's going on?" Viper's serious tone had Train lowering the wrench.

"With Rider's motorcycle or with Killyama?"

"Killyama."

"Nothing. We were just having a good time."

"Is that wise?"

"Why not? It was a Friday night; we let some of the women we want to fuck come to the clubhouse to party. I didn't think it was a big deal."

"They aren't Killyama. What she sees, she'll gossip about."

"Most of the men and women were at Rosie's last night. Sasha and Lily were babysitting at your house, so there wasn't anything to see."

"What about next Friday? She going to be there?"

"Maybe. If I decide to invite her, I'll talk to her and make sure she doesn't talk."

"The kids are getting older. Noah and Chance will be starting preschool. I don't want them to get hurt from the rumors that could be spread. All the brothers are picky on which hanger-on's they let come to the parties."

"Killyama isn't a hanger-on." Train stood up, going to his tool-box. Then Viper rose, preventing him from going back to work on the motorcycle after he grabbed the blowtorch.

"What is she, then?"

"Jesus, I don't know. Do you give Rider the third-degree when he brings in someone new?"

"Most of the women Rider brings are too stupid to remember where they are the next day, much less talk about it."

"Trust me; I know what I'm doing."

"All right. She's your responsibility. If shit goes down, it will be on you."

Train nodded. "I can handle Killyama."

Viper shook his head. "If you can do that, all the brothers will be amazed. Me included."

"She's not that bad."

Viper stared at him in bewilderment. "We talking about the same woman? Did you forget the night we all spent in jail because of those bitches?"

"She was only taking up for Beth. I can respect loyalty."

Viper shook his head. "Brother, you got it bad. Do I need to start picking another replacement if something happens to me?"

"Good luck. Winter hasn't let me back in your bed since she found out."

"She says I'm going to outlive everyone."

"From her lips to God's ear," Train said in all seriousness.

He was close to all the brothers, but Viper went beyond that. Gavin had been like the brother Train never had, and he had grown close to Viper through Gavin. They had spent a lot of time together in the military, and when they had been discharged, it was the three of them who had come up with the idea for The Last Riders.

Train couldn't prevent the twist of pain that hit his chest when he thought of Gavin.

"Something wrong?"

"I was just thinking about Gavin."

Viper's face echoed his own pain. "He'd be proud of what we've built."

"Yeah, he would. I still miss him. It's as if it were just yesterday when we planned out the clubhouse."

"I miss him, too." Viper brought his eyes back to Train after looking lost in thought out at the trees surrounding the property. "I wish you'd take my old room."

Train gripped the handlebar of Rider's bike, looking away from Viper. "I can't. It was the room Gavin planned to take."

"It made me feel closer to him."

"It just reminds me that he's not here."

"If you change your mind, let me know."

Train nodded. "I will."

"I better go. Winter has supper ready. You sure you don't need some help with the bike?"

"I'm sure. And, Viper, I'll make sure that Killyama behaves. You have my word."

Viper nodded. "I'll see you in the morning."

A little while later, he had finished working on Rider's bike and was closing his toolbox when Beth pulled into the parking lot.

Taking a cloth, he wiped his hands off as she got out of her SUV.

"Hi, Train." She smiled as she went toward the steps to the clubhouse.

"Beth, how's it going?"

"Good. It's been a long day."

As they walked up the steps together, Beth gave him a curious look. "Did you have fun at the party?"

Train snapped curtly, "Why? Did Killyama ask?"

Beth frowned. "No. I was just making idle chitchat. Should I have not asked?"

"I overreacted. I'm sorry. I'm just being paranoid. Viper's worried about Killyama spreading gossip about the club."

Beth paused on one of the steps. "I'm afraid that's my fault. When I broke up with Razer, I confided in them. They haven't told anyone about the parties, and that was years ago. I know they haven't ever told anyone else. They might comment about it around you guys, but it's not like you all don't know what's going on in the club. They would never tell anyone what happens here."

Train could tell she regretted confiding in the women she had grown close to. He could also understand how they had provided comfort when The Last Riders hadn't.

"I'm sorry. I shouldn't have said anything." He continued to climb the stairs with her, feeling bad he had upset her. "The brothers and I just don't want the life we have going on here screwed up."

"Killyama comes across as a hard-ass, but she wouldn't do anything to hurt Lily or me."

Train looked at Beth from the corner of his eye. "You're not going to give me the same assurance if she gets mad at me?"

Beth laughed. "If you hurt her, Killyama won't be the only one you'll have to worry about. Sex Piston and her whole crew will come after you like a pack of ravaging wolves." Beth patted him on his arm as they went into the club.

"I wonder if they still make silver bullets?" Train joked as he left her to go upstairs to his room. He didn't hear her retort as she went into the kitchen. He probably didn't want to hear it anyway. He had no intention of hurting Killyama. As long as they kept everything casual, both of them could have a good time, and then walk away unscathed when it was over.

He made a pit stop in the bathroom to shower. Then, wrapping a towel around his hips, he headed to his bedroom. Leaving the door open, he dressed and was putting his boots back on when Stori came into the room.

"What are you doing?" she asked as she plopped down on the bed.

"About to go down to eat dinner."

Train rose from off the side of the bed, but Stori caught his hand, yanking him back down.

"I'm hungry for some Train." Stori went to her knee, trying to maneuver the zipper of his jeans down. He caught her hands.

"Right now, I'm hungry for tacos."

Leaving her sitting on the bed, he turned toward the door.

"Dammit. Don't tell me you're going to turn into a one-woman man now, too. The women still aren't over losing Lucky. What's a woman got to do to get laid around here?" Stori pouted, falling back to the bed.

Train strode back. Lifting her, he tossed her over his shoulder then gave her a sharp whack on her delectable ass.

"I'm hungry, not neutered. Let me eat dinner. Then I'll keep you busy for the rest of the night." He effortlessly carried her through the house, enjoying the giggles that trailed after them.

Stori was sweet. She could fuck you in every position imaginable, and a couple he hadn't thought of until she had shown him. She was up for anything or anyone, though she usually snuggled up to him or Rider at night. He had yet to see her petty or bitchy. She was the perfect Last Rider woman.

Train knew he didn't stand a chance that Killyama would fit in as well. She would probably pull their hair out the first time she spent the night.

He set Stori down to make his plate, becoming frustrated at himself for thinking about Killyama. Train had hoped that having sex with Killyama again would get her out of his system. It looked like it would take longer than he expected.

He found a seat next to Rider, Moon, and Jewell. Then, when they were almost done eating and were just sitting around and talking, Stori sought him out, plopping down onto his lap.

"You ready?"

"I'm all yours," he said, helping her off his lap to carry his dirty dishes to the sink.

Taking out his cell phone when it started ringing, he saw it was Killyama calling.

"Hey," he answered, raising a finger to show Stori he needed a minute.

"I'm bored as fuck. You in the mood for company?" Killyama's voice came over the line.

Train stared at Stori, who was becoming irritated, waiting for the conversation to end.

"I'm kind of busy right now."

"Oh. That's a bummer. I was going to give you a blowjob so you can compare it to the women in the club. I don't expect you to give them up before I can prove who's better."

Did her voice have a sultry twinge to it? Or was it the lust that had detonated in his head?

"I'll be twenty minutes."

Stori stormed away huffily at his words, finding a space between Rider and Moon on the couch in the den.

"Wait! I can drive there..." The sultriness had disappeared from her voice. Train knew it had been a product of his imagination.

"I want the ride. See you in twenty." Train disconnected the call before she could argue about coming over.

The brothers were already taking Stori's shorts off. It hadn't taken her five seconds to replace him.

"Where are you going? Don't you want to join in?" Rider asked, taking off his jeans.

"No, I'm going out for dessert."

Chapter Eight

"Let's just go in and get him. It's too cold to sit here freezing my tits off," Killyama complained.

"You think it's any easier on me? I have news for you; Jonas needs to stop playing that dumbass game on his phone. And will you please quit chewing that gum? If you pop it one more time, I'm going to rip it out of your fucking mouth."

"I'm almost on level thirty-one. I need to kill one more zombie to level up, and then I'll stop."

Killyama leaned forward, placing an elbow on the back of each of their seats. "If he doesn't come out in one hour, I'm going to go knock on the door and pull Carter out." With little to do but wait for their bounty to come out, they passed the time trying to see who could be the most irritating. So far, she was winning.

Jonas closed the app, settling against the door so he could see her. "You're looking tired today. Late night?" Trust Jonas to amp the voltage.

"I'm not tired; I just didn't want to waste my makeup on you two."

"It didn't have anything to do with seeing Train's bike parked out front of the Destructors' last night?"

Belligerently, she stiffened. "You keeping an eye on me?"

"I was going to get a beer. Of course, I left when I recognized Train's motorcycle."

"He stopped by to say hi."

"I bet he got more than a hi."

"Does it matter?"

"I hope you know what you're doing. Train's one of two men I wouldn't cross."

Usually, it was Hammer who warned others about being stupid. Jonas was the more laid back of the two men. They were like uncles to her. Jonas was the cool one, while Hammer was the pain in the neck.

"I'm not a kid anymore; I can watch out for myself." She deliberately popped her gum again. "Who else wouldn't you cross? It's not like I'm scared or anything, but I can keep them on my radar."

"Shade."

"Shade? We're friends." She might be a tiny bit exaggerating.

Hammer and Jonas took their eyes off the apartment to cast her doubtful glances.

"Shade doesn't have friends," Hammer warned. "I raised you to stare into a man's eye and see his soul. Shade doesn't have one. If you don't see that, I failed."

"I saw it, but you haven't seen him around Lily."

"You're not Lily."

She dropped her arms, leaning back in her seat as she stared out of the window. No one was Lily. She had the extra special something that drew everyone around her into her world. Her sister, Beth, had the same capacity. They were charming and so nice they made you wonder which planet they had been born on. A woman like Lily could catch a man like Train, instead of taking leftovers.

She was the complete opposite. She could be refined or pleasant…if she had a knife to her neck.

Killyama perked up when she saw a car park in front of the apartment they were watching.

"Get ready." Hammer's low voice broke the tension-filled silence.

Killyama grabbed the door handle, preparing to jump out of their SUV, when a short, blond-haired man came out carrying a laptop.

"That's him. Go!"

Killyama jerked the door open, sprinting toward Carter. He was halfway to the parked car when the man driving saw the three of them running. He backed up before peeling out of the parking lot. Unfortunately for Carter, he didn't react as quickly.

"Jack Carter!"

The bail jumper dropped the laptop he was carrying as he ran back inside his apartment.

"Why in the hell do they run?" Jonas grunted, leaping to tackle the shorter man onto the ground.

Killyama and Hammer pulled Carter to his feet after Jonas handcuffed him.

"Let me go! I'm going to call the police."

"We're going to save you the trouble. The cops have been looking for you since you missed your court date."

They ignored the litany of verbal abuse Carter hurled at them as Killyama shoved him into the backseat, buckling him inside. Then she took the seat next to him as Jonas slammed the door closed. She was tempted to elbow him in the fucking face when he leered at her.

Hammer got in the front, handing the laptop to Jonas.

She kept an eye on Carter as Hammer drove to the police station.

"Whomever you stole that computer from won't be happy to get it back broken," Jonas remarked as he opened the laptop.

"It's mine."

"Sure it is. You have a rap sheet as long as my leg. You should wise up; you suck as a burglar."

"Don't mess with it. It's none of your business." Carter had been sitting docile until Jonas opened the laptop.

"Why you getting so bent out of shape?" Killyama egged him on. Deprived of chasing him down, she had to get her kicks another way.

"Maybe because it's none of your fucking business what I have on my computer," Carter snarled, struggling against his seatbelt and the handcuffs Jonas had placed on him.

"It's his. Dumbass has his picture on the log-in."

"Let me see." She scooted forward as Jonas lifted the computer high enough for her to see, which was close to Carter's face. His face turned red as he tried to reach for it but couldn't.

"Quit egging her on. Jesus, it's like I'm dealing with two kids when I work with you both," Hammer grumbled.

"You fuckwads don't know what shit you've walked into. I have friends who can make you disappear."

"Ooo, I'm so scared. Any of those friends bail your ass out of jail? Wait a minute. That was me, and I definitely don't consider you a friend."

"You fucking bitch, let's see how scared you are when..."

Killyama raised her eyebrows, waiting for him to finish. When he didn't, she rubbed more salt into his wounds.

"Couldn't think of anyone? I'll tell you what; I'll add you to the Christmas card list I send to all the losers who think they're going to screw me out of my money."

"Cunt, I'm going to fuck you up so bad—" Carter started to yell out until she couldn't resist the urge to elbow him the face any longer. "I'm going to have you arrested."

"For what? You hurt yourself when you fell. You see anything, Hammer? Jonas?"

"No," they answered.

"You're going to be sorry."

She became tired of the whiney pussy, ignoring him for the rest of the ride to the police station. Once there, Killyama climbed out as Jonas took Carter.

"I don't suppose you want to give me your password?"

"Suck my dick!" As they drew closer to the side door of the station, Carter dug his heels into the pavement. "What are you going to do with my computer?"

"Wipe it clean and sell it," Killyama lied. In actuality, Jonas would look it over and see if they could use any of the information on his drive. Sometimes their best clues on chasing other felons were handed to them when they were searching for another one.

"Hey, sexy lady, did you bring me a present, or did you finally decide to go out with me?" The booking officer was one she was familiar with.

"I brought you a present. I told you I don't date married men."

"I'd get divorced if I thought you would go out with me."

"Roberto, your wife is six months pregnant. One night, you're going to wake up, and she's going to be holding your dick in her hand."

"Nah, I sleep with one eye open."

Killyama moved to the side, letting Hammer deal with Roberto. She didn't flirt with married men. It grossed her out the way men could flaunt their wedding ring and brag about their kids, then hit on another woman in the same breath. She would cut out her tongue before she ever said, "I do."

"All done," Jonas said when Roberto led Carter away. "You sure you don't want to take Roberto to lunch? Don't let us stop you. Hammer and I can hang back."

"You're so freaking funny. Why don't you take him to lunch? You keep turning down my suggestions on who to date, so maybe I've been searching in the wrong direction."

"I've changed my mind."

"About what?"

"About Train. I think you're perfect together."

"Why?"

"Because neither of you would know a joke if it came up and bit you on the ass."

"Train tells jokes all the time." She didn't know why she was defending Train's somber temperament. It was just the principle of it. She was the only one allowed to give Train a hard time.

"Tell me one," Jonas requested as they got back in their vehicle.

"I can't think of anything off the top of my head."

"You can't think of one joke? How many times have you been out?"

Killyama shrugged. "Three times. I wouldn't call them dates, though."

Hammer stopped the SUV in the middle of backing up, turning to stare at her. "What would you call them?"

"I don't know. Boinking? Fucking? Take your pick."

Hammer slammed the gearshift into neutral, raising his voice so he was shouting into the confined space. "I raised you better than that! The least he can do is buy you dinner."

"I wasn't hungry for food."

"Hold me back, Jonas, or I'm going to give her the spanking I should have given her when I caught her smoking."

"Try it. You didn't do it then because you knew I would tell Mama. If you don't quiet down, I'm gonna tell her you've got a crush on her."

Hammer's face went white. "I do not."

"Yeah, right. She'll get that sad look on her face and give you a long speech on how much she still loves my father, and then you get sad."

"I have never considered her anything other than a friend, which is more than I can say for you and Train. You want to step

79

into a minefield, go for it. Just don't expect me to pick up the pieces when it explodes. You've always had to learn everything the hard way." Hammer put the gear back in and backed out. He was closing her out, showing her she had hurt him.

Regretting her words, she tried to make amends. "You know I won't say anything to Mama." It was as close to sorry as she was going to get.

He nodded.

Jonas remained silent, too. She hated it when they were mad at her.

She deliberately popped her gum. When that didn't get a reaction, she did it again.

"Jonas, taze her ass."

"What'd you say?" He turned his head, popping his own gum.

Hammer turned the air condition up to high. "I'm in fucking hell."

CHAPTER NINE

"That's the last of the packages." Train dropped the order he had finished boxing up into the cart that Rider would mail out on Monday.

"Whoop! Whoop! We're done for the week. I'm outta here." Ember cleaned her table off, hightailing it out of the factory so fast that Train winced at the sound of the slamming metal door.

Rider grinned at him, hopping onto a table as he waited for Train to clean up his table. "I wonder if she's more excited about it being Friday and she has the weekend off or the party tonight."

"The party. No one's had time to do anything but eat and sleep all week since we had to get the orders out."

The orders they had been working on all week had left two hours ago in their own truck, heading to the airport in Lexington. The supplies had filled all their waking hours, knowing it was going to a country that had suffered a catastrophic earthquake.

"Don't know if I'm going to make it tonight. I'm tired as fuck."

Train was surprised. Rider had never missed a Friday night party. The brothers always joked how he would fuck when he was half-dead, something he had actually done once.

"You're never too tired to fuck. Something wrong?"

"Today's Gavin's birthday."

Train had been busy, but he hadn't forgotten. This morning, he had gone to the cemetery where Gavin had been buried. He had seen Viper leaving as he rode onto the property Cash owned.

Rider had been just as close to Gavin as he had. They both had lost a good friend because of Memphis. Even now, they couldn't believe how a man they had considered a brother had betrayed them. Memphis had fooled them all. The Last Riders had taken the betrayal hard. Each of them would give their lives before another one would betray the club again.

Train wrapped an arm over Rider's shoulder when he jumped down from the table. "Come on; Sasha told me she ordered a new outfit for tonight. You'll get your stamina back when you see her in it."

"The one she let me pick out?"

Train hid his grin. The box she had carried up the steps had been big enough that it probably contained several outfits.

"Yes." He would stop by her room before he went to his own and make sure of it.

They raced up the steps to the clubhouse, taking the one hundred plus steps two at a time. Neither of them was out of breath. They used every opportunity to work out. Keeping their reflexes and body in shape was a way of life with them. Especially since some of the brothers contracted out to the military when their expertise was needed. He was one of them. Shade was another.

There wasn't a machine he couldn't fly in the sky or on the road. That was why he liked working on engines. If he or one of the brothers' lives depended on what they were riding on, it had to work.

Train used the opportunity of Rider stopping to talk to Moon to slip away upstairs to talk to Sasha. He didn't have to knock; she was standing by her bed, trying to put a necklace on.

"Need some help?"

"Please."

Train moved behind her, gently maneuvering the two ends together before closing the clasp.

"The brothers will be keeping you busy tonight."

The black halter accented the large swell of her breasts. It went around her neck, crisscrossing to dip in a deep V. Her midriff then tied behind her back, where he was treated to the sight of her ass cheeks peeking out from beneath her white shorts.

"That's the plan." She leaned back against his chest, giving him the cleavage she exposed.

"Is this the outfit Rider picked out?" Train let his hands rest lightly on her waist.

"How'd you know?"

"Lucky guess." The clothes would take Rider a second to get her out of.

"I'll wear the one you picked out next time." She rubbed her back against his chest like a cat seeking affection.

"I'll make sure you keep that promise." He dropped his hands, stepping away, then giving her a pat on her ass.

"You're leaving? I thought we could get the party started?"

"I can't. I need to shower and get changed. I invited Killyama to the party tonight."

Sasha gave him a friendly grin. "You going to leave your door open?"

"Not tonight. I want her to get used to us before I invite others to watch."

"Scaredy cat. Stori says she's fierce."

"I'm not scared; just cautious."

"Well, if you decide to let anyone join in, let me know. I'm up to the challenge. I miss being with you."

"You're going to have your hands full tonight without wondering what's going on in my bedroom."

"You never know. She might be into it."

"I'll keep that in mind. See you later." Train left, hurrying to get his shower before Killyama arrived.

He had been undecided about her coming. But if he had any chance of convincing her to join The Last Riders, he had to let her see the parties. He hoped the night went well. Otherwise, it was going to be a hell storm of massive proportions.

He took a quick shower and dressed with his eyes on his watch. He didn't want her to show up without him downstairs. The Friday night parties started anytime anyone wanted to fuck. With the hard week they had, they would be ready to blow off some steam soon.

Train was coming down the stairs when Killyama texted she was there. Opening the front door, he went outside to stand on the porch and wait for her.

He had to hang on to the balustrade when he saw her coming up the steps. The white jean top she wore was made to look like a bikini top that cupped her breasts lovingly. The material ended under her breasts, forming into fringes that gave him a glimpse of her waist. The fringes tapered to the hollow of her belly, which was exposed by her low-slung jeans that were so washed out they appeared almost white. There were so many holes, his eyes kept dipping to see the golden tan revealed through the frayed openings.

"Woman, I was already hard thinking about tonight. Now I could come just seeing you in that outfit."

"Slow your roll, lover. We need to get a few things straight before we go inside."

"Like what?"

"I know how this train ride goes. I'm telling you now, I'm not watching you fuck another woman."

Train tried to douse the raging fire in his dick as he got himself back under control. Leave it to Killyama to put the brakes on before the party started.

"I told you, we don't have to do anything you don't want to do. We'll leave the party and go upstairs to my room whenever it gets too much for you."

"Dude, as long I don't have to watch you fuck another woman, I can handle pretty much anything."

He smiled. "That's some brave words when you don't know what you're walking into. I've been with The Last Riders for a long time; they still surprise me."

He opened the door for her. The clubroom was already crowded.

"You hungry?" Train took her hand, leading her toward the kitchen.

"No, but I'll take a drink."

He stopped his progression, turning to take Killyama to the bar.

"What can I get you?" He stepped behind the bar, grabbing a cold beer for himself.

"Got any bottled water?"

"We have tequila."

"I'll stick to water for now." Killyama slid onto a stool, turning to study the faces around her.

Train shrugged, giving her the bottled water.

From her choice of profession, he could understand her trust issues. No woman, no matter how much she trusted a man, should ever lower their guards until they grew to know a man better.

"I didn't expect this many Last Riders to be here."

He slid onto a stool next to her. "They aren't all Last Riders. Members can invite anyone they want on Fridays."

Train didn't miss the dawning comprehension in her eyes.

"Only on Fridays?"

He nodded. "Unless you're property, celebrating something, or a new recruit, the clubhouse is closed to anyone else."

"That's why you put me off when I wanted to come over the last time?"

"Yes."

"All you had to do was tell me. It pissed me off."

"It didn't show." In fact, Killyama had sucked his dick as if it was her favorite sucker.

Shifting on his stool, he wanted to unzip his jeans and let her go at it again. The thought of fucking her mouth in front of the crowded room had him gulping down his beer to cool himself off.

She swung around on the stool to face him, one long leg sliding between his. "It's not as bad as I expected it to be."

"They're being on their best behavior."

"For me?" She shook her head at his nod. "Hell, tell them to have at it. The Destructors make The Last Riders look like kindergarteners."

"You sure? I'm trusting you, Killyama. You don't have the best record where the women are concerned."

"I'll keep my hands to myself if you do, too."

It wasn't exactly a promise to behave, but it was the best he was going to get.

"Moon, turn the music on!" he yelled out.

The brothers stared at him in silence. When he gave a nod, the music blared out from the expensive sound system Crash had installed.

"Sound of Madness" filled the air as Beth and Razer came out of the kitchen. Train saw Killyama's eyes widen as she took in Beth's clothes.

"Girl, you look hot."

Razer's wife gave her a self-conscious smile. "You don't look so bad yourself."

Train kept his eyes on Killyama as the members relaxed their guard.

Moon was dancing behind Jewel, grinding his hips against her ass. His hands were plastered to her naked breasts, the top pulled down to her waist.

Crash and Ember were sitting on a chair, going at it hot and heavy. She was on his lap as he rubbed her pussy through her jeans.

Razer hooked an arm over Beth's shoulder as he talked to Train about the week they had. Beth then asked Killyama what Sex Piston was doing tonight.

"Stud is racing in Illinois. Crazy Bitch went with her to cheer him on. Fat Louise and Cade promised they would stop by and let her mother see the baby."

"T.A. didn't go to the race?"

"No, she had to work late. If they had waited for her, they would have missed Stud's first race. She called me an hour ago to tell me she was going to bed with a book and a bottle of wine."

"A whole bottle?"

"You ever seen Stud race?"

"No."

"It takes a bottle of wine to get over missing that. He's hell on wheels."

Beth's gaze became interested. "Does he win a lot?"

"Every time. No one has beaten him yet."

Train and Razer stopped talking as Killyama bragged about Stud. Beth was practically fanning herself, and Train didn't miss the way Killyama's face became excited. Razer didn't seem much happier than he was about another man getting discussed in front of them. Train wouldn't describe what he felt as jealously, but it was close.

"When's his next race? I could tag along with Sex Piston and give you girls a break."

Razer and Train's conversation came to a screeching stop as they stopped pretending not to listen.

"I'll ask her and text you when I found out."

"Let's dance. I like this song." Razer guided Beth to the back of the room.

"He likes this song? He must be tone deaf," Killyama said with complete bewilderment.

"I like it, too."

He slid his leg between hers until his knee was resting against her crotch. "Does watching Stud race get you horny?"

"That's a leading question. You sure you want the answer?"

He pressed his knee harder against her. "Yes."

"Talking about Stud racing doesn't make me horny. What's tripping my wire is so much closer to me."

"Right answer." Train stood up then lifted her from the stool. He saw the overstuffed chair next to Crash and Ember was empty. Heading over, he sat down, pulling her down onto his lap.

He didn't pay attention to what everyone else was doing, unable to resist touching Killyama for another second.

"I've wanted to touch you since I saw you coming up the steps." He kissed the silky smooth flesh between her breasts.

She brought her hands to his shoulders as she tautened on his lap. "Don't you want to go upstairs?"

"Later." He covered her mouth with his, driving his tongue into her mouth before she could say anything else and ruin his mood.

"I was going to get you to show me around the club," she said when she was able to detach herself.

"You've seen most of it when you came over when Penni was here."

"I was going to say hi to Lily and see how Winter's doing."

"They aren't here."

His kisses weren't working. Deciding to go for it, he slid his hand over her flat waistline.

"Why aren't they here?"

Train lifted his head. "I don't know. Want me to call and ask?" He tried to keep the irritation out of his voice, realizing he failed when she shot him a withering look.

"Excuse me, but I ain't exactly used to being surrounded by people fucking."

Her humor drove his irritation away.

"I didn't take you for being shy." He glided his hand down to rest between her thighs.

"I'm not going to fuck you in front of everyone to prove I'm not shy."

"I don't expect you to. I wanted you to prove to me that being close to me makes you horny."

"You're always wanting me to prove shit to you. What about me?"

"What do you want me to prove to you?"

She didn't answer.

"Just ask."

"Okay. That you will trust me no matter what."

Trust didn't come easy for him. He never trusted anyone, except the brothers. However, she was out of her comfort zone, and she was trusting him with her body, so the least he could do was trust her. Within reason.

"I don't trust anyone like that."

"Not even The Last Riders?"

"Except for The Last Riders," Train clarified.

"And I'm not a Last Rider; is that what you're saying?"

"Not yet."

"You don't give up, do you?"

Train shook his head with a grin. "Not when I care about something."

"Do you care about me?"

Train held her stare, not letting her look away. "Yes."

Her body became limp as she twined her arms around his neck. "Do me a favor?"

"You need something to eat or drink?"

"No."

The hairs on the back of his neck stood up when she licked a path from his neck to his ear.

"I need more action and less talking."

CHAPTER TEN

Killyama allowed herself to become more comfortable. She wanted to switch the conversation from anything that concerned their emotions. Unsaid emotions couldn't come back to haunt you. When they weren't together anymore, she would eventually get over not having the sex, but feelings always came back to bite you in the ass.

He thought she was being shy, attending her first Last Rider party. It wasn't like she hadn't seen it all before in the backseat of her car.

All the bitches were jealous. They had all wanted to come. Cade had put his foot down, though. Sex Piston had kept mumbling that Stud would divorce her if she ditched his race to go to a Last Rider party, and she had told Crazy Bitch she wasn't going without her.

She let Train take over the kiss, knowing men liked that shit.

Killyama lifted one eyelash to see Ember had simply raised her short dress to her hips, sinking down on a condom-covered cock that Crash had readied.

"Holy Moses!" she said to herself, but Train had lifted his mouth from hers at the exclamation.

She hadn't seen *that* in the backseat of her car. She would have bitch-slapped any of her friends who showed that fancy shave job to their current dickheads.

Killyama had never been brave enough to go completely bare for three reasons. Number one: it hurt like a mother to have a complete waxing. Second: she preferred the runway effect—it gave the dickheads somewhere to aim for. The final and most important reason: it seriously hurt like a mother.

She might have to reconsider. She didn't want to be compared to Uncle Fester's Thing when Train went down on her. A girl had to do what a girl had to do to keep her man happy. However, he had to pass the final test before she decided to keep him, and she was willing to bet the last dollar sitting in her wallet that he would fail. She had never wanted a man to prove her wrong so badly.

The scary part was she was falling in love with him, and she knew he didn't feel the same. He didn't tremble when she touched him, nor did he worry about her when she wasn't there. When she had gotten shot, he had only come to the hospital with Lucky. She had even accepted that he would fuck around on her, which truthfully had never been a deal breaker with her.

Men could be faithful to a job, to their friends. Hell, they would even be loyal to their dog before they were faithful to their wives. That was why she had sworn never to get married.

She wiggled on Train's lap when he squeezed her thigh before going back to her crotch. He took it as an invitation when, in reality, she couldn't decide if she was into it or not. It was kind of distracting to see a woman get fucked a few feet away from where she was sitting. Therefore, she tried to focus on Train instead, but it was hard with the music blaring and the woman screaming, "Fuck me harder!"

She buried her head in his shoulder. "If I ever scream that loud, tape my mouth shut."

Train gave a low growl. "It doesn't bother me. I think it's hot to know a woman is enjoying what I'm doing."

"I don't think it's hot. I think it's called self-control."

"Don't you ever just loosen up?"

"No."

"Try. You might enjoy it."

"I'll take your word for it."

"You don't have to take my word for it. I can show you." He sprawled lower in the chair.

His hard body was always a source of temptation to her. Adding to that, his dark eyes turned slumberous, sending a tingle up her back. The possessive way he looked at her instantly made her wary to what he would do next.

He slid down one tiny strap that held her top up, lifting her up slightly to use his mouth to loosen the material and expose a nipple to his seeking lips.

Killyama wasn't thrilled about letting the club see her. Her fingers went to his hair, intending to pull him away, yet she somehow lost the will when his teeth bit down on the tender nipple.

She promised herself she would stop him in a minute. Then another one passed, and she found herself saying another. When he moved to her other breast, she almost jumped off his lap, but Train forestalled her, pinching the sensitive nipple he had been torturing and holding her in place as he licked her other nipple

"That's not fair," she gasped.

"I don't play fair."

She couldn't move, pinned like an unwilling captive. She was beginning to understand the draw of The Last Riders. They had the uncanny ability to make the women comfortable in their sexuality. They let the women know nothing was off limits. Hell, it was encouraged.

Killyama tried in vain to drag herself to solid ground again. She rose up, gasping out, which only drove her nipple deeper into his suckling mouth.

Staring down at Train with his mouth on her flesh, she let go of his hair to put her hands on his shoulder. She didn't know if she was trying to get away or give him more. He made up her mind for her, arching his hips so she could feel the hard ridge of his cock against her butt. Wiggling, she tried to ease the ache that had her growing wet, when the snap of her jeans was released.

As she put her hand over his to stop him, she became distracted as Ember and Crash came. She was so hot she felt as if steam was coming out of her jeans.

Train let her hand remain still as she got herself under control, making no effort to continue the heavy petting. Then, when Ember moved away and Crash went upstairs, she forgot all about the others in the room. No one could really see them, not unless they were standing at the bar, and most of them were dancing and playing pool.

Train slipped out of her grasp, and she let him slide his hand down the front of her jeans until he covered her pussy. She locked her thighs together, not to keep him away, but to increase the pressure. Then he stopped, pulling his hand back. She thought he would stop altogether. Instead, he lifted one of her legs over the arm of the chair then put his hand back on her pussy.

His shoulders blocked anyone from being able to watch as he pressed down on her, making circling motions that took all her willpower away. She wanted to stretch out her legs, but he controlled her movements, using his biceps to pin her. Killyama felt as if she were on a rack, breathlessly waiting for him to put her out of her torment.

Train then lifted his lips from her red, sensitive nipple, trailing kisses to the curve of her breast where he sucked hard at a tiny bit of her skin. It sent a jolt straight to her pussy.

"Let's go to your room…" she pleaded, unable to take his teasing any longer.

"Why? There isn't anything there that I can't do right here."

"I'm not going to let you fuck me here."

"We have all night to fuck."

"If you're not going to put me out of misery, then why are we fooling around?"

"Anticipation."

"You're so fucking funny." Her frustration had her snapping at him. "Hammer said you didn't have a sense of humor. Now I believe him."

As soon as Hammer's name came out of her mouth, she wanted to slap herself.

Train's lips curled up in a grin. "I never joked around with Hammer. We're usually too busy trying to get our ass out of Dodge."

Killyama narrowed her eyes on Train's unsurprised face. "How long have you known?"

"That you know Hammer and Jonas?"

She nodded abruptly.

"A while."

"Why didn't you say something? To me or to them? Hammer and Jonas have been running around Jamestown, trying to avoid you seeing them."

That fact caught his attention.

"Why wouldn't they want me to know?"

Thinking fast, she tried to regain her composure. "I guess they didn't want you to know they worked with a woman."

Train stared at her skeptically.

"You know how He-Man he is…"

"I can't say I've seen that side of him…or Jonas."

"Well, he is. They both are."

"I assumed he was your father."

"Hell to the fucking no." Lowering her lashes, she raised his mouth to hers.

"Do you know that you only kiss me when you try to change the subject?"

"I do?" She sighed. "Look, he's not my father. He's been in my life ever since I was a kid, and so has Jonas. They kind of became surrogate fathers."

"Your father didn't care that they took his place?"

"My father is dead."

"I'm sorry, Killy."

"I'd rather go back to making out than talking about it."

"I can do that."

He had continued rubbing her as they talked, not letting the desire inside of her die. Now she rode his hand harder as he finally gave her his mouth. Thrusting her tongue inside, she tasted heaven as she tried to clamp her legs together again.

"I'm not going to come," she whispered against his mouth.

"Who you telling? Me or yourself?" Train murmured back.

Her body was stretched over his. There was no lying about it, even though she wanted to.

"Both of us."

She brushed her hair out of her eyes. If he kept teasing her, she would be the one everyone was watching. He thought he could make her lose control and lay the foundation for more sexual experiences until she became as blasé as the other women in the room. Remembering the blowjob she had given him, she knew how she could get him to do what she wanted instead.

She deliberately wiggled her ass again. "You're so hard." She lowered her voice to a sensuous tone. Then, clamping her teeth on his lower lip, she nibbled it like a piece of candy. "You're so strong." She ran her hand over his bicep, feeling it flex under her fingertips. "Mmm...Rub me harder. Ooo, that feels *so* good, lover. You make me *so* horny. I could just eat—"

Train stood up so fast that Killyama almost fell to the floor. She hid her smile as he rushed her toward the steps.

"Killyama, have you had time to ask Sex Piston when…?" Beth started to ask as they passed her and Razer.

"She'll talk to her later," Train threw the comment over his shoulder as he kept walking, tugging her alongside him.

She laughed as they climbed the stairs. "That was a little rude."

He kept walking.

Yanking his bedroom door open, he pushed her inside, and then pressed her back to the closed door. "I didn't think you would want me fucking you in front of Beth. If she hadn't been in there, my dick would have taken what you were begging to give me."

"Dream on, lover. We gonna talk about it to death, or are we gonna do it?"

"Oh, we're gonna do it." Train tugged off her jeans, somehow leaving her stripper heels on. He slid a condom on, and then lifted her legs over his forearms as he raised her high up against the door. "I'm going to fuck you so hard, you're going to think that door is tattooed on your ass."

"Do it!" she whimpered, goading him on.

He positioned his dick at the opening of her pussy. With a lunge, he then buried himself halfway inside of her.

"God, that feels so good. Give it all to me."

Train lifted her legs higher over his biceps then wrapped his forearms over her legs, flattening her tits with his hands. Using her to brace himself, he drove his dick so high that she came instantly.

"Faster!" She wanted to ride out her orgasm as he fucked her.

She bucked against him as he fucked her steadily, his hair clinging to the sides of his face, obscuring her from seeing him. Gently, she reached out to brush it away.

"You're so tight…I'm afraid I'm going to hurt you."

"I'm not Humpty Dumpty; I don't break." She moaned. "Like that, lover. That's the way I want your cock…Deep and fast…"

She met each of his thrusts with one of her own. When he stiffened, he took her hands, lifting them over her head and locking them in place as he ground out his climax in her spasming pussy, giving her the weight of his body when he finally stopped moving.

"You're a dangerous woman."

She rubbed her cheek against his. "You going to let me down or keep me here all night?"

"Give me a minute. I'm trying to decide. I kind of like where you are, but I have plans for the bed and the shower."

"Can you let me use the bathroom first?"

"Do I have to?"

"Yes."

"Damn." He let her down, releasing her hands. "Hurry back."

"Dude, you won't have time to miss me." She started to open the door when she realized all she had on was her heels while her top was bunched around her waist.

Killyama pulled off her top then grabbed the one Train had taken out of a drawer. She started to take her heels off, too, when...

"Don't. I like fucking you with them on."

"Pervert." She grinned, going out the door and leaving Train's partially open.

In the bathroom, she did her business and washed off. When she came out, she came to a stop. In the bedroom across from Train's, there was a woman she hadn't seen around the club before. Rider was naked on the bed, and he was pulling her down on top of him. Crash was taking his jeans off when he looked up, seeing her staring at them.

"Want to join?"

Her mouth dropped open. The woman was going to do both men?

"No, thanks." She turned, nearly bumping into a grinning Train.

She slammed the door shut when he started laughing.

"She is going to fuck them both, and he thought he could fuck me, too?" she stormed, tearing off Train's shirt.

"Crash could fuck five women and have enough left over to give you."

She had imagined Train doing other women every night they weren't together, but she hadn't even thought that he would do two or more a night. Or a day. The sobering fact had her wanting to get dressed.

She picked up her clothes, going to the side of the bed as if she were going to lie down. "Who was the chick? I've never seen her before."

"That's Sasha. She became a member before Aisha was born."

"Did you give her your vote?"

"Beth told you about the votes?"

"Yes. And before you say anything, we won't say anything."

"Yes, I gave her my vote." Train held her stare, waiting for her reaction.

Killyama didn't react. She simply looked down at her clothes.

Sex meant nothing to him. It was about quantity to The Last Riders, not quality. She wouldn't even be second best to Train. She would be third, or fourth, or fifth. Hell, he probably couldn't remember which women he fucked the day before, much less the day before that.

She looked up, surprising him. "Why are you staring at me that way? Afraid I'm going to freak out on you?"

"It crossed my mind."

She tossed her clothes down then languidly stretched out on his bed. "Who has more stamina, you or Crash?"

She could tell he was debating on whether to tell her the truth or not. Like all men, his pride won out.

"Me."

"Prove it."

Train gave a relieved breath, lying down next to her and running a hand over her breasts. "I told you, you're a dangerous woman."

She raised herself over him, her nipples brushing his chest as she slipped between his thighs. Killyama brought her mouth to his cock, sucking the head inside before letting it pop out so she could lick the stem to his balls. She teased and tormented him the way he had done her downstairs, refusing to let him come, even when he broke into a cold sweat. She used her thumb every time she felt him almost climaxing, stopping it just short. It wasn't her yells that filled the bedroom when she finally let him come.

She didn't let him rest for long before she started in on him again, stroking him to his full-length. She made him prove his claim over and over again, not letting him fall asleep until the sun started rising outside his window.

"Go to sleep, lover." Killyama spoke softly as his breathing deepened.

She lay there, resting her head on her hand as she stared down at him, memorizing his face. With a tender hand, she traced his chiseled jaw, his stubborn chin, smoothing the tired shadows under his lashes. Then, brushing a soft kiss to his lips, she slid away, putting on her clothes.

She stood looking down at him, wanting to get back in bed. Instead, she tenderly covered him with a blanket before going to the door.

With her hand on the doorknob, she paused, then quietly opened and closed the door, leaving the man she loved behind.

Chapter Eleven

"You sure you want to do this?" Hammer asked as she was about to knock on the door.

Not pausing her knocking on the sturdy door, Killyama responded, "I'm sure."

She straightened her shoulders when she heard the door opening. Rider's face filled with shock when he saw her standing on the porch. Then his eyes went to Hammer and Jonas standing behind her.

"I want to talk to Viper," she declared.

"Come in. I'll get him. He's in the kitchen."

Killyama nodded, walking into the clubhouse she had left three hours before. She went into the large living room where all traces of the night before were gone while Hammer and Jonas stared around the club with interest.

"It doesn't look this big from the road," Jonas muttered under his breath as they flanked her.

Viper came out of the kitchen with Shade a minute later, not showing his surprise as Rider had, but his eyes were wary.

Shade and Rider followed their president's lead as he came to stand in front of them.

"Morning, Killyama. Hammer, Jonas, it's been a while since I've seen both of you."

The men shook hands as Killyama heard doors opening from upstairs. She wondered sardonically which of the men had alerted the others above to come downstairs.

"Viper, Shade, it's good to see you, too." Hammer took his hand back.

Killyama raised an eyebrow at Hammer's diffident tone. Then she got the men back on the track she wanted.

"If we're all done shooting the shit, I want to talk to you."

Train hurried down the steps, while Moon and Crash stayed at the top, looking over the banister. Ten to one, they were told to protect the women still sleeping.

"Go ahead. We're all brothers here."

She shrugged. "Fine. I'm here to call in the favor you owe me."

Viper narrowed his eyes. "I was wondering when you were going to call it in."

"Today's the day." She could see the men didn't find her wise-crack humorous.

"What do you want?"

Killyama met Train's eyes as he moved behind Viper. Fury glowed in them as they waited for her answer.

"Sasha. She has a warrant out for her arrest in Ohio. We're here to take her back."

"Sasha isn't going—" Train tried to take a step forward, but Viper held out his arm, stopping him.

"You owe me, Viper. I didn't ask for anything when I saved Winter's ass. *You* made the offer. Now I'm calling it in. I want Sasha. It's not a hard decision to make; you're either going to keep your favor or not. I'm actually doing you a biggie. I could have called the State Police and told them where she was."

"But you wouldn't collect the bounty for that, would you?" Viper's expression turned harsh.

"Well, there is that." She shrugged. "Kentucky has been a pesky problem for me. The state doesn't allow bounty hunters to make arrests. They have to go to the courthouse, and a judge orders the sheriff to make it. But I'm sure you all knew that, with Knox being on your payroll. Him and Diamond have been able to keep her from being re-arrested." She grinned, trying once again at humor she didn't feel. "I have to hand it to you guys; you managed to keep Sasha hidden in Ohio before stashing her where no one could get to her."

"Ohio doesn't have bounty hunters, either, so why do you care? Did Kane pay...?"

She tsked Viper. "Crash fucked up. You should consider hiring Jonas when you're having someone investigated. I may be a licensed bounty hunter in Tennessee, but in Ohio, I'm a licensed surety bond agent. It's amazing what you can accomplish on the internet, like earning a Criminal Justice degree and applying to different states for licenses."

Viper's lips tightened as he looked up at Moon. "Get Sasha."

The man nodded then gave her a thunderous glower before he disappeared from sight.

"She is facing a hung jury. Her ex-boyfriend fabricated the charges. She didn't steal any jewelry from Kane—"

"That's not for us to decide; it's the court's decision."

"Diamond is working on her case—"

"I would have gotten a lawyer in Ohio, one who knows how the good ol' boy system works there. But that's just me."

Sex Piston was going to be furious when she heard that she had insulted her sister's skills.

"What's going on?" Sasha asked. The female Last Rider came down the steps, apprehensively moving toward the men.

Train and Rider moved closer to her in a protective gesture, and Sasha immediately put her trembling hand into Rider's. She wanted to rip off the arm Train placed around her shoulders.

Moon must have told her to get dressed because she was wearing a T-shirt and jeans. Even without makeup and casual clothes, Sasha was an attractive woman. It had taken Killyama two hours to get dressed for the party last night, and that was with Sex Piston doing her hair and makeup. Still, she didn't look half as good as Sasha looked this morning right after getting out of bed.

Killyama assumed a cheerful smile as she continued to annihilate the men. "I'm here to take you back to Ohio. You missed your trial date, and your bond has been revoked."

"I don't want to go! Viper…"

Viper moved his condemning gaze away from her to look at Sasha in sympathy. "You have to go with her."

"But—"

"Listen to me. I'll get you out as soon as I can. I promise."

Sasha started crying as Killyama stepped forward to take Sasha's arm, but Rider and Train didn't release their hold on her. Killyama didn't back away, either.

"Viper, are we going to have a problem here?"

"Train, Rider, let her go." Viper ordered.

When they angrily stepped away, Killyama took Sasha's shaking arm, dodging the impassive look Shade gave her. He was the only one guarding his expression as she led her fugitive toward the door where Viper opened it for them, yet forced Killyama to stop when he didn't move.

"I'm letting you take her because The Last Riders keep their word. We're even now. I don't want to see you in this clubhouse ever again. You got me?"

She refused to show how his words had deeply affected her. "No reason to come back. I got what I came for. I'll get paid for taking Sasha back to Ohio, and sex with Train was just an added bonus."

Train had moved so she would have to brush past him when she went out the door. And when she did, he flinched as if she had contaminated him.

"You fucking bitch. You had this planned all along, didn't you?"

"Nothing gets past you, does it, lover?" Mockery might not have been the best choice when a man had been betrayed, but she never did anything half-assed.

Train sprung toward her, but Shade caught him around his waist, pulling him back before Hammer or Jonas could.

"Cool it. We'll get Sasha back."

"Yes, we will," Train snarled. "Don't worry, Sasha; I'll keep your spot in my bed warm until you get back."

His hate-filled tone had been directed toward her, and it struck like a hot poker to the heart. She made sure not to look around as she went out the door, afraid one of the intuitive men would see the hurt she tried to hide.

Knowing the club watched as they loaded Sasha into their vehicle, Killyama climbed into the backseat, sitting next to Sasha and never looking back at the clubhouse.

As Hammer pulled out of the parking lot, the only sound that could be heard was the cries of the woman sitting next to her.

"Quit crying," she snapped. "It's not like you're going to the electric chair. You stole a couple of necklaces; you didn't kill the fucker."

"I didn't steal anything," she sobbed out. "Kane gave me one necklace, not two. He lied about that and the rest of the jewelry he claimed I stole."

"Listen, I don't care if you're guilty or innocent. I leave that to twelve people to decide."

"They are going to lock me away for years. I'm innocent, and you don't care?" She sniffed her tears back.

"Nope." She turned to stare out the back window, expecting to see some of The Last Riders following. So far, the road behind them was empty.

"What kind of person are you?"

Killyama shot her a glare. "One who works hard for her money."

"Are you saying I don't?"

"Bitch, what do I have to do to get it through your thick head that I do not care about anything to do with you? Not the charges brought against you, nor anything else concerning you, except the check I will get for bringing you to Ohio."

"I feel sorry for you."

"Feel sorry for yourself." Killyama could stand a lot of things, but pity wasn't one of them. "I'm not the one who hooked up with a loser who was sick of you banging a clubhouse full of men and pressed charges against you for stealing."

While it didn't make Sasha stop crying, that comment shut her mouth.

"Well, that was interesting," Jonas remarked when they crossed the city line and entered the neighboring county. Finally relaxing, he reached for his coffee cup, and then handed her one.

"Thanks for the backup," she said caustically. "Were you wait-ing for Train to punch me?"

"Did you see Shade?" Jonas mimicked Shade's motions. "It was like watching a master at work."

"Wow. I see where I am on the scale of importance to you fuckwads."

"Be real. Hammer or I would have stepped in if we thought he would have hurt you. He might have shaken you, but you would have crushed his nuts if he had."

"Train wouldn't have touched you. He's the sweetest man I know," Sasha said.

Killyama should have known she wouldn't stay quiet for long.

"I'll take your word for it."

"You shouldn't have to. I heard you in his room all last night. Any woman who spends any time with him knows how considerate and gentle he is. Train's my favorite. Well, him and Rider are pretty good, so it's hard to pick."

Killyama slouched down in her seat. "Jonas, shoot me."

"Why, already regretting that Train won't be inviting you over for any more sleepovers?"

"I don't regret a damn thing. Why would I care? Train's not keeping a spot warm for me," she snapped.

When Sasha nodded, Killyama wanted to punch her in the face.

"No, he won't, and you'll be missing out. He's the type to go downstairs and fix you something to eat when you're hungry, buy your favorite body wash, and when you're on your period, he rubs your belly."

"Pull over!" Killyama ordered, practically yelling.

"What for?" Hammer took his eyes off the road to stare at her in the rearview mirror.

"I want Jonas to switch seats with me."

"I'm not pulling over. The Last Riders could be behind us out of sight."

"Oh, and did I forget to mention that he would work your shift if you want to get ready for the party?"

Killyama tried to climb into the front seat, but Jonas wouldn't budge. Giving up, she had to listen to Sasha talk about Train's attributes until they reached the interstate, which took an hour. When she ran out of things to say about him, she started talking about Rider. Apparently, he wasn't as perfect as Train, because she started discussing Crash after five minutes.

"Oh, my God. Will someone shoot me already? Bitch, I know you're making this shit up."

"I'm not lying, I swear. If you take me back, they won't be mad anymore. Well, maybe just a little." She stared at her beseechingly then started crying again.

Killyama reached into the console, taking out the tissues and handing them to her.

"Thank you. Do you know if the other women prisoners are going to beat me up or make me their bitch?"

Killyama rubbed her forehead. They were still two hours away from the jail.

"You've been watching too much television. You've been in jail before."

"I was only there for two hours before Moon bonded me out."

"Moon must have someone in his back pocket to have you bonded out so fast."

Sasha wiped her eyes with the tissue. "Not enough to manage to get the charges dropped. Please take me back."

"Running away doesn't solve anything. You need to face the charges. Were you just going to hide out for the rest of your life?"

"No, Diamond was trying to fix things for me."

"Diamond and The Last Riders were putting their ass on the line by protecting you. It was only a matter time before the authorities in Ohio grew tired of waiting for Knox to arrest you. Would you be happy if Knox was arrested? Or Diamond lost her license to practice law? You say you care about Train and Rider; would you have cared if the State Police came knocking on the clubhouse door and one of them were hurt trying to sneak you out?"

Shamefaced, Sasha stared down at her lap. "I didn't think of that. I'm so used to Viper and Moon taking care of things that I didn't consider they could get hurt."

"You're a grown-ass woman. The only one who needs to be handling your business is you. Do you know how many women are behind bars because they trusted a man?" Killyama shook her head at the woman. "Do what you have to do to get this trouble taken care of without getting any of your friends hurt, and then get a new start on a future *you* control."

Sasha's crying stopped, and she remained quiet for the rest of the trip. Killyama expected her to start the waterworks again when they stopped at the jail and she helped her out of the back seat, but she remained calm.

Killyama watched as she was taken into the in-take room while Jonas filled out the paperwork. She could see Sasha pulling out her empty pockets.

Killyama asked a standing guard nearby if Ron was on duty. Then she asked if she could talk to him.

Waiting impatiently for him to show, Killyama watched as Sasha was told to remove her shoes by a female guard. The woman's lips were beginning to tremble again.

"Hi, Rae. How can I help you?"

Hammer and Jonas frowned at her in puzzlement as she turned toward Ron.

"I have a favor to ask."

"I'll see what I can do. What do you need?" Ron was one of the few men she had grown to like since she had started working in this field. He was fifty years old and thirty pounds overweight, with a wife who was as in love with him as he with her.

Killyama walked to the side so no one could hear their conversation. "Could you give the woman I brought in her own cell and make sure no one messes with her? If you can lose her paperwork for a few days, I would appreciate it."

"What was she wanted for?"

"Theft. She's going to get her charges cleared. Her ex framed her."

"We've heard that one before."

"I believe her." At his doubting look, she put her hand on his arm. "Come on; she's scared."

"She should be."

"Please."

He sighed heavily. "Okay, but this is the last time. When are you going to stop listening to the sob stories these runners are feeding you?"

"I guess when you get promoted out of here, I won't have anyone to help me out."

"You're too kindhearted. The last one you tried to help was back in jail the next day."

"She's different." Killyama gestured toward Sasha. "When she gets out of here, she won't be back." Viper would see to that.

"Fine. I'll watch out for her."

"I'd hug you, but I don't want the other guards to get jealous," she teased him good-naturedly.

"Better not. Deb gets mean when she thinks someone is flirting with me."

"You think I can't take her?" Killyama grinned.

"Hell no! You might be younger, but I married a tough cookie."

"I guess we're not fated to be together, then."

Ron blushed. "I better get back to work."

"Thanks, Ron."

"We done?" Killyama asked as Hammer and Jonas took the paperwork from the officer at the desk.

"Yes. What were you talking to Ron about?" Hammer asked.

"Nothing. I was just asking him about his wife and kids."

"Sure you did," Jonas said, handing her the completed paperwork.

"I saw the hundred you slipped him." Hammer pushed the button so the guard would open the door for them to leave.

"You need to get your eyes checked." Killyama swiped the keys away from Hammer. "I'm driving."

Getting behind the wheel, she started the SUV. "It's getting late. How about we stay the night?"

"You never want to stay the night. What's up?" Hammer took the gum she had been about to put in her mouth, throwing it out the window.

"Nothing. I had a long night, and we have a long drive. I'm tired."

"That's cool with us. We can get an early start in the morning."

"I'm going to take a couple of days off. We can rent a car before we find a hotel room for me to use until I come home."

Jonas nixed the idea. "We're not going back home without you."

"I need some space and rest. I'm not going to get that with you two here."

"You believe this bullshit, Jonas?"

Jonas leaned forward, sniffing the air. "I smell the bullshit, too."

"You're going to stick your nose in it, aren't you?" Hammer looked at her with disapproval.

She knew they weren't going to believe whatever lie she came up with, so she admitted, "Yes."

"Then I guess we're all staying," Jonas stated.

"What's the plan?"

Killyama grinned at Hammer. "When you're dealing with someone who has a lot of power and who can get a lot of strings pulled, you know what you have to do?"

"What?" Hammer and Jonas both asked.

"You have to call the puppet master."

CHAPTER TWELVE

Train watched the SUV pull out onto the road. Then he started to go inside the clubhouse to get his wallet and keys.

"Where do you think you're going?"

"To Ohio."

"You're staying here. Shade, Moon, go. And take Rider."

"I want to go," Train protested.

"There isn't anything you can do."

The men went back inside the clubhouse as Viper took out his phone. Train waited impatiently as Viper called Knox then Diamond, listening as Viper recounted what had happened, not sparing the embarrassment of how Killyama had known Sasha was there.

Unable to listen anymore, Train went to the bar, getting a glass and the whiskey, pouring it to the brim.

"What did Diamond say?" Train asked when Viper walked up to him, putting his phone away.

Viper took the bottle away from him, pouring himself a glass. "She said, 'I told you so'."

Train downed his drink then turned to smash the glass against the wall. "It's all my fault."

"No, it's mine. Diamond warned me two months ago this would happen, and she told me to hire a different lawyer in Ohio. I put it off, thinking I'd take care of it when I had the time. I've been so busy with the new contracts, Aisha, and making sure Winter's cancer is gone that I let Sasha slip through the crack."

"You've had your hands full. I'm the one who invited Killyama. We've been so careful not to let anyone see Sasha in town, and then last night Killyama saw her and asked who she was. Like a fool, I told her." Train gave a harsh laugh. "She's been playing me like a fiddle since we had the party at Rosie's. I even believed I was making headway in getting her to join The Last Riders."

Viper poured himself another drink at that confession.

Imagining all the brothers' angry thoughts, Train stormed out of the clubroom, going to his room then coming back downstairs where he threw his leather on the floor at Viper's feet.

"I don't deserve to be a Last Rider."

"Pick it up," Viper said on a sigh. "You let your dick do the thinking. It's happened to us all. We'll get Sasha out of this trouble, and then we will go back to normal. The one change we will make is no further contact with the Destructors. Stud might have married into the crew of conniving women, but The Last Riders haven't."

Razer, who had come over when Killyama was walking out the door with Sasha, didn't say a word of protest against Viper's order. However, Train knew that Beth and Lily, and maybe some of the other wives, were going to be hurt by the order.

A line was going to be drawn between The Last Riders and the Destructors, and it was all Killyama's fault. It would be better this way, though, because if he ever got close to Killyama again, he would break a vow he had made to never touch a woman when he was angry. And right now, he was beyond angry at the bitch.

He wanted to pay her back so badly that she would never betray another man. The problem was, the coldhearted woman had to have a heart to learn her lesson, and she didn't have one.

Jewell peered around the door of the kitchen. "Is it okay if I come out now?"

"Yes." Train took the bottle away from Viper before he could drink it all, pulling out another glass.

"I hope you don't expect me to clean up this mess?" Jewell gingerly stepped over the broken glass.

"I did it; I'll clean it up."

"Will someone tell me what's going on?" Jewell demanded, staring at the men's faces.

"Killyama used the favor Viper owed her to take Sasha back to Ohio. Seems she's some kind of surety bond agent there."

Jewell didn't look as upset as Train would have expected. "You're not mad?"

"At Killyama?" Jewell prevaricated.

"Hell yes. Who else?"

"Sasha." She shrugged. "Don't get me wrong; I'm not crazy about what Killyama did. But let's be real, Train. You were asking for trouble when you started messing around with her. Everyone in Treepoint and Jamestown knows she's a psychopath. Did you forget the fight at the Pink Slipper? I know I haven't. You men may have forgotten, but I still remember T.A. shaking me like a rag doll then trying to strangle me. Do any of you remember what Killyama was doing?"

Train racked his memory. Truthfully, he didn't remember. He had been too busy trying to fight off one of the larger bikers from the Destructors.

Jewell shook her at the men's blank stares. "All the women were taking each other on except for Killyama. She went for you guys." She looked around, asking, "Where's Rider?"

"He left." Viper put his glass down.

"I bet he remembers that night. She nearly broke his nose with a chair. She also gave you"—she pointed at Train—"one of those two black eyes you got that night."

"I would have remembered Killyama giving me a black eye. Dozer did…" Train trailed off as he thought back to that night.

"Yes, he did. He hit you so hard he knocked you out. Killyama hit you when you were falling down."

"She hit me when I was down?"

"You hadn't hit the floor yet, but you were down and out for a few minutes."

"I'm going to pay that bitch back. I won't lay a hand on her, but when I'm finished with her, I'll make sure she's paid back for that and betraying my trust."

"If you're going to make her pay, know what you're making her pay for. Killyama doesn't owe any loyalty to The Last Riders. Sasha should have let her ex-boyfriend have time to get over her before she rubbed his face in the fact she had become a Last Rider. I'm not excusing her ex"—Jewell raised her hands in defense—"but Sasha could have made better choices. Sasha and Killyama are both guilty of screwing men over."

Train almost lost his cool. His voice turned deadly as he told Jewell, "Sasha didn't betray The Last Riders' trust. And Killyama may not owe The Last Riders loyalty, but she did betray the personal trust I had in her."

Viper looked down at a text message. "Shade said he'll call as soon they get to Ohio. Diamond has been trying to find a lawyer to take Sasha's case. Crash, are you positive you didn't miss anything on Kane or his family we can use against them?"

"You want me to hire Jonas to double-check my work?" At Viper's glare, Crash changed his sarcastic tone. "I'm sure. His family hasn't had so much as a speeding ticket on their record. I searched the phone number Sasha gave me for Kane; it only shows run-of-the-mill text messages. He goes to work and goes back home every night. Once a week, he goes to play golf, but that's pretty much it. Sasha said he always had two phones on him, but I don't have access to those messages without the phone number."

"He isn't carrying two phones without a reason. I'll tell Shade. Maybe he can find out."

"Nickel has been trying to figure it out since I got here," Moon spoke up. "He's had no luck. He talked to three women Kane had dated. None of them knew, either."

Sasha was going to do time for a crime she hadn't committed unless they found something on Kane to make him tell the truth. Killyama's treachery had limited their options.

Train wanted to defy Viper's order and go to Ohio. It was hard to stand idly by as each of the members awoke and learned what had happened that morning.

"Do you think Sasha will get mad if I borrow her new black dress?" Stori came up from behind him, running her hand over his ass.

He shoved himself away from her, moving to the other side of the counter. "What do you think?"

"Sorry," she mumbled, escaping into the kitchen.

Jewell took the whisky bottle away from Viper, refilling Train's glass for him. "You going to make us all pay for Killyama stabbing you in the back?"

He gave a humorless smile. "No. It wasn't the first time I ever got stabbed." Train almost spilled his drink onto the jacket he had laid there. The night she had been cold, he had tried to get her to wear it. She wasn't worthy to touch him or the jacket now. "But it will be the last time."

Chapter Thirteen

"Get your ass off my bike. I told you last night I had nothing to say to you."

Killyama got off Shade's bike, snidely asking, "You have any luck getting Sasha out of jail yet?"

"No, but if you came to gloat, you're barking up the wrong tree. You need to leave before anyone comes out and sees you. I can guarantee Hammer and Jonas won't be enough to pull them off you."

"They aren't here. They're asleep in their hotel room. They told me I'm wasting my time."

"They're right."

"Where are you going?"

Shade remained silent, getting on his bike and starting the motor.

"Fine, don't answer. You can say hi to Sasha when they arrest your ass." Killyama turned and started walking toward the SUV she had parked at the convenience store across the street.

Shade rode his bike across the street, waiting for her to reach him.

"You could have offered me a ride."

"I thought you don't ride with married men?"

"I'm tired," she excused. "I haven't slept in two nights."

"I bet Train isn't getting much sleep tonight, either." Shade's penetrating blue eyes studied her reaction as Killyama winced while thinking about how the women would be helping Train repair his wounded pride.

"I thought of a way to help Sasha," she spoke quickly, trying to keep him from reading too much.

"What? Have her plead to the charge? Or throw her to the mercy of the court?"

"You haven't been able to find a lawyer in Ohio?" she asked, ignoring his stab.

"No."

Killyama reached into her pocket then gave him a card. "He'll help, but he's expensive."

Shade took the card, shoving it into his jacket pocket without even looking at it. "I hope you're not expecting me to say thanks."

"No." Killyama gave him a wry smile. "It doesn't matter which lawyer you get. The DA has an air tight case against her, which is why Diamond hasn't been able to get the charges dropped. Until you can find some new evidence, Sasha is only going to be a memory for the next five to seven years."

"What's your idea?"

"Kane still has one of the necklaces he accused Sasha of stealing. He has it stashed at his father's house. There's no breaking in there; you'll get caught before you get a foot inside the gate."

Shade didn't seem surprised, and he was still listening. "I don't get caught."

"You will. Jonas says there is no getting past the security. It doesn't make a difference anyway. You can't steal them then take them to the police. You can't tell them you stole them from him, even if you tell the police or Sasha's lawyer the jewelry is there. They have to have probable cause to get a search warrant." Killyama took a deep breath, relieving the tension that had been building as she talked. "Once a week, Kane goes golfing."

"Crash will be relieved that he hasn't lost his touch. You're not telling me anything we don't know."

"Did you know Kane's not actually golfing? He borrows the caddy to drive over to a small hotel that has a massage parlor attached."

Shade turned off his motor. "How did you find this out?"

"One of Kane's ex-girlfriends told me. She managed to get ahold of his burner phone when they were dating while he was taking a shower. He had told Cassandra the extra phone was for clients; that he was dappling in real estate. What he has been dappling in is hookers.

"While Kane's at the massage parlor, Hammer, Jonas, and I are going to try to grab his burner phone as an insurance policy. We don't know what's on it, so I don't want to put all of our eggs in that basket. What I suggest is you break into Kane's car at the golf course. Cassandra said he keeps the gate opener to his father's house on the window visor. He's on vacation in the Hamptons, by the way, and the staff is off. Kane keeps his keys in the console. Apparently, he doesn't even take his wallet into the massage parlor. He pays in cash."

"Like you said, I can't take the jewelry."

"You won't have to. Just arrange for it to be seen easily. The cops won't need a search warrant if the jewelry is in plain sight when the police and the fire department put out the fire you set."

"Sounds like you have everything all planned out. What I don't understand is what you need me for? You, Hammer, and Jonas can do this on your own. If you think you're going to win points from Train, you won't. He hates you right now. The whole club does. You've broken a friendship with the Destructors, and the fallout will affect Beth, Lily, and Diamond, too. Viper ordered them not to have any association with you."

Killyama didn't blink an eye, knowing any response she made would be recounted to The Last Riders.

"Dude, is that supposed to get me upset? I don't give a fuck about The Last Riders, and if Beth, Lily, and Diamond listen to Viper, that's on them, not me. The only fallout I need you to care about is when the shit hits the fan, and daddy big bucks comes racing back from his vacation. Then you make sure it doesn't get swept under the rug. To do that, it's going to take lots of money and finesse. You wouldn't have caught Lily's attention if you couldn't handle that. The dude whose card I gave you can help you and will point you in the right direction."

"I take it he wants his own cut?" Shade took the card out of his pocket to look at it. "He's not a lawyer? How can a Professor of Economics at the university help?"

"He has money and connections, and he's running for mayor. He's trying to get into politics, but two things have stopped him: Kane's father and the current mayor. If Yates helps us, it eliminates daddy big bucks who holds the mayor's purse strings. One thing Kentucky and Ohio have in common is the good ol' boy system. Yates wants to prove corruption in the courts system and slide into home plate. But does it really matter as long as Sasha gets out?"

"Moon will be all over this plan. The mayor has been breathing down his neck ever since he found out his daughter wasn't the virgin she was pretending to be."

Killyama laid her hand over his when he would have reached for his cell phone. "No. You're the only one I want to know what's going down…now and when it's over. I don't care how you explain it to The Last Riders; just keep me out of it. That's my price…Take it or leave it."

Shade scrutinized her expression, pulling his hand away from her touch. "Why?"

"As long as you come out looking and smelling like a hero, and Sasha goes back to fucking everyone's brains out, we all get what we want."

"I'll play it your way, but you're making a mistake you're going to regret."

"What am I going to regret? That The Last Riders can't stand me? They never did. The Destructors? Hell, Stud is going to be just as mad at me as The Last Riders. The women? They'll work it out by telling Viper to shove his order up his ass." Killyama sidestepped around his bike, going to her ride.

"Will you at least tell me why you did it?"

She stepped up into the black Escalade. "I was bored." Slamming her door closed, she drove away.

Train was the only one who mattered, and he wouldn't care that her heart was breaking at the lie she had told Shade.

She turned the window wipers' speed up faster when the drizzle turned into a downpour. She drove easily as the streets to the hotel were beginning to flood. She wasn't timid on slick roads; she liked everything about rain—the way it made everything smell new, the way it sounded on a roof, the way it felt on your skin…the way heaven could weep the tears she refused to shed.

଒ ଓ

Shade watched the taillights until she was out of sight before taking out his phone again.

"Any news?" Train's low voice answered.

"You alone?"

"No. What do you need?"

Shade heard Jewell mutter something in the background.

"Never mind. I'll talk you later when I find something out."

Hanging up, he started his bike, riding back to the clubhouse. Once there, he shook off the rain as he ran into the clubhouse where Rider was waiting for him inside.

"What did Killyama want?"

"Wake Moon up. We have work to do."

CHAPTER FOURTEEN

Crash raised his eyes from his cards. "Who was that?"

Train set his cell phone down on the kitchen table. "Shade."

"What did he want?"

"He didn't say. He was acting weird."

"Shade weird or weird-weird?"

"I don't know. I can't explain it. Call him back and ask him." Using the tip of his cards, he shoved his cell phone toward Crash.

"I was just asking." He shifted in his seat as if Shade would yell at him from the phone.

Jewell folded her cards, stretching as she rose. "I have to get to bed. I need to try to get a couple of hours sleep before work."

"See you in the morning." Train dropped another twenty in the pot.

"Why don't you come with me? You haven't slept in three nights."

"I'm not tired."

"Suit yourself. Crash, make sure you shower before work; you reek. That pizza you ordered had enough garlic on it to make a vampire comatose."

"Want to give me a goodnight kiss?"

"Hell no. Besides, it's morning." Jewell shoved away from Crash when he jokingly tried to pull her down onto his lap. Dodging him, she escaped out of the kitchen.

Train showed his cards, pulling the pile of cash toward him.

Crash grunted, leaning back in his chair. "I'm all in, brother. Then I'm going to bed."

"You don't want to play another game?"

"You have all my money."

Train took out his wallet and precisely tucked the bills inside. "I can give you a loan if you need it?"

"No thanks. I'll borrow some money from Razer if I need it. He doesn't charge interest." Crash left, complaining about having to take another shower.

Train made a fresh pot of coffee, glad he hadn't eaten a slice of the bizarre pizza Crash loved to order. It had five different meats and enough garlic to kill a horse, with jalapenos, onions, and pineapple on top. It always made his eyes water when Crash would carry the pizza box into the room.

He was cramming the box in the trash outside of the kitchen door when Razer stepped out of his house, heading toward him.

"Crash ordered pizza again?"

"He lives on that stuff." Train held the door for him as they made their way inside. "I told him he was a heart attack waiting to happen, but he says the garlic keeps him healthy." Train picked up his coffee cup as Razer poured himself one. "What has you up so early? You don't have to be at work for another couple of hours."

"Beth will be getting Noah and Chance ready for pre-school in an hour. I didn't want the boys to see me sleeping on the couch."

"You slept on the couch?"

"Beth and I got into a fight when I told her not to talk to Sex Piston and her crew anymore."

"I can imagine how that went."

"Like a ton of the bricks. She threatened to hurt me when I fell asleep."

Train made them breakfast, and they were fixing their plates when Viper showed up. His face was haggard as he poured his coffee.

"I'd ask how your night went, but I can see that for myself." Train offered him a piece of toast.

Viper shook his head, sitting down at the table with them.

"I take it Winter didn't take your order any better than Beth did?" Razer bit into a piece of crispy bacon.

"Do you know how hard it is to live with two women who are mad at you?"

Train and Razer stared at him like he had lost his mind as Stori and Ember came in, arguing over which of them would cook breakfast and who would do the laundry.

"When Winter stopped yelling at me and locked me out of the bedroom, Aunt Shay let me have it. I should have stuck to my plan about building Aunt Shay her own house instead of building a two-story to give us our space. Now I'm stuck with two women who refuse to fix me a meal."

"I wouldn't eat it if she does. Winter can have a mean streak when she gets mad," Train advised. "Did Shade call you last night? He was acting strange."

"He called me an hour ago. What do you mean by strange?"

"He didn't tell me why he called. What did he say to you?"

"He said he thinks he found a way to get Sasha out of trouble. He'll call back tonight with more info."

"That sounds good, right?"

"Let's hope so. I feel like I dropped the ball on this one," Viper said.

"You didn't. I did. I wanted to punch myself in the face when Jewell told me about Killyama giving me that black eye."

"I knew they were trouble the minute I walked into the Pink Slipper." Razer stood up to refill the men's coffee.

"I knew we weren't getting rid of them when Winter invited them to our wedding."

"If you three are all done feeling sorry for yourselves, can I wash your dishes?" Stori asked with her hands on her hips. "I need to get to work, and I want to start the dishwasher."

Train helped Stori carry the dishes to the sink as the club members filed in to eat.

"Shade's probably the only one who had a good night's sleep, being away from Lily. Lucky called to tell me he was sleeping at the church, and Rachel spent the night at her brother's house." Viper stood up. The coffee had revived him, but he still looked exhausted.

"Which one?" Train asked as they headed toward the factory.

"Tate's."

"At least it wasn't Greer's. He wouldn't let Cash live it down."

"I'm sure he knows by now. The problem is, the women keep dragging everyone into our lives. I'm standing firm on this one. The wives need to know I mean business this time."

The three men angrily turned around as Stori and Ember, who had walked out behind them, listening, started laughing.

"Seriously, those women have you by the balls. What about Diamond? You can't expect her to stay away from her own sister." Stori hastily wiped her laughter from her face.

"I don't know. Why not? They fight off and on with one another. Knox said they once went two years without talking."

"That's because they were mad at each other, not because a man told them to."

"I'm the president of The Last Riders, and the women are all part of the club, for better or worse. When they married into the club, they became my responsibility, and having anything to do with that underhanded bitch is detrimental to us all."

"I don't remember that part of the wedding vows." Skeptically, Stori stared at the two married in the group.

"It was implied," Train spoke up, agreeing with Viper.

"I agree," Razer backed up his president.

"I don't think the women will agree, but what do I know? I just thought I would give you a woman's opinion." Stori linked her arm with Train's. "Can you talk Jewell into letting me get off early?

I want to make pork chop casserole for dinner. I know how much you like it."

Train smiled down at her. She was like a breath of fresh air. Killyama had used him to achieve her own ends, but Stori didn't want anything from him, only to make him happy. She catered to all the men in the club and was one of the few women who didn't argue with the other female members. She was the opposite of Killyama, and exactly what he needed right now.

"I'll see what I can do." He was supposed to get off at three. He would ask Jewell if he could work until four so Stori could get off.

⁂ ⁃

By afternoon, Train felt as bad as Viper had that morning. When Stori left, giving him a hug, he regretted offering to let her off early. The three sleepless nights had taken their toll on him. He had finally succeeded in driving himself to exhaustion.

The delivery truck had to be loaded with Cash's help. When they were done, he went back inside the factory to see most of the workers had left. Cash had already gone up to the clubhouse, and Jewell was about to leave.

"A package came for you," she told him. "I laid it on your workstation. Lock up when you leave."

"Will do."

Curious, Train picked up the small package. He had seen the UPS arrive when he was loading the truck, but he had thought it was for the factory. He never received packages. He had no family, all of his friends lived at the clubhouse, and he hadn't ordered anything.

He took out his pocketknife, running it across the top of the box. Closing his knife, he opened the package, finding another box inside.

Lifting the lid, he stared down in astonishment. Wrapped in tissue paper was a brand new black wallet with a chain attached.

Train touched it, feeling the buttery soft leather in his hand as he ran his thumb over the Navy insignia at one corner.

The expensive wallet was something he would have never bought for himself. He would think it was a mistake and that Jewell had gotten the name of whom it was meant for wrong, except the wallet was engraved with his nickname across the top.

He searched for the invoice to see who had sent it, or if there was a card he had missed, but there wasn't anything. Then he took out his phone to search the company found on the return address on the main box, wanting to see if they could tell him who had sent it. However, they were closed. He would have to call back tomorrow.

Maybe Sasha had ordered it. She was always ordering something, but he didn't think so. Usually, he or Rider gave her their credit cards when they wanted to splurge on the women. He couldn't see any of the brothers buying the wallet for him, either.

Train locked up the factory before heading into the clubhouse. The brothers were already in the living room, relaxing and waiting for dinner.

"What do you have there?" Cash held on to his pool stick as Crash took his turn.

"Someone sent me a wallet." Train lifted the lid of the box so that Cash and Crash could see.

"Nice. Who sent it?" Crash lifted the wallet so the others could get a look.

"I don't know. There wasn't an invoice or a card."

"You have a secret admirer you haven't told us about?" Viper lifted it out of Crash's hands.

"No. Maybe Sasha bought it for me. It's not like I can ask her right now."

"Nope," Crash denied that belief. "I keep an eye on the credit card statements. No one bought a wallet."

Train didn't know who would have done it then. He scoured his mind. The only person outside of the club who could have possibly ordered it for him was unlikely. Killyama didn't seem the type of woman to give gifts. The bitch wouldn't give him the time of day, much less buy him a wallet. But if she had, Train didn't want it.

Seeing the stares of the brothers, he could tell they were thinking it was from her, too.

Going to the trashcan beside the bar, he threw the box inside.

"Don't throw it away. If you don't want it, I'll take it." Cash strode to the trashcan, taking it out. "I can give it to Greer for his birthday."

Train snatched it back from Cash. He had overreacted. He would keep it until he found out who sent it. If it was Killyama, he would give it back to her. Greer Porter wasn't getting it.

"I changed my mind. Willa could have sent it to me." Train hadn't considered Willa before, but she liked giving presents out, so did Lily. Until he knew for sure, he would put it in his dresser.

"If you change your mind again, let me know. Greer's birthday is next week."

"You give Greer a wallet with my name, you're practically begging Rachel to divorce you."

"I don't know why. It's not like Greer can spell." Cash laughed as he went back to the pool table.

"Greer might not be able to, but Rachel can."

"Dinner's ready!" Stori poked her head around the kitchen door to yell. Seeing Train, she came further into the room as the brothers nearly ran him down to get into the kitchen. "I saved you a big pork chop, and I put plenty of potatoes on it, just the way you like."

Stori eagerly anticipated his praise for fixing his favorite meal. However, fatigue hit him and what appetite he'd had disappeared.

The thought of spending the next hour gushing over how good the food was soured his stomach.

"Go ahead. I need to take a shower and get some sleep. Save my plate, and I'll reheat it when I wake up."

Stori's face fell in disappointment. "Want me to join you? I snacked while I was cooking. I can—"

Train shook his head. "There's no need for you to wait around for me to wake. Go keep Cash company. He's probably missing Rachel."

"Okay. Call me when you wake up, and I'll warm the food for you."

Nodding, he then went upstairs, trying to shake off the thought that Killyama had sent the wallet. Was it her way of saying she was sorry? Or had she ordered it before she had decided to bust Sasha? Either way, he placed it in his dresser before he showered, so he wouldn't see it.

Train let the cold water run down his head, wetting his long hair. He needed to cut it. He liked to keep the length to his shoulders, but slicking it back, he realized it was down his back.

Naked, he stepped out of the shower then searched through the drawers until he found his scissors. Pulling his hair back, he braided it. Then he cut it at the length he wanted, dropping the end into the trash. Going back inside the shower, he finished washing off.

Wrapping a towel around his waist, he went to his bedroom, closing and locking the door before turning the light off and lying down on the empty bed. The silence struck him. Usually, one or more of the women stayed in his room at night. Well, they had before he had been an idiot and talked to Killyama that night at Rosie's.

"Fuck." Train raised his arm to cover his eyes. He had never been affected by a woman so much that he couldn't fuck another to take his mind off her. That Killyama had accomplished the impossible feat filled him with self-loathing.

He would grab a couple hours sleep. When he woke up, he would fuck Stori, Jewell, and Ember. By morning, he wouldn't remember Killyama's name. If that didn't work, he had a couple of the new recruits he hadn't given his vote to yet. One way or another, he was going to forget she had ever shared his bed.

Unable to doze off with her on his mind, he reached for his cell phone. Viper answered on the first ring.

"I want to go to Ohio. A few days is all I'm asking."

"Go then. Check with Jewell to make sure your shifts are covered."

"I will. Thanks, brother."

"Train...it's not your fault that Sasha is sitting in jail."

"I made it possible. You tried to warn me about Killyama, and I didn't listen. Now Sasha is paying the price."

Train could hear Viper's sigh through the phone. "You didn't let Sasha down, you didn't let your mother down, and you didn't let Gavin down. You don't know how to let anyone down. That's why I didn't promote you to VP, even though you deserve it. It's why I chose you to protect Winter and Aisha if anything happens to me. You were born a soldier; you don't give up, no matter what hell is waiting."

Chapter Fifteen

"Shade's here." Hammer turned to stare at her in the backseat. "You want me to give it to him?"

"No, we all will." Killyama reached for the door handle.

"You can wait here. Me and Hammer will go."

She ignored Jonas's gruff offer, stiffly getting out of the car and heading toward Shade, who had his motorcycle parked at the back of convenience store, out of sight of The Last Riders' clubhouse.

"We need to quit meeting like this," Killyama joked, tossing Kane's burner phone to him.

Shade deftly caught it. "How did it go? I was getting worried. You're an hour late."

"I stopped for a hamburger. Jonas checked the phone out. There're a couple of pictures of Kane and several of the women at the massage parlor. He must have paid extra to let them take it. Sick fuck likes to strangle them as he fucks them. When you talk to Yates, tell him he should check and see if there are any unsolved murders in town. He gets off on it too much for there not to be a skeleton in his closet."

"If not more."

Hammer's sickened agreement had Shade's discerning gaze moving from one to the other.

"You have any problem finding the jewelry?" Hammer asked.

"No. You could have warned me about the guard dog, though."

"I couldn't make it too easy for you. A little dog shouldn't have been a problem for you."

Shade's gaze settled on Hammer. "There wasn't anything little about that Doberman. He ripped my favorite pair of jeans. It was a trained attack dog. If I hadn't worked with them in the military, it would have had me for lunch."

"Couldn't have been too bad; I don't see a mark on you." Hammer drew Shade's gaze back to him as it had once again wandered to Killyama.

"We were best friends by the time I left him tied to a tree outside." His eyes cut back to Killyama. "I've never seen you with a scarf. Maybe you should get a thicker jacket."

Killyama shrugged. "I'm cold-natured. You should know that by now. If we're done here, I'm ready to head back to Jamestown… unless you need me to dig you fuckers the rest of the way out of the hole you dug for yourselves?"

"No, I think we have it." Shade's eyes were like blue lasers as she turned to walk back to the Escalade.

Killyama counted the steps, breaking out in a cold sweat. "Is he still watching?" she whispered hoarsely so Shade couldn't hear. The son of a bitch hadn't started his motor. He was waiting for them to leave.

"Yes."

She didn't know what she wanted to do more: faint or vomit.

Jonas hurried to open the door for her, blocking Killyama from sight, and Hammer climbed in beside her.

She watched as Jonas waved at Shade as he got inside to start the SUV. Jonas slowly drove past The Last Riders' clubhouse, maintaining the speed limit until he turned down a dark street where he accelerated, the streets passing in a blur.

Dropping her head onto Hammer's shoulder, she unzipped the tight leather jacket and let him help her out of it before sinking against him, seeking comfort she would never accept if she weren't hurting so badly.

"Get me to the hospital."

"We're almost there."

"Do you think we fooled him?" She weakly tried to reach for the blood-soaked bandage that was wound around her neck, but Hammer pulled her hand away, holding it tightly in his hand.

"He bought it, hook, line, and sinker. Now, will you quit worrying about Shade and let us take care of you?"

She didn't talk the rest of the way to the hospital.

When Jonas brought the SUV to a screeching halt, Hammer was already jumping out, reaching inside to lift her out then carrying her into the emergency room. Thankfully, she passed out before the electronic door could close behind them.

ॐ ☙

She awoke in the dark, not remembering where she was. She tried to speak, but the fire in her throat prevented anything but a guttural sound to escape.

Feverish, she imagined Train was in bed with her and sleeping, so he couldn't hear her. She had to wake him up. She needed his help.

Afraid she was being held down by mysterious hands in the dark, she needed him to get them off so she could breathe.

"Tr-Train...help me."

The light came on, but Train wasn't staring down at her.

It was Hammer who drew her out of the nightmare.

"Jonas and I are here. Go back to sleep."

"It wasn't a nightmare, was it?"

"No, it wasn't a nightmare."

The plan had gone to shit when they had been sneaked into the massage parlor by the mama-san through the back door.

"You have my money?" the woman had asked.

133

Killyama had felt a tingling warning at the back of her neck as Hammer had given the mama-san the envelope of cash.

"This isn't what we agreed." She shoved the envelope back at him. "You go."

"You get half now and the other half when we leave." Hammer pulled the cash out of the envelope, letting her see the amount of money she was walking away from.

"How do I know you're not the cops?"

Killyama pretended to give her an embarrassed look. "We only want to watch. My boyfriend wants me to learn how you make your customers so happy."

The mama-san's doubts didn't vanish, but her greed won out.

"Kane only pays for thirty minutes. He cheats me out of fifteen minutes. If he goes happiness-ess longer, you pay?"

"Yes. It will make my man happy." She should think of another line of work.

The mama-san snatched the money back before leading them to a hallway that had several doors. She was chubby, but she moved fluidly along the hallway, the white coat giving her a business-like appearance.

The parlor wasn't what Killyama had expected. It was clean and looked professional. She was reminded of the spa days Sex Piston had treated them to whenever Stud had sold a bike.

The mama-san opened a door at the end of the hallway, and Killyama looked around, seeing a massage table with a towel folded at the end. It was clean and had a fresh odor.

They all stepped inside, closing the door behind them.

"You go in there." The mama-san motioned to a black curtain. "And stay until I come and get you when he leaves." The mama-san pointed at Hammer. "He comes with me."

Killyama and Hammer shook their heads. "That's not the deal. He wants to watch, too—"

"The lesson for you, not him. If Kane sees you, my business over." She snapped her fingers in front of their faces. "Your choice. You stay. He goes."

"I'm not leaving you alone." Hammer tried to take her arm, but Killyama shook him off.

"I'll be fine. Go with her. Pretty boy won't even know I'm here. You know I can handle myself. If I can beat your ass, Kane won't give me trouble if something goes wrong."

"Kane good customer. You cause trouble, you deal with me."

"No trouble, only happiness," Killyama assured the woman.

She hid behind the curtain as Hammer reluctantly left with the mama-san. Jonas was going to kick her ass for this. Hammer was protective of her, but Jonas didn't share the same confidence in her abilities. The two men had always been by her side for as long as she could remember, unless they were deployed, usually making sure a girlfriend was left to keep watch of her.

Killyama stayed to the side of the curtain, not sure if Kane would be able to see her outline through the thin material.

Stiffening, she heard someone enter the room. A charming voice was greeting the mama-san. When their voices began arguing over money because Kane wanted to use a coupon, Killyama became so frustrated she wanted to shout she would pay for the fucking hand job. Thankfully, the mama-san was satisfied with the money and left the room.

The sound of Kane undressing had her waiting tensely, worried he would look behind the curtain. When the room then went quiet, Killyama bravely peeked through a gap in the material, seeing Kane lying on his back, the white towel tenting his hard-on.

Killyama nearly screamed as the minutes ticked by before the door opened again, and a tiny Asian woman's high heels tapped on the floor. She was wearing a tiny black dress that was so short Killyama could see she wasn't wearing anything underneath when she bent over to light the candles. Then she dimmed the overhead lights.

Killyama watched as the petite woman oiled her hands. Then she looked toward Kane's clothes. They were sitting on a table a foot from her.

Dammit, she had expected him to be on his back. Kane would be able to easily see her if she moved from her hiding spot. That meant she was forced to watch the woman slide her oiled hands over Kane's body before giving him a blowjob that put the one Killyama had given Train to shame. She was furious at herself for letting the erotically charged atmosphere excite her.

There were no emotions between the two adults, other than lust from Kane. The woman looked positively bored. At least, she did until Kane grabbed the fragile wrist stroking his cock.

"No touch," the small woman protested to no avail.

Kane slid himself out from her hands, using the grip he had on her wrist to twist her arm behind her back as he hopped off the table, forcing her to lean her upper body over the table.

"No," the woman objected, whimpering in fear.

Killyama's grip tightened on the curtain, unable to decide if this was part of the services the parlor offered.

The frightened cries escalated when Kane pulled the woman's dress to her waist, about to sink his dick into the struggling masseuse.

Dammit, Killyama couldn't watch the woman get raped.

When she started gasping at the forced weight of his hand that circled her throat, Killyama darted out from behind the curtain, pushing Kane off the crying woman.

"Who the hell are you?" Kane yelled as she helped the woman rise. "MAMA-SAN!"

Killyama held the woman as the mama-san ran into the room, Hammer rushing in behind her, restraining Kane. She couldn't catch many of the words the mama-san spat at the terrified worker.

When she would have backhanded her, Killyama caught her hand.

"What's going on in here?"

Kane's yells had doors opening and closing as customers from other rooms fled.

"Is this a shake down? If you want my money, take it," some stupide asshole asked.

"We don't want your money," Hammer barked at him before turning toward Killyama. "What happened?" His calm voice broke through all the other voices.

Seeing Kane's diverted attention, Killyama used the opportunity to grab the cell phone, barely missing getting caught as Kane started dressing. Sliding it into her pocket, she quickly moved toward the door.

"Tell her this is too much happiness-ess for me. I'll wait outside." She turned her glare on Kane. "Fucker, next time you want something off the menu, ask first." Bolting out of the room, Killyama ran down the hallway and through the back door.

Jonas, seeing her coming, got out of the Escalade. But before he could ask what happened, she told him to go help Hammer.

"Shit." Jonas took off running inside the back of the parlor. She wanted to go back inside with him, but she didn't want to be there when Kane discovered his cell phone was missing.

She was climbing into the backseat when she was hit from behind. Falling forward, she twisted over to see Kane was over her, the bastard's face filled with fury.

He didn't give her a chance to react before wrapping a coat hanger wire around her neck.

"Why watch me fuck someone when you can experience it for yourself, cunt?"

She tried to shove him off her, forcing herself to disconnect from the pain around her throat. However, she didn't stand a chance of breaking his hold, and she would run out of air if she concentrated on breaking his grip.

Every lesson Hammer and Jonas had taught her flashed through her mind. Arching her body, she tried to shove Kane off her. When that didn't work, she crossed her arms, reaching for his wrists. Managing to get her feet on the seat, she used her thighs to push Kane over her head. It didn't work. The Escalade was big, but there wasn't enough room for her to successfully perform the maneuver.

The wire around her neck twisted tighter, making her almost black out. Using her last chance at survival, she tried to hit him in the nose with the palm of her hand, but he blocked her, which meant he released the coat hanger.

Killyama couldn't see what he was doing. By the time she saw the flash of a knife, she didn't have time to respond. The searing pain in the same spot she had been shot two months ago filled her with agonizing pain.

Digging her nails into his wrist, she was able to keep him from plunging it any deeper, but her grip was becoming slippery from the blood oozing out of the wound.

He was ripping her pants off when Hammer jerked him off her, flinging him back. Then Kane ran as Jonas unwound the coat hanger, Hammer on his heels.

"Hammer! Get back here!" Jonas yelled, trying to help her sit up. "You need to drive us to the hospital!"

Seconds later, Hammer slammed the back door shut then jumped behind the wheel. "You okay, Rae?"

Gasping, she held her burning throat.

"Stop, let me see." Jonas cussed when he saw the wound then asked Hammer to hand him the first-aid case out of the glove box.

Hammer passed it to Jonas. "I told you to wear the fucking Taser!" He drove expertly as he screamed at her.

"Give her time to catch her breath before you start yelling," Jonas reproved him as he stemmed the blood on her shoulder. "Her throat's a fucking mess."

"Is it still there?" Killyama croaked out.

"What?" Jonas asked as he wrapped a bandage around her throat.

"Kane's cell phone. Is it still in my pocket?"

Jonas helped her pull her pants back on. She was hurting too much to feel embarrassed.

He took out the phone, showing it to her.

"The hospital's ten minutes away." Hammer honked at a car going too slow.

"No, drive to our hotel room." Killyama's order was given in a hoarse whisper. "I don't want Shade to know anything went wrong."

"Fuck that!" Hammer growled. "I'm driving you to the hospital. I can meet Shade."

"He'll know when I don't show."

"I don't give a fuck what Shade or Train figure out. I had to watch for years as your father turned you inside out. I'll be damned if I watch The Last Riders do the same."

"Please, Jonas." He was always the one she went to when she had to get Hammer to see reason. "As soon as I give the phone to Shade, I'll be out of there. If Shade finds out, he'll call Train. I don't want him asking any questions."

Jonas stared at her sympathetically before telling Hammer, "Go to the hotel. Hurry. She'll disappear if The Last Riders show up."

"They won't show, but they will want to know why I helped."

The good part of being hurt was that Hammer and Jonas stopped arguing when they reached the hotel. It took the two men an hour to get her cleaned up enough to pass Shade's inspection. She carefully redid her makeup, concealing the lower portion of her jaw that was turning purple.

"Hand me a jacket." She was afraid to bend over to pick up the leather jacket.

Hammer's face was grave as he zipped it up, hiding the bandage at her throat. "Little girl, you're breaking my heart."

Killyama forced a smile before going to the mirror to apply a cherry shade of lipstick. "You don't have one."

"Yes, I do." Hammer's pain-filled expression showed she had hit a nerve.

"I was joking. I'm going to be fine. I'm looking forward to the painkillers the doctors are going to hook me up with."

"Like you'll take them. You hate to take a Tylenol."

"That shit is bad for you."

Minutes later, Killyama let Hammer help her into the SUV.

"Let's get this show on the road, Jonas. If she groans one more time, she's going to the hospital."

Killyama pouted. "Don't be mean to me. I'm hurt."

"No, shit. You are your own worst enemy."

"Not anymore. The Last Riders are."

When they didn't contradict her, she wished she were capable of crying.

"I wish it would rain."

"It rained last night. The skies are supposed to be clear tonight."

Even the Heavens were frowning down on her. It didn't matter, anyway. It would take a flood to wash away the damage she had done to herself.

⁋ ℈

"Rae? You need me to get the nurse?"

Jonas's concern brought her back to the present.

"I could use some water…and a Tylenol."

The men fussed over her until she told them to leave and let her sleep.

"We'll go when you fall asleep," Hammer promised, settling into a chair by her bed as Jonas stood by the door.

She was about to doze off, but she forced her sleepy eyes open.

"Go to sleep, Rae. No one is getting past us. Have I ever broken a promise to you?"

"No, never." Letting her eyelids close, she started to drift off to sleep, confident the two men would keep her safe.

They had filled her father's shoes even before he had died. She used to aggravate them sometimes, talking her father up like a hero, bragging about his military accomplishments. What she could never put into words was that Jonas and Hammer were truly the meaning of the word hero, and she was blessed to have them both. She had learned early on that a father wasn't a word; it was deeds.

Damn, being hurt brought the sensitive side out of her. She needed to get better so she could show them she could still beat their asses.

"Hammer?"

"Yeah, Rae?"

"When you come back, bring me a pack of gum."

CHAPTER SIXTEEN

Train was starting his bike when he felt his cell phone vibrate in his jacket pocket.

"Where are you?" Viper barked out as soon he answered the call.

"In the parking lot, getting ready to pull out. What's—"

"Stay there. I'll be out in five." Viper disconnected the call before Train could ask what was wrong.

He looked over at Viper's house, seeing the lights were on. Earlier when he had come down the steps, both houses were dark since he had slept longer than he had intended. By midnight, most of the brothers and the women had already turned in for the night. Turning to face the clubhouse, he saw lights had been turned on inside there, too.

"Fuck," Train swore, impatiently waiting for someone to come out and tell him what was going on.

He was almost ready to get off his bike when Viper finally appeared.

"Shade called and told me that he wants you and Crash to come to Ohio. When I told him that you were already on your way, he said I might want to be there, too."

"Did he say why?"

"No, I figured we could find out together. We can talk when he gets there." Viper went to his bike. He was starting it when Crash, Nickel, and Razer came out of the clubhouse to find their bikes.

Train backed his up to pull alongside of Viper's. "I thought you said Shade only asked for me and Crash?"

"I'd rather have too much backup than not enough."

The brothers were ready in seconds, Viper taking the lead down the winding road leading into town. Razer and Train rode at the back of the pack.

As they passed the sheriff's office, Knox's and Lucky's bikes' headlights hit them. They decelerated through the empty street until Knox was riding next to Crash, and Lucky sped ahead to ride with Viper.

Other than for gas, the brothers didn't stop until they were the on the outskirts of Ohio, where Viper texted Shade, letting him know they would be there in thirty minutes.

"Shade sent the address to a hospital fifteen minutes away," he informed everyone.

They made it to the rendezvous point ten minutes later, where Shade was sitting casually on his bike with his arms resting on the handlebars. Moon and Rider were waiting with him.

The brothers circled Shade's bike so they could hear what he had to say.

"What's up? Something happen to Sasha?" Viper motioned for the men to turn off their bikes.

Train felt Shade's critical gaze on him before it settled on Viper. "No. Nothing has changed so far, but I expect the charges to be dropped."

"How'd you manage that?"

"Killyama."

Train wasn't the only one who stared at Shade in astonishment. "What did Killyama have to do with getting Sasha's charges dropped?"

Shade took a cell phone out of his jacket pocket, handing it to Viper. "It's Kane's burner phone. She stole it from him. She also found a way for me to get inside his father's house. The police now know that Kane and his father lied about the jewelry. Arrogant dick left it in a drawer in his office. She also hooked me up with a profes-sor who won't let it get swept under the rug."

"A professor?" Train asked, stunned.

Shade's lips curled up in mirthless smile. "A Professor of Economics. He wants to take down the man keeping him from get-ting his dream job. Mayor. Not only did she fix Sasha's problem; she fixed Moon's, too."

"Why would she help?" Train stared at the phone in Viper's hand.

"You'll have to ask her that question."

Train moved to turn the key to start his motorcycle, determined to do just that. He was going to drive to Jamestown and shake her until she answered all of his questions.

"Save the gas. She's not in Jamestown." Shade read his mind. "Killyama is still in Ohio. She never left after dropping Sasha off at the police station."

"How'd she steal Kane's burner phone?" Train asked as he removed his hand from the key.

"Should have been nicknamed Crazy Bitch. She found out from Kane's ex-girlfriend that he has a taste for hand jobs. Apparently, she convinced the owner of a masseuse parlor to let her watch. When he was occupied, she stole the phone."

Train couldn't sit still for another moment. Getting off his bike, he paced back and forth as he tried to blow off steam. "I'm going to wring her fucking neck."

"Kane almost saved you the trouble." Reaching into his pocket, Shade took out his own phone, holding it up. "She was an hour late to give me Kane's phone. When she arrived, she was wearing a leather jacket zipped up to her throat. It was cold out, but she was also wearing a scarf to her jaw. When I asked why she was wearing it, she made a joke, telling me she was cold-natured."

"What's wrong with her wearing a scarf?" Viper asked.

Train was thinking the same thing. In the time he had known her, though, she had only worn a jacket when it was freezing outside. A scarf, never. That seemed too feminine for Killyama. He was beginning to get a sick feeling in his stomach.

"The whole time they were there," Shade continued, "Jonas and Hammer didn't take their eyes off her. After they left, I looked at the Kane's cell phone. It had blood on it. So I followed their car." Shade ran his finger over the screen on his cell phone, pulling up a picture.

Train expected Shade to hand the phone to Viper. Instead, he held it out to him.

He stopped pacing, heading over to Shade's bike to take the phone, seeing it wasn't a picture but a video. All the brothers except Rider and Moon got off their bikes to watch it.

The video showed the black Escalade braking at a hospital's emergency entrance. Hammer jumped out of the back then reached inside, lifting Killyama out. Train barely managed to finish watching as Hammer carried her inside the hospital with Jonas. From her limp body, it was clear she was unconscious.

Giving Shade his phone back, Train climbed back on his bike. "I have to see her."

"No. She made me promise not to tell you or any of the brothers that she helped. Think about it, brother. Why did she go through so much to help Sasha out? And why go through the trouble to keep us from finding out?"

The brothers stared at each other, all trying to figure out Killyama's motives.

"I might know," Knox spoke up in the extended silence. "Diamond has been on my case to talk Sasha into turning herself in when she found out a warrant had been taken out for her in Ohio. I told her there wasn't anything to be worried about. Then, remember about a month ago, when I received a call from the DA? He wanted me to stake out the clubhouse to see if she was there. Diamond was also called, asking her to convince Sasha to turn herself in, and was asked if she knew where she was. We both lied, saying she was hiding out with family in Wyoming."

Knox's thoughtful expression and the account of the increased interest in Sasha's whereabouts had all the brothers starting to connect the dots.

"Sex Piston," Train stated, staring at the large hospital.

Killyama was behind one of those windows. She had deliberately put herself at risk to relieve Sex Piston's fear that her sister would be held culpable for lying to the courts.

"You think Sex Piston told her to do it? Or did she do it on her own?" Train asked the question more to himself than the men.

"On her own," Knox answered. "I think Diamond confided in her sister that she was worried about losing her license and me losing my job as sheriff. Then Sex Piston bitched about it to Killyama. I can see her throwing herself under the bus to protect them."

"I can, too," Viper agreed, looking at the cell phone with the blood she had shed to protect those she loved. "She did nearly get herself killed when she protected Lily and Winter. With Sex Piston, she would try to walk on water to protect that bitch."

Train's heart was so heavy he had to sit down on his motorcycle to get his strength back.

"That's why she waited to call my debt in. She waited so Sex Piston couldn't be blamed. She didn't even tell Stud, so it wouldn't cause a rift between him and Sex Piston." Viper was taking her sacrifice as hard as Train was.

"And between me and Diamond." Knox didn't leave his own guilt out of the conversation. "If anyone found out that Diamond had confided in Sex Piston, she could have lost her law license for breach of privacy."

Train laughed so hard his head fell back. Staring upward at sky, he saw the sun was beginning to rise. "I am such a dumb fuck," he castigated himself. "When she came to Rosie's, she told me that if I broke my rule of not fucking anyone who didn't belong to The Last Riders, she would give me the go-ahead to fuck the club women. Deep down, I knew she was lying to me. Killyama would never put up with any man who slept with others, even if it was a casual hook-up."

Train was a man who knew when he was beaten. Instinctively, he had known Killyama wasn't as laid back about their arrangement as she had pretended, but he had believed it because it achieved his own goal. He had wanted her on his terms: no relationship, no caring, and especially no love. She hadn't been the only one lying to him. He had been lying to himself.

"Brother, I could have warned you if I had known she said that. Those bitches don't even share clothes. If Diamond asks to borrow something from Sex Piston, she tells her no, or that she doesn't want it anymore."

Knox rarely talked about the dynamic between Diamond and the bitches. Train thought it was because the antics they got into grated on his more reserved personality. Now he could see that Knox had grown to like his sister-in-law and her friends.

"When Killyama asked Lily to borrow those high-priced heels I bought her, she told Lily she wasn't getting them back."

"You like her, don't you?" Train asked, knowing Shade would rip off anyone's head who denied Lily what she wanted.

"It's hard not to like the woman who saves your wife's life." Shade didn't admit nor deny it, which meant he technically admitted it.

"Like is a strong word for how I feel about her, but I can respect why Killyama did what she did," Viper conceded. He clearly wasn't going to get over his hurt pride anytime soon.

"I don't think Sex Piston was the only one she tried to protect." Train replayed the words that Winter had told him. "Winter tried

147

to tell me that Killyama is in love with me. I blew it off when she told me, but I think she's right. Getting the charges dropped against Sasha is her way of saying she is sorry."

"I wouldn't take it that far. That bitch doesn't know the meaning of the word. She talked you into inviting her to the clubhouse to make sure Sasha was there. She also used the opportunity to have sex with you again. If that's not enough, not one of us with wives has been laid since then."

Yeah, Viper was still pissed. Train tried to think of a way to soothe his ruffled feathers but came up short. Viper didn't forgive easily, especially where his dick was concerned.

Train could sympathize. He hadn't had sex since he had been with Killyama. Viper had gone without even longer after the birth of his baby.

The law he had laid down about the members having nothing to do with Killyama had come back to bite him in the ass, and with him making such a big deal about it, it wasn't going to be easy for him to admit he had been wrong.

"Damn, a devious woman gives me a hard-on." Moon stood up to adjust his jeans. "Train, if you don't make her your woman, I'm going to make her mine."

Moon said the wrong thing at the wrong time.

Before the other brothers could react, Train swung his fist out with lightning fast reflexes, punching Moon in his gut and knocking him backward onto his bike. It took several minutes before Shade and Knox took pity on him, lifting a struggling Train off him.

"You try to touch her, brother or not, I'll kill you." He wiped his bloodied knuckles on the side of his jeans.

None of The Last Riders tried to help Moon to his feet.

Train put his hand on his handlebar. "I'm going to the hospital to find out how Killyama is doing. You all can come with me or stay here. I'm done talking."

"Train, she doesn't want you knowing." Shade moved to stand in front of Train's bike. "Have you changed your mind about wanting her to become a Last Rider?"

"You know I haven't." Train stared challengingly at Viper. He couldn't make it any plainer to his president that Killyama was going to be a part of his life. If the club couldn't accept that, they wouldn't be a part of the future he was determined to have with her.

"You go in that hospital, telling her you forgive her and everything is all hunky-dory, Killyama will chew you up and spit you out."

Train dropped his hands from the handlebars. Shade's logic made sense. As badly as he wanted to go to the hospital, it wasn't the best move.

"Learn from us, brother. Some of us have been right where you are. Build her trust first. Show her what you can give her that the Destructors can't."

"Like what?"

The Destructors were not The Last Riders, but the years she had spent with them, building strong relationships, Train couldn't compete with that, not anytime soon.

"You already know that answer. She's in love with you." Shade fixed his steely gaze on him. "Killyama is devious as hell. Use it against her. You're the best soldier in the club. You fought like a warrior when we were in the field and in the air. I never once worried that you wouldn't fight your way through to bring us home." Shade moved away from him, leaving the choice to him on whether they were going to force their way inside her room to see her or stay away for now. "A smart warrior would try to win her hand and win the war. Bring your princess home on her terms when she's ready. We'll all be waiting."

Chapter Seventeen

Sasha's dejected expression vanished the second an attractive police officer opened the green door, allowing her to leave the jail behind. Then a shrill scream could be heard in the air when she caught sight of the large group of the men who had been waiting for her, now walking toward her, which prompted a blossoming wide smile out of her.

"Train!" Sasha jumped into his arms, wrapping her legs around his waist as he lifted her into his arms, twirling the excited woman around in a circle before he passed her over to Rider, who gave her the same excessive greeting.

Moon took his turn next, planting a kiss on her mouth as she hurled herself into his arms. When it was Razer's turn, he set her down after he caught her, giving her a tamer hug. Viper's casual hug ended with him turning her toward the motorcycles. All of the men were smiling as they got on their bikes.

Sasha practically skipped to Train's bike when Viper dropped his arm from her. Using Train's shoulder to balance herself, she climbed behind him and snuggled close, wrapping her arms around him as they drove out of the parking garage. Train's bike was swallowed up by The Last Riders who protectively surrounded them.

Killyama forced her eyes down to the cell she was holding. After a series of swipes on her screen, she walked down the ramp to the garage below, alighting the sidewalk outside the police station.

The taxi she had requested took fifteen minutes to arrive. Giving the driver the address, Killyama buckled her seat belt as he darted into the morning traffic. She had the cash ready, paying when the cab arrived at the hotel. She knew she had been busted before the driver could count his money and leave.

Hammer was angrily throwing his suitcase in the back of the Escalade. Jonas lifted his and her cases into the trunk, showing more restraint, but the infuriated glance he gave her as he closed the truck showed he was just as upset.

"You were supposed to get something to eat then rest until we got back from filling your prescriptions. Do I need to hire an interpreter so you can understand me?" Hammer asked snidely as soon as she was within earshot.

"I was tired of waiting and decided to go get my own food." Killyama took her usual spot in the back seat as Hammer programmed their trip into the GPS.

"You need to take the medicine. There's a drink in the bag." Jonas handed her the bag that was sitting on the console next to him. From the aroma, there was food inside it, too. When she reached for the medicine bottles, Jonas watched as she took the pills before he turned back around. "You'll get nauseous taking them on an empty stomach. Eat."

She pulled out the wrapped biscuit, squirting a dollop of honey from the packet Jonas always remembered to get for her. She had no intention of antagonizing the men further. And she hadn't missed their looks of concern when she had gotten out of the taxi.

The men's stubborn silence lasted until after they hit the interstate. When she finished eating, she used a pack of wipes to clean her sticky fingers.

"I was thinking…" Killyama's raspy voice had Hammer turning down the music so they could hear her. "We should find an apartment in Lexington. It makes more sense to live there instead of Jamestown. It doesn't take long to drive to Tennessee, but the drive to Ohio is further. It will make it easier going back and forth between the two. Or we can just say fuck it and stop working in Ohio, concentrating only on jobs in Tennessee. What do you think?"

"Why not just focus on Ohio?" Jonas asked.

"That way, I can see the gang when I get a day off."

"What about your mom?"

"I'll get her an apartment, too. Her place is falling down around her. When she sees I'm serious about moving, she won't argue too much."

"If you're sure, I'll start hunting for a place," Hammer said. "It'll take time. We have to finish a couple of jobs in Ohio. Then it won't be easy to find three places that will make us all happy."

"It shouldn't take that long. The jobs in Ohio—"

"We're going to wait until you're back in shape." From Hammer's tone, Killyama knew it would be useless to argue with him.

"Fine."

"Jonas, record this conversation on your cell phone."

Jonas's expression began to thaw. "Why?"

"Because she's finally agreeing to something I told her we should do three years ago."

Killyama rolled her eyes. "Turn the music back up. I don't want to hear you gloat all the way home." When she heard what came on over the radio, she said, "Change the song." The melancholy music of "Ruin Me" was abruptly switched to "Love is a Battlefield."

"That better?"

"No, but it's better than your country shit."

She slept until Hammer woke her by lifting her out and carrying her up the flight of steps to her apartment. Groggily, she tried to protest.

"I can walk."

Hammer stared down at her in concern as Jonas unlocked her door.

She lowered her lashes. "I'm okay, Hammer."

His tenderness wasn't exhibited often, but when it was, it was hard for her to deal with it. It was the same way with Jonas.

Hammer lay her down on her bed, nearly tripping over the vicious cat that swiped at him from under the bed.

"I'll pay for you to get that cat declawed," he offered as the cat came out of her hiding spot to jump on her bed.

"He's my burglar alarm. If anyone breaks in, all I have to do is search the hospitals for anyone who needs a rabies shot."

"If I don't kill it first." Hammer sat down on the side of her bed, using a pillow to swat the cat away.

Jonas came inside, carrying her suitcase and setting it by her door. Placing her medications on her nightstand, he left, and then came back with a bottled water. "There. You should be good for a while."

"You have your cell phone?"

Killyama wiggled her cell phone in Hammer's face.

"Call if you need anything. Want me to stop by tonight and bring you some dinner?"

"No. If I need you, I'll call. And no, I don't need a blanket."

Jonas dropped the blanket he had picked up from the bottom of her bed.

"Go get a beer, get laid, or better yet, do both. I'll check in with you tomorrow."

The men finally left her in the peace of her apartment.

Seeing she was alone, Gollum lost his haughty attitude, rubbing against her and purring before rolling into Killyama's side and curling up against her waist.

"You miss me?"

The purring response had Killyama lovingly stroking the sleek fur.

"I bought you a new toy. I'll get it for you when we wake up."

She was about to drift off when Gollum jumped off her. The cat only acted that way when he sensed someone was at the apartment door. Thinking it was one of her neighbors, she expected him to come back or to hear a knock at her door. When neither happened, Killyama got out of bed, seeing the cat's eyes glinting from under the couch.

She went to her door and opened it. Confused at seeing no one on the landing, she looked down, finding a long box.

Locking the door behind her, she carried it inside, setting it on the counter. After removing one of the knives from the butcher block, she cut the ribbon on the box, opened it, and found herself staring down at two dozen red roses.

Picking one up, she held the fragile flower as she searched for a large tumbler in her kitchen cabinet. The blue tumbler nearly toppled over after she filled it with water and the flowers.

Gollum jumped on the counter to sniff the flowers, nearly sending them falling again. Killyama lifted the troublesome cat off the counter.

"I should call Jonas and tell him, the next time he sends me flowers, to buy me a vase, too," she complained out loud, knowing she wouldn't even mention the flowers to him, afraid she would hurt the sensitive man's feelings if she didn't get mushy. Letting the men be nice to her this past week was as much as she could take before busting some heads.

After digging out the catnip toys she had bought from her suitcase, she watched a movie before scooping her cat up to go to bed.

About to turn out the light, she paused, fear momentarily overriding her. She would be damned if she let Kane into her dreams. Like all monsters, they only hurt you if you let them.

Her hand went to her throat. The bruising on her neck would eventually go away, and so would the memory of him staring down at her with bloodlust in his eyes.

Turning off the light, she let herself be lulled to sleep by the purring by her head, unaware that the cat wasn't the only one watching over her.

ঙ০ ০১

Moon lit a cigarette before offering one to Train.

Train shook his head. "No, thanks. I quit." He had only occasionally smoked, and usually only when one of the brothers had offered him one.

Moon peered at him through the smoky haze of his exhale. "Go get some sleep. I'll stay here until you get back."

He nodded. "Archer is watching the back. I'll be back in the morning." Train hated to leave, but he had some business to take care of with Shade.

"I've got it covered. Enjoy yourself and get some sleep."

"I will." Train grimly kicked up his kickstand. Seven members were waiting for their own share of the fun, all eight original members must be present for the Last Riders to serve their own brand of justice.

His bike sped down the winding roads toward Treepoint, its headlight guiding his way as lightning streaked across the sky. Knowing the road like the back of his hand, Train seamlessly rode, determined to beat the storm.

Gliding over the pavement at breakneck speeds like a thunderbolt waiting to strike, at the journey's end, the damage wrought would claim a victim.

CHAPTER EIGHTEEN

"Which color?" Killyama held up the two fingernail polishes for Star to choose from.

Sex Piston's youngest stepdaughter had her little mouth pursed as she debated which one to pick. "Why can't I have that one?" Star pointed at the deep red that Killyama had used to paint Fat Louise's nails earlier.

"What's wrong with these?" Killyama tried to steer her toward the more subdued colors.

"They aren't as pretty."

"Your daddy will like these." She wiggled the two polishes enticingly. "He'll yell at me if I paint your toenails that shade of red."

"Is he going to yell at Fat Louise?" The soft-hearted little girl looked worried.

"Yes," Killyama lied unrepentantly. Sometimes with kids, you had to put the fear of God into them. If not God, then Stud was a good second for one who worshiped him. "That's why she left before your daddy comes home."

"The pink."

"I like the pink, too." Killyama shook the bottle as she reached for Star's foot. The little girl began falling to the floor, catching herself. When she kept tickling her unmercifully, Star's giggles had Killyama laughing with her as they rolled on the floor.

"Do I need to send you girls to time out?"

Killyama quickly sat up at the sound of Stud's voice. She tugged her top back down that had inched up during the skirmish, turning toward the door and projecting the patronizing attitude she always wore unless her guard was down.

The sight of Stud and Train standing in the doorway had her nearly exposing the shock of seeing The Last Rider in Stud's family room. She had avoided him during the holidays by refusing Beth's and Lily's invitations to celebrate with them, saying she was too busy with work. Since then, she had been glad they lived in different counties so she hadn't run into him when she was around town.

"What's he doing here?" That wasn't the choice of words she wanted to use, but the little girl's presence had her filtering her words.

The corner of Train's mouth quirked up.

"I invited him to lunch, if that's okay with you?" Stud's expression showed he didn't care if it was or wasn't. "We're taking a break from designing the new bike Train ordered."

"Did you include the price of lunch in the quote for the bike? If not, there's a McDonald's ten miles away."

"Yes."

Damn, the bastard used her own trick against her. She would have to warn Sex Piston he could lie as easily as she could.

"Where's Sex Piston?" Stud asked.

"In the kitchen."

"Take a seat, Train. I'll go tell her you're eating with us."

If the fucker expected to get a nicer response from his wife, he was going to be disappointed.

"Ready, Star?" Killyama turned back to the little girl.

Obediently, the child sat down on the floor, holding her foot out. Killyama sat cross-legged as she opened the nail polish. She delicately proceeded to brush the pink polish on the nail beds, trying to hold her hand steady as Train made himself comfortable on the couch.

She felt his eyes taking her in, going from the bright red polish on her toes to her black shorts, and then raising his eyes to her black and white tie-dyed shirt. She almost touched the skull and cross-bones bandana at her throat. Forcing the new habit back, she made herself keep painting Star's nails nonchalantly, as if his presence in the room didn't bother her.

"You're looking good."

"You talking to me?" she asked snidely.

"Yes."

She scoffed. "I always look good."

"Yes, you do." Appreciation glowed in his eyes. "You're a beau-tiful woman. It would be hard for you not to see that when you look a mirror."

"Dude, save your compliments for the w-h-o-r-e-s." Conscious of the little girl listening, she spelled out the word.

"You want to go for a ride?"

"Viper cool with that?" Killyama set the foot she was working on down, reaching for Star's other foot.

"Viper doesn't tell me who to spend my time with when I'm not working. I'm off for the rest of the day." He paused. "There's a movie showing at the park. We could take a blanket and watch it."

"I'm busy. Ask…Jewell." She had almost mentioned Sasha but managed to stop herself from revealing that she knew the woman was out of jail.

"I'm asking you. If you don't want to, I can hang out here with you. Or we could go to the Destructors' clubhouse."

Killyama set Star's foot down, telling the girl, "Go see what is taking your mom so long?"

"It'll ruin my polish!"

"If it does, I'll fix it before I leave."

"Promise?"

"I said so," Killyama said calmly, not wanting to take her frustration out on the child.

As soon as Star was out of earshot, Killyama lithely stood then advanced toward Train. "Since when do you want to take me riding? The only sucker in this room is you. If you want payback, take your best shot. If not, then get the fuck out of here."

Before she could blink, Train dragged her down to his lap. When she would have punched him, he twisted her hands behind her back with one of his.

She fiercely tried to struggle out of his hold. Using her legs—the only part of her body she could still use—she attempted to throw herself off the couch. However, Train circumvented her move by using one of his long legs to pin her down.

She reared her head back when he lowered his to hers. At first, she thought he was going to kiss her. Instead, he stared deeply into her eyes. Unlike her, Train was eerily calm.

Seeing she wasn't going anywhere until he was ready to let her go, or she yelled for help, which she refused to do, Killyama settled down on his lap.

"That's better." Train stroked his thumb over her collarbone, just beneath the bandana.

"Don't touch me!" she hissed.

Train moved his hand to her waist, her abdomen quivering under his touch.

Remaining quiet, she hoped he would go as soon as he said what he apparently wanted to say.

"I do want to pay you back, but not the way you're thinking. I want to pay you back for the last night we were together." Train brushed his lips over the corner of hers. "You can't fuck a man like that and not expect him to come back for more. It's been two months since I felt you under me."

"I would think the only thing you'd remember about that day was Sasha."

"I was angry, but I'm over it. It actually worked out for the best. Shade found a way to fix Sasha's problem, and Moon's, too. You actually did us a big favor. If you hadn't forced our hand, Sasha would still be hiding out. Now she can do anything she wants—stay in Ohio or Treepoint."

"She didn't get jail time?" Killyama pretended not to know.

"No." Train travelled his mouth to her jaw before slipping down to her neck. When his lips would have nuzzled the bandana, she used her forehead to move his head away. The mark on her neck was barely noticeable, but she kept it covered so Sex Piston wouldn't ask questions.

His eyes crinkled in amusement as she carefully watched his reaction, trying to ascertain whether he knew she was lying or not. Other than humor at her situation, she didn't see any tells. He could be deceiving her, though, but why would he? Shade had given his word not to tell The Last Riders she had helped Sasha out of jail.

Payback is the only reason he's here, she told herself, despite his denial.

Train must have seen the distrust in her eyes.

"I'll tell you what. Spend another night with me, and we can call it even."

"I'm done making deals with The Last Riders."

"Not even one more?" He inched his hand up higher to cover her breast, searching for the nipple that was aching for his touch.

Her mind kept switching sides. One part of her wanted him so badly it was worse than the addiction she'd had when she quit smoking. The other part of her could imagine him standing over her dead body, using his boots to grind her into the dust.

"I don't do one-nighters anymore."

He raised his head up at that. "Why not?"

Fucker thought he was going to get his something-something from her again. That wasn't happening.

"I decided I deserve more than leftovers."

"You're going to get married before having sex again?" The horrified look on his face had her smiling.

She almost lied, but she had no intention of cutting off her nose to spite her face.

"Hell no. I'm never getting married."

"What's wrong with marriage?"

"Husbands fuck around on wives."

"Not all the time."

"Most of the time. A woman who kills a man who cheats on her gets a lighter sentence if she's not married to the fucker."

Train's mouth dropped open. "You've looked up the statistics?"

She rolled her eyes. "I didn't have to." He thought she was being ridiculous. "Wives get charged with first-degree murder. Girlfriends get charged with involuntary manslaughter. I want to get out of prison when I can take a piss without using a bedpan."

He released her hands, laughing so hard she had to put a hand over his mouth.

"Sh...Sex Piston will—"

Star came jumping into the room with her mother and father behind her.

Killyama clambered off of Train's lap, giving him a scowl as she righted her clothes.

"Were you tickling Train, too?" Star asked innocently.

"Yes. I was trying to find his funny bone. Lunch ready?" Killyama tried to delay the inevitable questions Sex Piston would ask, not caring that Killyama wouldn't want to answer in front of Train or Star. Her friend couldn't care less if she was embarrassed or offended.

"Did you find it?" Star giggled, taking her hand and skipping by her side as they went into the dining room.

Rocky, Sex Piston and Stud's son, was already sitting at the table, eating a grilled cheese sandwich. Sitting down next to her brother, Star began eating her lunch, as if afraid he would swipe the grapes from her plate. The boy just might. He would shove anything in his mouth, which was why Stud had nicknamed him Rocky after he had to pull rocks from his mouth more than once. He wasn't outgrowing the habit, either. The adventuresome child would eat anything. Killyama had suggested calling him Iron Man, because his stomach could handle anything.

"No, he doesn't have one." Killyama started to pull a chair back from table, but Train did it before she could.

"Yes, I do." Train smiled at Star, mumbling aside so only Killyama could hear, "Want me to help you find it?"

She elbowed him in the stomach as she sat down.

Killyama ate her sandwich, listening to Train and Stud talk about motorcycles and ignoring Sex Piston's discerning gaze.

After lunch, Star kept fidgeting in her seat, waiting for Killyama to finish eating. When she did, Star jumped out of her chair.

"Can we go now?" Star grabbed her hand when she stood up.

"Why are you in such a hurry?" Stud's eyes tried to slow his daughter as she tried to drag Killyama out of the dining room.

"Killyama promised to help me wash my Barbie's hair. Mama says I make a mess when I do it by myself."

"Don't let her talk you into washing the one that has the hair that grows. It's been washed so much that the hair is falling out."

"I won't." She let Star lead her to her bedroom.

The little girl's excited chatter had her straining to hear the men leave. It took ten minutes before she could detect the sounds of Stud and Train heading toward the massive garage he had built behind his house.

Killyama was leaning over the bathtub with ten Barbies lined up to take their turns when Sex Piston came into the bathroom. Putting down the lid of the toilet, she micromanaged the Barbies getting their baths.

"Star, what have I told you about going to my bathroom to get my things?"

A soapy hand left a trail of suds on Star's cheek when she pushed her hair back to eye her mother guiltily. "Your shampoo smells so pretty."

Killyama wiped her cheek with the edge of a towel. "I'll buy you another bottle."

Sex Piston sighed. "It's the third time she's taken my shampoo. They're thirty bucks a pop. You going to buy those, too?"

"Yes." Killyama squirted even more shampoo on the lifeless doll she was currently holding.

"I don't care if she uses it. I just want her to ask first before she takes something out of my room."

"She will next time, won't you, Star?"

"I promise, Mom. I won't do it again."

Sex Piston reached into the cabinet next to her, pulling out a tray of pretend hair tools mixed with real ones she no longer used that she had brought home from the shop, setting them on the counter for them to use later after the Barbies' hair dried.

"Star, will you go get the white towels on the bottom shelf in the hall closet for me?"

"Yes, Mama." Star handed Killyama the doll she was washing. "Don't let Angie drown. She doesn't swim as good as Kassandra."

"I won't." She turned on the water to remove the shampoo as Sex Piston sunk down next to her, choosing one of the dolls. She gently dunked the doll then shampooed it as if she were doing one of the rich bitches who frequently visited her shop.

"Don't do it." The bitch lifted her troubled eyes to hers.

Killyama couldn't be closer to the woman if they had shared the same blood. Probably closer. She and Sex Piston didn't fight often, whereas Sex Piston and Diamond fought constantly.

"I won't." She knew they weren't talking about the shampoo.

"I can't watch you get hurt like that again."

Setting the doll down on the edge of the tub, she reached for another one. "I've gotten him out of my system."

"Men like Train aren't easy to get over. I tried to stay away from Stud. So I'm asking you to do something I couldn't do."

"Train isn't Stud and never will be. I'm moving to Knoxville when Hammer finds me an apartment." She had given in to the idea of Lexington. However, business had become so steady they hadn't had any time to go look at the apartments Hammer had selected before they had been taken off the market.

Sex Piston bowed her head, meticulously washing the doll. "This is all my fault," she said, biting down on her trembling lip.

"Stop. I don't want to hear you say that again. It's not your fault I like the dude. I swore I wouldn't be like my mother, and I fell for a man just like my father, if not worse. I should have left town the day I came back from taking that ride from him, but I knew I would miss you all. I'll get over him. I'll find someone I will care about more, and then move back home."

"What if you don't? What if you never come back?"

Killyama nudged her with her shoulder. "I'll be back."

"You swear?"

"I swear. Have I ever lied to you?"

"Yes, when you swore to me you wouldn't get involved when you heard Stud and me arguing about talking to Knox about Sasha." Her eyes dropped to the bandana at her throat. The bitch was smarter than others gave her credit for.

"Well, other than that time?"

"No, you never have."

"You'll see. I'll be back before you know it. It's not going to be hard to find someone. Hell, my only requirement is a big dick."

Star came back in, holding enough towels so each doll could be dried separately. Setting them on the counter, she slipped between her and Sex Piston.

Seeing her mother's sad expression, Star handed her the doll she was about to wash off. "You can do Ken, Mama. He likes his hair washed."

"You do him, Star. I'm afraid I'll drown him." Sex Piston stared at the doll vengefully, as if it were Train incarnate.

"I'll do him." Killyama took the doll from Sex Piston, not wanting the girl's feelings to be hurt.

"Careful," Star warned. "His head falls off. Mama broke it accidently, and Daddy glued it back on, but it falls off a lot."

"Does it?" Killyama took her eyes off the doll for a brief second to look at Star. When she turned back, the doll's head was floating in the sudsy water.

Star fished his head out then took the headless body from her.

"I'm sorry, Star. How about I buy you a new one?" Killyama apologized to the upset girl.

Mollified, she wiggled the head back onto the body. "Can you just buy me a different Barbie I don't have? I don't want any more boy dolls. They break too easily."

Killyama laughed, flicking water on Star's cheek and starting a water fight. Then the three of them dried off before they finished the dolls.

Killyama enjoyed the afternoon with Star then went into the backyard to play with Rocky as Sex Piston cooked dinner. It was midnight when she drove home to her apartment.

She hadn't wanted to leave. The love and intimacy in the family always drove home what was missing from her own life, what she never had: her own family.

Growing up, it had been her and her mother, with spurts of appearances from Hammer and Jonas. The only one she had always wanted to be there would show up when no one would know, keeping his identity a secret.

Inside her apartment, she carried her laptop to her bed. After showering, she rested on the bed, letting the cat snuggle next to her as she searched for the doll Star had told her she wanted. Clicking on "purchase," she checked out before going to another site.

She scrolled down the options available, choosing what she wanted, checking out, and then closing the laptop when the receipt flashed across the screen.

Turning off her bedside lamp, she nuzzled her cat. "Who do you think he's with tonight? Sasha, Jewell, or both?" The stupid game she played in her mind ripped her to shreds, but she couldn't help from playing it. The scenarios of what went on in the clubhouse at night played differently every night until she fell asleep. It was a fucked-up way of replacing counting sheep.

Before she had seen Crash and Rider the night she had spent at The Last Riders' clubhouse, she had imagined Train with only one of the women. Since then, she had begun imagining him with two or three of them a night.

Unable to fall asleep, she reached for the radio on her nightstand, pushing a button on the top. The soothing sound of thunder and rain filled the dark room. She started to count the seconds between the claps of thunder.

She had lied when she told Sex Piston she had ridden Train from her consciousness. There wasn't going to be any getting over Train. She had instinctively known she would fall in love with him when he had walked across the parking lot the day they had gone for a ride.

She had inherited her mother's flaw. Only one man had been able to hold her heart. Even in his death, she still mourned him.

Though several men had tried to capture the heart that had already been taken, none had succeeded. Her father had made sure of that, secreting her mother away in a small town where no man could live up to the hero worship her mother felt for him.

Train was on the flip side of the same coin. Neither one truly cared about the women in their lives. He would happily share her with any of the men in the club. Hell, probably the women, too.

He was never going to love her. He would only care for her like he did all the women, but there wouldn't be anything special between them. She bet if the women were grouped in a dark room, none of the men would be able to tell them apart, other than the tits.

Killyama took the thought back. Shade would be able to tell. He watched Lily with a hawk-like intensity. The woman didn't take a breath before he made sure it was pure enough to enter her body.

Killyama didn't know if she wanted a man so possessive, but damn, it would be nice to see what it could be like. To feel the warmth of someone's love battle the frigid emotions that were seeping into her soul.

"I have a better chance of catching Dalton Andrews," she said out loud to the cat.

Lily had met the movie star when she had visited some friends. He had made the news last year when his wife had succumbed to cancer, leaving him a widower. She would give herself a couple of years to get over Train, and let Dalton Andrews get over the famous fashion model, before she asked Lily if she could hook them up.

"What do you think, Gollum?" She nodded in the dark as if the cat agreed with her ludicrous plan. "I could buy you all kinds of toys if I nabbed him."

Giving up trying to fall asleep, she turned on a movie that she had watched dozens of times. She was asleep before the first fight scene, tossing and turning as Dalton Andrews and Train fought in her dreams. She could see herself cheering the two men on.

Just as she thought Train was winning, another man grabbed him from behind.

Killyama woke up terrified, gasping in fear. She almost fell out the bed as she searched for her cell phone on the nightstand.

It took five seconds for Sex Piston to answer. "Bitch, do you know what time it is?"

"You don't sound like you were asleep." Killyama could hear Stud grumbling in the background, telling Sex Piston to hang up the phone.

"I wasn't," she snapped, her voice coming and going as if she were struggling for the phone. "What do you want?"

The terror of her dream was ebbing away like most nightmares do when you wake up. She should have washed her face before she made the call. The shock of the cold water would have saved her from making a fool out of herself.

"Do you need me to come over? Are you okay? Give me time to get dressed—"

"No! I'm fine! I just need you to do something…" Feeling ridiculous, she was also too afraid to go back to sleep until Sex Piston did what she wanted. "Uh…Could you go throw that Ken doll away?"

Silence meant her request.

"Sex Piston?"

"What'd you snort?" The sound of Sex Piston and Stud tussling for the phone stopped.

"Nothing! Just do it. And don't throw it out in the kitchen trash. Make Stud throw it away outside."

Again silence.

"Listen, I know it's crazy as fuck, but just do it, okay?"

Sex Piston's long drawled out "Okay" had Killyama gritting her teeth.

"Thank you. Tell Stud I'm sorry for bothering him."

"I will. You know I'm never letting you play with Star's dolls again, right?"

"Believe me; I won't be going near them." Killyama started to disconnect the call. "Sex Piston!"

"What!"

Killyama winced. Sex Piston had cruised past concern for her friend's mental state and had moved on to aggravation.

"Make sure you don't forget the head."

CHAPTER NINETEEN

"Good luck!" Stud hit Train on the back as he lifted his helmet to put it on. Train buckled the strap as the man he was beginning to think of as a friend took his own motorcycle.

He had called Stud and asked him for help getting into the race after Shade had told him that Lily and Beth were planning to take a mommy day off to watch Stud race with Sex Piston and her crew.

He had raced when he had first started riding a motorcycle, wiping out more than winning. He had stopped when he had entered the service and hadn't picked it up again when he was discharged. It didn't provide the same excitement he had grown used to after he had been picked for a secret unit controlled by the president.

Members from several different military branches had been hand-selected to try out once a year for the unit. Each current team member also had to be re-invited to try out, with over two hundred candidates chosen to compete. Only twenty-four would be picked for the elite unit. Train had made the unit each time. Hammer had made the team five years before he had and had continued to get picked.

The last time they had been called out, they had rescued a group of four men taken hostage. When he arrived to gather intel, Hammer had informed the fellow members that it would be the last time he would try out if asked.

Losing Jonas the year before that had been a shock. The members had always joked that Jonas and Hammer were attached at the hip. Losing two high-ranking members hurt.

When Train had asked Hammer why he was giving it up since Hammer had lived and breathed the American flag, he had evaded the question, saying he was giving the young guns a chance to make the unit.

Train had figured out the why when he had read Crash's reports. Jonas had quit the unit when Killyama had begun bounty hunting full-time in the business the three of them had formed. He wanted to be there to protect her from the caliber of fugitives she had been chasing the previous year.

She was taking her life in her hands each time she accepted a job, which was why Hammer had decided not to try out for the unit again. He was placing Killyama over the job he loved, afraid Jonas couldn't do it alone.

He wanted to know what tied the three of them together. Even Shade couldn't figure it out. Shade was a member of the same team, except he was given special consideration over which jobs he took and how. He was the lone wolf in the unit; often sent out without other members' knowledge.

Stud gave Train a thumbs up as he started his bike. Train tightened his gloved hands on the bike he would ride in the race, one Rider had loaned to him from his personal collection. He was going to have to get one of his own if he was going to continue to compete to impress Killyama.

He took a quick look around while he waited for the race to start. Killyama was sitting in the front row on the second floor of the stands next to Sex Piston, who was sitting next to Beth and Lily. Crazy Bitch was sitting on the other side of Killyama, with the rest of the bitches seated down the rest of the row. The women looked excited as they waited for the race to start.

The men seated behind them didn't exhibit the same of air of excitement. Their set faces showed how much they wanted to be anywhere else. That was, everyone except Rider, who was munching on popcorn, drawing killing gazes from Shade and Razer.

Train readied himself for the race. He would focus on the man in front of him—Stud—whose racing suit was black and covered in sponsors' logos. His bike was also black, sleek, and made exclusively for him. Stud's reputation building motorcycles was only eclipsed by his racing.

The suit Train was wearing was one of Stud's practice suits. It was black without the logos. Stud had told him he usually wore it when he didn't want others to know he was practicing.

From the yells coming from the stands, Train could see Stud's problem. The man had a huge fan base, including Killyama, who was decked out in a T-shirt with Stud's name embossed across her tits.

Train got Rider's bright red bike in position, waiting for the flag to drop. As soon the leggy blonde dropped it, Train took off, letting the riders in front fight it out for the lead position.

The course had one long turn before leading to a straightway that turned into a series of four intermittent curves. A racer had to repeat the course four times and come in first to win.

Train took the first curve easily, still staying behind the other riders. Taking the rest of the curves, he let himself become more familiar with the track.

As he passed the stands where Killyama was, he shot a quick glance to see that her head was turned to the side, talking to Crazy Bitch. He was risking his neck for a woman who wasn't even watching him. Meanwhile, Sex Piston, Beth, and Lily were leaning over the rail, shouting Stud's name.

When Train came out of the first turn again, he hunched over his bike even further, setting his sights on Stud. It took another lap to bring him even to Stud, the two riding side by side through the series of turns.

Leaning into the curves, Train felt his kneepad ride the track due to making the last turn so fast. He expertly righted himself, preparing for the next turn.

This time when he passed Killyama, he didn't have time to look, the danger and the thrill of the ride taking over.

As they passed the first turn again, they saw one of the racers had crashed. Train skillfully went one way, while Stud went in the other direction to miss the wreck, adroitly handling the bikes until they rode side by side again.

When they passed the stands for the third time, Train accelerated again, increasing speed to pull away from Stud. Stud wasn't giving the race up without a fight, though, accelerating until they rode at the same dangerous speed.

When they reached the last turn, Train was hanging so low to the ground it wasn't his kneepad riding the track; it was his elbow pad. The forward momentum gave him the extra inch he needed to win the race.

Using his boot to right himself, he managed to stop his bike before crashing into the stands.

When he took off his helmet, he grinned at Stud, who was there to shake his hand.

Getting off the motorcycle, he pushed it into the winner's circle. He waited for third place to be given before Stud stepped up to accept his second-place trophy. The screams had Train turning to see Killyama and all the others standing as his name was called.

When Stud stepped down, they shook hands again. Then Train's name was called to accept his first prize. The huge trophy was held by a buxom brunette with leather shorts.

He turned again to see if Killyama was cheering for him, only to see that the spot where she had been standing was now empty. He hadn't expected Killyama to cheer for him, but he was disappointed that she hadn't even watched him receive his trophy.

When the brunette would have kissed him, Train dodged her, turning to leave the stage.

Rider met him at the back gate, helping him load up his borrowed bike onto the trailer while Lily and Beth congratulated him.

"Wow, Train, I was terrified you were going to wreck when you came out of that last turn!" Beth hugged him before letting her sister shyly take a turn.

"I knew you were going to win! You were so awesome!" Lily was barely able to get her compliments out before Shade snatched her back to his side.

"Thanks. Where's Razer?"

Beth laughed. "I made him go buy some of Stud's T-shirts. Hopefully, the next time you race, we can buy one of yours."

Train shook his head. "This is my last race for a while."

"Why? You won." Lily's smile faded. "All of us were cheering for you to win."

"Not all of you." Train scuffed his boot as he kicked a rock.

Realizing that Beth and Lily were staring at him quizzically, he made an excuse to give himself time to bury the feelings of jealously toward the exuberant cheering Killyama had given Stud.

"I want to tell Stud I'm leaving to go back to the clubhouse. Rider, if you're done tying the bike down, I'll be back in a minute."

"Take your time. I'm going to go buy myself a couple of T-shirts."

Train stopped in his tracks. "You're going to buy some of Stud's T-shirts?"

"Hell no. I'm going to buy some plain ones. The women can paint my name on them. That way, all the brothers will see who's their favorite. You want me to buy one for you girls, too?" Rider stared at them expectantly, missing the glowering frown from Shade.

"That's okay," Lily delicately refused. "We can wait until Train has some made."

Shade stared down at his small wife with a gleam that promised retribution.

Rider loved to rile The Last Riders' enforcer. One day, though, he would go too far. Train hoped he would be there to witness it when it happened.

He found Stud's trailer where his bike was parked next to, but Train didn't see him. However, Sex Piston was sitting on the hood of the truck, her legs hanging off the side.

When he approached, her eyes narrowed on him, making no effort to hide her contempt for him.

Braving the woman's surly manner, he drew closer.

"I wanted to tell Stud I was leaving. Is he going to be back soon?"

"He's busy. I'll let him know you left."

Another man would have cut and run from her attitude. Train wasn't that man. He had dealt with women long enough to know what made them tick, and he knew what made Sex Piston tick. The bitches watched out for each other.

Train was determined to have Killyama, and Stud's wife was just as committed to keeping her from getting hurt. What she didn't know was that he had no intention of hurting her.

"I can wait." Train stubbornly leaned against the truck door, crossing his arms over his chest.

Her mouth set in a hard line. "If you're waiting for Killyama, you're wasting your time. She already left."

Train's lashes lowered. He had hoped to see her before she left. "That's fine. I'll still wait."

"Fucker, what are you not getting? Are you stupid? You think you can try to use my man to get back in my bitch's panties?" She agilely hopped off the hood of the truck. "I'll rip the pitchfork out of the devil's hand if I have to, to keep you away from her." She waved him away from her with a shooing motion. "Go back to those hos you keep your bed warm for."

"The only woman I'm keeping a spot warm for is Killyama."

Sex Piston rudely snorted her disbelief. "I'll believe that when I see it." She tried to shoo him away again. "You're wasting your time getting Stud to help you. The only one who is going to talk Killyama into giving you another whirl is me, and that won't be happening...no matter how many races you talk Stud into losing."

Dumfounded, Train's mouth dropped open. "You think Stud deliberately lost the race because I asked him to?"

"My man doesn't lose."

"I have news for you. He did today. I'm not ashamed to admit I wanted to win because I wanted to impress Killyama, but I certainly didn't ask Stud to let me."

"I can vouch for that," Stud said, walking up from behind the trailer. "He beat my ass fair and square."

Train took the hand held out to him. "I wanted to thank you again for getting me into the race and letting me borrow your suit."

"No problem. I was glad to help. It gave me someone new to race. In this arena, it's usually the same ones who show up each time. I hope to see you here again. Maybe next time you'll take it easy on me."

Train moved, avoiding the truck door that Sex Piston slung open, nearly hitting him.

"She gets easier to tolerate the more you get to know her." Stud excused his wife's behavior with a shrug.

"I'll have to take your word for it."

"If you think she's bad, wait until you have to deal with Crazy Bitch. She'll drive you over the bend. Fat Louise and T.A. aren't much better, but you can feed them to get them to back off when they get cranky."

Train didn't try to hide his interest.

Stud's humor vanished. "Killyama is hard to describe." Leaning an elbow on the hood of the truck, Stud studied him. "I saw her beat the hell out of some of the brothers in the club when they pissed her off. Then she bought Rocky a mini-bike when I told her I wanted to wait. She paid for Fat Louise's mother's rehab. When Star got sick and the doctor didn't want to admit her, she left, and ten minutes later had her admitted." Stud gave a low laugh. "Sex Piston said Killyama cornered the doctor in the doctor's lounge."

"I think she bought me a new wallet. It came in the mail without a card."

Stud nodded. "That sounds like her. She's sneaky as fuck, but you already know that, don't you? If she sent it to you, it means she likes you."

"How do you know?" Jealousy reared its ugly head. Train had never been jealous over a woman in his entire life. That Killyama could bring out those feeling was going to take some getting used to.

"How do you think I got all those sponsors? Killyama called them when I was thinking of giving up racing. It takes time out of my work schedule, and Sex Piston's shop was going through a slump when she ticked off one of her biggest customers. With four kids, it was hard to justify my racing."

"If you need—" Train had started to offer a loan, but Stud stopped him.

"It's all good now. The money made from the sponsors picked up the slack, and Sex Piston's customer came back. She's good at her job, and the rich bitches like to look good."

"If you need anything, the offer is there."

"I won't. Congrats again. I better be going before she rips out my radio." Stud started to leave then stopped. "I heard what Sex Piston said. She is right about one thing. If you want Killyama, you will have to go through Sex Piston first."

"I'm figuring that out for myself. Any ideas?"

Stud rubbed a thoughtful finger across the bridge of his nose. "Find something she wants, but don't let her have it."

Train drew a blank. "Like what?"

"Damned if I know. I had to use my kids to get her attached to me." He gestured toward Sex Piston. "And brother, I might like you, but you can't have my kids. You're more than welcome to drop in for a beer when you want to see Killyama, but it won't earn you kudos from either of them. You'll think of something...You have a clubhouse at your back to bounce ideas off of."

Only one brother was smart enough to help him out of this dilemma...Shade.

"I'm going to take your advice. Later, Stud."

Stud waved back as he got in the front of the truck.

Train waved politely at Sex Piston, seeing her raise up her finger in a fuck-you gesture as he turned away.

Rider was waiting when he slid in the front seat of the truck. He had to shove the large pile of T-shirts over so he could get in.

"How much did you spend?"

Rider put the truck in gear, heading home. "Two hundred."

"You spent two hundred dollars just to piss off Shade?"

"Yep." Rider grinned unrepentantly. "Making him mad is worth any amount of money."

"I'll remind you of that when I'm covering your casket with dirt."

"Shade won't kill me. He might want to, but he won't. It'll hurt Lily too much."

"Brother, a woman is going to bring you down to earth, and when she does, you're going to hit hard."

"That woman doesn't exist," he stated cockily. "You need me to give you some lessons? I didn't see Killyama hanging out with you after the race. Did you at least get a kiss for winning when you went searching for Stud?"

"No, she already left. But Sex Piston made sure to congratulate me when she told me to fuck off."

"Damn, that must have hurt." Rider's cheerful attitude had him wishing he had caught a ride with Shade and the women. "What's your next move, since that one didn't work out so hot?"

"I don't know. Sex Piston told me I had to get past her first."

"She said that?"

Train nodded. "She came right out and told me I wasn't getting into her bitch's panties without her say-so."

"You going to ask Shade what he would do?"

"I don't need Shade's advice." He would, but he wouldn't admit it to Rider if his balls were on fire.

"You need more than Shade's advice; you need a fucking miracle."

Train looked up to see they were stopped at a red light. Rider was waving at an attractive woman in a sports car who was waving back. Maybe the person he should be asking was sitting right next to him. If Rider knew he wanted his advice, though, he would never hear the end of it.

Trying to be cool, he nonchalantly asked, "What would you do?"

Rider took his eyes off the blonde, who looked like she was ready to jump out of her car and into their truck, and looked at him. "What would *I* do?" he asked in shock.

Flushing, Train clenched his jaw. "Yes, how would you make Sex Piston like you?"

The light turned green. "Give me a minute to think." Rider's face turned thoughtful.

He should have just kept his big mouth shut until he could talk to Shade.

"I know." Rider snapped his fingers.

"What is it?" Train asked when Rider didn't tell him right away.

"What's in it for me? I did my good deed for the day when I loaned you my bike."

Train sighed. "What do you want?"

"You know what I want."

Train did. Rider was curious about how Killyama was in bed. He had repeatedly asked what she had done to him the night she had spent in the clubhouse to make him yell out. Train had never answered his questions. Now Rider wanted to watch when Train had sex with her.

"I'll tell you what. You help me figure out how to get past Sex Piston, and if Killyama ever lets me invite anyone to watch, you have first dibs."

Rider shrugged. "I can live with that."

"So...?" If the brother didn't wipe that expression off his face, Train was going to deck him when the truck came to a stop. The randy bastard was anticipating more than just watching. He was going to be shit out of luck, unless Killyama was on board.

He listened to Rider's plan for the rest of the ride back to the clubhouse. Then, when he pulled into the parking lot, Train could only stare at him.

"Viper will never go for it," was all Train could say.

"Convincing Viper is up to you. I'm only telling you what I would do."

"It'll never work."

"You'll never know if you don't ask. If he won't do it, ask Winter to try to persuade him."

"I stand a better chance asking Stud if I can adopt one of his kids. I'll try it on my own. If not, then I'll ask Viper."

They got out of the truck to unload Rider's bike.

"I don't envy you. I don't know what's worse: Sex Piston liking you or hating your guts."

"I'll just be happy if she doesn't try to poison my beer when I'm not looking."

"I take it you're going to take up Stud's offer of a beer sooner than he expected?"

Train nodded. "As soon I get cleaned up."

"I've got this. Go ahead," Rider offered when they unloaded the bike.

"You sure? I was going to wash it for you."

"I'll do it." Rider was meticulous in caring for his bikes, and he hardly offered to loan them out.

"Thanks, brother."

"I'd say any time, but I would be lying," Rider joked as he pushed the motorcycle through the back entrance of the factory where he kept his collection under lock and key.

Train took the steps two at a time. Killyama or Sex Piston might not be at the Destructors' clubhouse when he showed, but he would use the opportunity to become more at ease with the men in the club. So far, he had only gotten to know Stud and talked a time or two with Cade. If he was going to make a relationship with Killyama work, he needed to get used to hanging out with all of them. If they were as close-knit as The Last Riders, Sex Piston wasn't going to be his only challenge.

He heard everyone in the kitchen when he came through the front door. The living room was empty. From the aroma, The Last Riders were settling down to dinner. He wanted to join them, but he continued up the steps.

When he had tried to talk Killyama into joining the club, he had expected her to make the sacrifice of giving up a club she loved for him. Staring at himself in the bathroom mirror, he thought, if they couldn't come up with a compromise, he could be the one choosing another club to make someone else happy.

Shaking the depressing thought off, he decided not to worry about it yet. He needed to catch the woman first, and if he didn't bring Sex Piston around, the only thing he was going to be worried about was picking which plot in the cemetery he wanted to be buried in.

CHAPTER TWENTY

"You want Stud to make him leave?" Sex Piston poured a shot of tequila into her empty glass.

"You need to go easy on that," Killyama warned. "You have a conference with Meri and Keri's teacher in the morning."

"I didn't forget. The bitch keeps sending me reminder emails."

"That's your fault for missing two meetings with her."

"Because I was working. I told her I couldn't get off till six."

"That has nothing to do with it. You don't want to let Meri and Keri become foreign exchange students."

"I'll miss them too much."

Killyama didn't doubt she would, but she was also sure the other half of the request was causing a problem, too.

"It might not be bad being a host family." T.A. winked at Train when she saw him watching Killyama. Then T.A. turned her flirtations toward Calder who was avoiding her attempts by giving his back to the room. "What does a girl have to do to get laid?" T.A. scowled, trying unsuccessfully to entice Rock next.

"Quit talking about their dick," Killyama reminded her for the umpteenth time. Then she went back to her conversation with Sex Piston. "Maybe it won't be so bad. You get along great with most kids."

"These aren't kids. They're a pain in the ass, hormone-filled, one shady move away from jail. I have my stepdaughters whipped into shape; why should I take someone else's sixteen-year-old and start all over? With my luck, they'll end up in juvie or knocked up. I'll probably end up with another girl like Sissy or T.A."

"That's not it. You're afraid you'll get attached and won't see them anymore when they go back home." Killyama scooted her chair to the side as she saw Jenna practically licking the head off Train's beer.

"Anyone else want another beer?" T.A. asked, her ass half on and half off the chair as she started to rise.

"I'll get everyone a round." Killyama stood up so fast she nearly knocked down the chair she had been sitting on.

She weaved through the tables and around the pool table to elbow her way between Train and Calder.

Jenna straightened when she saw her staring her down.

"Give me four beers, and try to keep your tits out of them."

The slut was smart enough not to argue, pouring out four beers while Killyama watched her every move. She didn't trust her not to spit in them.

"You need some help with those?" Train offered.

"No." Killyama took two mugs in each hand then turned to go back to the table.

"You want to dance after you take them to the table?"

"My beer will go flat."

"I can sit with you until you finish it."

Killyama slammed the beers into Calder's chest, drenching his T-shirt. "Take those to my table and tell T.A. mine better still be full when I get there."

Leaving Calder juggling the beers, Killyama grabbed Train's arm while Stud and Cade watched in amusement. She shoved him toward the door, not releasing him until they stood in the gravel parking lot.

"Dude, I'm trying to be as nice to you as I know how! What does it take to get you to learn I'm not interested?"

"You're interested. You're just scared."

She gaped at him. "You think I'm afraid of you?"

"Not me. I think you are afraid of how good we are together."

Killyama poked his chest. "You"—she pointed at herself—"and I are not together."

"We will be." Train gave her a once over. When he started to say something, she covered his mouth with her hand. Train laughingly pulled his head away. "What did you think I was going to say?"

She tucked her curly hair behind her ear. "You were going to say something nice, and I'm not in the mood to hear it."

Train took a step forward. Unconsciously, she took a step back, trying not to let him get close to her.

"I was going to tell you those boots look as good as those heels did, and I want to rip that top off of you." Train's chest brushed up so close to her that she knew she wouldn't be able to see Stud's name if she looked down.

She took another step backward, coming into contact with the front wall of the club.

"Go home, Train. There's no place for you here."

"Make room for me, then." He placed one strong arm on the wall next to her head. "I don't need much room." He braced his other arm on the other side of her before sinking his body against hers. "I only need this much room."

When he tried to kiss her, she turned her face away.

Resting her head against his chest, she clutched fistfuls of his T-shirt, trying to decide if she was going to pull him closer or push him away. Train made the decision for her, burrowing his hands in her hair then lifting her mouth until there wasn't an escape for her. Claiming her lips, he drove his tongue into her mouth, tilting her head so she had to part her lips wider until her jaw started to ache when she didn't respond.

"Kiss me back."

"I don't want to."

"Don't lie to me. Kiss me…please."

It was the plea that did her in. Hating herself, she responded to him the way she had promised herself she wouldn't. Then, when the hard ridge of his dick rubbed against her waist, she melted into the wall at her back.

"Let's go inside…" His throaty murmur had her sliding out from under him.

"No." If she took him inside, Sex Piston and crew would know she had caved.

She started to open the door, but Train's arm came around her waist, pulling her back into his chest.

"We could get a motel room, or go to my club. I don't care where we go."

Killyama wavered, letting him pull her away from the door, while she half-heartedly tried to struggle free.

"I can't." This time when she managed to get loose, she turned to face him. Her rampant heartbeat and the throb in her aching pussy were signs it took only a touch from the man before she reconsidered taking a chance with him.

"Why not?"

Killyama had never let herself be vulnerable, and she didn't plan to start now. How could she tell him that she wanted to have sex with him again so badly that her body was growing wet just thinking about it? That she already had feelings for him, and she was afraid he was going to break her heart? That if he wanted payback for Sasha and left her hurting to get revenge for The Last Riders, he had already succeeded?

Killyama couldn't tell him, because she wasn't able to voice her fears, unlike most women were willing to do. It was useless to stay and continue talking to him.

She pivoted on her heels…

"What if we each picked one make-it-or-break-it rule?"

Killyama turned back, staring at his face in the moonlight. "Are you serious? We tried this before."

His eyes were unwavering, staring back. "I remember. Deep down, I knew you were lying, but I wanted you in my bed bad enough that I took a chance. I'm willing to take another. Shade says I'm terrible at poker, at gambling, but I'm willing to roll the dice and try again."

"Why?" Her raspy words brought a tenderness to his gaze that had a lump rising in her throat.

"Because I care about you. I like spending time with you." He reached out to take her hand, pulling her to him. "You make me laugh."

"I make you laugh?"

"Yes. That's important to a man."

Laughter was good. Laughter was a good and open emotion that men usually didn't talk about wanting from a woman. They weren't explicit emotions any woman could make him feel. It was how a part of her affected him that he couldn't get from any other woman, even from those he had ready access to.

"I'm not saying I'll think about it, but what would be your rule breaker?"

"That you would never lie to me."

Killyama licked her lips. "You won't like my rule."

"Try me." His sensual lips curled into a smile that had her wanting to say fuck it. Regardless, she was the one who had to live with herself in the morning.

"No other women. That's my rule breaker."

"Would you be able to take my word that I'm not fucking around on you when you're not there, knowing the women in the club will be giving it to the other brothers?"

"If a man is going to cheat, he is going to cheat, regardless of where he's at. Stud could cheat anytime he walks through the club doors without Sex Piston, but he doesn't. Or, if he does, none of us would know. Sex Piston trusts him, and I do, too."

"Then let's give it a try."

He lifted their clasped hands to her breasts, rubbing his knuckles across her nipple.

She gave him a quick half-smile. "I'll think about it."

Train laughed, letting her hand drop to her side. "You want to spend the day with me tomorrow, thinking it over?"

"I'm busy tomorrow."

"Doing what?"

"I need to help my mom with a few chores."

"I'm off tomorrow. I could help."

"You sure you want to? I can spring for pizza when we're done," she magnanimously offered. "I'll text you the address."

Hearing the door open, Killyama turned to see Sex Piston blatantly eavesdropping.

"Your beer is getting warm."

"I'm coming." Killyama took the silent hint that her friend wasn't going to leave her alone with Train. She went through the door that Sex Piston held open, telling Train, "I'll see you in the morning."

Sex Piston slammed the door on whatever he had said in response.

She almost laughed when she saw Train come back inside the clubhouse seconds later, finding a spot next to Calder.

"Bitch, you need your head examined for even talking to him." Sex Piston's hard eyes bore into her.

"I'm not stupid. I took everything he had to say with a grain of salt." Killyama winced when she took a sip of her beer. It tasted like warm piss. She hated the taste of beer unless it was ice cold and had a shot of tequila to follow it.

"Why give him the opportunity? You're going to get sucked in—"

"Is that so bad?" Killyama snapped. "Beth and Lily are happy. Willa, Winter, and Rachel seem happy. Why would it be such a stretch of the imagination that Train could make me happy?"

The women seated around her gazed at her in sympathy.

"You think everything he says is bullshit, don't you?"

T.A. nervously twisted her beer mug by the handle. "Yes, but if you want to go for it, I'm with you."

Out of all the bitches, T.A. was the most optimistic about men. She would give any man a chance, which was why she had slept with most of the Destructors and the Blue Horsemen. She kept hoping she would find the one man who wouldn't let her down, in bed and out. So far, her hook-ups had ended in failure.

"I think she should go for it, too. It's better than her moving away," Crazy Bitch gave her own two cents, which didn't make Sex Piston any happier. "You want me to call Fat Louise and see what she thinks?"

"Hell no. I know what Fat Louise would say. She'd tell you to fuck him." Sex Piston's lips tightened when boisterous laughter came from the bar. It didn't take a rocket scientist to know the men were talking about them. "I'm not going to play the bad guy. You're going to do what you want to do, regardless of what I say. I don't want you to move, either, but if he's why you want to move away from us, then I'd rather you do it now. At least you'd come back when you got over him. I'm worried that, if you did get serious with him and it didn't last, you'd move away anyway, and after being with him, you wouldn't ever come back."

To Sex Piston, it wasn't a decision between if Train would hurt her but when.

"Or maybe I can spend some time with him and find out I don't want him. That's what normal people do."

T.A. shook her head. "We're not normal."

"If you fuck him…" Sex Piston started.

"I'm not going to fuck him."

The women stared at her in shock.

"I'm not," Killyama stated. "Yet. Or at least not until I'm sure he can keep his dick to himself."

T.A.'s eyes widened. "How?"

"It's not like Beth or Lily won't tell me." She shrugged. "I just want to find out if the man can stop banging every tail that comes within sniffing distance, or if he will be content to wait until his balls are blue, if that's what it takes to get me in his bed."

"What if Beth and Lily don't know what's going on in the club-house when they're not there?" T.A. waved Pike away as he started to approach.

"Do you really think that if Train starts cheating on me, I won't know? There isn't a man alive who can pull that wool over my eyes. A man acts differently when he has blue balls than he does when he has a happy dick. If he lies to me about cheating with those hos, you won't have to worry about me moving to Knoxville; you'll be visiting me in Danville." Killyama wasn't joking, and they knew it.

Danville was where the state penitentiary was.

If Train did manage to pull the wool over her eyes, she would kill the fucker. She might beat the living hell out of the woman, but she would kill Train. The only one who would be doing a happy dance was her when the coroner wheeled his cold dead body out of the clubhouse.

"I'd be sitting in jail with you, and then my kids would be motherless," Sex Piston said glumly.

"No, they won't. I'd take care of them for you," T.A. happily offered without hesitation.

"I bet she'd take care of Stud, too." Crazy Bitch's snide aside had Killyama drinking the nasty beer to keep from laughing at Sex Piston's menacing expression.

"You'd do Stud if I were in prison?"

"It's not like you'd still be married to him. Stud would divorce you."

"Bitch, you wanna help me out, then go get Jenna and tell the slut to come here."

"Why?" T.A. asked innocently, preparing to get out of her chair.

"I want to tell her that you're out of my crew, and she's in."

T.A. sank back down in her chair. "That's kind of hurtful."

"And you telling me to my face that you would fuck my man isn't?" Sex Piston scoffed at T.A.'s hurt expression.

"At least I'd take good care of your kids. You see Jenna doing that?"

"I'll tell you what. You can have Stud when I'm dead. Okay?"

"All right. You work with all those chemicals; I'll outlive you."

"Killyama?"

"Yes?"

"When you move to Knoxville"—Sex Piston stood up angrily, her beer sloshing over the side of the mug as she picked it up—"and you will be moving...take T.A. with you."

CHAPTER
TWENTY-ONE

Train turned the blinker on, signaling the turn onto the street where Killyama's mother lived. He had expected other houses on the road, not familiar with Jamestown as he was with Treepoint, but it was further out of town than what he had expected. No man's land.

The house was a mile down from the turnoff, the road turning into gravel. He almost lost his struts on the first pothole.

"Son of a fucking bitch."

Train had taken the back road to the Porters' house many times to purchase pot from the brothers, but the one Killyama had directed him to made theirs look like the yellow brick road.

The next rut almost buried the truck in the mud. He had to saw the truck back and forth before he could find enough traction to free his tires.

Becoming aggravated, thinking Killyama had sent him to the boonies to make a fool out of him again, he was ready to turn around when he went over another rut that had his truck dipping so low he expected to see his bumper in his rearview mirror.

Turning a corner, he was searching for a place to turn around in the knee-length grass when he saw a trailer sitting on the side of the gravel road. He knew he was in the right place when he recognized the Escalade Killyama had been in when she had taken Sasha.

Train parked Cash's borrowed truck beside the Escalade at the back of the house. Getting out, he saw Hammer and Jonas, shirtless and on the roof, nailing shingles down. Killyama moved into view from behind the house, wearing blue jeans tucked into work boots and a tank top with a bright red bandana tied around her throat. Her curly hair had been swept up on top of her head into a careless knot.

"I was beginning to think you chickened out of meeting my mother."

"Nothing could have kept me away, not even what you called a road." Train brushed a smudge of dirt off her cheek, letting his fingers linger before dropping his hand. Then he looked up at the two men on the roof. "Hey, Hammer, Jonas."

The men didn't stop hammering to greet him.

"That's one of the chores we have to work on today. Come on inside and meet my mama."

Train's nerves went on high alert. He still had to get past Sex Piston and the rest of her friends. Plus, Hammer and Jonas were giving him the cold shoulder. The last thing he needed was another person keeping him from making headway with her.

Killyama casually held the screen door of the trailer open for him. He caught a glimpse of her anxious expression as he stepped inside.

"Mama, this is Train. He's a friend of mine. He offered to come and help with the roof."

"Hi, Train." Killyama's mother removed her hands from the sink, drying them on a dishtowel.

The woman who came over to hold his hand was so delicate he was afraid she would disappear like a whisper of smoke. He knew her age from Crash's report, but she looked more like Killyama's sister than her mother.

The only characteristic of her mother's he could see they had in common was their hair color. Her nose and cheeks had a sprinkle of freckles, while Killyama's complexion was flawless. Her eyes were brown, and she was so small Train thought she might need a step-ladder just to shake his hand.

"Train, this is my mother...Peyton."

"It's nice to meet you," Peyton said. "We've already eaten, but I could fix you some breakfast if you're hungry?"

"I already ate, but thank you."

"I appreciate you offering to help Hammer and Jonas fix my roof. That last storm decided to take a chunk out of it."

"I'm glad to help out," Train said, releasing her hand.

"I'll be mowing the yard, Mama. If you need us, just yell out."

"I'm going to vacuum and get started on white washing the front porch before I make lunch."

"Don't bother; I promised to buy pizza when we finish."

"Oh, I don't mind."

"Anything you fix would be fine." Train smiled gently at the soft-spoken woman. She was dressed as if she were going to an afternoon tea, and not the housework she had described.

"I don't want to disappoint Hammer and Jonas if they're expecting pizza." She stared at her daughter as if she didn't know what to do without her say-so.

"You know they'll like anything you fix. Okay?"

"All right. If you're sure."

"I am. We better get started." Killyama went to the door, and Train followed, carefully shutting the screen door behind them so it wouldn't slam shut.

When he was sure her mother couldn't hear them, Train said, "That can't be your mother." He shook his head in disbelief.

"I don't know why everyone says that when they meet her."

"You don't see the differences?" Train lifted a mocking brow. "You're twice her height, and I don't think you inherited that attitude you carry around your shoulders from her."

"No, I didn't."

Train jumped out of the way when a hammer fell between them. Looking up, he saw Hammer's head peeking over the side of the roof.

"Sorry, it slipped out of my hand," Hammer apologized.

Train wanted to throw it back at him but restrained himself. He waited beside Killyama as Hammer climbed down to retrieve his tool, politely giving it back handle first instead of burying it in the arrogant asshole's head.

"Is it safe to leave you three working together while I mow?" She stepped between them as they stared at each other challengingly.

"It depends on whether you have another hammer I can defend myself with," Train drawled. He wouldn't make the first move to pick a fight with Hammer, but he would be damned if he backed away from one.

Jonas stood overhead with his hands on his hips, watching the standoff. From their contemptuous stance, both of them wanted a confrontation.

Killyama raised her voice. "I invited him here. You can deal with it or leave. If Mama doesn't hear any work going on, she'll be out here, wanting to know why."

"Everything is fine. Go mow," Hammer gritted out.

"That's what I wanted to hear. I'm going inside to make some lemonade. All this testosterone is making me hot. Train, anytime you want to take that shirt off, feel free. It'll give me something to stare at while I mow."

Killyama was teasing, yet she didn't go inside to make the lemonade until he nodded that he would ignore the men's attempts to start a fight.

"The extra hammer is in the toolbox in the back of the Escalade," Jonas called out as Hammer started climbing the ladder.

Train found the hammer before he followed, keeping a cautious eye for any other missiles to mysteriously go sailing over his head.

The men worked steadily, nailing down the shingles, while he wondered where the lemonade was. That's when he heard the mower start and saw Killyama driving it through the grassy field.

"Hammer, Jonas, Train, I brought you something to drink."

Train let Hammer and Jonas go first, worried they would accidently push the ladder over. Once he was safely on the ground, he took the lemonade Peyton handed him.

After Train thanked her, she blushed before going back inside.

"You hurt that little girl, the squad will be searching for two new members." The warm smile Hammer had worn for Peyton dissolved.

"Killyama isn't a little girl, and I have no intention of hurting her."

"You think I've forgotten the women you and Shade bragged about fucking when we were on a mission? The times we visited you in Ohio, you weren't hurting for company there, either. If you think Jonas is going to sit back and watch our girl getting the same treatment as those cunts you claimed for The Last Riders, you better buckle up, because it's going to take more than a parachute to save you."

Train set his drink down on the porch bannister, taking off his shirt then turning so Killyama could see his muscular back. "Killyama has no problem taking care of herself. The Last Riders have all tried to guess where she came by the skills to fight the way she does. You two have done an excellent job training her." He paused before asking, "Which one of you is her father?"

"Crash's skills let you down again?" Jonas scoffed at Train's lame attempt to discover who her father was. "Let me make it easy for you. Neither Hammer nor I are her father. A day hasn't gone by that I wish it were true, but she's not."

Train sighed. He had worked with them on missions for years, so he knew that, if Jonas said one of them wasn't Killyama's father, they weren't. Ultimately, it didn't matter. They considered her their daughter, blood or not.

"I'm not going to apologize for my past. I'm not the only man here who enjoyed a good time. The only reason you and Jonas haven't settled down yet isn't because you haven't met the right women, but because both of you haven't met the right woman. I can sling mud just as easily, or we can call a truce and admit we want what's going to make Killyama happy. I promise to do that to the best of my ability, but if you're expecting me to cut off my left nut to keep you two happy, then I guess we're all shit out of luck."

Hammer reached for Train's T-shirt, tossing it back at him. "Right now, I'll be happy if you put that back on. She's mowed the same patch of grass three times."

Train grinned as he tugged it back on.

"Truce?" Holding out his hand, the men reluctantly shook it.

The window in the kitchen opened, and the men turned to see Killyama's mother.

"The only one I see out there working up a sweat is my daughter. Do I need to put my jeans on and show you how to nail on a shingle?"

Killyama would have snarled profanities at them. Peyton did it much more delicately, but her message was the same.

"No, ma'am." Train winked at her as Hammer and Jonas scrambled back up the ladder.

The rest of the afternoon passed without incident as they worked in unison, sweat pouring down their backs.

Not caring if he made Jonas or Hammer angry, he removed his shirt and was about to call in a favor to Cash to help when he realized they were on the last row.

As he worked, the aroma of whatever Peyton was cooking wafted upward, competing with the sun to torment him.

"I hear your stomach from over here. Didn't you have breakfast?" Jonas nailed a shingle with more force than was necessary.

"Only coffee and toast." Train brushed the sweat out of his eyes.

"Don't expect us to feel sorry for you. You have a clubhouse of women cooking for you. Peyton only cooks for us when Killyama invites us over."

"I would have thought you were as close to Peyton as you are to Killyama." Train didn't expect either of the men to answer, so he was surprised when Hammer did after a slight hesitation.

"Peyton stays pretty much to herself…other than Killyama."

"That's hard to believe. She's a beautiful woman."

"She's a one-man woman," Jonas chimed in.

"Is Killyama's father dead?"

Hammer stood up, giving Jonas a hard stare. "We're done. Let's go see if lunch is ready."

The men climbed off the roof and went into the trailer that had seen better days. Train could tell it was cared for, but he bet the couch was the original one, and the curtains and the carpet were frayed around the edges.

Guessing they weren't going to feed him any more information, Train found himself studying the woman who fussed over them after they had washed up in the bathroom while Killyama was washing up at the kitchen sink.

"You sit by Killyama, Train. Jonas and Hammer can share the other seat."

The table was a four-seater booth that was at the side of the kitchen. Train slid over on the seat so Killyama could sit down, while Hammer and Jonas elbowed each other for room on the other side, fitting like two sardines in a can.

"Where are you going to sit?" Train asked as he started to get out, but was pinned in by Killyama.

"I'll pull over a chair after I put the food on the table."

Train expected Killyama to help her mother. Instead, she slid the huge bowl of hamburger pasta her mother had set down toward her, leaving Jonas and Hammer to start on the modest bowl of salad. They stared at the pasta that took up most of the table like ravaging wolves.

"Guests first." Killyama gave him the serving spoon as Peyton placed her chair at the edge of the small table.

Seeing Peyton nibble at her salad, unobtrusively watching him, Train took a modest spoonful, placing it on his plate. He had learned to take small portions until he decided if he liked it.

"You sure you don't want more?" Killyama asked, taking the serving spoon from him and ignoring the sulks from the other side of the table.

"I had a big breakfast." Train stabbed a lone noddle with his fork.

"You snooze, you lose at this table. It's Hammer and Jonas's favorite. Mama makes it for them whenever they come over."

Train waited until Peyton had taken a small serving before he took a bite of the dish. Not caring about being overly polite, Hammer filled his plate with enough pasta to feed three grown men. Jonas had no problem doing the same, leaving the bowl empty.

"I tried to warn you." Killyama dug into her own large portion. "It's kind of addicting."

Train enjoyed the one bite he had taken. It was good, but it wasn't great.

"It's really good. Thank you for lunch," he complimented.

"You're welcome. It's just poor man's goulash. I used to fix it for Killyama when she was a little girl, when the budget was tight.

A neighbor of mine gave me the recipe years ago. Her trailer used to be further down the holler. She would come over for visits until she passed away."

Train listened as she talked. Looking down, he saw his fork was scraping an empty plate. Frowning, he stared at the empty bowl then at Hammer's and Jonas's still full plates.

Killyama used tongs to place a mound of salad on his plate. "I tried to give you a heads up. That was a double batch, too."

"I'll leave my number so if you need any more chores done around here, I can swing by and help any day you feel like cooking." Train politely smiled at Peyton.

"I'll get Killyama to key in your number on my phone." Peyton smiled back, blushing at the compliments the men gave as the two women packed the dirty dishes to the small sink.

Train was about to volunteer to do the dishes when they each returned carrying two delicate dessert plates. This time, Train made sure to nab the largest serving, trying not to flinch as the men used their boots to stomp on his foot.

He forgot about the pain when he slid the warm spiced peaches with ice cream into his mouth.

"This is delicious," Train complimented.

"I can the peaches myself. Next time you come over, I'll make you a cobbler."

Train tucked his feet behind Killyama's, having no problem being a coward where food was concerned. He even scavenged hers for her last bite.

"Why haven't we had this before?" Jonas plaintively asked, staring down at his empty plate.

"Usually, Killyama hides the spiced peaches when I get finished canning them. She set out a couple of jars to use today."

Train slid his hand under the table to squeeze her thigh when she would have slid out from the table. "It was delicious. Thank you for sharing them. I can understand why you hid them. Some things are just too good to be shared."

"Jonas, go get the air fresher out from under the kitchen sink. The smell of bullshit is making me want to lose my lunch," Hammer quipped.

Peyton, who had stood to gather the dessert plates, crashed a plate down on the side of Hammer's skull. Hammer shrank back from the fury that had Peyton shooting sparks.

Train gaped, too scared at the sudden attack from the delicate woman to laugh at Hammer's discomfort.

When Killyama would have taken his plate, Train stopped her. "I take it back."

"What?" Her eyes twinkled in merriment. Killyama had enjoyed Hammer getting struck upside his head.

"You and your mom could be twins."

"You think so?" Killyama cocked an eyebrow at him as her mother cleaned the shards of glass off Hammer's shoulders.

"Hell yes." He helped her carry the dessert dishes, enjoying Peyton scolding Hammer for his bad manners. "I have to admit; I didn't see it coming, and neither did he."

After doing the dishes, Peyton cleaned the table as the group sat down in the small living room. When she was done, she sat down on the recliner, while Hammer and Jonas sprawled out on the couch. There wasn't a place for Train and Killyama to sit, so he started to bring in the chair that Peyton had been sitting on at the table when Killyama solved the problem.

"Scoot over, Jonas. Let Train sit down."

Train would have rather have gotten the chair, but he sat down on the couch when Jonas made room for him.

Killyama sat down on the floor, settling against her mother's legs. He was struck by the closeness of the two as Peyton rocked the recliner and Killyama laid her head on her mother's thigh.

Conversation flowed around the room much easier than he had expected. Train listened without taking part as Hammer talked about repairing the underpinning of Peyton's trailer.

"Let me know the next time you go out for a few hours. I'll have to jack the trailer up to get underneath it. I want to lay some more support beams. I'm afraid the floor in the kitchen is going to give if it isn't fixed soon."

"A piece was ordered last week. I was going to get started on it tomorrow, if that's convenient for you?"

"That works for me."

Peyton, seeing Train's curious look, explained, "I sell my pieces at a shop in town. Sometimes customers come in and commission me to make something for them."

"You're an artist?"

"Yes."

"Do you paint or—"

"I do a little bit of everything. I paint, but my favorite is sculpting."

"I would love to see some of your work. Do you have any pieces here?"

Peyton's cheeks turned pink. "No. There isn't much room to store them here. The neighbor I was telling you about who gave me her recipe passed away three years ago. She had no family, so she left her trailer to me. I've been using it as a studio. I make a mess when I'm working, and it gives me a place to store the finished items until I'm ready to sell. Killyama, hand me my album, and I'll show him—"

"Mama, Train wouldn't be interested—"

"I would really like to see your pictures." He couldn't understand why Killyama didn't want him to see her mother's work. Maybe she was embarrassed Peyton's work wasn't any good. Jamestown wasn't exactly New York, where exclusive shops exhibited artists' pieces.

Killyama rose to her knees to open a drawer in the side table, pulling out a thick photo album. Instead of immediately giving it to him, she opened the book toward the back before leaning forward to give it to him.

Train straightened on the couch, staring at the beautiful picture of a bridge. Unlike most pictures that focused on the idyllic beauty of a summer day, the sky in Peyton's painting was grey and gloomy. The bridge was old, and part of it was broken. The water below seemed to toss with dark undercurrents. It was striking and thought provoking that the bridge had stood the passage of time, still standing, though withered with age.

He turned to see picture after picture, each brought to life by Peyton's brush. Train turned one page, taking in the intricate beauty of a sculpture of a mother and child. The woman's face was lined with age and worry as she kneeled at the child's feet. The little girl was wearing a dress that was too big for her, slipping off her shoulders. She was crying while the mother wiped her tears away. Train had never been affected by art in his life, but the statue touched a part of him that he had never known existed.

"Have you sold this one yet?" Train asked gruffly.

"Which one?" Peyton looked as he lifted the book to show her. "I'm sorry. That one isn't for sale. That is in my private collection."

"If you ever think of selling, I would love to buy it," he said sincerely, staring down at the talent that showed an almost tangible bond between the mother and child.

Train flipped another page, his heart stopping. It was another statue, except this one was in bronze. It had the same features of the little girl from the previous page, but this one was an older girl. Her features were partially obscured by windblown hair curling tumultuously around her. Behind her stood a man with his hand on her shoulder. The man's features were hidden, his head turned to the side, showing only a profile that was also obscured by the girl's hair that had blown upward, seeming to strike him in the face. It was as beautiful as the other one, maybe even more so. The pain in the girl's face struck a chord in him, which the artist had intended.

"Is this one for sale?" Even as he started to lift the album, Peyton was already shaking her head. "You're very gifted. If you take commission, I would be willing to have both of those pieces redone."

"I don't do duplicates. Even if I tried, I don't think they would come out the same," she said apologetically. "When I finish the current painting I've already sold, I have another piece I'm looking forward to starting. When I finish that, I'll give you first choice before I sell it."

"I would appreciate it. Your talent is remarkable."

"Thank you. I started a class when Killyama went to kindergarten. Since then, I've been fortunate to make a living off what I had only expected to be a hobby."

"I can see why. It's a shame that collectors haven't seen your work. I wish I knew someone…"

Peyton shook her head. "I'm happy just piddling around in my studio, making the pieces I want at my own speed."

Train flipped through the rest of the pages, deciding to go to the beginning of the portfolio where he saw snapshots of Killyama.

She tried to take it away from him.

"Uh-uh. Let me look." He snatched it out of her reach.

"Dude, if I wanted you to see them, I would have shown you."

"Behave, Killyama," Peyton reproved her daughter.

Train intently stared down at the pictures of Killyama from birth through her high school years.

"I see why you don't want to sell your sculptures; you used Killyama as your model."

Peyton nodded, leaning back to avoid Killyama's glare. "I hid them at first. She hated having her pictures taken. She was always running away from the camera, and she hated sitting still long enough for me to sculpt her. I hate to have to tell you this, Train, but my daughter can be a little difficult."

He didn't lift his eyes from the pictures. "I'd have to agree." Train lifted the album higher when Killyama tried to snatch it away again. "You played the flute?" Train turned his head to the side to see her mortified reaction.

"Keep laughing, and I'll shove it up your—"

"Killyama..." Peyton tapped her daughter's hand where it lay on her thigh as Killyama braced herself to try to take the book away from him. "Train's our guest, and I raised you to be a lady...Or, I tried to."

Killyama's ass obediently hit the floor, but she scooted farther away from her mother's reprimanding hand.

"I don't know why you get so embarrassed about those pictures. She was a very good flute player. When she was in sixth grade, her middle school band was asked to play for the president's inauguration. It made the local papers in Jamestown, and one of the news stations in Lexington even covered it. Everyone in town was so proud of them. I was, too. Let me see if I can find the tape of when I recorded it."

"I threw it away." Killyama scooted even farther away from her mother until she was sitting next to Jonas's legs.

"Why did you do that?"

"Because the tape broke."

"But—"

"I would have liked to see it. It's a shame you don't have it anymore. I would have loved to hear you blow your flute." Train's amusement set a match to Killyama's temper.

"Wait here, fuckwad. I have it in my old bedroom. I still remember how to play the funeral march."

"You're killing me!" Peyton yelled. "One more vulgar word out of that mouth of yours, and I'm going to wash it out with soap."

"So that's why you nicknamed her Killyama…" Train had managed to stop Killyama from taking the book from him; however, Hammer, seeing how furious she was becoming, took it and gave it to her.

"Killyama was such a sweet baby. She was so precious when she was little. Then she grew up."

"Mom!"

"What? Why are you getting so upset? I didn't tell him…" Peyton broke off when Killyama got off the floor.

Train caught her hand as she tried to pass him. "Where are you going?"

"To get the soap."

Chapter
Twenty-Two

"You sure I can't give you a ride home?"

Killyama wrapped her arm around the post on her mother's porch, trying to keep herself rooted to the spot. She was tempted to go with him, despite her promise to Sex Piston not to fuck him.

"Mama likes it when I spend the night with her. She'll be upset if I don't stay."

"We could go for a drive, and I could bring you back?"

She shook her head at his suggestion. "We both know I won't come back until morning."

Hammer and Jonas had just reluctantly left, leaving them alone. She should have gone back inside before they had left, but she wanted to spend a little time alone with him, thinking she could control the situation with her mother on the other side of the trailer's thin, metal walls. She told herself she would be able to keep her panties on in the short time she would walk him to his truck. Staring into his eyes, though, she was beginning to doubt her decision.

He took her free hand, tugging her down the steps. Then he lifted her into his arms when she reached the last step.

"This isn't a good idea."

"Why?" His sultry expression as he stared down at her was one he would give any bitch in his clubhouse. It wasn't going to be easy not to at least take a dip in what he was offering.

Train was a sexy man, and he knew it. He knew he was attractive to the opposite sex. Hell, to half the male population, too.

All she wanted from him was to make her feel as if they were on a level playing field. She wasn't going to stop until he wanted her as much as she wanted him.

"Because I'm not going to fuck you." Her staunch declaration didn't faze him.

Her panties might be getting damp, but Train hadn't worked up to category five blue balls yet. Damn, he might have been at a D1, which was a little twitch, but she was going for level five blow-your-fucking-balls-off-to-get-relief. Maybe spending the day with her mother wasn't the best idea for the level of devastation she was hoping to accomplish.

Train put his foot on the running board of the truck, sticking one of his hands in his back pocket that sent a metal chain swinging to the top of his thigh.

She lifted her eyes from the dancing silver chain to his, seeing the sensual curl of his lips.

"I…" Killyama lost her train of thought as she imagined sucking that bottom lip into her mouth. "You said you like spending time with me. Your wish came true today. You spent the whole day with me. The night wasn't part of the deal."

"I see. What about we hang out at your club—dancing, drinking a few beers—and then we spend the night together?"

"How about we do the half part and leave the rest of the night up to we'll see?"

Train buried his face in the fold of her bandana. She was about to push him away, but he forestalled her by gently placing a kiss on her chin then her lips before pulling away. She had to step back as he swung the truck door open.

"I'll see you tomorrow when I get off work. I'll try to be good until you get there."

Killyama curved her fingers over the window seal as he rolled it down. "Then don't get into more trouble than I can handle when I get there."

He started his truck after giving her another parting kiss.

She watched as Train backed out of the yard, then watched as the red taillights jumped as Train hit a rut in the road.

Killyama laughed softly to herself as she turned back to her mother's trailer, coming to a stop when she saw her mother sitting on the top of the porch, staring at her.

She nonchalantly walked toward the bottom of the steps. "I didn't mean to take so long. You ready for bed? Or do you want to draw for a while?" Her mother had asked her to pose for the piece that had been commissioned.

"If you're not too tired, I'd like to draw for a while."

"Doesn't take any energy to sit," she drawled, starting up the first step, but her mother didn't move to go inside.

"You like him, don't you?"

Killyama looked away from her mother's knowing eyes. "Yes."

"Be careful, Rae."

"I will."

"Are we still moving to Knoxville?"

"Not yet. Maybe in a few months."

"Good. I'm not anxious to move."

"I know you aren't."

Killyama saw the relief in her eyes. The sorrow she carried around her like a shroud was still there. What was missing was the conflict that had been brewing since she had asked her mother to move. She hadn't given her acquiesce, but Killyama had known her answer was going to be no.

"Mama, even if we don't move to Knoxville, we need to find you a place closer to town. I don't feel safe with you out here by yourself." Her shoulders sagged with worry for her mother. "I'm constantly worried. If I can't get back into town when I'm working, then I definitely won't be able to reach you in time if anything goes wrong."

"Nothing will go wrong."

"No one knows when something bad is going to happen. You're miles away from the fire department or an ambulance. Your trailer has been broken into twice while you were at your studio, because everyone in town believes you're out here in the boonies to grow pot or make meth. This trailer is falling apart. Please, at least let me buy you a better trailer, or have a house built here on your property."

Her mother smoothed her slacks down over her thighs. "I love this trailer."

"What you loved was my father who bought it for you, and he's gone. He's not coming back, Mama."

"I know he's dead, Rae." Tears slipped from the corner of her eyes.

"I don't think you do. I think you still imagine him sitting in that recliner. That's why you never let anyone else sit there. That's why, when Mrs. Ford left her trailer to you, and you could have moved there and used this place as a studio, you didn't. Even that place is bigger and in much better shape."

"I needed more room for my workspace. It would have been wasted if I had moved in there."

"I could move back in with you—"

"We both know that won't work. I like being alone when I'm working, and you have your own life without worrying about me."

"If you want me happy, then at least let Jonas set up some alarms. You're a sitting duck out here by yourself."

"Will you quit asking me to move if I do?"

Killyama sighed. She had learned a long time ago to pick her battles with her mother. "Yes."

"Fine. I'll call him in the morning." She stood up, patting her hair down. She never could stand having a hair out of place. She always wore makeup as though she were expecting company, and always had enough food in the house that she could put a meal on the table in thirty minutes.

As far back as she could remember, her mama made up her face in the bedroom mirror every morning as Killyama sat on her bed, watching her. She would fix her hair the way her father had told her he liked it. She had done it all for him, never knowing what day or time he would show.

On the days he hadn't shown, her mother would hide her disappointment until night came, and then she would make yet another excuse for why he hadn't come to visit them. The days he had shown, the house had been filled with joy and laughter as they tried to make him happy so he wouldn't leave again. And when he did, that he would want to come back.

Her father had played her mama like a fucking yo-yo, and as she had grown, he had played her, too; making promises he had no intentions of keeping; making them dance to his tune by being the perfect daughter, the smartest student, accomplished at anything that would help her fit into his life away from them. She had repeatedly told herself that, if she made him proud, then, even if he didn't want to live in Jamestown, her and her mother would be able to move to where he had lived when he was away from them.

In hindsight, she had been doomed for disappointment. Her father had wanted to play and have a good time when he had been there. Then, like a child at a playground, when he was finished playing, he had wanted to go home, leaving the toys he had been playing with behind, laying in the dirt.

It was how Train would treat her if she wasn't careful.

"Come on." Killyama held her hand out to her mother. "It's getting late." She lifted her mother to her feet, opening the screen door to let her enter first. "So, what did you think of Train?"

"He's very handsome. Is he always that polite?"

"Usually. I have never really seen him lose his temper."

"That's good. That quality is important to have if you're thinking of marrying a man."

"Train and I won't be getting married. We might be doing the midnight limbo—"

"Let's keep it PG rated. We're close, but I really don't want to hear any details about your sex life." Her mother laid a blanket on the floor, positioning Killyama's legs and arms the way she wanted them.

"But that's the best part. You have to miss that…" Killyama tried to find a way to phrase it delicately so it wouldn't get her smacked upside the head with her mother's drawing pad.

"No, I don't," Peyton said firmly before changing the subject back to Train. "How long have you known him?"

Her mother curled up in her father's recliner as she drew. Killyama was used to her mother not talking as she worked, giving herself free reign to talk about Train now that she had decided to introduce him to her.

By almost one a.m., she couldn't sit still any longer. She stretched when they finished for the night.

"Mama?"

Her mother looked up from placing the pencils she was working with neatly back into their case. "Yes?"

"Will you draw me a picture of Train?"

"You've never asked me to draw a picture before."

"I thought, if we work out, I could give it to him."

"And if it doesn't?" Her mother arched a curved brow.

"Then I'll make a dartboard out of it."

80 ⋈

Killyama could easily see out to the parking lot from where she sat. If she got any freaking closer, her nose would be pressed to the tinted window. The parking lot in front of the Destructors' was filled with motorcycles, except for the one she was waiting for.

She propped her legs up on the chair in front of her, using them to silently warn the men not to join her. Then her eyes dropped to her cell phone that was staring blankly up at her. Train had texted her two hours, saying he would be there by now. Thankfully, Sex Piston wasn't there to witness her being stood up.

"Come dance with me. You're wasting time waiting for a man who's not going to show."

Killyama didn't take her eyes off the window, telling Bear, "It's mine to waste."

"I don't get it. What does he have that you can't get right here?"

"Rhythm. You suck at dancing."

She heard his boots walking away.

Dropping her legs to the floor, she started to scoot out from the table when she saw Train turning into the parking lot. He held the heavy bike steady as he found a spot at the end of a row.

She turned her chair so she was facing the bar and pool table. Out of the corner of her eye, she saw Train coming in through the door, scanning the crowd for her. Spotting her, he made his way directly to her table, despite several of the men yelling out greetings to him.

"I'm sorry. Viper—"

"Dude, I'm not married to you; I don't need to hear your excuse."

Train's mouth closed with a snap.

Standing, she walked to the edge of the dance floor. "You coming?" It wasn't one of her favorite songs, but she began dancing to the loud music.

Train took his jacket off, setting it down on a chair before coming to stand next to her. "You never act the way I expect you to."

"How am I supposed to act?"

"I don't know. Cuss at me, dance with someone else…I even thought you might have gone home."

"That's a lot of deep thoughts for a man. Why didn't you just call and find out; save yourself the suspense?"

"I didn't want you to tell me to fuck off, or to not bother coming."

Killyama slipped one thigh between his. "You thought I'd be a bitch to you?"

"Yeah."

"If you show, you show. It's no big deal. I was hanging out, anyway. I save my bitching skills for stuff that's important."

"I don't know if I should be relieved or pissed off." Train brought his hands to her hips, pulling her closer until her pussy was riding his thigh as they danced.

"Take your pick. Just keep moving. What you're doing feels good."

"Next time, I'll call."

"Maybe I'll answer." She pressed her breasts against his chest as she slipped her arms around his waist, tucking her hands into his back pockets so she could guide his hips where she wanted them.

She wanted to drag him to one of the spare bedrooms and fuck him until he begged for mercy. Instead, she continued to dance, trying to appear as if his closeness wasn't getting to her.

"You smell good tonight." She wanted to take back the compliment as soon as it slipped out of her mouth.

Train grinned down at her. Bastard knew he was punching her ticket.

"It's just soap and water. I don't have to worry about the brothers borrowing the expensive shower gels most of them use."

"I knew you had more in common with the Destructors than the brand of beer you like. They don't use the expensive shit, either."

She was teasing, but Train's expression grew grim, and he dropped his thigh, no longer moving.

"You shower with the men often?"

"You being serious? If I asked you that question, you'd think I was all in your grill. If you want to ask if I fucked any of the men here, ask. If not, move those feet; you're going too damn slow."

His feet didn't budge. "I'm asking."

"I thought me lying to you was your rule breaker, not if I'm fucking other dudes."

"I didn't say it was a rule breaker. I just want to know."

"And if I am?"

"Then I want to know who." Train ignored Bear when he bumped into him as he danced with Jenna. The big man had two left feet, and Train wasn't getting out of his way. "Then I'll need to have a talk with Stud. I wouldn't want to start a fight without letting the president of the club know."

Bear was becoming irritating. The burly man was dancing like a bull in a china shop. He always managed to miss Killyama, but kept bumping into Train.

"I'm not saying I haven't fucked one or two of the brothers here, but I haven't in a few months." Killyama caressed Train's buttocks. None of the men could see her hands in his pockets, but he could feel her pacifying gesture.

Train started moving his feet again. "Have you decided if we're going to do this?"

"I guess so." She shrugged. "I'm here dancing with you, aren't I?"

His hard expression finally relaxed.

"Damn, dude, I didn't expect you to get so hot under the collar about me doing other men. I didn't take you for the jealous type. Is it just the Destructors you don't want me fucking, or does that include The Last Riders?"

From his brooding gaze, either Train didn't want to answer her question, or he couldn't. She was glad he didn't, because she wouldn't have been happy with the answer she was sure he would have given.

The Last Riders didn't share pussy with other clubs, but sharing it among themselves was expected. Beth and Lily had never shared the details of the Friday night parties they had attended. How far the sisters went during those parties was anyone's guess. Killyama was guessing not far, though. Or, at least that was the hope she clung to. That, and her and Train could somehow work out a relationship they could live with, and wouldn't leave one—meaning her—doing what they didn't want to do.

She didn't want to have sex with any other Last Rider, and she sure as hell didn't want to watch Train giving it to another woman in front of her.

Maybe renting a porn would be a compromise they could both live with.

"Who are you smiling at?" Train looked over his shoulder suspiciously.

"Do you see me staring at anyone but you?"

"Just checking."

She gripped his ass tighter as they danced a couple of songs before deciding to play pool. She won all three games and, when Rabbit asked if he could play, she let the two men have it, taking a stool to watch.

She ordered beers for the men who gathered around to watch Train beat Rabbit, and then he won against Bear. When he won against Pike, she ordered them all a shot of whiskey.

"Where you going? Let's play another game."

Train shook his head when Pike tried to coax him into another game. "Another time. I don't want Killyama getting bored."

Killyama tipped her shot glass, saluting him. "Good save. You know they're all scared of me and wouldn't bug you to play after that excuse."

He grinned. "It worked, didn't it?"

She smiled back, giving him the beer she had ordered for him.

He was thirstily drinking it when Jenna held out her hand. "That'll be a hundred and seventy-five dollars."

Train lowered his beer bottle, staring down at it like it was somehow made out of gold. "I thought a beer is five bucks if you don't belong to the club. If it costs me a hundred and seventy-five dollars for you to bring it to me, next time, I'll get it out of the cooler myself."

"It's not for one beer. Killyama said the last three rounds for the men were on you."

Train tilted his beer to his mouth, finishing it before setting it down on the table. Then he reached for his wallet.

Killyama humorously watched him fork over the money he had just won.

"Nice wallet," Jenna complimented, counting the cash he had given her.

"Thanks. It was a gift." Train waited until Jenna went back behind the counter before he took the shot of tequila Killyama was about to drink.

"Hey...That was mine." She couldn't help laughing at his disgruntled expression.

"Want to tell me why I bought, not one, but three rounds of beer?"

"The first two rounds were beer. The last one was whiskey."

Train choked on her shot of tequila.

"And it was cheaper than a visit to the emergency room, which is where the brothers would have sent you if you had won another game. The only reason your ass isn't in an ambulance right now is because I was smart enough to buy those rounds for them, and because they're slow as shit and didn't know they were dealing with a pool shark until you beat Pike." She swiveled on the stool she was sitting on. "Jenna, bring me another shot of tequila and another beer for Train," she yelled out before turning back to him.

"Am I buying that, too?"

"No, it's on me. Don't be pissy. You're lucky I got over my mad spell with you and we're friends now. Before, I would have warned them. I'm a good pool player, but I'm not that good." She rolled her eyes at his lame attempt to get on her good side by letting her win all three games.

"Lucky me," he grumbled.

It took another beer before she could talk him into dancing with her again. When they sat down to take a break, several men pulled chairs up to join them.

"Where's the rest of the crew tonight?" Calder asked. "I haven't seen Stud tonight, either."

Killyama cocked her head at Train as he deliberately pulled her chair closer to his, dropping an arm over her shoulder. He was practically pissing on her chair to stake her as his property.

"Stud and Sex Piston had a teacher's conference with Meri and Keri's teacher. Sex Piston keeps making up excuses for missing, so both of them went this time. Crazy Bitch and T.A. are out on a double date, and Fat Louise and Cade are hanging out at their house with their baby."

"The girls in trouble?" Before Calder had gone to prison, he wouldn't have cared less if the girls were in trouble. Then prison and the rehab Stud had sent him to had given him the opportunity to get clean. It had taken time for him to mend fences within the club and form relationships with his nieces and nephew.

"No, the girls want to be foreign exchange students next year, and Sex Piston is fighting it all the way."

"What does Stud think about it?"

"You know Stud; he isn't crazy about it, either, but it's not like he can spring for a family trip to Paris."

"I'm with Sex Piston. Two young girls in Paris? Stud would just be asking for trouble."

Killyama stiffened. "I don't know why not. I told Sex Piston she should let them go," she lied. She wasn't about to offer any advice when it was Stud and Sex Piston's call to make. If they felt the girls could act responsible, then she was all for it. "You think they'll bang any man with a French accent?"

"Wouldn't you?"

"Hell yes, but that's me, not Meri and Keri."

Train dropped his arm from around her shoulder. "You'd fuck a man just because he had a French accent?"

"Hell yes." She wasn't about to back down in front of the men. "What woman wouldn't? It's called the city of love for a reason." She fucking cracked herself up. Crazy Bitch was usually the one who enjoyed baiting the men in the club, but since she was AWOL, Killyama decided to fill in for her. "All I'd have to hear is three simple words: 'Welcome to Paris,' in French, and I'd do him."

Train rose to his feet. "Really? That's all it would take to get you in bed?"

Killyama had meant to aggravate Calder, not Train. That was just a bonus. He was sexy as hell when he was jealous...

"Bienvenue a Paris."

"What'd you say?" Killyama put her finger in her ear, trying to pop the plug that kept her from understanding what he had said.

Train repeat the unintelligible words again. Then he repeated it in the only language she understood.

"I said, Welcome to Paris."

CHAPTER
TWENTY-THREE

"Go home, asshole! You're going to wake my neighbors!"

Train tried to reason with the furious woman, but she ignored all of his attempts to cool her down. The only reason he had managed to get her on his bike was because she had been damned by her own words. Then she had taken off like a scalded cat as soon as he had parked at her apartment building.

If he hadn't kept up his military training, he wouldn't have made it to her door in time before she could lock herself inside. He had barely managed to jam a boot in the door to keep her from closing it.

She braced her shoulder against the door as he tried to reason with her to let him inside. She was still trying to lock him out when she heard her next-door neighbor ask if there was a problem.

Frustrated, she let the him inside, and Train held his hands up in the air as he shut the door with his boot.

Train cautiously eyed her over as they faced off. Her hair was a tumbled mass of curls as she held his helmet, and he could see her perfect breasts trembling under the silky black top she wore.

He chose his words wisely, not wanting to find out the hard way if she had inherited her mother's habit of head bashing.

"It better be English," she warned when he opened his mouth.

"Don't blame me because I took you at your word. How was I supposed to know you would get mad for calling your bluff?"

She began pacing in her high-heeled boots, going from one end of the room to the other. "I. Am. Not. Going. To. Fuck. You just because you started mouthing off a bunch of mumbo jumbo." She raked her hair back, making it more disarrayed.

"It's not mumbo jumbo; it's French. I speak it fluently. I took it in high school, college, and used it a few times in the military. Want me to show you that I can repeat what you want in French?"

"La te da." She threw him a nasty look at she continued pacing. "Can you say 'go home' in French?"

"Yes, but I want to know why first. Why don't you want to have sex with me now? You said you wanted to think it over—obviously you have or you wouldn't have invited me to meet your mother, or meet you at the clubhouse. So, what's up?"

Sighing in defeat, she admitted, "I told Sex Piston and the other bitches I wouldn't."

"Why in the hell would you tell them that? Personally, I don't think it's any of their business, but I know you are all tight. Why would they care as long as it's what you want?" His stomach sank at a sudden thought. "Did you tell them you don't want me?"

"No. They just want me to be careful. They don't want me to get hurt."

"You're not the only who can be hurt here."

"It's not the same."

"Why not? I'm taking a chance, too. I should be the one worried…Have I done anything you asked me not to? You're the one who almost ran me over."

She stopped pacing to stare at him. He could see what she had been hiding from him; what Winter and everyone had been saying. She cared for him, and she was afraid he would want her only physically. However, if he gave her the breathing room she wanted, he might never get her back to the point they were now.

He moved to stand in front of her, tracing a lone finger along the bottom of the black bandana that curved around her throat. This was as close to being vulnerable as she was going to show him.

She put her hand up to stop him from touching her.

Sliding out from under her restraining hand, he drew an imaginary line down her chest, coming to a stop at the button between her breasts. "Do you want to know who the woman was who's name I covered up?"

"Yes." Train wanted to kiss the lip that she tugged between her teeth.

"Her name was Nalin, and she was my mother." Train unbuttoned the first button, sliding down to the next one.

"Why did you cover up your mother's name?"

"Because she lied to me. My father was a drunk." Train's lips twisted in mockery. "Not only was he a drunk, he was a mean drunk. Everyone on the reservation was afraid of him. I was seven when my mother saved enough money from cleaning houses to move us to Louisiana, where my father found a job with an offshore drilling company. My mother was so excited. She thought it would be a new start for us. I wasn't as excited. I didn't want to leave my grandparents behind, but my two little sisters and I had no choice.

"My father stayed sober when he was on the job, but when he came home, a bottle was in his hand. Our mother never told us when he was coming. I doubt she even knew herself. I would usually find out he was home when I heard him walking down to my mother's room at night after the bars were closed. My sisters would sneak into my room when they heard them fighting." Train slipped another button free as Killyama's pale face watched his movements. She didn't stop him.

"I was nine years old when he made the mistake of trying to beat my sister when she had gone into our mother's bedroom. The days my father wasn't there, Lenna would snuggle with my mother until it was time to get ready for school. We hadn't heard him come home that night.

"My father was still drunk and started beating Lenna. My mother tried to pull him off, but he just beat her, too. I still remember lying on my bedroom floor as he tried to rape my baby sister." Train unbuttoned another button. Her skin was like satin where his fingers touched, keeping him rooted in the present as he recounted the memories of his past.

"I lost it. My father wasn't used to us fighting back, so I managed to get him off of Lenna. It was the only time in my life my mother called the police. She knew he would kill me for fighting him.

"The police came and arrested him. He lost his job, and the courts wouldn't let him back in our home." Train shook his head at the turmoil that erupted because of that night. "My mother wouldn't take him back after that happened. Me and my sisters wanted to move back to the reservation, but my mother wouldn't. She was determined we would have a better life." Another button was undone.

"She scrimped and saved, and we moved into an apartment in a good neighborhood that had the best school in the state. I would go with her to clean businesses at night, and go to school in the morning, grabbing a few hours' sleep as she would finish the few jobs she didn't need my help with. By my senior year high school, she built up her business so that she could hire other workers. That was when I decided to go into the military. I didn't think she needed me anymore."

Train paused before flicking the next button undone. "I was in my second year in the military when I found out from my sister that our mother was seeing our father again. I made my sister put my mother on the phone, and we talked a long time. She swore to me that she wasn't taking him back, that she was seeing him because she felt sorry for him. She said he was living on the streets. She swore to me that she would never let him come near my sisters. She lied.

"A week later, I was staring down at my mother and sisters' graves. Lenna, Ela, and my mother had all lied to me. My mother had let my father move back in before Lenna had even told me that she was seeing him." Train spread the silky blouse away from her, staring down at her rose-tipped breasts. He gently pressed a kiss on the flesh between them.

"That's why you covered up your tattoo?"

"Yes, and that's why I would never lie to you, and I don't want you to lie to me. Lies affect everyone around you." Raising his head, he pulled the two parts of her top back together. "And since I have no intention of making you a liar, I'm going home." He turned to leave.

"Train?"

He stopped, but he didn't turn around. His self-control had limits, and seeing her hazel eyes look defenseless was more than he could take.

"I told them I wouldn't fuck you until I was sure you wouldn't fuck around on me."

Train turned. "I already told you I won't."

"I believe you."

"I want to be upfront, Rae. Neither us knows how this will work out, but I will be honest."

"I will, too."

When he started to leave again, she reached out, looping the wallet chain that was clipped onto his jeans around her finger.

"How do you say 'fuck me' in French?"

His eyes narrowed on her sultry expression. One minute, she could have a man cringing in fear, and the next...she was a modern day Delilah.

She shrugged her blouse off then moved closer to brush her breasts against his T-shirt. Train unsnapped her jeans, speaking softly in French as he started tugging them down. She then brought her hands to his biceps so she could maintain her balance as her boots prevented the jeans from dropping to the floor. Train tangled his foot with hers as he gave Killyama a small push backward.

She stared up at him without comprehension, asking, "What did you say?"

"I said, 'fuck me' in Apache. I also asked if you're wet?"

"If I wasn't before, I am now. That's hot. Say some more."

Train took off his T-shirt. "How about I show you instead?"

She leaned forward, unlacing her boots then taking them off and slinging them to the floor.

They kissed as they finished undressing each other. Train was so excited about having her willing and submissive under him that he ignored the pain coming from his ankle. When it became a trail of fire, he broke free from the kiss to see a cat staring up at him with beady eyes.

"What the hell?"

Killyama reached down to pick up the hissing cat that was doing his damnedest to scratch him again. "This is Gollum."

"It's a cat?" He was looking at Gollum as if he had never seen a cat before. "That doesn't look like a cat. Cats are cute, fluffy fur balls. What you're holding needs an exorcist."

Killyama laughed. "He's not that bad."

Train saw the whatever-it-was swat Killyama, leaving a thin scratch on her forearm.

She hugged the cat to her, soothing his ruffled fur. "He was Fat Louise's sister's cat first. When she wanted to kill him, Fat Louise took him. Then, when she married Cade, Crazy Bitch took him. When Crazy Bitch threatened to kill him, I took him and renamed him Gollum. It used to be Manson."

"Manson suits him better." Train jerked his wrist back when the cat tried to scratch him again.

"I'm not giving my cat away."

Train had never seen hurt in Killyama's eyes in the years he had known her. She was showing it now.

"Killy, my sisters had a cat. It was nicer and would rub against my leg. Gollum and I will eventually get along, too. What do you usually do with Mans—Gollum when men come over?"

Killyama buried her face in the cat's fur.

Even if he hadn't heard from Shade and Viper about how courageous she was in the past, it showed now. Train couldn't think of any other woman who would put her face near that hissing, spitting spawn of some fucked up creature.

"I've been meaning to ask..." Killyama started. "Does a little lie count?"

"Yes."

"Even a little, little one?" She pinched two fingers together with her free hand.

He stared back at her sternly until she unconsciously lowered her gaze.

"I've never invited a man into my apartment."

"Ever?"

"Do we have to be precise?"

"Yes."

Train couldn't keep his stern expression. When Killyama was embarrassed, she was cute. She would never be kitten cute—she had too much personality for that. She reminded him of a sleek leopard, instead.

"Then, I've never let anyone spend the night."

"Did that hurt?" Train started to pull her up for a kiss, then hastily jerked back when Gollum bared his teeth at him.

"Yes, it did," she snapped, taking the cat into the kitchen.

"Wait. Where are you...?"

Killyama walked through kitchen and out the back door, naked as the day she was born.

Train started cussing, bending over to pick up his jeans. "So help me...If she doesn't quit flashing..." He stopped the litany of what he was going to do when she came back inside. "Where in the hell did you go?"

"I put Gollum on my screened-in back porch."

"Anyone in the back parking lot could have seen you naked!"

Her shrug had him wanting to paddle that ass she had just flashed.

"Do me a favor; when you get him in the morning, put on a robe."

"You're being squeamish about me being naked when I'm in my house?" she asked with an arched brow.

Train's voice rose. "You were skinny-dipping at Mrs. Langley's house, too."

"So? I bet you don't bitch to those hos walking around your club naked."

Train was getting so angry that he had to bite his tongue from snapping at her. He still wanted to fuck her so badly, but he was afraid she would hold a grudge if he paddled her ass red and not let him have it. Therefore, he started counting to ten, then twenty.

Her eyes widened when he went to the front door and locked it. Then he went to the back door and did the same.

"Dude, what are you...?" She watched in confusion as he unclasped the wallet's chain from his jeans.

"Where's your bedroom?"

Killyama pointed at the door to the side of the living room.

"Lead the way," Train ordered, holding the chain loosely in his hand as she walked toward her bedroom.

"Dude, I'm giving you fair warning; I'm not into any freaky deaky shit that involves pain. I'd hate to have to beat the living hell out of you, instead of you thinking you're getting me hot."

Train closed the bedroom door behind them. He didn't think the cat could get in, but he wasn't taking a chance with his dick as an easy target.

"You need to expand your horizons," Train taunted.

She wasn't taking the bait. "If those horizons are filled with pain, I'm good."

"You haven't ever wanted to try it?"

"What do you not understand? I do not enjoy pain. I don't need to be spanked with a whip to figure that shit out."

"Women aren't always the submissive ones." He pulled her comforter to the bottom of her bed. "Lie down."

Interest sparked in her eyes. He could tell the thought of him being submissive to her was appealing.

"Have you ever played submissive to a woman?"

He stared at her matter-of-factly. If she wanted his answer, she was going to have to follow his commands.

She pursed her lips but laid down.

Train sat down next to her hip. He considered telling her to take the bandana off, yet decided not to press his luck.

"I've never been submissive to any woman, but that doesn't mean I wouldn't do it if she wanted me to. Sexually, I'm pretty laid back."

Train bent down to lick her nipple, laving it with his tongue until it tautened. Then he slid his tongue between her parted lips as he used his fingers to tug and shape her breast, winding half the chain around it before he released her lips to suck her other nipple into his mouth.

She gave a soft moan, arching under him as he switched to her mouth again, now winding the other half of the chain around her other breast.

His cock was hard, the head riding her belly as he bent over her.

"If I have something made for you, will you wear it?"

She had to clear her voice before she could answer him. "Depends on what it is."

Train fiddled with the chain until it was exactly where he wanted it. Then he kissed the flesh on the underside of the chain, licking down to her bellybutton and playing with her navel ring. It only took her a couple of seconds to agree.

"Yes."

Train lifted her legs over his shoulders, licking his way down to her cunt. He found her so wet and needy he had to grip her legs to keep them on his shoulders. His tongue slid through her slit to find her clit, laving it, twirling his tongue, before sliding back down her slit to find her opening.

He savored her before breaching her defenseless pussy, thrusting his tongue inside of her carefully and watching her abdomen muscles react to what he was doing.

The muscles in her pussy tried to clench his tongue to keep it still, but he used his teeth to rake her clit, loosening her hold, and then driving his tongue higher inside of her.

"Lover, please…"

Hearing that word out of her mouth again was like a firecracker to his nuts.

Using his shoulders, he pushed her legs higher until they were beside her tits. Reaching for the condom he had placed on the nightstand, he covered his cock, angry at himself for not already having it on. He almost climaxed before he could sink his dick inside her pussy, each thrust driving his climax closer.

"Damn, I don't want to come yet," Train groaned.

Looking at her through the strands of his dark hair that she had loosened, he took in every detail of her expression.

He'd had so many women through the years as a Last Rider, and even before that. In fact, he had lost count of how many women. He had watched as they climaxed, learning what they liked and didn't. But he had never seen the response or emotions Killyama expressed when he touched her.

When his hand brushed her cheek, she turned into his hand. When he thrust hard, her lashes would quiver. When his chest flattened her chain-covered breasts, her lips trembled. Every nuance of her expressions was a new experience for him.

When he sped up, driving them both to an orgasm, he held his breath, not wanting it to end, and wanting to see the breathtaking love shining through her eyes. He then watched it all disappear in an instant when she realized he was watching her.

"Dude, you can get off of me now."

Train didn't slow his movements. He drifted his fingers to the chain at her breasts, slowly unraveling one then the other as she sucked in a deep breath before screaming as she reached another peak.

Massaging the blood back into her breasts, he whispered in Apache a phrase his grandfather used to say to his grandmother every night.

"When you sleep at night, dream of me, as I will dream of you. So even in our dreams, we will never be apart."

"What did you say?" With a curious expression, she twined a stand of his hair around her finger.

All of The Last Riders' women would want to be held at night, yet Killyama scooted away, maintaining her own space. When he tried to pull her closer, she rose to go to the bathroom. The only time he had seen her accept a display of affection had been from her mother.

"I said, sweet dreams," he told the empty room.

CHAPTER
TWENTY-FOUR

"No."

"Come on, Viper. All I'm asking for is a favor. I don't know why you're complaining; it'll solve your problem, too." Train handed Viper another package to be loaded onto the delivery truck.

Rider gave him an encouraging nod when Viper still didn't look convinced.

"How does inviting Sex Piston and her crew to a Friday night party solve any problems for me? It will only add to it when they tear it apart."

"They won't cause a fight," Train reasoned. "And it's not like they'll be sneaking in…We're inviting them. Plus, it'll get you off the shit list with the wives, and some of the brothers, too. None of the wives are putting out since you laid down your order not to have anything to do with Killyama and her crew. Even though you rescinded the order, they're still pissed and say they won't put out until she comes back. I've asked her twice. She's not coming. She makes me drive to Jamestown. The way it's going, neither you or any of the married men are getting any anytime soon."

"Winter and I aren't having sex because she's mad at me; she's getting over Aisha's birth."

"Really?" Train rolled his eyes at Viper's delusional comment. Aisha was six months old now. Even Train knew Winter was well passed the convalescent stage. The president of The Last Riders had more experience with women than most of them had, but where his wife was concerned, he was a sucker every time. "How about you, Razer? Cash? You two getting any?"

Razer tore his work gloves off, shoving them into his back pocket. "No."

Train dodged a box Cash threw into the back of the truck. "No, and I wouldn't ask Shade that question either when he comes out to check the boxes off."

Viper put his hands on his hips, his stance becoming aggressive. "Don't blame me if you pussies can't control your women. They *aren't* coming to the party."

Train's shoulders fell. He would have to wait until Shade was in a better mood to ask him for his advice on how to turn Sex Piston around. He knew she was the reason Killyama still refused to come over. When he went to the Destructors', she could maintain the image that what was going on between them was a casual hook up. If they went to The Last Riders and saw they were a couple, then maybe Sex Piston and her bitches would thaw out and get off Killyama's case.

"It doesn't matter to me, Viper." Rider placed the smaller boxes to fit between the larger ones. "But seems to me that, if Sex Piston came, she would bring Stud, and Stud could keep the bitches in control. Everyone would get what they want. If Train and Killyama get serious, and we all know that he wants to, then we're not only making Train suffer, but the other men, too. You can't tell me that having Shade snapping heads off is for fun. And Knox has practically ticketed the whole town for jaywalking. He even gave Willa a ticket the other day."

Cash and Razer looked away from Viper's hard stare.

"Go ahead and invite them. But I won't be there, and if Lucky doesn't agree to be in there, it's a no go."

"Thanks, brother!" Train held out his hand to Viper.

Viper shook his head, not accepting his hand. "That's not all. If there are any damages, it's coming out of your pocket."

"They'll behave," Train promised. "I'll talk to Stud, and Cade will come with Fat Louise. The only two I have to worry about is Crazy Bitch and T.A., and with a clubhouse of men to keep them occupied, they won't want to leave." Train tried to be upbeat to ease Viper's fears.

"That's what I'm worried about." Viper frowned, but he did finally take his hand. "So, did you come up with this bright idea yourself?" He glanced accusingly at Razer and Cash.

"It was Rider's idea." Train believed giving credit where it was due. Besides, he could always blame Rider if his plan went haywire.

"I better go get the other cart." Rider hightailed it into the factory.

"You took advice from Rider?" Razer straightened a stack of boxes to make room for the ones Rider would bring out. "If he gave you the idea, he must have an ulterior motive. Rider doesn't do anything unless it benefits himself."

Train didn't mention the promise he had made to Rider. It didn't matter, anyway. It was only conditional on Killyama's agreement, and there was no way Killyama would let Rider watch. If Train was honest with himself, he wasn't sure he wanted Rider to. He was beginning to understand why the married men didn't share their women.

"Be careful, brother. Rider has a way of stealing the women's heart. He's their favorite. Hell, he eats at Lucky's house more than he does here, and even Rachel will fry extra fish for him when he goes to her house. If I hadn't made a play for Beth first, Rider would have been the one married with two kids."

Train laughed, seeing Razer had Shade bring out the other cart. "Now you're exaggerating. Beth was too scared to give any of us a second glance."

"Go ahead and laugh. When Killyama is cooking breakfast for him, I'll remind you I told you so."

"The day she makes breakfast for Rider, we're going to need more than a factory full of supplies to survive, because that means the world has come to an end. She doesn't even make me a coffee of cup when I stay the night."

"You're not cute. Rider acts cute. It gets past their guard," Cash gave as his own warning.

"Watch it, Shade. That box is heavy," Viper snapped out, going to help him when Shade made to lift the heavy box himself. "Rider hasn't gotten past Winter's guard," he grunted out.

Train eyed the man who was walking toward Viper's house. "Is that Rider going to your house now?"

Viper turned to see Winter opening the door and letting Rider inside. He made a production of looking at his wristwatch.

"Shade, you take over. I'm going to see if Aisha is awake from her nap."

The men watched as Viper strode toward his house.

"Ten to one, Winter's fixing him lunch."

Razer's comment had Train worried, but he was positive Killyama wouldn't be taken in by Rider. The men were only trying to rile him up, like they used to do to Lucky before he married Willa.

"What in the fuck are you all jabbering about?" Shade snarled.

Train decided to put Shade out of his bad mood by telling him the plan that Rider had suggested, finishing by telling him the men were giving him a hard time about Rider. "...So Razer and Cash say Rider is the women's favorite. Who do you think is?"

Shade stared at him as if he was a card short in a full deck. "Me."

৪০ ৫৩

"Did you bring me my mascara that you borrowed?" Crazy Bitch wiggled to adjust her short skirt that had ridden up when she had slid into the backseat.

"I didn't borrow it. You put it in my purse because you didn't want to take your purse." T.A. rummaged through her purse then gave Crazy Bitch her mascara back.

Using her elbow to make T.A. give her more room, Killyama was growing more nervous the closer they drove to The Last Riders' clubhouse. She wished she hadn't let Sex Piston talk her into driving their car. Sitting between T.A. and Crazy Bitch made the twenty-minute drive seem longer.

Sex Piston rolled down the window in the front seat. "T.A., how much more of that cheap perfume you going to spray? We can't breathe up here."

"Try to breathe back here," Killyama complained, waving a hand in front of her face. "I don't know why you're spraying so much. it's not like you're going to be able to get close enough to any of The Last Riders for them to get a whiff. Stud already read us the riot act to behave."

"I don't know why you are allowed to fuck Train, yet me and T.A. have to keep our hands to ourselves," Crazy Bitch protested as she skillfully put her mascara on despite the moving car.

"Stud doesn't want it to be a habit," Sex Piston told her. "He's only going because I promised we would behave."

"He's become a stick in the mud since he married you," T.A. chimed in. "I take it back; if you get arrested, Stud's on his own."

"I'll make sure to tell him." Sex Piston slowed as they neared the sheriff's office, blowing the horn as they passed. "You think Knox will be upset if we didn't stop by to say hi?"

"No." Killyama smiled despite her nerves.

Knox had probably taken the night off to bunker down with Diamond. If Sex Piston did anything to make the club angry, her brother-in-law would want to be as far and inaccessible as possible.

"That's a cool corset. Can I borrow it the next time I go out with Slim?"

"No, your tits will stretch the leather out." Killyama had lost too many clothes to T.A. to let her borrow one of her favorites.

When they parked, the women took the time to give each other a once over. Then they waited as Stud and the Destructors Stud had asked Viper if he could bring along drove up.

Now that she was outside the car, she could breathe again. She adjusted the four buckles on the front of her corset, cinching it tightly until her breasts nearly spilled over the top. She took the lint roller from Sex Piston, making sure none of Gollum's hair was on her leather pants.

"Thanks," Killyama said, giving the roller back. "Sex Piston, I...Do...?"

"Bitch, I ain't stupid. We'll behave."

"Okay. Then let's have some fun," she said as Stud, Cade, Calder, and Pike got off their bikes.

"Looking good tonight, Calder," T.A. flirted as they climbed up the steps.

"You're all looking good tonight. Why don't you all look this good when you're hanging out with the Destructors?"

"Because there aren't any Destructors we haven't done or want to." Crazy Bitch's caustic reply had them taking a couple steps faster to get between her and Calder.

At one time, they had seemed attracted to each other...That was before another woman had come between them, offering him more than Crazy Bitch was willing to give. Candi had led them both down a road that Calder was damn lucky to get off of. He had chosen drugs over Crazy Bitch, and she had every intention of rubbing his nose in it.

Their eyes met as they took the steps together. Killyama felt bad for her. She had sworn off men, and other than the occasional hook-up T.A. had talked her into, she had stuck to it.

Moon was standing on the porch with a trampy blonde who had a cheap dye job and shorts up her crack.

"Hey, Killyama, ladies. Come to see how The Last Riders roll?"

"I see you're already enjoying yours, Moon. Viper know you're out here doing guard duty with your own party going on?"

The blonde blew the smoke from the joint she was enjoying into T.A.'s face as she crowded up the last step. The porch light shining down highlighted the flush she felt at the disdainful look the ho was giving them.

The night was starting off just the way she had expected it to. She didn't know why she had let Train convince her to come and bring her friends. She was dreading having to put up with the men when she knew they despised her because of Sasha, which was why she had made excuses when he had wanted her to come over. When he had invited her friends, however, she knew he wanted to get on friendlier terms with them because of her. Plus, she wanted them along as a buffer.

"I'm giving Crash a piss break, so no, Viper won't mind." Moon didn't seem insulted by her smart-ass comment as he opened the front door, stepping aside so they could enter. "Save a dance for me."

She had to give the ballsy man kudos for not being afraid of her temper. His provocative attitude was one she could appreciate.

The club was packed, so it wasn't until a couple of women moved from around the crowded pool table that she saw Train.

Sex Piston saw him, too.

"You need backup?"

"No. You get yourself something to drink. I've got this."

"You need me, just yell."

"I won't be the one yelling." She maneuvered around Cade and Fat Louise, weaving through the crowd until she was standing next to the two bitches. She didn't have to be told to know they were hanger-on's. The sluts wore dresses to get laid, which didn't bother her, as long as they kept their hands and tits off Train.

When he sank the eight ball in the front corner pocket, he caught sight of her. Laying the pool stick down, he immediately came over.

"I didn't expect you for another ten minutes."

"I let Sex Piston drive. That way, if we got pulled over, Knox could take care of the ticket."

"Good thing she wasn't pulled over, then. Knox has been writing so many tickets lately that the county gave him the okay to hire another deputy."

"She'll be riding home with Stud. She's planning on getting shit-faced."

"I stocked her favorite brand of tequila." Train took her arm, moving them away from the pool table. "You want a drink?"

"No, I'm good." She saw the two bimbos' disappointed gazes move to Moon who had taken Train's place.

"I see T.A. and Crazy Bitch are making themselves at home."

Killyama looked over to see they were dancing with two men she didn't recognize. Both of them loved to dance. With a room full of men, loud music, and a free bar, they were giving the two bimbos a run for their money.

"They're not shy."

"I wouldn't use the word shy to describe any of you." Train's mouth lifted humorously. "I'm going to grab a beer. You want to save me a seat on the couch?"

Killyama turned to where Train had pointed.

"Lily's here?"

"Yes, I told you she comes sometimes."

Killyama took another look around the room. It was a couple of seconds before she realized that something was different from the last party she had attended. The women were dressed as slutty as before—she certainly couldn't throw rocks in that direction since she was dressed just as suggestively. What had changed was their behavior.

"I get it. Who is the club putting on the show for? Lily or my friends?" She raised her brow, daring him to deny it. The men might not be keeping their hands to themselves, but the atmosphere was still PG rated.

"I don't know what you mean," Train deadpanned. "You sure I can't get you a drink?"

"I'm sure. Dude, be real with me." She placed a hand on his arm to keep him from slipping away.

Train sighed. "For her and them. Lily doesn't feel comfortable—"

"You don't have to explain it to me." She stared down at her painted toenails. "You wanted my friends here a lot tonight, didn't you?"

"I want you to be as comfortable in my club as I am in yours. I love living here. We're like a family, like your friends are to you. If I have to make peace with them, that's what I'm going to do."

She hated it when men made flowery speeches, but Train had hit her heart with a punch she hadn't been expecting. Her friends were her most vulnerable spot. She loved them. That Train wanted them to like him as much she wanted his friends to like her put her in an awkward position, one she had never been in before.

"I was dreading coming here tonight. If you hadn't invited Sex Piston, I don't know if I would have," she confessed, still staring down at her toes. She could walk into a room stark naked and not feel embarrassed, but exposing herself emotionally was almost impossible for her.

"Why?"

"I know the club hates me after what went down with Sasha. I don't want you to have to pick between me and your friends any more than you want me to have to choose between you and my friends."

"Look at me." Train's commanding voice had her raising her eyes. "None of the brothers or the women hate you. Sasha told us how you had one of the guards watch out for her, and she's had her charges dropped. If we hadn't been forced to act, she would still be running from the law. So it's all good, okay?"

"Okay." She made sure to keep her eyes steady when he mentioned being forced to act, feeling relieved that Shade had kept his word about her involvement in getting Sasha's charges dropped. "How about you get me a shot of tequila, and I'll find us a place to sit?"

"I can do that." He brushed his knuckles over the globes of her breasts. "Did I tell you I like your top? Leather suits you."

She turned so he could get a look at her ass in the tight leather pants. "I was wondering when you were going to say something. A woman likes to be appreciated when she dresses up for her man."

The desire blazing in his eyes was better than any words he could use to compliment her.

"So, you're admitting I'm your man?"

"I guess I am."

Train frowned. "Damn."

"What?" she asked, instead of angrily drilling one of her heels into his foot. If he didn't want to be her man, he could go...

"I told Mick I didn't have a woman. You made a liar out of me."

As satisfied as Gollum with a can of tuna, she strutted away from him, calling out, "Don't forget my tequila."

She was so busy strutting she accidentally bumped into a woman who was going toward the same couch.

"Sorry, my bad," Killyama apologized to the gorgeous redhead next to Cash.

"It was my fault. I was admiring your top." Rachel's friendly flattery would normally have her returning the compliment with one of her own, or thanking her. Before she could do either, Rachel's face turned blood red and she changed directions toward the bar with a surprised Cash following.

Killyama searched her memories to remember if she had insulted the woman before. If what Train had said was true about The Last Riders not holding a grudge against her, Rachel's behavior was inexplicable.

Shrugging, she went to the couch. Stud stood up to let her have his seat, sitting on the arm of the couch next to Sex Piston. Shade had taken the chair in front of it, with Lily on his lap. Evie was standing next to them, talking to Lily. When she saw her taking a seat, she gave her a smile before saying she was going to find King.

"Do I stink or something?" Killyama lowered her voice so Shade and Stud wouldn't hear her embarrassing question.

Sex Piston inconspicuously sniffed. "No, why?" she answered from out of the corner of her mouth as she lifted her beer to disguise their conversation.

"Rachel and Evie took off like their tails were on fire. Evie, I can understand, but I never laid a hand on Rachel."

"Maybe you're imagining it?"

"Maybe." She shifted away from Sex Piston as Train managed to find room to sit down next to her.

"You're a little close, aren't you?" Killyama wiggled on the couch cushions, managing to give herself breathing room and regretting cinching the corset so tightly.

"I like being close to you. If you don't have enough room, you could sit on my lap."

"Never mind. I'm good." Sex Piston had said she didn't smell, but she didn't want to take any chances.

She tried to remember what she had eaten that night. Maybe she should go to her car and grab the pack of gum she always kept stashed there.

She was sidetracked when Stud and Train started talking about his new bike.

"Have you decided what color you want to paint it?"

Train turned toward her. "What do you think?"

"Black," she answered without thinking.

"Can't be black. That's Stud's bike's color."

"Why does that matter?"

"When I race him again, it'll be easier for you to see which one of us is in the lead."

Stud laughed. "Should I be worried?"

"Yes." Train placed a possessive hand on her thigh. "It's hard for a man to see his woman rooting for another man, even if you like him."

"Can't say I blame you. It's why I started racing again. Sex Piston didn't give me the time of day until she saw one of my races."

Sex Piston didn't deny the accusation because it was the truth. Stud had been going nowhere in his attempts to catch her until she had seen the race they had all gone to.

"Watching you race might have gotten you in my bed, but it was your kids that let you steal my heart."

Stud leaned down to whisper something into Sex Piston's ear that had love simmering in her eyes.

"How did the conference go with your girls' teacher?" Train asked, turning to Stud and taking his attention away from Sex Piston.

"Sex Piston and I decided we don't want them to become for-eign exchange students. It's an excellent program, but we don't feel comfortable having another couple we don't know take responsibil-ity for them. The girls haven't talked to us in a week."

Train nodded in agreement. "If I had kids, I wouldn't have been able to do it, either." He stared down at the beer in his hand. "You remember Penni, Shade's sister?"

Stud's mouth twitched. "Yes, she's hard to forget."

"Yeah, well, I don't think you know this, but Penni has a friend who was born in Paris. Grace moved to the United States when she was older. She actually works with Penni. I mentioned to Penni that you two were having a problem trying to decide what to do, and she talked to Grace. She called a friend of hers who still lives in Paris, and she offered to let the girls stay with her for the summer or a school term. Seems when her daughter was vacating in America, she was killed. She said it would give her something to do—taking the girls shopping and sightseeing."

Sex Piston and Stud stared at Train, speechless at the offer. Killyama melted against Train.

"I'm sure Jonas could check her out for you before you two decide whether that would be an option worth considering. If you want, I can text you her information. She said to think it over, and if you decide not to do it, she wouldn't mind letting your family visit for a vacation. You would have to pay for your plane tickets and expenses, but it would save you money on hotel rooms."

Killyama gave Sex Piston the drink she hadn't touched yet, watching the stunned woman suck it down in one gulp. Then Stud and Sex Piston stared at each other. For once, she let Stud take the lead.

"That's very generous. If you text me her number, I'll check her out and talk to Sex Piston before I contact her. If we watch our pennies and save, we might actually be able to take them ourselves if we take her up on her offer and stay with her."

"I hope it works out for you. I'm sure it sucks with the girls giving you the silent treatment."

"I can handle that. It's when they start charging us for babysitting that I get mad. Tonight, they're charging me twenty bucks an hour, a piece for Rocky and Star. They offered to babysit Fat Louise's baby for free, just to rub it in."

"That's why, when I have kids, I'm only having boys," Train joked.

"Take it from me, boys are a handful," Beth disagreed as her and Razer joined the conversation. "Chance and Noah have me afraid of having more children. Lily, Evie, and Stori are the only ones who can babysitting for us anymore."

"They aren't that bad. They're just a little rambunctious," Lily spoke out in her nephews' defense.

"I don't mind babysitting if they can't help you out," Killyama offered.

Beth gave her a warm look. "I know. They still ask when you're coming to babysit them again."

"When did you babysit them?" Train asked.

"I don't know…A couple of times." Killyama looked at him curiously. His troubled expression had her wondering what he was thinking. Did he think she couldn't handle the two boys? Like Lily said, they were rambunctious, but they weren't any worse than all four of Sex Piston's kids.

Train stood up, asking her to come with him.

Letting him take her hand, she followed him to where the members were dancing.

"Something wrong?"

"No," he answered shortly, staring across the club room. When she saw his attention was on the women, she began moving stiffly against him.

"Dude, if you want to dance with another bitch, I can leave."

"I want to dance with *you*. I just had something on my mind." He shook off whatever was bothering him, his eyes once again intent on her.

"You know, if it works out with Meri and Keri, you're going to become Sex Piston's new best friend."

"I doubt that. You pretty much have that job sealed."

"Sex Piston is my best friend, but I'm not hers. She doesn't pick favorites."

"Women always pick favorites. They say they don't, but they do," he ruminated out loud.

She didn't question him, trying to be sensitive, which was hard for her. Was he thinking about his sisters when he had said that? Or his mother? She couldn't blame him for feeling resentful that his mother had chosen his father over the safety of his sisters. Or was he thinking about the women in the club?

She stared around the room as Train had done a few minutes ago, wondering which man was the women's favorite. It was a toss-up. She thought it might be Train, but she was biased because he was the most attractive to her. However, the other women had more intimate details that could make another more attractive. Sasha had certainly been able to list Train's attributes. Shade, Rider, and Viper wouldn't have a problem finding a bed to share, either. She would have to ask Beth or Lily the next time they had their monthly lunch date.

Killyama almost lost her balance in her borrowed high heels when she saw some of the women avert their eyes when she was caught staring directly at them.

She got a deathly sick feeling in her stomach. Train had wanted to know when she had babysat Beth's kids in the past, because he was worried she might have seen something when she was coming and going from Beth's house.

He had said women chose favorites. That meant he didn't think the men did. In fact, Train didn't need to pick a favorite woman. Her man had done them all.

CHAPTER TWENTY-FIVE

"Show me where the restroom is." Killyama commandeered Beth as soon as the men left to play a game of pool.

Beth broke off her conversation with Sex Piston. "You know where it is. It's around the corner and passed the steps. You can't miss it—"

Killyama linked her arm with hers as they made their way through the crowd.

"It's a small bathroom. It doesn't have stalls…" Beth protested.

"I know."

Beth stopped arguing, following meekly beside her.

She heard Sex Piston and Lily fall in step behind them, curious to what was going on.

Killyama had noticed Rachel went in the direction of the bathroom. When she saw the group of women going in the same direction, Rachel started heading back into the main room.

"Keep going, bitch. I want to talk to you." Killyama knew her suspicions had been correct when she saw Rachel blanch.

"Killyama, please don't make any trouble," Lily pleaded.

"I'm not going to touch the bitch. I just want to talk to her."

Rachel fell in step with the group of women.

When Killyama opened the bathroom door, the women crowded inside. Sex Piston had to stand on the other side of the toilet just to make room for everyone.

Her eyes going to Beth and Lily for assurance, Rachel stuttered, "Wh-What did you—"

"You've done Train, haven't you?"

Her pale face turned red, her shaking hand going to the sink to steady herself. "No...Yes...But..."

"That's all I needed to know. I don't do men who have fucked around with married women." She tried to press through the women to reach for the doorknob.

"Beth, please stop her!" Rachel yelled over her head.

Beth didn't move from the door, blocking her exit.

"Bitch, I don't need details." She turned back to face the humiliated woman, her hands clenched at her sides.

"Please let me explain...Please?" Rachel avoided both Killyama and Sex Piston's gazes. "This is so embarrassing."

"Just spit it out," she snapped.

"All right! You know how the men aren't shy about letting others watch them have sex?"

"Yes."

"Cash let Train watch," she delicately explained. "Sometimes the men invite them into their beds, too."

"You could have said no."

Rachel nodded. "Yes, I could have, but I didn't. The men have a way of getting you so wound up that you kind of...lose—kind of...like it."

"How many times have you liked it?" she asked sharply.

"Two...Maybe three," she confessed. "But not since I found out he was interested in you. I don't think he's been with any other women since you spent the night here."

"That's why you were avoiding me earlier?"

"Yes. It's so embarrassing..."

"What about the other women? He's done them all, hasn't he?"

"No," Lily sputtered.

"No," Beth denied.

"Maybe not you two, but I think he has all the others." Rachel bit her lip at the confession.

"Move," Killyama ordered Lily so she could put down the lid of the toilet. Sitting down, she stared at the three women.

Sex Piston stayed put, listening to every word. Shockingly, she didn't confront Rachel. What she did do was turn toward Killyama and put her hand on her shoulder.

"Beth, tell her."

Beth's face went as shamefaced as Rachel's, her eyes going to Lily's.

Killyama could tell that Lily didn't know what her sister was going to say, but she gave her support, anyway. "Go ahead."

"I was intimate with Rider. It was before I was married to Razer," Beth hurriedly clarified herself. "Killyama, all of the married women have been intimate with at least one of the men."

"I haven't, but...I did have sex with another couple in the room." Lily looked like she was going to pass out from her admission.

Killyama stood up, letting Lily have the only seat in the room.

Sex Piston gave a low whistle. "I want to know what they're selling. If I bottle it, I would make a fortune." She mused for a moment. "I know my uptight sister hasn't..." She broke off when Lily buried her face in her hands.

"Oh, my fu—" Killyama broke off when Lily rose her eyes to hers.

The woman wasn't shy about another couple watching her and Shade, yet she was getting upset because Killyama was about to take the Lord's name in vain? It was screwed up.

"I give the fucker's credit. They're smarter than the Destructors. If they find out..." She broke off as she began laughing.

Sex Piston didn't share her amusement.

"If Stud invited any of the brothers in our bedroom, he'll need a surgeon to pull my boot out of his ass."

Rachel shook her head. "You think that now, then it happens somehow." She raised her hands up in question.

"I think I know why." Beth looked undecided about telling them something.

"You might as well tell me. It's not like I won't find out, anyway," Killyama said shrewdly.

"I don't know if I should. I could get trouble...If anyone else finds out—"

"We're all sisters here." Or, they were until that bathroom door opened. Right now, Stud wasn't the only one who would need a surgeon when she was finished. There wouldn't be enough surgeons in Kentucky to put Train back together.

"Winter told me something, and when I asked Razer about it, he said Viper may have, but he hadn't. I don't believe him, though." Beth's troubled eyes met theirs. "Winter said that the men pick their replacement in case something happens to them. I think, when they share like Cash did, or let them watch like Shade had, it's with the one they chose to watch over us if something happens."

"That can't be true," Lily protested.

"It better not be." Rachel's red hair practically bristled.

"Rider comes over a lot. He goes to Willa's a lot, too," Beth mused.

"That's because you both are always cooking." Lily shook her head. Then her eyes grew thoughtful.

"So Train is Winter and your replacement?" Killyama looked at Rachel's furious expression.

"He must be. Cash could have at least given me a choice if that's true."

"Who would you have you chosen?" Killyama couldn't help asking.

Rachel's face turned fire engine red. "I really hate to admit it, but I would have chosen Train, too. Of course that was before he became involved with you."

"Of course." Killyama rolled her eyes up to the low ceiling. "Who would you have picked, Beth?"

"Rider." Beth's red face was the only explanation she needed.

"Lily?"

"Knox."

"You think Winter would have chosen Train?"

Both Beth and Lily answered, "Yes."

"So, it stands to reason, Shade is Diamond's replacement."

The women nodded their agreement.

"If—and it's a big if—Train gets serious, I wonder who he would pick for me?"

Rachel, Beth, and Lily stared at each other, and then turned toward her in unison.

"Rider," Killyama repeated Beth's answer, seeing if the three women agreed.

They all nodded.

"Rider it is, then." Killyama squeezed through the women.

"What are you going to do?" It was easy to see that Rachel was the smartest of the three. Sex Piston didn't count; she knew her well enough to know she was going to turn the tables on the men.

"If Train thinks he needs a replacement for if anything happens to him, who am I to argue? I think he should be afraid of dying."

"Really? Why?"

How Lily could still be so innocent when she was married to Shade beat the hell out of her. Seeing she still didn't understand, though, Killyama took pity on her. The other women's panicked faces showed they didn't need a picture or a map drawn out for them.

"Because I'm going to kill the fucker."

Chapter
Twenty-Six

"Where did Killyama go?" Train asked Razer when they finished their game, giving Stud and Cash the pool sticks.

"I think she went to the restroom." Stud rolled the four ball across the table so that Cash could rack them.

"Thanks." Train left the pool table, circling around Moon and the two women he had invited. The brother was half-lit as he yelled out to Rider that he needed some help. From his expression, Shade was going to send Moon on upstairs soon.

Train was irritated. Moon knew the rules. When Lily was in the room, none of the men were allowed to get shitfaced in front of her. Concerned that Lily was close by, yet not seeing her, he looked to Shade, who was looking for her, too.

Deciding to save the fool-hearty brother, Train waylaid Moon as he lifted one of the women's dresses.

"Moon." Train reached for his arm. "Brother, take it upstairs."

"Liz and Deja want me to see who has the sexist thong. Want to help me choose? I asked Rider, but I don't see—"

"Go upstairs," Train repeated the request, seeing Shade was getting angrier by the minute due to not being able to find Lily and Moon's loud voice.

"I will. Let me—"

"Now, Moon." Lucky's harsh voice had Moon realizing he had fucked up.

"I'm going. Let's go, Liz, Deja. Tell Shade I didn't mean any disrespect."

"You can tell him yourself in the morning."

Lucky blocked Shade as he neared. "I took care of it, Shade. Moon's taking his party upstairs."

"Moon, I warned you. If Lily gets upset—"

"She's fine, Shade. She's with Beth and Rachel." Lucky nodded to where the women were standing.

"Where's Killyama? I thought she was with them." Train's gaze came to a halt when he saw where she was.

The woman had somehow gotten past him without him noticing. She was leaning over the pool table to make a shot while Rider was standing on the other side, practically drooling at the bounty she was giving him.

Train brushed past Moon, striding toward the pool table.

"Where have you been?" he asked her as he stared Rider down. The man was too enthralled to notice.

"I saw you were busy, so I asked if Rider wanted to play."

The woman didn't clear her throat, so Train knew the seductive tone she used had been deliberate.

"Are you pissed at me because I played a game with Razer and left you alone?" Train couldn't understand what had happened to the woman.

"Lover, I don't need a babysitter."

Train almost swallowed his own tongue when Killyama called him lover. The sensual tone had his dick pressing against his jeans.

"Then explain to me what—"

"Can any of your bitches make this shot?" Killyama turned her back to the pool table. Leaning backward until her head was on top of the pool table, she braced the pool stick between her tits. Then she turned her head to the side, and with a flick of her wrist, the stick struck the cue ball, sending the blue ball spinning into the pocket in front of Rider.

"No." Train burrowed his hands in his pockets to keep from taking the pool stick away from her.

"Can you show me that again?" Rider asked when she straightened.

"I didn't know you were so…limber." Train picked up one of the pool balls and lightly tossed it in the air. Rider received his silent threat and closed his mouth.

"You think you know all my secrets just because you fucked me a few times?"

Train rested his hip against the pool table when he heard a quarrel taking place by the bar. He looked away from Killyama to see who it was, and saw Beth and Razer arguing. Lily and Shade were also fighting by the kitchen door. Evidently, Lily wasn't ready to leave, and she was telling her husband no.

Sex Piston, T.A., and Crazy Bitch were sitting on top on the bar. At first, Train thought they were enjoying Razer and Beth's argument, then it dawned on him who they were watching. Him and Killyama.

"I don't need you to drive me home!" Train heard Rachel's yell as she threatened Cash with an empty beer bottle. "I texted Greer to come pick me up."

Train could see her fury from across the room. Cash was trying to placate Rachel, but she wasn't listening to anything he said.

Giving the beer bottle to Willa, who was trying to calm her down, Rachel shook her head toward Cash as she told Willa what started the argument. Train couldn't hear why, but from Willa's reaction, it was bad.

"Lucky!" Willa quit trying to play peacemaker between Rachel and Cash, hunting for her husband with the beer bottle in her hand, and her other hand on her pregnant as if the unborn baby was just as upset as it's mother.

"What did you start?" Train tried to take the pool stick away from Killyama before he left to try to calm the escalating arguments in the room.

He nearly tripped over his own feet when she spun around, the pool stick swinging through the air. Train felt the whoosh of air and managed to duck in time to save himself.

"What are you doing?" You almost hit me—" Train ducked again.

Fed up, he tried to take the pool stick away. Then he quickly backed up a step when she pointed it at him.

"Move along, fucker. Next time, I won't miss." She was waving that pool stick like a teacher would wave a ruler.

Train debated if he should take it away from her forcefully, when Cash and Rachel's argument went from bad to worse. Greer had arrived to pick up his sister and wanted to know why she was so upset. From there, it became hell. The fight that broke out between Cash and Greer became the priority.

When he started to go break up the fight, he heard Killyama ask Rider to rack the balls. Train stopped in his tracks, seeing Killyama shove the rack across the table toward Rider as he pulled two balls out of the side pocket in front of him.

"Don't want to miss those…lover."

Those last four words caused a bloodcurdling yell to come instinctively from Train. He dragged Rider across the pool table as Rider tried to defend himself, but Train gave him no chance before his fist shot out, nailing Rider in the mouth.

When he would have punched him again, Stud tried to pull him back.

"Let me go," Train grunted.

"We need to help Lucky. Rider didn't even try to hit you back."

Train tried to gather the shards of his temper when he saw Killyama fawning over Rider.

"Woman, get away from him...now."

"Why the hell did you hit him? You were supposed to swing at me!" Killyama laid the pool stick down as if she were afraid she would hit him with it. He should have known her well enough by now to take that as a warning.

Train stared at her, dumfounded. "I've never hit a woman in my life."

"Then I suggest you start."

Train caught her fist before it could land.

"I'm not going to hit you, no matter how mad I get, so I knock it...Ow!" Train doubled over. He literally saw stars. He had done two tours in the military and had never felt pain like what was coming from his nuts.

Rider hopped off the pool table to help him as Train landed on his knees, hanging on to the pool table for support. He kept sucking in air to keep himself from passing out.

"I can see why you men need replacements. You all are a bunch of pussies."

"What are you talking about?" Train tried to focus on the venom spewing from her mouth instead of the stars floating behind his eyes.

Killyama didn't show any mercy. She grabbed his ponytail, lifting his head and forcing him to look up at her. "Are you Viper's and Cash's spare?"

"Yes."

She released his hair in disgust. "I'm going to save you the trouble of picking one for me. If you're dumb enough to pick one, then I'm okay with Rider. Is that okay with you, Rider?"

Train managed to get to his feet by holding on to the pool table and Rider's arm.

"Well?" Killyama snarled.

"I'd rather you pick someone else. How about Moon?" Rider turned to search for Moon, who was no longer in the room.

"Actually, I had already asked Shade. But if you want Rider, maybe we need to convince him. What do you think, Rider?"

"Do I have to?"

Train snatched the pool stick away before Killyama could pick it up again. He couldn't tell who she would have aimed for, but him and Rider would have been going to the dentist's office if it had landed.

"Give it back." When Killyama tried to snatch it out of his hand, Train tossed it to Rider.

Before she could react, Train threw her over his shoulder, stumbling backward into the pool table when she clawed his back, going for his hair.

"Bitch, I'm going to paddle that ass of yours when I get you to my room." He fought the vertigo from having his nuts smashed and his head nearly ripped off his shoulders.

"Fucker, you're going to be sneezing your balls out of your nostrils if you lay one hand on me."

Train raised his hand, smacking her on her ass.

"I thought you didn't hit women?"

"I hit a wildcat. When you start acting like a lady, I'll stop."

Train stepped over Cash and Greer on the way to the stairs, hearing Rider reluctantly coming up behind them. Then he stopped when he was halfway up the stairs to see Rachel sitting there, crying.

"You okay, Rachel?"

"I didn't mean for Greer and Cash to get in a fight." She sniffed.

"Bitch, what are you crying for?"

Train smacked her ass again. "This is all her fault. You and Cash will make up in the morning. Let him and Greer fight it out. They've been building it up for a while. Maybe they'll get it out of their systems now."

"You think so?"

"Yes. Just pretend it was all Cash's fault, and I'll make sure he brings flowers to apologize. Rider, take her home."

Train hugged the side of the staircase to let Rachel take Rider's hand.

"Don't take long. I don't want to keep her waiting," he said as he continued carrying a struggling Killyama up the steps. Train had to hold on to the handrail to keep the woman from throwing them both down the steps.

"Do I have to?" Rider's whiney voice floated upward to the landing where Train was spanking Killyama's ass to keep her still.

"Don't make me come and get you." Satisfied that his threat had lit a fire under Rider's ass, Train carried Killyama to his room. If she had wanted to make him jealous by using Rider, she could handle the consequences. He hadn't made his mind up about sharing her, but she had made his mind for him. She could have chosen any of the Last Rider's, and she had chosen Rider. Who was he to argue?

Getting her through the doorway proved to be a challenge. The bitch held on to the doorway and refused to let go.

He slid a hand between her struggling thighs, rubbing her slit through the thin leather of her pants, promising, "It'll feel better with the pants gone."

"Motherfucker, I'll castrate you!"

Train rained a series of small slaps down on her ass until she released the door to protect her bottom. Slamming the door with his boot, he then dumped her onto his bed.

"Whew, I've never had to work so hard to get a woman in my bed before." Train chuckled.

Killyama raised herself up onto her knees, her hair a tumbled mess of curls, which she brushed out of her eyes to aim her fury at him. "You are so dead."

He wasn't stupid enough to sit down on his bed to pull off his boots. Going to the chair he kept at his desk, he saw her about to jump off his bed, her sights set on the door.

"You won't make it, but go for it. I enjoy tussling with you." He took his boots off, keeping track of her every move. When he stood up to unbuckle his belt, she sprung.

If she would have made it, she would have landed right in front of bedroom door. However, he caught her in the air like she was an acrobat giving a performance. Turning back with her over his shoulder once again, he tossed her unceremoniously back down onto the bed.

"Dude, this stopped being funny about ten minutes ago. I'm done playing with you. If you don't move and let me out that door, I'm seriously going to hurt you."

Train removed his T-shirt then slid his belt out from his belt loops. She watched his every movement.

"I'm not the one playing a game, Killyama, and I've had enough. Every man and woman in this club knows not to push me to a certain point. You went beyond pushing tonight and straight to bulldozing to get what you want."

"I don't want a fucking thing from you."

"Yes, you do. You want me on your terms. You want to play on what I feel for you to make me do what you want." He drilled her with his glare. "What scared you the most tonight? When I mentioned kids? Or was it the thought of another woman having a stake on me if anything happens?"

"I don't care if you—"

"Don't think of lying to me. You do care…So much that you were willing to walk away from me to prove to yourself you don't."

"The only thing I care about right now is getting my bitches and leaving."

"That's the first problem we've got to get past, because I'm not letting you leave."

CHAPTER
TWENTY-SEVEN

A knock on Train's bedroom door had Killyama tensing, her fingers itching to grab Train's laptop sitting on his desk. She had every intention of beating him with it if he made the mistake of getting close to her.

She watched as Train opened his door, and Rider appeared in the doorway.

"She cooled down yet? I can come back later if she hasn't." His plaintive voice grated on nerves.

She eyed the computer again, deciding to switch targets.

"Cut it out. Killyama isn't Willa. She isn't buying that load of crap you're selling."

She lowered her lashes, shielding her perceptive eyes as she watched Rider close the door and lean back against it, crossing his arms over his chest. If she hadn't already figured out Rider's game, the expression he wore now would have scared her senseless. She had been a bounty hunter too long and was too well trained by Hammer and Jonas to let Rider fool her. She wanted to give him an A for his deviousness, hiding behind that mash and the behavior he acted out toward the women in the club. They didn't have a clue who they were dealing with, but she did.

"She gonna sell me out?" His mama's boy persona disappeared as Rider stared calculating back at her.

"If they're dumb enough to believe that you're only after what's in their kitchen cabinets, why should I care?" She shrugged. Hammer hadn't raised no fool.

Rider's mouth curled into a sensuous smile. "She'll tell, but they won't believe her."

Train smiled back.

The men were staring at her like they were about to take down a defenseless deer.

Her heart sped up unexpectedly, adrenaline pumping through her bloodstream like she had been chasing a wanted fugitive, only to find herself unexpectedly cornered by two.

"It was only a matter of time. I don't know how you fooled Winter and Rachel this long, anyway."

"Because they only want to see what they want to see. I always give the women what they want. You might like to spoil them to get what you want. Me? I like to be the one pampered."

His comment raised her hackles. She dug her fingers into the bedspread underneath her, forcing herself to stay still. When you were up against two hungry lions, you didn't attack; you stared them down.

Rider laughed again. "She didn't like that. Your woman is jealous as fuck."

"Yes, she is." Train chuckled with Rider.

Killyama became frightened. They were toying with her, getting ready to pounce.

Train finished taking off his jeans, kicking them out of the way.

"Am I getting undressed or just watching?" Gone was the whiney voice he had used downstairs. Now he was all business, staring at her as if she were the main course at dinner.

He had never been frightened of her like he had pretended. He was a cold-blooded chameleon. She thought she was good at masking her emotions. Rider was the true expert, putting on a different face for each of the wives.

Train moved slowly forward, trailing a finger over the top of her breasts, then snatching his hand back when she tried to scratch him.

"Get undressed. She's breathing so hard that her tits are about to come out of that top."

She carefully slid her cell phone out of her corset.

"Who are you going to call? Sex Piston? You think I didn't notice that you could have stopped me anytime when I carried you up here? All you had to do was yell for her, and Sex Piston, Stud, and Calder would have made me let you go. Why didn't you?" he asked as if they were all talking about the weather, and not that she was faced with two hungry men who were already looking forward to slacking their appetites on her.

She had seen Sex Piston, Crazy Bitch, and T.A. sitting on top of the bar, while Stud had been trying to get them off. Each of them had seen Train carrying her upstairs. Stud had even made a move toward her, but Killyama had signaled Sex Piston behind Train's back not to interfere. The last she had seen of them, Sex Piston was fighting with Stud, and Crazy Bitch was fighting Calder to hold them back.

"Because I didn't want them to kill you," she snarled, not able to explain to herself why she had held them back.

"She lies a lot, doesn't she?" Rider had removed his shirt as she had debated calling Sex Piston.

Train gave a weary sigh. "Yes, and it's a rule breaker for me."

"She know that?"

"Yes. I'm working on her being more honest with me. So far, she's not getting the message that I won't tolerate it."

"You need my help to get the message through?" Rider gave her a lascivious grin, taking off his boots and jeans.

Killyama swallowed hard at her first sight of Rider's muscular body.

"I think she likes what she sees." Rider swept his eyes over her body with his own carnal smile.

"They usually do." Train gave her a searching look. It was then she saw Train wouldn't do anything she didn't want to do. "Rider spends a lot of time working out to keep in shape for the women."

Where was that jealously he had exhibit when she had teased Rider at the pool table?

The fucker gave her benign smile as Rider carried his clothes over to Train's chair at the desk.

"We ready to get this party started?" Rider looked at Train instead of her.

"That's up to Killyama. You calling Sex Piston or Hammer?"

Killyama stared down at her phone, making up her mind. The fuckers needed to be taught a lesson, and she was the woman to do it.

The brief flash of emotions toward her had exposed his weakness for her, building her confidence that she wasn't going to be the one taken down.

"I don't need to call either of them. I can take you two pencil dicks myself."

"Then bring it on, Killy. If you want to leave, all you have to do is get past me."

"I can't help?" Rider protested, moving away from the door to give her a fair chance.

"No. When I need your help, I'll ask."

She slowly set her phone down on the nightstand, freeing her hands. When she slid off the bed, Train didn't move, giving her time to ready herself. It was a mistake. The man was underestimating her. He was like a lamb to the slaughter, and she was going to deliver him a world of hurt.

Seductively sliding the leather out of the buckle at the top of her corset, the leather gaped but didn't fall because it was too snugly fit to her ribcage.

"You mind if I take my shoes off?"

"Saves me the trouble."

Train might be looking at her in amusement now, but he was going to pay for it when it was her turn to laugh.

She didn't take her eyes off the two men as she toed the heels off before kicking them out of the way. She didn't want anything to break her concentration when she administered their ass kicking. Tripping and falling over her shoes would give them a chance to pounce.

She placed her weight on the balls of her feet, her hands going to her sides. She focused on Train's nose, making that her target.

"She looks sexy as fuck, doesn't she, Rider?"

"Yes, she does." If the women could see Rider's expression, they would run screaming from their husbands. He watched every move she made intently. No show of warmth in his eyes. "Why don't you open another buckle so you can breathe better?"

"I liked you better when you pretended to be lame."

He grinned. "Most women do."

Train didn't take his eyes off her, either. "Rider takes it a whole new level in Willa's bedroom."

Furious, Killyama flew the heel of her palm toward his nose. She knew she was in trouble when he easily blocked her with his wrist. He should have at least winced at the force of her strike; instead, he stared back at her steadily, waiting for her next move.

"That might have hurt if you were successful," Train complimented her. "Hammer's done a good job training you."

"Jonas taught me that move."

"He couldn't have prepared you for me, Killyama. You can't beat me, and you certainly can't beat Rider. We're wasting time. We could be having fun—"

Her foot flashed out, nailing him on his thigh. "I'm having fun. Aren't you?"

"No. And I appreciate you not getting my balls again."

"I was aiming for them, but with your pants off, it's hard to guess where they're hiding."

Rider's laughter filled the room. "I like her. I'll make sure she loses that bitchy attitude when I have to replace you."

"Brother, I plan on living a full life, despite her trying to end it."

He deflected every kick sent his way. She was working up a sweat, whereas Train appeared bored.

"You never answered my question, Killy."

Confused, she stared at him, not comprehending. "What question?"

"What got you so mad tonight? Because I mentioned children, or that men chose replacements?"

"I don't give a damn if you want kids. They won't be mine. I'm never going to have children."

"Why not?"

She avoided his serious expression, finding Rider's impassive face that made it easier to hide the emotional upheaval Train was trying to elicit from her.

"I'm not getting married, and I'm not raising a fatherless child."

"I'm not ready to go down that aisle, either. But I'm not saying never, and they wouldn't be fatherless if they were mine."

"Don't know how you'll be making them with those M&Ms." She turned back to look at him. It was easier to do so when she insulted him.

"That was a low blow. It's a good thing I remember how much you liked them when you gave me that blowjob last night."

"I was faking it."

"You do that a lot, don't you?" He wasn't getting upset. He was methodically wearing her down, something Hammer had warned would happen with more skilled adversaries. "So, if it wasn't the mention of kids that upset you, it was because the men chose their replacements?"

"It's fucked up."

"Why? The men want to know their women are taken care of if something happens to them."

"Nothing is going to happen to you unless one of you shoot yourselves in the foot, or you fuck yourself to death."

"It will happen. It already did."

Train's serious statement had her freezing in place.

"Gavin."

Train gave a nod. "Yes, it was Gavin who came up with the idea when he was moving to Treepoint. He was engaged to a woman he had met in Ohio. He wanted to make sure Taylor was taken care of if something happened to him."

"Who did he pick? Viper?"

The pain in Train's eyes had her wanting to hug him close. Rider's brown eyes were filled with the same pain. She made herself suck back the sympathy she felt for them at the loss of their friend.

"Me. Gavin and Viper had an argument before he left."

"Did you enjoy her as much as he did?"

She had never been truly afraid of Train. She was now.

"I never touched Taylor, not once. I was by her side when we found out he was missing. I was also there the day she tried to OD when she finally realized he wasn't coming back to her. I was there when she sold the house they had bought together because she didn't want to live there, surrounded by his memories. I was there to tell her it was okay to see other men. And I was there to walk her down the aisle when she married another man who took the responsibility of caring for her." Train stared her down. "When we pick our replacements, we don't pick them to share their beds. We pick the one most able to care for their needs."

"What did Rachel need?" she snapped.

"That wasn't for Rachel; it was for Cash. He gets off on watching me tongue-fuck her."

At his smirk, she lost her temper. She attacked, intending to maim him. He deftly evaded her attempts, blocking her in a flurry of movement she could barely keep up with. Frustrated, she raised her knee to remove his opportunity of ever becoming a father.

"That's so fucked up! I hate you! *I fucking hate you*!"

Train blocked her knee jab, trapping her knee between his thighs. "You think that sounds fucked up? I think you trying to save Sasha was fucked up. You could have just talked to Viper, but you were so worried about Sex Piston and Diamond getting in trouble that you put your life in danger." He twisted one of her hands behind her back.

Killyama frenziedly scratched his cheek with her short nails, and Train just calmly tucked it behind her back with her other one.

She fought against him as he went to the back of her neck with his free hand, untying the bandana. She stared at the blank wall over his shoulder as he pulled it away, exposing the permanent mark that Kane had given her.

"Poor, baby." Train traced the line at the base of her throat with his lips.

"Don't *poor baby* me. I'm not one of your stupid hos. Let me go. I'm ready to leave."

"I bet you are. You hate being vulnerable." He took a step forward. With her leg between his, she couldn't get her balance, so with a push to her chest, Train released her hands as she toppled onto the bed.

She stared up at the ceiling as he placed a hand beside her head.

"I told you that you're not the only one who can get hurt." Train took one of her hands, placing it over his heart. "You don't have a mark on you that I caused. I have sore nuts, a bruised wrist, several bruises on my legs, and you scratched my face. If we're counting wounds, you're winning the war. If that's what it takes for you to trust me, go ahead." Train straddled her hips without weighing her down. Then he opened his arms wide. "Have at it."

She stared stupidly up at him. "You're letting me hit you?"

"Yes, go ahead." Train took her hand again, putting it in the middle of his chest. "Scratch me again." When she didn't make an attempt to do it, he balled her hand into a fist. "Punch me. Go ahead. I know you want to."

"I don't want to anymore. You took all the fun out of it," she confessed wearily.

"Killy, I don't want to take anything from you without replacing it with something better."

"Something that every woman in the clubhouse can have?" She continued to stare up at the ceiling. "I knew that Jewell, Stori, Sasha, Ember…and the other hos were competition, but the wives, too? I didn't expect them to have a piece of you, too."

"The women members are no competition, baby. They aren't even in the same league. And the other wives…yes, they have a piece of me, the piece I want them to have. I messed with Rachel, and it felt good, but I don't get anything from her anymore. Babe, it wasn't a regular thing."

"Even if it was once, it's too much! You messed around with a married woman."

"Yes, I did. But both of their husbands were there. All of The Last Riders like to share to some extent. It can be some of the best sex imaginable. But if you don't want to, we won't. That's not my rule breaker; it's yours. And I already told you no other women, and that means the women member and the wives.

"Cash and Viper, they don't expect me to fuck their wives because I'm their replacement. They shared their women with me so it will make them more comfortable around me if something happens to them. If I was in a relationship, that wouldn't have been part of the deal. For sure, I have every intention of being faithful to the woman I care about, and that is you."

She dropped her hands limply to her side. "So, Winter and Rachel are the only two you've accepted responsibility for?"

"Yes. And Rider is responsible for Beth, Willa, and now you."

"I'm everybody's favorite."

Killyama turned her head on the mattress to see Rider lying sideways on the bottom of the bed. The chameleon was back, showing her the easygoing man the women were used to seeing.

"I can't believe they fell for your bullshit." She had also fallen for it the first couple of times she had been around him. She would have continued to do so, too, if not for Hammer and Jonas's warnings.

"They did." He obviously had no conscience or remorse in attaining the trust the women had given to him.

She turned back to Train, unsettled by Rider's unblinking gaze. "Is it too late for me to choose Shade?"

"After tonight, I'd say yes. But I'll ask him tomorrow."

"Wait until morning to make up your mind. You might change it after tonight," Rider suggested amicably.

One minute she was dealing with Jack the Ripper, and the next, she was staring at Ryan Gosling. The fucker should have gone into acting instead of wasting his skills on a clubhouse filled with women. He could have had thousands at his beck and call.

Killyama felt Train unbuckling her corset. "You look like you could use a breather."

She looked at his face as he spread her top, baring the upper half of her body. Then he massaged the red lines caused by the corset.

"Just so there's no misunderstanding; I'm not letting Rider touch me."

"I'm content to watch. Just pretend I'm not here, babe."

That would be an impossibility. In fact, she didn't know why she wasn't demanding he leave. She had never had sex in front of anyone before, though she certainly wasn't shy about her body.

Train's cock on her belly made her wiggle underneath him.

"Rider, make yourself useful." Train's hair provided a shield for her face as he kissed her.

The mattress bounced as Rider must have gotten up. Then she felt the tight leather of her pants slide down her legs as she sucked Train's tongue into her mouth.

"Let me know if you need anything else." Rider's voice was filled with tension as she felt the mattress bounce again.

Train raised his leg so he could lie by her side. He broke the passionate kiss to smooth a hand down her belly, sliding between her thighs. Lifting the leg closest to him, he raised it to his side, then brought his hand to her hip, turning her so she was facing Rider at the bottom of the bed.

She closed her eyes as she heard him putting on a condom. Then, unable to stop herself, she opened them to watch Rider's reaction.

There were several inches separating them, but his eyes ate the distance. His gaze traveled down her breasts to her sparse curls where Train slipped his hand between them, not blocking Rider's view of him playing with her.

She closed her eyes again, almost telling Train to stop. It was too much having Train behind her and Rider in front, although he wasn't touching her.

When she opened her eyes again, Rider's gaze was pinned on her pussy, his hand going to his thick cock and sliding over the long length in a slow pace as Train sank a finger into her.

"You're so wet. I could fuck you now, and my cock would slip right in." Train slipped his arm under her neck so he could reach her breast, tweaking the nipple as he sank another finger inside of her.

She bit back the moan that tried to slip from her lips.

Rider began pumping his dick faster as Train increased his speed, driving his fingers into her. His lust-filled gaze fueled the tendrils of need in her as if Train wasn't using his fingers but Rider's cock. It was the most erotic experience of her life, knowing Rider could see but not touch.

Train maintained his masterful control over her body as if he were the only one who could give her the climax she was silently screaming she needed.

"Train…" His name was the closest she could bring herself to beg.

He didn't make her. Moving closer to her, his wet hand came to her waist as he tried to fit his hard cock into her tight opening. He had to shift his position before he could easily thrust into her.

Train buried his face in her hair. "She's so fucking tight."

"How tight?" Rider asked on a groan, continuing to slide his hand up and down his dick as Train moved in and out of her.

Shuddering, she turned her head and sunk her teeth into Train's arm.

She saw Rider inching closer. She was so close to coming. If he spoiled her orgasm by touching her when she was defenseless, she would split his lip.

Unexpectedly, he took her hand in his, holding it tightly as she came, stroking his thumb over her knuckles as Train continued to thrust into her from behind.

Droplets of sweat slipped down between her breasts as Rider raised her hand so her fingers could capture them before lifting her fingers to his mouth. He sucked on one finger, his tongue twirling over it.

"You taste so good," he murmured as Killyama let him slip another finger inside.

Train bucked against her, driving her into the mattress and forcing Rider to release her fingers.

"Fuck me back, Killy. Let Rider watch you come. Show him how your little cunt is stretched tight around my cock and how he'll never know how fucking unbelievable it feels."

She shoved her ass back into Train's hips, following his commands. Her muscles tightened then shook as her climax drove him higher until he came with her.

Self-consciously, she watched as Rider came, too, gliding his hand over his cock when his dick grew even longer as he moved to his back and let his climax play out on his waist.

Killyama burrowed her face in the messed up bedspread, but Train flipped her over so she was staring up at him. Unable to bear his steady gaze, she buried her face in his shoulder.

"Since when do you get shy?" he teased.

She was trying to come up with a smart-ass reply when she heard a pounding on the bedroom door.

"Bitch, you have five seconds before I'm coming in!" Sex Piston threatened from the other side of the door.

"Please tell me you locked the door," Killyama whispered, horrorstricken.

When she saw their faces, she scrambled off the bed and picked up her clothes, throwing them under Train's bed. Hastily, Killyama then dropped to the floor, lifting the bedspread so she could crawl under the bed.

The men had frozen at Sex Piston's threat, expecting Killyama to keep her out. They couldn't understand what she was doing until it was too late, missing their chance to get dressed.

"What is she doing?" Rider asked Train, both of their faces perplexed.

"I'm hiding, assholes. Tell her I'm not here."

CHAPTER
TWENTY-EIGHT

"Are you coming or not?" Train held his phone tighter to his ear, swiveling the stool he was sitting on as he turned to see Jewell wasn't in her office.

Getting up from his worktable, he went into the empty office, shutting himself in so he could hear Killyama.

"I'm thinking about it. I'll let you know in a few hours."

Her vague answer rose his suspicions.

"Where are you? I thought you were hanging out at Sex Piston's shop today."

"I am."

She was lying. The woman wouldn't consider lying if they were face to face.

"Let me talk to her. I want to say hi."

"Dude, she doesn't want to say hi. She's telling her customer what happened last weekend."

He was going to kill her. The woman knew exactly what buttons to push to distract him, and she didn't just push; she took a sledgehammer to them.

"Gotta go. She has a customer coming in, and I need to check them in for her."

Train stared down at the phone. She had hung up on him without telling him good-bye.

Gnashing his teeth, he dialed another number.

"Where is she?"

"Hammer and Jonas just picked Killyama up. I don't know where they're headed yet. When I do, I'll call."

"Thanks. Keep me posted."

"Will do."

Train shoved his cell phone back into his pocket. There wasn't anything else he could do until he heard from Crash.

Someone had been on her day and night since Shade had told them she had been hurt. She tracked anyone who had a bounty on their head, and she was good at it, too. She had no concept of danger, though, and that scared the fuck out of him.

Hammer and Jonas were always by her side, but it didn't relieve his worry. They had fucked up when she had nearly been strangled and raped by Kane. Train didn't believe in giving second chances where her safety was concerned.

He tiredly went back to his worktable, filling the numerous orders. He had been spending the evenings and nights with Killyama, and switching between working at the factory and keeping an eye on her during the day.

He owed Crash big time. All the brothers had stepped up to take shifts for him on watching her, but it usually fell on Crash to keep an eye or her because most of the computer work he did could be done at night. If the brother kept volunteering when he had to ask for help, Train was going to start paying him.

He had just settled back down at his worktable when Stori handed him a couple of letters and a small package.

"You coming to the dinner tonight? Willa made you a birthday cake."

"Yes." Train reached for the box cutter.

Stori hesitated from delivering the rest of the mail, finally telling him, "I plan on making your favorite casserole, but I wanted to make sure you were going to be there before I do."

He stopped opening the box to give her a friendly grin. "I wouldn't miss my own birthday party."

"So, how are you and Killyama doing?"

Train set the box cutter down to give her his full attention. "I'm planning a future with her, if that's what you're asking."

She placed a caressing hand on his arm. "I was just checking. I miss spending time with you."

Train pulled his arm away. "You can spend time with me at the party tonight. Killyama will be there, too. I want all the women to become friends with her."

Stori's mouth drooped in disappointment. "Sure. Well, I better get busy. I'll talk to you later."

"Okay." Train went back to opening the package.

Looking inside, he pulled out a tool roll. It was made out of a soft, oil-tanned leather that felt like butter in his hands. Unwinding the thin strap from the metal toggle that kept it closed, he unrolled it until it was flat. The pockets had snaps that kept him from seeing inside. He unsnapped each of the pockets, taking out motorcycle tools. Then, carefully placing them back in the pockets and snapping them closed, Train rolled it back up and just stared at the gift.

He had always kept a kit in his saddlebag, but his old one was nowhere near as nice as this one. It would fit perfectly in his saddlebag. He would let Rider or one of the other brothers have the old one if he didn't need it.

Train looked for where it came from, already knowing he wouldn't find it. He would get Crash to check out the return address, though he didn't expect to find anything more this time than he had the last when his wallet had been mailed.

He rubbed the soft leather. It was beautiful and would increase in beauty with age, like Killyama.

Train swallowed the lump in his throat. He knew she had sent them both, but she didn't want any acknowledgment. If he asked, he knew she would just deny it. Stori wanted credit for everything she did for him, yet Killyama went out her way to keep him in the dark.

With every step he took toward her, he took two steps back. She didn't even want to admit aloud they were a couple, she avoided any outward signs of affection, and she maintained her space when he was in bed with her at night. The only time he could see what she felt for him was when they had sex, and she always tried to control it for as long as she could. He was never going to understand her until she opened up to him, yet she refused to.

If he asked about her father or her past relationships to try to find out what had made her so closed off emotionally, she would turn her waspish tongue on him. It had become easier to let it ride, hoping she would loosen up when she realized she could trust him.

"Yeah, like that's ever going to happen," he muttered to himself as he answered his cell phone.

"Killyama is in a small town in Tennessee. Looks like they are trying to get someone. They're parked in an alleyway, watching a vacant building across the street."

Son of a bitch. The woman had promised to tell him when she was going on a hunt. He wouldn't have let Crash take over for him if he had known she was working.

He was about to disconnect the call when he heard Crash cursing.

"What? What's going on?"

"It's cool. They're taking down an old woman who was going inside the building. They're taking her to their Escalade now. Looks like she will be making your party tonight, after all," Crash joked, then started cursing again.

"What?"

"The old bat tried to pull a gun on Killyama when she tried to frisk her. She took it away…Ow, that looks like it hurt—"

"Who got hurt?" Train stood up, knocking his stool into Razer who was working behind him.

"The old woman. Killyama put her hand on the gun's chamber, and then twisted it out of her hand. From what I can hear, she's screaming that Killyama broke her thumb."

Breaking out in cold sweat, Train used his foot to slide his stool back under him. "Is she okay?"

"I don't know. She's still yelling at Killyama."

"Not the old woman." Train's voice rose. He didn't even notice that the workers had stopped to eavesdrop on the one-sided conservation. "Killyama? Is she okay?"

"Oh, yes, she fine. The old woman is crying, though."

"Crash, I don't care about the old woman!"

"Brother, stop yelling at me. She's helping the old bitch get into the SUV. They're leaving. I'll call you back when I know where they're going next. Later." The line went dead.

He was going to stra—He was going to yell…Dammit, he wasn't even going to be able to yell at her because he didn't want her to know he was watching her. She would be the one strangling him if she found out.

"Trouble?"

Train turned toward Razer who was openly curious. In fact, several of the other workers were waiting attentively for his answer.

"No. Killyama must have caught a fugitive, and she pulled a gun."

"She pulled a gun on a fugitive? I didn't know bounty hunters could carry a gun?" Razer's expression filled with concern.

Train didn't know if Razer's concern stemmed from worry of another brother's woman or Beth's.

"No, the fugitive pulled one on Killyama," Train explained, beginning to understand Crash's predicament of explaining the incident.

"I'm glad she wasn't hurt."

"The fugitive or Killyama?" Train tried to joke off the fear he had felt when he had heard a gun had been pulled on her.

She was going to have to find another job. He didn't give a shit that she worked with Hammer and Jonas. There had to be safer jobs she could do; ones that didn't involve guns, knives, and old women who wanted to shoot her.

"Killyama wouldn't have hurt the old woman. That's her weakness."

"Why do you say that?"

"Because, she takes trays of cookies to women living in nursing homes every Christmas. She even sends some to Beth to bring to the one in Treepoint. She also gives Lily coats to give to the elderly women who come to the church store needing them. Killyama told Lily to tell her when she runs out of them so she'd buy some more."

The woman was beyond unbelievable. She came off as a bitch and a shrew, yet she was so tenderhearted, not wanting elderly women to miss out on Christmas or be cold. Train had been a big believer in actions speaking louder than words, and she was proving him correct.

He didn't want to change the woman; he just wanted to become a part of her world so she didn't feel the need to hide that part of herself. She had let Beth and Lily in. He hoped she would let him in, too.

When Crash called again, he said they had taken the old woman to the E.R., and then drove her down to a restaurant where they were now feeding her.

Train shook his head as he went back to work, wondering if Killyama would also take her shopping before jail.

When Jewell walked past his workstation, he asked her if dinner could be an hour later than usual. He wanted Killyama to be there, and with the detours she was making, she was going to be late.

He was getting off work when Killyama texted him to say she was coming, but she would be late. Train tucked his phone away after texting her not to eat dinner, that it had been delayed because they were getting off late.

After showering, he raced to get dressed then went downstairs to hang out with the brothers until Killyama arrived.

Lily and Beth had decorated the dining room with balloons and had set up a table where everyone could place their gifts. The table was mainly filled with liquor from the brothers, and the wrapped ones were from the women. All of the gifts would be inexpensive— free gas cards or free dinners at the local restaurants.

He was looking forward to seeing what Killyama would surprise him with. She knew it was his birthday; that was why he had made a big deal out of her being there. He had even picked out what she would wear tonight.

The leather tool roll had to have been ordered in advance for his birthday. Train wished she would have given it to him in person and let him thank her for it. It was a gift he would treasure, especially knowing it was from her.

He took a bottle of whiskey that Shade had given him off the table, carrying it to the club room. It would stop the complaining from the men about when they were going to eat.

The bottle was empty and Train was about to go get another one when Killyama walked through the door with a plain brown bag in her hand.

"I see a couple of grey hairs I didn't see last night. You must be getting old." she teased, giving him the bag.

"Let me know when you see five. I'll get Sex Piston to dye my hair." Train pulled out a cheap bottle of whiskey from the bag she had given him.

"I figured I didn't need to splurge for the expensive stuff when you're just going to share it with the brothers." She lifted her brow at the bottle he had just packed from the dining room.

Train shrugged. "It all tastes the same to me. Shade's the one who likes the expensive brands." It was true. He would end up drinking the cheaper whiskey and let the brothers enjoy the one Shade had gifted him.

"I'll have to remember that when it's his birthday. What's for dinner? I'm starving."

Train set the whiskey bottles on the bar then pulled her close. The club was empty except for them.

"Not until you give me my birthday kiss."

She had taken off the bandana since her scars had healed. Tonight she wore a silver necklace with a sunburst pendant that covered what was left of the thin line. The silver halter made of a mesh and her black flowy pants gave an elegant appearance until you looked closer and realized the top revealed every curve of her breasts. If he wasn't a gentleman, he would swear he could see her nipples. He had to raise his eyes to hers, afraid he would go blind if he stared too long.

"I gave you a birthday kiss this morning in the shower." She tried to sneak past him into the kitchen, but Train blocked the doorway.

"You gave me a blowjob; that doesn't count."

"I wish I knew that before I gave it. That would have saved me a lot of trouble."

"You consider giving me a blowjob trouble?"

"Dude, I was sound asleep at six when you woke me up to shower with you. Meaning I was half-asleep and the water was cold; what do you think?"

Train frowned. "Then why didn't you say something?"

"Duh…" Killyama tapped a finger to his forehead. "Birthday boy, remember?"

Train's frown vanished, a smile tugging at his lips. "Okay, I'll let you give me a kiss later."

She stopped him before he could go through the kitchen door. Putting her hands on his cheeks, she gave him an inviting kiss that had him wanting to miss dinner.

"How hungry are you? We could get something later."

She struggled out of his arms. "That's why I didn't want to kiss you—you have a one-track mind."

"Believe me; I have two or three things on mind right now."

"As long as it doesn't involve Rider, I'm game," she taunted, pushing the kitchen door open.

Train let her escape. She was going to need her strength for what he had planned for tonight.

They made their plates in the kitchen where Stori and Jewell had set a dinner buffet. Then they carried them into the dining room.

Train sat at the end of the table where Lily told him to sit, and Killyama sat down next to him with Lily and Shade sitting on his other side. Beth and Razer were on Killyama's other side. The two women started talking immediately to her while Train ate, watching her reaction to them.

She asked who they had suckered into babysitting for them, and they laughingly said Bliss, Darcy, and Drake. Then she sat quietly as she ate, listening as they recounted how excited the boys were that they were going to eat out at the diner.

The longer Train listened, the more he understood it was deeply engrained in her personality to not draw notice to herself. She would respond to them when they talked to her, but she never said anything that would turn the conversation toward her. When he thought about it, he realized she would make a cutting comment or insult someone only if she wanted to be noticed.

In some point in her life, she had to have been taught how to be a shadow of herself. The times she couldn't handle being invisible, she struck out. Train didn't think it was her mother, or Hammer and Jonas. They had been the ones who had taught her to strike back. That left only one person. The man Killyama refused to name: her father.

CHAPTER TWENTY-NINE

Killyama stared at the plate of food, cutting a piece of the delicious pork chop surrounded by potatoes and cheese. She would have to ask Beth for the recipe. Hammer and Jonas loved meat and potato dishes.

She finished her plate, refusing Train's offer to get her seconds.

"I'll have to go to the gym tomorrow to work off what I've already eaten."

"You can eat another plate. I plan to work it off you tonight."

"You eat another plate as big as the one you just ate, you won't be able to walk up those steps, much less fuck me when you get there."

She rolled her eyes at Lily's and Beth's flushed faces. Bitches acted like they had on chastity belts under their dresses.

Shade and Razer trailed after Train to refill their plates.

"They eat any more of that casserole, I won't be the only one not getting laid tonight." She stared down at the women's only partially eaten dinner. Neither of them had put the best part of the dinner on their plates. "Are you two sick or something? You didn't eat much. You should have tried that casserole..."

Beth cut her green beans into tiny dots. "We've eaten it before."

"It's a little heavy on my stomach," Lily explained.

"Mine, too. Thank God I didn't wear my leather pants tonight. The ones I'm wearing have elastic. I saved room for the cake Willa made for Train. Before I forget, can you text me that recipe for the casserole? Hammer and Jonas will eat that shit up..."

A light finally went on over her head when she saw the secretive look the two sisters shared.

"If you don't—"

"That's not it," Beth hastened to stop her.

"Then what is it?" She narrowed her eyes at them.

"It's the men's favorite dish, especially Train's."

"Which bitch makes it? Or do all the women make it for them?"

"Stori, and don't bother asking her for the recipe. She won't give it out. I even tried to make it several times from recipes I found on the web. Razer says it's good, but even I can tell it doesn't taste the same."

"I wouldn't worry about it. Saves you from making dinner when she cooks it." She gave them a speculative look. "It doesn't look like it bothers you when Razer and Shade scarf down that candy Willa makes."

"Stori isn't Willa. And Willa gave us her recipe. She even helped us make it the first couple of times."

She stared at the women, shocked. Beth and Lily weren't like her. They were nice. She could even see Rachel, who was sitting further down, was agreeing with them.

"I thought you would be mad about it, too. Train usually drools over her when she makes it for him."

Killyama shrugged. "I don't worry about what other women put on a plate to give my man. It's under the covers I worry about. You bitches are just being sensitive."

"I told Beth that." Lily avoided Beth's glare.

"Then why don't you go get some, then?" Beth challenged.

"I'm full."

The women started talking about the church store when the men came back. Killyama noticed that Train had filled another plate with an even bigger helping of the casserole. She then saw Beth, Lily, and Rachel look at their men's full plates when they sat down.

She saw Stori take a seat at the other end of the table, talking animatedly with Viper. Winter, who was sitting next to him, didn't seem any happier than the other women at the table.

"I'll be right back. That looks too good to resist," she told Train as she got up.

He grinned up at her. "I told you. You'll be lucky if there is any left."

"Then I'll swipe some of yours," she said as she made her way into the kitchen.

He was right; there wasn't any left. Dishing the spoonful that was left, she went back to the dining room, stopping by Stori's chair.

The woman glanced up and saw her standing by her side.

"You make the casserole?"

Stori's fork paused by her mouth as she nodded.

"It's delicioso."

She lowered her fork to her plate. "What…? Thank you?"

"Train is teaching me French. I thought I'd throw that word out there. That casserole is *so* good it deserves the effort."

Stori beamed. "Thank you. Next time I make it, I'll make sure to save you some extra for later, like I do for Train. But, I think delicioso is Spanish."

"Whatever." Killyama shrugged. "It's still good. Do me a favor, text me that recipe. Sex Piston and Stud will love it. I'm going to call her tonight so she can get the ingredients."

"Uh…I don't…" She stopped, fear flashing across her face as Killyama's shrewd gaze captured hers. "I can do that," she finally said with a nod.

"Thanks. You have your phone handy? I'll give you my number."

"Sure."

Killyama left the defeated bitch after rattling off her number with a last parting shot. "And don't forget any ingredients.

Sex Piston gets pissed when a recipe doesn't come out the way she expects it to."

Train shook his head at the minuscule portion on her plate when she sat back down. "I told you there wasn't much left. Shade always eats as much as I do."

Lily stood jerkily to her feet. "Are you ready to cut your cake?"

"I've been ready." Train patted his flat belly.

Killyama watched him get up and move to stand by the cake where Willa was waiting. She laughed with the others at the table at the raucous birthday song Viper had started as Train cut into the first slice. Then he let Willa and Lily serve the others.

The loud cheers and claps slowed as Train started opening his presents one at a time, thanking the brothers for the liquor.

The gifts were a mixture of useful, off-the-wall items meant for enjoyment. Jewell had given him new motorcycle gloves, Lily had given him a gift certificate to the diner, and Evie and King had gotten him a gift certificate for a steak dinner.

"I hope those certificates are for two," Killyama joked to Beth.

Viper had gotten him a card he had printed off the computer for a week off anytime he wanted it. Beth and Razer had gotten him a mini beer pong set. Rachel and Cash had gifted him a fishing knife. And Knox and Diamond had given him a police scanner. She enjoyed watching Train open his gifts. After opening each one, he would thank each brother with a man hug, and a kiss on the cheek for the women.

He then opened the last one, a present that had been obscured from view by cake.

Reading Stori's name aloud from the small card that was attached to the present, he tore it open. His face said it all. He liked it a lot.

He raised it up so the room could see the silver skull and crossbones belt buckle. The upper teeth were set on top of the metal of the buckle, with the lower jaw missing. From each side of the skull was a metal bone that had engraved words that together said *The Last Riders*.

Train took off his belt and put it on, and then wrapped the belt around his lean waist again.

The men stared at it enviously. Rider and Razer were both asking Stori where she had bought it from.

"You like it?" Stori got out of her chair as Train approached her.

"I love it. Thank you." He lifted her off her feet, giving her a bear hug.

Killyama watched as several women glanced her way while she thanked Lily for giving her a slice of cake, eating it without concern.

Train came back to where she was sitting, carrying the large slice he had cut himself. The men sitting around them complimented him on his gifts.

"You gonna share that steak dinner with me? I don't have anything to do tomorrow night," Moon shouted out from beside Winter.

"Depends on when Killyama wants to go." Train winked, eating his cake.

"She going to share that massage Sasha promised you when she comes over next week—" Crash howled when Willa slammed his piece of cake down onto his hand.

"No, I gave that to Rider."

"Why not me? I'm the one who...Fuck, that hurt. Willa, you could have just handed me the damn fork."

"Brother, it might be safer for you to eat your cake in the kitchen."

Killyama couldn't see Lucky, but his stoic threat had Crash leaving the table with his dessert.

Crash's comment hadn't upset her. She was used to men teasing each other. She didn't expect Train to watch every comment he made around her.

"You better insure that belt buckle. Some of the brothers look like they are eyeing it."

Train tilted his head to the side, studying her. "The brothers always ask before they borrow anything."

"You lend anyone that belt buckle, you won't get it back."

Train took a bite of his cake. The intensity of how he was watching her made her curious.

"It doesn't bother you that Stori gave it to me?" he finally asked.

"The only thing I'm jealous about is how much better that belt buckle would look on me," she answered candidly.

No matter how good or expensive a present was, it wouldn't make a person care about the person giving it. A big diamond might get you a piece of tail, but when a woman walked out the door, she was taking the ring and leaving the husband behind. That was why she couldn't understand why the women were upset over the men complimenting Stori on her dish. A woman could prepare a four course meal, and their man would still slip a donut when she wasn't looking. If she was going to get jealous over her man, it was going to be because of something big, like Train finding happiness with the massage Sasha had offered.

"You want me to help you carry some shit upstairs?" she asked as they placed their plates in the kitchen sink.

"Can I trust you?" he teased as he went toward the dining room where the cake was all but demolished with only a fourth left, which Willa was carving into smaller pieces.

"Of course. I mean, you're wearing the one I want." She picked up the six-pack cooler and the beer pong set, careful not to break the shot glasses that had titties stenciled on them. What the man didn't know wouldn't hurt him. She was just as envious of some of his gifts as the brothers were.

In his bedroom, he had to search for a place to set his gifts down. She found a spot for the beer pong on a wall shelf.

"Where do you want me to put this?"

Train set most of his things on his desk before reaching out to take the cozy cooler from her. She curled a finger through the opening, refusing to give it up.

"Did I ever tell you I hate to drink hot beer?"

Train laughed, leaning his hip against his desk. "No, you haven't."

"Well, I do. And Crazy Bitch always brings a six-pack of beer when she makes me cruise around with her and T.A."

Train's smile slipped. "Where do you cruise?"

"Around Jamestown…after the high school has a basketball game."

"Do you ever stop when they want you to pull over?"

"Fuck no. We just like to piss off the high school girls."

Train released the beer cozy. "I can share. I'll use it for when I go fishing or hunting, and you can have it until basketball season is over."

"That works for me. I'll take it home with me. You don't have enough space in your room to keep it, anyway. Let me know when you need it, and I'll let you borrow it."

She slipped off her high heels, and then slipped her pants down her legs, showing him the birthday thong she had bought for him. Leaving the top on he had asked her to wear, she stepped between his leg, bringing her hands to his belt buckle.

"You need some help getting out of those jeans?"

He stopped her from unbuckling his belt. "Depends. Are we going to have a custody dispute over my belt buckle?"

She suggestively dropped to her knees. "No, I'm going to let you keep it." She started to slowly remove the belt. "It says The Last Riders, not the Destructors." Once his jeans were open, she licked a path from the blue jean snap down to where the zipper began. "You taste like birthday cake."

Train ran his fingers through her hair, using it to tilt her head back. "I love you."

She burrowed her face into his thigh, despite his restraining hand, not looking up. "You're on a sugar high."

"The only high I'm on tonight is you."

"Lover, I'm trying to give you the best birthday blowjob you've ever had. Don't ruin it."

"No blowjob is going to beat the present I got earlier today." His husky voice had her lifting her head.

"What was it? A pillowcase with a pair of tits stenciled on it?"

"Do they make those?"

"Lover, you can make anything, if you want it bad enough. If it wasn't that, what was it?"

"Someone sent me a bike roll of tools."

"Who gave it to you?" She reached into the front of his jeans to pull out his cock.

"I don't know. I like it almost as much as the wallet someone sent me a few months ago."

She flicked her tongue over the head of his cock. "The one with the long chain?"

"Yes…" Train groaned, not taking his eyes off her. "I thought maybe you sent them."

She shook her head as she rubbed her lips over him, blowing on the spot after she had licked him, which caused Train to straighten, his hip jutting forward as his hands went behind his back to lean against the desk.

"You think I have a diamond mine in my thong? I didn't send them. I don't give presents like that. They cost too much," she added.

Presents like that were like giving a part of your soul to the one receiving it.

"Are we done jabbering?" She looked up at him. "I want to end your birthday with a bang."

CHAPTER THIRTY

Train opened his blurry eyes, barely dodging the swinging kitchen door he had just pushed open.

"Have you seen…?" He cut himself off, his grouchy mood mildly improving.

Going to the coffee pot, he poured himself a cup of coffee before sitting down next to Killyama at the kitchen table.

"Why didn't you wake me up? I could have eaten with you."

She finished a bite of her toast before she answered him. "I was going to bring you a plate in bed."

His sour disposition vanished in a second. "Damn, I wish I had known."

"Sorry about your luck. You want me to make you a plate?" She didn't look anxious to get up, buttering another piece of toast.

"No, I'll do it. Thanks, anyway."

"No problem." She shrugged, eating her toast.

Train was fixing himself a plate when he realized they were alone.

"Who cooked breakfast?"

"Dude, do you see anyone here but me and you?" Indignant, she got up to pour herself another glass of orange juice.

He shook his head. "No, I'm just surprised."

"Why, that I cook or that I beat the other bitches out of bed?"

"Both, I suppose. You even made pancakes." He placed a stack on his plate, smothering it in butter and syrup. "If I didn't know better, I'd think it was still my birthday."

"Hell no. I don't have time for another present. I'm meeting T.A. in an hour."

Train sat down to dig into his pancakes. He wished he had taken the time to heat up the syrup, then they would have been perfect.

Train cut off another bite of his pancakes. "You could borrow a T-shirt from me. Or, if you had woken me up, I could have borrowed some clothes for you to wear."

"Why wake anyone else up? Doesn't my outfit look as good this morning as it did last night?"

"Yes, but it must have been hard to cook in it," he tried explaining.

Her acerbic reply had him wishing he had just kept his mouth shut.

"A woman always suffers when she tries to do something nice for her man and he doesn't appreciate it."

He stopped talking, giving his food all of his attention.

Rider came in, giving him a reprieve from Killyama who was watching him eat every bite as she leaned lazily against the counter with her arms crossed in front of her.

"What's for breakfast?" Rider asked, staring curiously down at his plate, missing the tension between the two of them.

"Pancakes and bacon," Killyama told him. "Sit down, and I'll make you a plate."

Train eyed Rider over his bite of pancakes. He had sat down and was happily watching Killyama make him a plate. Frowning, he saw her microwave the syrup before pouring it over his large stack.

"There you go. You want coffee or juice?" Her sweet voice had Train's hair rising on the back of his neck.

"Both. I'll—"

She put a hand on Rider's shoulder. "You go ahead and eat while it's still hot."

Train chewed off a piece of his crispy bacon, seeing Rider's gloating expression. The brother was knocking on Heaven's door, and Train was going to answer it if Rider wasn't careful.

Killyama went behind the counter to load the dishes with the pans she used to make breakfast as the kitchen gradually filled and the members piled up their plates.

Viper, Shade, and Cash sat down at the table with him, while the rest of the members went to the dining room to find a seat.

The men ate as their wives were drawn into a conversation with Killyama while making their plates. When they didn't come to the table where the men had saved them a seat, the men tried to eavesdrop on their conversation, but their low discussion was hard to hear.

"Rider, go see what they're talking about?" Viper encouraged, staring at Winter, who held Aisha, not making any attempt to join him.

"I'm eating. Make Train. It's his fault Killyama is here and they're listening to her."

Train started to get up, but then sat back down at Viper's glare and Killyama asking him if he wanted anything.

"I was going to get another cup of coffee."

"I'll get that for you," Lily offered.

The men's table went silent as Lily refilled his cup, bringing it to him and then hurrying back to where the women were talking.

"Why didn't you ask Lily what they're talking about?" Train whispered out of the corner of his mouth to Shade.

"Because I'm clearly the only one at this table who has a dick, and I'm not worried about what they're talking about."

When Killyama said something to Rachel and Winter that had them arguing, Lily hushed them. Four pairs of eyes turned to the table where they were sitting before resuming what they were talking about with lowered voices.

"This is bad." Cash was the closest to the counter, but his back was turned to it. He leaned back in his chair until it only had two legs on the floor, trying to overhear the conversation.

"Can you hear anything?"

"I thought you weren't worried?" Train asked Shade.

"I'm not. I'm just curious."

"Then walk your curious ass behind the kitchen counter and see what they're talking about," Viper snapped.

Rider started to get up. "Jesus, I'll do it."

"You need anything, Rider?" Killyama asked irritably.

"Uh…Is there any bacon left?"

"No, it's all gone."

"Never mind, then."

Train and the rest of the men at the table blasted Rider with a look, causing him to hide behind his coffee cup.

"Killyama, I thought you were supposed to meet T.A.?"

Train didn't know which brother kicked him under the table, but it hurt like a motherfucker.

"She texted to tell me she's running late. Finish your breakfast."

Killyama's sharp response had him scooting his chair backward from the table, out of range from another kick.

"Yes, ma'am." Train found it hard to choke down his late bite.

"I'll give you another ten percent of the company if you break up with her. I'll even let you pick which woman you want here. You like Dawn? She hasn't been here in a while." Viper's cajoling voice dropped to a whisper as the women finally started toward their husband's sides.

"I'll give you my truck. I know how much you want it." Cash barely managed to stop from falling backward as Rachel moved by him to take a seat.

Train nearly jumped out of his chair when Killyama placed a hand on his shoulder.

"I have to go."

He was conscious of the brothers listening to every word.

"I get off at four. Am I going to see you tonight?"

Viper's and Cash's scowls had him wishing he had texted her that question after she left.

"Nope. T.A., Crazy Bitch, and I are spending the night in Berea, Ohio. We have tickets for the first two days of the Cleveland Brown's training camp. A few of the players are looking forward to seeing us again. They're going to introduce us to some of the rookies. One of the players offered to pay for our hotel room tonight. It might be a couple of days before I see you again. We won't back for three days. Could be longer if we can score another ticket for the third day of training."

Train frowned.

When she started to move away, he caught her hand. "Aren't you going to give me a kiss before you leave?"

Laughing, she patted him on the back. "You're so cute when you're being silly."

She started toward the swinging door before changing her mind and going to the counter. All of the men's eyes watched her as Killyama picked up a brightly colored pink box, and then went to the refrigerator to take out a plastic container, stacking it on the pink box. Closing the fridge with her hip, she then opened a drawer, pulling out his six-pack beer cozy, dangling it from her pinky.

"I almost forgot my stuff," she said, beaming proudly that she hadn't forgotten her pilfered items.

"Is that the rest of my birthday cake and the pork chop casserole Stori saved me for lunch?" He didn't mention the cozy, knowing he would never see it again.

"Yes, you have a problem with that?" Glaring at him, she stopped by his chair.

"No." If he hadn't felt the heavy metal of the skull and crossbones buckle on his belt, he would have been tempted to make sure it was still there.

"Good. I volunteered to bring a snack for the road trip. This will be enough for the three of us. If Sex Piston and Fat Louise were going, we'd have had to make a pit stop."

"Why aren't they going?" Thankfully, it was Lily who asked the question he was too afraid to voice.

"It's only the single ladies today." Her cell phone started shouting, "*Answer the phone.*" "Gotta go. You all have a great day. Have some fun! You all look like a bunch of sour pusses in the morning. Too much partying will make you old before your time."

Killyama left without telling him good-bye, her phone now shouting obscenities from the club room.

The silence around the kitchen was so loud it could be cut with the butter knife Shade was holding.

"Brother, I'll give you the pick of my motorcycles," Rider offered.

Train thought over Rider's vast collection. Collectors had hounded him to sell two of the them. He might have just received an offer too good to refuse.

Ignoring Rider's offer, he met Shade's eyes. The man knew what he wanted. Hell, it was what all the men wanted. And it didn't take Shade long to get Lily to confess that Killyama had told Rachel and Winter they needed to find new replacements for their husbands; saying, if Train couldn't handle Killyama, he didn't have a shot in hell in taking care of three women if anything went wrong.

"Who did she suggest?" Viper questioned Lily so aggressively that Shade placed an arm over her shoulder.

Lily paled, trying to roll her eyes toward Rachel and Winter to answer for her. When they remained curiously mute, Lily answered for them.

"Moon."

"Why Moon? She didn't mention me?" Rider's fork dropped to his plate.

"She said the whole idea of having replacements was to have a man who could help you in need, not to be saddled with or one who would need caring for."

"Did she happen to mention who she wanted? Because, Train, as much I consider you a brother, I—"

"She doesn't want you, Cash. She wants Shade. Killyama asked if it was okay with me," Lily told them.

Shade's emotionless façade nearly broke when Lily continued.

"She said, if she had to see anyone naked, she could deal with it being Shade because she wanted to know if your...if you..."

"I know what she wants to know," Shade answered grimly. "Brother..."

"I already know." None of the brothers would step up to fill his shoes if something happened to him. The way it was going, she wasn't even going to swing enough votes to become a Last Rider.

⊗⊘ ⊗

By the time he was seated at his workstation, he was tired and cranky, and he had a splitting headache that was turning into a migraine. He was furious at Killyama for her behavior.

He had only been working for thirty minutes before Crash called him.

"Where is she?" Train knew she wasn't heading to the Brown's training camp, but he wanted to give her the benefit of the doubt.

"She's heading toward Knoxville with Hammer and Jonas. I'll call you when I know more."

Train texted Jewell, telling her he was going to take the day off. He needed some sleep if he was going to tail Killyama for a couple of days, which was why she had lied to him about being gone for three days. That meant the fugitive she was tracking was one they anticipated being difficult to find. Train would meet up with Crash and send him back to Treepoint.

The next time she stayed the night at the club, he was going to sneak into her phone and put a tracer on it. It would save him and Crash a lot of effort.

When Jewell gave him the okay, he went to his room, getting the much needed sleep he needed, knowing it was going to be a while before he would be able to again.

೮ ೪

It was almost midnight when he pulled into the Waffle Stop across from the hotel Killyama, Hammer, and Jonas were staying in.

Train sat down in a booth facing the hotel. Ordering a black coffee, he gave Crash his attention.

"They're tracking a fugitive who broke parole."

"What's he on parole for?"

"He beat up his baby's mama. They already checked out the family in the area. The baby's mama has gone into hiding. She's got a restraining on Cooper—the fugitive—saying he threatened to hurt her and the baby when he was sent to prison." He gestured toward the hotel. "They settled down for the night about an hour ago."

"Who's sleeping where?"

"They're sharing the same room. You want me to stay?"

"No, go on home. I'll see you in a couple of days."

"Where'd you get the wheels?"

"It's Moon's. Sasha drove it down for me."

"Sasha's at the club?"

"Ready and waiting." Train slid Crash's check next to his own. "Drive safe, and thanks."

"Let me know if you need a break. I can come back."

"If it takes longer than two days, I might have to. Someone told me I'm getting too old to burn both ends of the candle, and I'm feeling it tonight."

"If she was my old lady, she wouldn't be running around, chasing felons."

"If Killyama was your woman, you'd be dead."

Crash shook his head, leaving.

The waitress approached him for refills several times, each time making a beeline toward the cook tending the grill who kept eyeing him suspiciously. At four o'clock, two cops came in, doing the same thing. Train saw them running the license plate on Moon's car when they left with their coffee.

He went to his car at five, expecting Hammer would want to get back on the hunt with the sun. Plus, he needed to hide out in case they stopped at the Waffle Stop for breakfast.

He was glad he had moved the car when Killyama, Hammer, and Jonas came out of the hotel. The three looked wide awake, talking as they made their way inside the Waffle Stop, staying inside only thirty minutes before they were on the road again.

Train spent the day following them, holding back so they wouldn't see him.

It was getting dark when Hammer and Jonas went inside a burger joint and left Killyama outside. A few minutes later, Train felt his phone vibrate with a text message. He took his phone out to see Killyama had texted him.

He was glad she couldn't hear him laugh as he stared at the picture she had sent him. It was of three football players, holding their helmets as they talked to whoever was on the other side of the camera.

The first message read: *Missing you.* Underneath, another one read: *Not.*

Train texted Jewell to send him the picture he wanted. When she sent it back, he sent the picture to Killyama. Sitting back, he waited for the fireworks to start.

Who took that picture of you?

I did. It's a selfie, he replied.

Selfie, my titty.

Train waited a second to see if she was going to say anything else. She did.

You have a selfie of Shade like that?

He wondered what she would do if pulled up to that Escalade and paddled her ass.

Why don't you find out when come over tonight? If you don't have tickets for tomorrow, come on back now. I can meet you at your apartment. I miss you.

Sorry, lover. One of the players gave us tickets for tomorrow. Guess you're just going to keep missing me.

Just one time he wished she would give him a small sign that she cared about him. Just one that she didn't hide behind pretenses or insults.

Train didn't respond and was about to shove his phone back into his pocket when she got out of the Escalade. When he saw her face, he could see that she knew he had been mad at her texts. With no one around, she had let her guard down.

An aching loneliness filled her expression, and his hand went to the door handle. He had suspected the deep emotions she held for him, but he had never witnessed them before. Now he was.

She bleakly watched a small family walk past her. The father carried a little girl in his arms while the mother carried an infant. It hit Train that she believed she would never have what that family had.

Train couldn't understand why Killyama believed she couldn't have her own like that. She had even told him she didn't want to have kids.

He wanted to hold her close and ask the questions that were going to drive them apart if she didn't learn to trust him with her answers.

Pulling his cell phone back out of his pocket, he texted her before she could go inside the restaurant.

Have fun. Text me when you get back, and we'll meet up. Love you.

Her smiling face was worth the cut to his pride. The smiley face she texted back was as good as it was going to get for now.

Train ducked into a convenience store to use the restroom and grab himself a snack. He had just resettled back in the car when Killyama, Hammer, and Jonas came running outside the restaurant. When Hammer pulled out with wheels screeching, he knew they must have received a hot tip.

He had already been listening to the police scanner as he waited for them, so when the alert came from his phone and the scanner, his blood ran cold.

There had been an alert issued for a two-year-old boy. The child had been taken by his non-custodial father who was wanted for a parole violation. Train knew it was the same man Killyama was searching for when Cooper's name verified by the dispatcher.

Train cussed, almost hitting a blue truck that had pulled out of a shopping lot. It blocked him from keeping a clear view of Hammer's vehicle. Then, when the truck stopped at a yellow light, Train lost sight of them, still stopped at the red light behind the truck while Hammer had sped up.

Train nearly rear-ended the truck. Slamming his hand down on the steering wheel, he backed up then swerved to the right into the turning lane. Gunning Moon's motor, he shot out into the traffic, dodging cars until he saw a turn he could make that led into a drug store.

He shot through oncoming traffic, did a U-turn to make a left, and then another right onto the street he had lost Hammer. Passing cars at a speed that would have gotten him a ticket if the cops hadn't been searching for the little boy, Train gave a sigh of relief when he saw Hammer's SUV turn down a side street. He made the turn three cars behind them.

The streets became tree-lined as they moved farther into a residential neighborhood. He was about to follow Hammer down another street when he saw him break and park in front of a house.

Train braked, too, stopping his car. He then watched as Killyama and Jonas walked away from Hammer, who started running catty corner from them. Their bright vests were clearly visible as they walked toward a house that had a "For Sale" sign posted in the front yard.

Train jumped out of Moon's vehicle and ran to the side of the neighboring house. He climbed over a fence on the opposite side of the tree line, seeing Hammer trying to look through the side windows then disappearing behind the house.

Train brought his hand behind his back, clutching his gun handle, as Killyama knocked on the door then fiddled with the lock box on the door handle. Jonas must have called the agent, requesting to see the house.

When Killyama raised the key in her hand triumphantly, Train tensed as she put it in the lock and turned it. Killyama and Jonas then barged inside.

Train wanted to run inside when he heard yells. Then he heard a crash from the backyard, assuming Hammer had broken in through the back.

"Get your fucking hands up!" He heard Jonas's loud shout from inside.

Train was about to charge toward the house when Killyama came running out with the little boy carried protectively in her arms. At the same time, the police swarmed the neighborhood.

Seeing her holding the crying child brought a lump to his throat as he hurried back to his car, driving past the squad cars. He drove by a traffic jam as he headed back to the hotel where Killyama was staying. He knew she would be busy for the next few hours doing the paperwork on the capture. He could get some sleep before heading back to Treepoint.

He was about to check in to a room when he changed his mind after staring at his watch. Instead, he grabbed a bite to eat at the Waffle Stop then drove back to Treepoint. If he was wrong, then she would still be safe with Hammer and Jonas for the night. However, with the fugitive captured, she would more than likely go right back to Jamestown.

He was exhausted when he arrived back at the club.

Parking behind the factory, he changed the license plates before he covered the car up with a tarp. Too tired to take the steps, he walked the pathway around the club, not speaking to any of the brothers as he went upstairs, where he simply nodded at Moon as he passed him in the hall.

He didn't want to shower, but two days without one had him taking a quick one before he dried off and made his way to his bed. He thought about locking the door, but he knew no one would come in without knocking

He kicked the covers to the bottom of his bed, tossed onto his stomach, and shoved a pillow over his head to drown out the blaring music. He was glad he had invested in a good pair of black out shades; the pitch dark room would be welcoming in the morning.

He was asleep in less than a minute, naked.

Train didn't know how long he had been asleep when a gentle hand slid down his back to curve intimately over his ass. He shoved the pillow off his head, opening his mouth to snap at whichever woman had come inside his room without knocking, then froze when he felt a head drop to his shoulder.

"I missed you, too, lover." Her voice was filled with the emotion she couldn't show him in daylight.

He swung out his arm and lifted his chest so he could pull her underneath him. Silently, they made love, the loud music muffling their gasps and moans. He tried desperately to reach her the only way she would allow him to, trying to show her with his body how much he loved her. Trying to drive the words out of her he needed to hear, kissing each part of her body until she was begging for release. Giving up when he couldn't hold his own climax back any longer, he moaned his love for her in the dark room.

Wearily, he shoved the pillow under his head when she rolled over. Train expected her to scoot over more like she usually did, but she placed a thigh over his instead. He didn't touch her, though.

She lived in her own self-imposed exile, briefly leaving it when she was with her friends, her mother, or when she was having sex with him; returning to her solitary existence when someone grew too close, wanting more than she was willing to give.

Killyama used her lies as a barrier between them. He kept trying to find a way around it, but she just built it taller and wider. Train was terrified he wouldn't be able to reach her in time to keep her from enclosing herself without a chance of escape.

CHAPTER
THIRTY-ONE

"What are you lazy fuckers sitting around for?" Killyama stomped up her mother's porch where Hammer and Jonas were waiting. "You were supposed to pick me up an hour ago. We're wasting time. We should be halfway to Knoxville by now." Seeing the men's steely gazes staring back at her, her tone went from criticizing to concern. "Is something wrong with Mama? Is that why you texted me to meet you here?" She started to run inside the trailer.

"Peyton's fine." Jonas's words stopped her in her tracks. "We need to talk."

"Where's Mama?"

"She's making us lunch."

Killyama stared at Jonas's poignant face, while Hammer turned toward the road, so she couldn't see his. For a badass, she could read him like a book.

She braced herself. If neither of them wanted to be the one tell her, whatever it was had to be bad.

"Just spit it out. If it has something to do with Mama—"

"It's not about Peyton; it's about The Last Riders."

She shook her head. "I don't want to hear it." She took a step down from the porch. "I don't care what Train's done. I don't even give a fuck who he killed. And if The Last Riders have done something criminal, I don't even care—"

"Rae, listen to me." Jonas put his hands on her shoulders.

"I don't want to. Please, Jonas."

"They bugged your phone."

She tried to shrug out of Jonas's grip. "Train's just worried about me. We knew he was watching when we went on a hunt."

"It's more than that, Rae. Listen to me—"

"No! I can't, Jonas. I can't lose him…" It was the closest she had ever come to cry in front of them since she had been a child.

"Leave her alone, Jonas. We can deal with this ourselves."

It took Hammer's gruff statement to show how bad it really was.

She wanted to sink down on the steps to lessen the impact of what they were about to reveal. Instead, she turned to face them. Jonas was the one who always tried to shield her, Hammer would get angry at him, and tell them that what she didn't know could get her killed. That was why he had put hours of work developing her skills.

"Tell me."

"I need my computer. I left it in the Escalade."

As they walked the distance to the vehicle, no one said a word. It made Killyama feel like she was being led to her execution.

Hammer held the back door open for her. "I meant what I said, Jonas and I have this."

Killyama rested her hand on the door, pausing. "Can you or Jonas get hurt if I don't help?"

"Yes."

"Then there's your answer." She jumped inside Hammer's SUV, hearing the door close behind her.

What her and Train had going these last few months would have ended sooner or later. Jonas and Hammer had always been the ones who had been there when she needed them. Her friends were like sisters to her, but she looked over them more than they did her. Even her mama had lost herself for a few years until she could find her way back to her. Jonas and Hammer hadn't, not ever. They were a team, and a team stuck together, even though one's heart was about to break.

Jonas and Hammer got in the front seat, setting the laptop on top of the console so she could watch the video.

"Ready?" Jonas's silver eyes met hers.

"Shut up and press play."

֍ ֍

"What are you doing tonight?"

Train tossed his soda can into the trash. He hated Curt Dawkins, who was staring at him as he sucked smoke into his lungs that wouldn't be working for him much longer. If the cigarettes didn't kill him, The Last Riders would.

"Rider, Moon, and I are going to grab a beer at Rosie's after work. Wanna go?" Curt continued after he took another draw, pulling his jeans up that had slipped down with every puff he took. Train didn't know why the disgusting shit made the effort. His beer gut would just have it slipping down again.

"No, thanks. I'm busy. I need to get back to work. I don't want Jewell docking my pay if I don't clock back in after break."

"She doesn't dock me. She always tells me to take my time."

Probably because she enjoys having you out of sight, Train thought.

None of The Last Riders could stand the braggart, but Jewell, as the factory's manager, had to deal with him the most. The club kept hoping he would slip up and say something to one of the brothers, or he would really fuck up and make a play for Jewell. He hadn't, and the club was getting tired of tolerating him.

Shade just wanted to kill him and be done with it, but Viper wouldn't give the go-ahead because Curt had family in town. If he went missing, it would draw suspicion toward The Last Riders, and without proof, he wasn't willing to take that risk. Therefore, until

Viper had proof that Curt had been raping women in town, something they had been told had been happening for years, they had to let the fucker keep breathing.

"Who's the wallbanger? You guys need to hook me up in becoming a Last Rider if you're getting that piece of ass."

Train turned to see who Curt was staring at with his tongue practically hanging out of his mouth. Killyama was walking toward the front of the factory.

Train took a step forward so she would see him, giving a whistle. Stopping, she swerved and walked toward him.

He almost chuckled when he saw the anger glinting in her eyes as she drew closer.

"You see a leash on my neck?"

"I was trying to save you a trip inside," Train explained, noticing Curt was putting out his cigarette with his work boot.

"Next time, just yell," she snapped.

"I'll do that. What—"

"Are you going to introduce me or what?"

The way she was staring at Curt made his flesh crawl. Stiffening, he made the introductions, deliberately giving Killyama's nickname as an introduction.

Curt's eyes widened, taking in her T-shirt that read "Try This" in bright red letters, her blue shorts, and her tan ankle boots that had a strap crisscrossing the front to tie at the back with fringes dangling down.

"It's nice to meet you. You here to place an order? I can help—"

"She's here to see me," Train cut Curt off, shifting away from the door to move beside Killyama.

"You work here?" Ignoring Train, she didn't take her eyes off Curt.

"Yeah, I can take care of anything you need," Curt insinuated, puffing his chest out at her interest.

Train was ready to blow all efforts The Last Riders had done in the months since Curt had been hired, wanting to plant his fist in the man's smirking face.

"Then don't you think you should get your ass back to work? I'm sure The Last Riders don't pay you to shoot the shit with me."

Curt's face turned ruddy red as he jerked the back door open.

"Dude, I'd lay off the beers, or buy a bigger pair of pants." Killyama couldn't help adding an insult to the injury she had done to his pride.

Train slung an arm over her shoulders despite her trying to wiggle away from him. "You just made my fucking day."

She tried to hide her smile as she used her hands to try to push away from him. "Lover, that dick doesn't have enough socks to shove down his jeans to make me give him the time of day."

"I was getting worried," Train admitted.

"You were jealous of that wiener? *Please...*"

"So, what are you doing here? Why didn't you tell me you were coming?"

"I thought I'd make your fucking day." She looked around the parking lot to make sure no one was watching. Then she brought her hands to his belt buckle to pull him closer, planting a kiss on his lips before taking a step back.

Train licked his bottom lip, still wanting to taste her after the brief kiss was over.

"Is it my birthday again and no one told me?"

"Not yet, but you never know. How much longer before you get off?"

"Not for a few hours. I told Jewell she could take off when I came back from break." He had made the offer when Jewell had complained about wanting to go shopping. He was trying to make up the time he had spent chasing after Killyama.

"I'll call Beth or Lily and see what they're up to."

"Why not just hang out with me?"

"You won't get in trouble?"

"No, I won't get in trouble." Train stared at her poker face. "You know that I'm part owner of the factory, right? I might get in trouble for not putting my time in, but I won't for letting you keep me company."

"How should I know—"

"Jonas is good. As good as Crash. I'm sure you had me checked out, even though Hammer and Jonas know me from serving with me."

"Crash does a sucky job. I wouldn't bet the bank on what he knows." Her blithe answer had Train shaking his head.

"I didn't need Crash to tell me you had checked me out. You never asked me about what happened to my father when I told you he killed my family."

"I didn't have to ask because I know what I would have done."

"Then you're smarter than the detectives who have been trying to make a case against me for years."

"Smart enough to know that they don't have a chance of ever pinning his murder on you. What would you have done if he hadn't escaped the psych ward they were evaluating him in?"

"We'll never know now, will we?"

"Guess not. So, are we going to stop chit chatting so you can earn more moola? I need a new pair of shoes."

Train opened the door for her. "I think you have enough shoes. I haven't seen the same pair on you since I've known you."

She rolled her eyes heavenward. "You don't live with all these bitches and not know better than that. A woman never has enough shoes."

"Just admit you have a shoe fetish," Train joked, not missing the workers watching them as they walked through the factory.

"If you're keeping track of my shoes, I'm not the one with the shoe fetish."

Train pulled up another stool so she could sit next to him, and once she sat down, she used the heel of her boot to swivel the stool to stare at the work being done around her.

Train sat down, picking up the order he had planned to fill when he came off break.

"So, what do we have to do?"

Train took his attention off the order form to gaze at her interested eyes. "You're going to help?"

"Why not? I don't have anything better to do. The shop is closed today. Sex Piston is home with Rocky and Star—they have a virus. Fat Louise and T.A. are at work. And Crazy Bitch is using the day to clean her apartment."

"You didn't volunteer to help Crazy Bitch?"

"Hell no. Some of the brothers came over last night. They trashed the place, so she made a couple of them stay to clean up the mess."

"Her loss is my gain. You want to work, I have plenty to keep you busy."

Train decided it would be easier for him to fill the orders and for her to box the items for shipping. He searched for a smaller order that needed to be filled, and then found the items required. After showing her how to package them, he started filling another order.

She was quick. Killyama was already done before he could return to his station, setting a toilet kit on top of the table.

"How in the fuck am I supposed to pack that?"

Going to the wall in front of his deck, he slid out a large flat box, showing her how to use the heavy tape on the box flaps to close the bottom.

"Got it." She placed the toilet kit inside.

"We use popcorn so it won't slide around in the box."

"Popcorn?"

"I'll show you." He lifted the box, carrying it to a machine that sat a few inches away from his station. Setting the box under the machine, he pressed the button that would let synthetic popcorn fill the box.

"That's cool."

"Let's see how cool you think it is after you've done thousands of packages."

"I'll pass on that. Next time Rocky or Star are blowing chunks, I might give Sex Piston a day off."

He saw Jewell walking out of the office and told Killyama, "I'll be right back."

By the time he was done listening to what Jewell needed done and switched the office calls to his desk, he found Killyama had completed three orders and was waiting for him to check them before she closed the boxes.

"You're quick. You ever want to quit hunting fugitives, I'll hire you."

"The Last Riders would fire you if that happened."

Train sat down next to her. "No, they wouldn't. They would give me a raise."

"Dude, you steal some of Rider's bullshit cologne? I know they can't stand me."

"No, babe, they can," Train insisted.

"Ember looks like she needs your help." He felt the hurt she was masking when she stood up, sending the top of the stool spinning.

Train carried a large box to the mail cart for Ember, and when he came back, Killyama was working on another order. Then he was called away again by someone else. With Jewell gone, he had to troubleshoot any problems the workers had. He was then helping Rider fix the postage machine when Killyama tapped him on the back.

"I'm done with the orders on your desk. You have any more?"

"You're done with the whole stack?"

"Yes, and Stori checked the boxes for me to make sure I did them right."

"You could help me with mine until we get this machine working again." Rider swiped an ink-stained hand across his cheek.

She raised the bottom of her shirt to wipe the smudge away. "Whatcha gonna do for me if I do?"

Train had never seen Rider flustered. If he hadn't seen it himself, he wouldn't have believed it was possible.

"What do you want?"

"When's your birthday?"

"Why do you care when Rider's birthday is?" Train narrowed his eyes at her.

"Because I want to be there. You guys get some good shit."

"Next month," Rider answered.

"I'll finish your orders for you if you let me have the stuff you don't want."

"If I don't want it, why would you?" he asked suspiciously.

"I'm not as picky as you fuckers are. We got a deal?"

Rider nodded. "Only if I don't want whatever it is."

"Okay. Where's your work desk?"

Rider pointed toward the back of the factory.

"I see who's got the brains between you."

"Why?" Rider stared at her then looked at him.

Train shrugged, not knowing what she was inferring.

"Sucker. Train's workstation is by the boxes, popcorn spreader, and the mail cart. You have to practically walk through the entire factory every time you need those things."

Train bent down to look at the postage machine as Killyama strutted off toward Rider's desk.

Rider fumed. "We're switching stations."

"Don't blame me. I gave you first choice when we started working here." Train tried to keep from laughing.

"After you talked me into the one I'm at now. You told me it was farther away from Shade's desk. He doesn't work out of the office anymore, so you can switch me—"

"You really want Jewell watching every move you make? She already stays on your case for texting so much."

Train finally fixed the postage machine without Rider's help since he was busy studying the layout of the factory so he could move his workstation closer to the equipment and not have Jewell's censuring gaze on him.

Train lost track of what Killyama was doing when Stori came to complain that the seed refrigerator was leaking. He thought Rider wasn't the only sucker in the factory. Jewell had probably wanted the day off to keep from having to deal with the problems that were waiting to be fixed.

The rest of the day flew past. Every now and then, he caught sight of Killyama as she worked. But, as the workers started to leave, he didn't see her.

He walked through the factory and was about to go out the back door to see if she had decided to take a break when he saw her coming out of the door marked PRIVATE.

"How did you get in there?" Train asked her sharply. The only ones who had a key to that part of the factory were the founding members. They were never allowed to let anyone inside.

"It was open. I was looking for a packet of seeds. I must have gone in the wrong room."

Train clenched his teeth in fury at the lie. "That door is *never* open."

"Dude, I don't know what to tell you; it was open."

He stared at her angrily. "Tell me the fucking truth for once. How'd you get in the door?"

She narrowed her eyes at him, her lips tightening. "I'm. Not. Lying. What's the big deal, anyway? The bikes and cars in there are nice, but they aren't anything I haven't seen before."

"The big deal is that, unless you have a key, no one is supposed to be in there, so you couldn't have gone in there unless you have a key." Train looked down at his keys that were attached to his wallet, seeing the one to the door was still there.

"Maybe I picked the lock." Her smartass answer didn't lessen his anger.

"No, the door is solid steel, and so is the lock. Unless you have a blowtorch, no one is going through that door without a key. What was in there you wanted to see?"

"I was looking for the s-e-e-d-s," Killyama ground out. "You need me to spell it out again?"

"No, I got it the first time. Empty out your pockets."

"Are you serious? You really think I'm lying?"

"Empty your pockets, Killyama. Prove it to me."

"I'm not proving shit to you. The door was unlocked. Why would I lie?"

"I don't know," Train snarled sarcastically. "Why do you lie about anything? You lied about going to the Brown's training camp. You lied about working in Sex Piston's shop. Shit, you lie about what you eat for breakfast if you don't want me to know, even though I told you lying was a rule breaker for me."

"I only lie when it's none of your business. I don't need you keeping tabs on me!" she snapped.

"Well, that's not going to be a problem for you anymore."

"What'd you mean by that?"

"It means, I'm done. I won't take the safety of the club over you."

"I am not lying, Train."

"I don't believe you. Are you going to empty your pockets, or do I have to empty them for you?" He had to give her one last chance, praying she would empty out her pockets and prove she wasn't lying to him.

She crossed arms over her chest. "Go fuck yourself."

"Don't make me do this, Killyama. Just give me the key, and I'll forget about it." Again, he gave her a chance to redeem herself. It was a chance he would never offer another man or woman.

"No."

Train sighed, motioning to Rider who had been slipping up to Killyama as they argued. She caught the movement too late to react as Rider caught her in a bear hug, pinning her arms to her sides.

"Did you lock the front door?" Train asked Rider.

"Yes." Rider looked as coldly furious as he did.

Train caught Killyama's foot when she tried to kick him, holding it by his hip. Moving to her side where she couldn't use her free leg, he shoved a hand down the pocket that was closest to him. Coming up empty, he had more difficulty in the other pocket, finally succeeding, just to find it was also empty. She stopped moving as he reached around her to search her back pockets.

"Son of a fucking bitch," Train snarled, jerking away from her and touching blood on his shoulder. "Bite me again, and I'll call Viper to come search you."

She spat in his face when he moved to search her back pockets, but she didn't bite him again.

When they were done checking her, she tucked her T-shirt back into her jeans, frostily telling him, "I told you I didn't have the key."

"Do you have your key?" Train asked Rider.

"Check my keychain on my desk."

Train nodded at Killyama. "Don't let her go."

"I wasn't going to," he said coldly as Train went through the back area to where the workstations were, coming back with the keychain in his hand.

"Is it there?"

"No," Train answered, staring at Killyama, who was staring back at him stonily. He put Rider's keychain in his pocket. "Hold her tighter," he warned.

When she started kicking out again, he caught both of her legs. Using all of his strength, he managed to pin her thighs against his side with one arm, his free hand going under her T-shirt to her bra. He ran his fingers under the bra, feeling for what he was looking for and pulling the key out.

Releasing her legs, he stepped back, showing them both the key.

"Let her go, Rider."

Rider released her like he had just let a rattlesnake go.

"What were you looking for?"

"The bathroom." She put her hand under her T-shirt, not embarrassed by the proof of her deception.

"You want me to call Viper?" Rider asked.

"No, I will."

Train made the call, and then stared at Killyama while they waited.

When Train heard the knock on the back door, he opened it to let Viper and Shade inside. Then he stayed by the door, letting Viper deal with the situation. When she had refused to give him the key, he had lost the ability to interceded for her.

"How'd she get the key?" Viper asked grimly, staring down at the key Train handed over to him.

"She must have taken it off my keyring when she offered to fill the orders for me," Rider explained, glancing at Killyama before moving even farther away from her, as if revolted from merely being near her.

"If you wanted to see what was in there, why didn't you just ask Train?"

"I was just curious, okay? I didn't realize it was a big deal until Train got pissed." Her shrug didn't set Viper's temper off, but it did his.

"When you saw I was mad, why didn't you just tell me what you had done?" Train questioned, still hoping she would come up with an explanation for her behavior.

"I lost my temper."

"You lost your temper?" Viper gave her a deadly smile.

"Yeah. What can I say? I have a bad temper."

Her offhand answers had the brothers simmering. Her attitude wasn't helping her. It was making things go from bad to worse.

When Viper moved toward Killyama, she didn't so much as flinch, but Train saw the brief flash of fear on her face before she was able to cover it up with a sneer.

Viper brushed past her, going to the door behind her. When he opened it, he called for Shade and Train, and then turned toward Rider.

"Can you watch her on your own?"

"I got her," Rider answered as the three of them went through the door.

"Do you have any idea what she was looking for?" Shade asked as soon the door was closed.

"No," Train answered, knowing there was no way Killyama could hear them through the soundproof walls unless the door was open. "I don't know how long she was in here, either," Train admitted, staring stoically ahead. He would be damned lucky this time if Viper didn't take his jacket when he offered it. He had been the one who had given Killyama the chance to betray them twice now.

"I'll check the security room." Shade went to the back corner of the room, past the motorcycles and a few of the brothers' cars. The one he had borrowed from Moon was up on a hydraulic lift, waiting for him to change the oil.

Shade pulled a key out of his pocket that only him and Viper had and opened the lock. Train saw the light flip on, and then they waited as Shade went inside.

"What do you think she was looking for?"

Train looked around the large room. "She could have been checking to see if she recognized any of the cars in here. I've borrowed most of them when I was watching her."

"Could be. Hammer and Jonas are experienced enough that they might have seen you tailing them," Viper agreed thoughtfully.

It took five minutes before Shade returned to their sides. "I don't think she got in there. Whatever she was looking for must have been in the garage."

"Okay, so maybe she was just trying to see if you were tailing her, but brother, we still have a problem."

"I know. I already told her that, if she didn't hand over the key, I was done with her."

Viper nodded, satisfied the problem had been dealt with. "I'm sorry. I know you care about her."

"I love her, Viper, but I can't deal with her lies."

"I'm not going to ban her from the club this time. You brought her back to the club, you can deal with the fallout."

"I will." Train understood what Viper was telling him. He was going to take the heat for Beth and Lily's anger because Killyama would never again be allowed to step any part of herself on The Last Riders' property.

Viper left through the bay so he wouldn't have to see Killyama again. Meanwhile, Train went through the cars to satisfy himself that Killyama hadn't been snooping through them.

"You're being quiet," Train said to Shade, who had made no move to leave when he had finished.

"I'm thinking."

"What are you thinking? I'd love to hear it, because I'm so fucking mad I want to bust a wall."

"I think she was searching for something, but I don't know what or why."

Train grimaced. "I should have known something wasn't right when she showed up this afternoon. She never comes over until I call or text her."

"You didn't plan on her being here today?"

"No, she was supposed to be hanging out with Sex Piston. She said Rocky and Star had a virus. I believed her. She lied to me, and it wasn't the first time. Usually it's when she's with Hammer and Jonas. I've been telling her I don't like her bounty hunting."

"Why not? She's good at it. Damn good. She earned a reputation she deserves. Other than me, she couldn't be in better hands than with Hammer and Jonas when she's not with you." Shade paused before telling him, "Every month, Lily mismanages our checking account. She gives most of her paychecks to anyone who comes into the church store with a sob story. Every month, when we balance the checkbook, she hates to admit what she's done, saying she bought a new pair of shoes or a new dress, despite knowing I don't see any new clothes or shoes. When you're in a relationship, you get used to it."

"I don't have to anymore," Train said starkly, going to the door. "You coming?"

"You go ahead. I'm going to check around here some more. I don't need to be there to hear what you're going to say to her."

Train went into the other room. Killyama had climbed onto one of the tables that was used for items that had been ordered as presents. She swung her long legs back and forth as Rider stood nearby watching her.

"We'll walk you to your car." Train motioned her toward the door, not showing a hint of emotion.

Killyama jumped off the table, and Train and Rider followed her out the back door, Rider lagging behind them. She never looked at Train as they drew closer to her car.

Crash was standing on the club porch, staring down at them. From his face, he had already heard what had happened.

"Killyama, tell me the truth. Why did you do it?"

"How do you say fuck off in French?"

Train had trusted her, given her a part of himself he had never given another woman, and she was telling him to fuck off?

"I hope whatever reason you gave yourself was worth it."

Killyama's back was toward him as she opened the car door. Without a word, she got inside and shut the door. She was driving away from their relationship seemingly without a care in the world. Train wished he could say the same.

Then, a brief glance he caught of her reflection in the window stopped his thoughts. A flicker of hope remained lit in his heart. It was flickering, but it was still there.

Hope was a gossamer thread that tied someone to their beliefs. It could be strengthened by faith, or broken when it was stretched too tight. He believed that Killyama had a reason for breaking into the back room, but he was struggling with the faith he had in her that it was a reason that could justify what she had done. The only reason that thread between them hadn't been broken yet was his love for her. One more twist on it, though, and it would be severed forever.

There was no rebuilding his faith in her without an explanation, which she was refusing to do, so he had to either find his own answers or cut the thread himself.

Train gave Rider his keys back before going to his bike.

"You going after her?" Rider asked incredulously when Train started his bike.

He backed his motorcycle up. "No. I'm just going for a ride."

Peeling out, he drove out of the parking lot without any sense of direction, letting faith lead the way.

CHAPTER THIRTY-TWO

Train stared at the bedroom window, waiting for the light to come on. It was still early; the sun having come up an hour ago. He had no intention of waking her up so early, but the waiting was starting to get to him.

Sitting where she could see him if she looked out her window or open her door, he didn't want to startle her, yet he hoped she would see him before he had to knock on the door.

It was eight a.m. when he saw her bedroom light come on. He waited until he saw the light come on in the kitchen before he got off his bike and knocked on her front door.

"Train? What are you doing here?" Peyton asked as she opened her screen door, staring at him with a frown of concern. "Is Killyama all right?"

"Yes. May I come in? I'd like to talk to you about her." Train didn't expect her to let him in since he had only met her once, yet she opened the door without hesitation, inviting him inside.

"I'm making some coffee. Would you like a cup?"

"No, thank you." Train racked his brain, trying to find a way to start the discussion.

"You said you wanted to talk to me about Killyama?" she prompted.

"Yes, ma'am. I've been seeing your daughter for several months—"

"I know." She tightened the knot at her waist that held her housecoat together.

"We broke up yesterday. She did something that I consider a breach of my trust—"

Peyton held her hand up, stopping him. "I don't want to hear the details. If Killyama decided not to see you anymore, then I respect her privacy. I won't try to change her mind."

"I broke up with her. And it's not her mind that needs to be changed. It's mine." Train stared at her, willing her to see what was in his heart. "I love her. I have for some time, yet she continues to push me away by lying. Yesterday, she went so far as to steal a key off a friend of mine."

"She must have had a reason. Killyama never stole from anyone before." Her troubled eyes met his.

"That's why I'm here. I guess I was hoping you would know something that Killyama wasn't willing to tell me."

"No." Peyton went into the kitchen to make herself a cup of coffee. Without her makeup on, Train could see Killyama in her. Her mother wasn't as skillful as her daughter at lying.

"I'm sorry I can't help you. Are you sure I can't offer you any coffee?"

"No, what I want, you aren't willing to give."

"Call her. Try to talk it out…Maybe you will be able to work things out with her."

"I've tried. Believe me; I've tried. Do you know that she swears she'll never get married, that she doesn't want children?"

"She'll change her mind." Peyton's dismay showed he had exposed a sore spot.

"She might be pretending it's a joke to you, but she's serious about it. I tried to find out why she doesn't want a future with me, or any man, but she stonewalls me. A man can only take being told to fuck off so many times before he starts to listen. Either you help me or, so help me God, I'm going to walk out that door and I won't look back." Train gave the same opportunity to Peyton he had given to Killyama. If she didn't help him, he was done, and he let her see that truth in his eyes.

Tears welled up in Peyton's as she set her coffee cup back down on the counter with a trembling hand. "Will you give me a few minutes? I need to get dressed. There's something I think you need to see."

"All right." At this point, he was willing to do anything to shed some light on Killyama's behavior.

"Have a seat. It won't take me but a moment," she excused herself.

"Take your time. I'm in no hurry."

Peyton nodded then went through the narrow trailer toward her bedroom, while Train took a seat on one of the benches at the kitchen table. From there, he could stare out the kitchen window. He almost expected to see flashing blue lights, or Hammer and Jonas's vehicle pull up. He had offered to leave, but Peyton could have become frightened and used the opportunity to call the police or someone else she could trust.

When she returned, she was wearing slacks and a blue cowl neck sweater. It was early spring and the mornings outside were cool.

"The grass is damp in the morning," she explained as Train watched her slip on a pair of rain boots before going to the door. "Ready?"

"Yes."

Once they were outside, she stared wide-eyed at his motorcycle as if she had never seen one before. "You're not driving the truck?"

"No. Where are we going?" He got on his bike, holding his hand out for her to take.

"To my studio. The road there is even worse…We can walk."

"Get on. I'll go slow," Train promised.

Peyton took his hand, faltering as she got on behind him. Then she hesitantly placed her hands on his sides.

"Hold on," Train warned as he started the bike, turning it around in the yard before he went in the direction she pointed down the rutted road.

She was right; it would have been quicker to walk since it took them ten minutes to get to the trailer that was set off from the road. He had expected it to be the same as Peyton's, but it wasn't. It was much larger and newer, and definitely in better shape; that's for damn sure.

"You use this place as your studio?"

"I know. Killyama wants me to live here and use mine as the studio," she said as she got off the bike.

He followed her to the door of the trailer. It didn't have a front porch; stone steps led to the doorway. Peyton went up the steps first, unlocking the door, then Train followed her inside.

The outside wasn't the only difference between the two trailers. The trailer he entered was much more open and modern than Peyton's. Peyton's had a small booth for guest to eat at, whereas this one had a table with six chairs, the living room had a sectional couch that could easily seat many, and it even had a fireplace which Peyton easily flipped a switch to start. Train tried to hide his expression from her knowing eyes.

"I'm more comfortable in my home. I feel guilty this one's going to waste."

"It's not wasteful if you're using it."

"I made the master bedroom my studio. It's this way."

They walked down a hallway that was big enough for two people to walk side-by-side, leading to a door at the end.

Peyton reached for the doorknob but hesitated before opening it. "Killyama is the only one who has been inside. I'm trusting you, Train. I don't know why...but I do."

"Anything I see or hear will be just between us. I give you my word as a man of honor."

A wry smile curled her lips upward. "*Honor?* That means different things to different people. I hope it means something to you."

He nodded. "It does."

She gave him a searching look. She must have been satisfied with what she saw reflected in his gaze because she opened the door, stepped inside, and allowed him to enter.

Train leaned against the doorway, taking it in. The pieces he had asked to buy were there. The pictures hadn't given justice to the magnitude of seeing them in person.

"Rae never liked taking pictures, even as a baby. She would cry or make faces every time I tried. It was easier to get her to pose for me. Sometimes, it took several sittings to get the look I wanted to capture."

Rows after rows of sculptures replicating Killyama showed her growth from a child to the independent woman she was today.

"They're beautiful." Even the word spoken out loud didn't describe the beauty of the sculptures she had created. It was as if each piece had caught that part of Killyama that she didn't want anyone else to see. All the bravery she had shown when she had saved Lily and Winter's life was there, her sense of humor that always brought a smile to his lips, her stubbornness that drove everyone crazy. Train stared at them all, not touching as he took his time walking past the shelves until he came to the end.

"I just finished that last week."

"May I touch it?" he asked gruffly.

"Yes, just be careful."

He nodded as he picked it up gently.

"It took me several days to figure out which material I wanted to sculpt it out of. I usually do bronze, but I had a piece of emerald green soapstone that called to me." She gave a nervous laugh. "I know it sounds silly."

Train couldn't get any words out. Cradling it carefully, he stared down in awe at the expression she had managed to capture.

"You can have it if you want it."

Train raised his head at her offer. "Yes, I want it. I'll pay for it. How much do you want?" The emotions he felt weren't easy for a man like him, but the sculpture he was holding made it impossible to keep them in check.

"I couldn't take your money." She gently took it out of his hands before going to the window and letting the morning sun hit it. "Rae was talking about you when she posed for this. I know she loves you. She may not have told you, but she does."

Train felt the fragile thread of hope strengthen.

"Do you know why she would have stolen my friend's key?"

She shook her head. "No." Then she briskly set the sculpture on a worktable that had some drawings. "But yesterday morning, Hammer and Jonas came by and told me they were meeting Killyama. They didn't want to come inside, so they stayed out on the front porch until she arrived." She rubbed her temples with her slender fingers as she recounted what happened. "I was in the kitchen, and I couldn't hear much..."

"What did you hear?" Train moved nearer to the table.

"She was begging Jonas not to tell her something about The Last Riders."

Train felt his stomach clench in dread. The Last Riders kept a lot of secrets. One in particular that could destroy the whole club was buried a mile away from the clubhouse, on more property they owned. There was no way Hammer or Jonas could know about it, because it was *only* known by the founding members. None of the other brothers knew about it. Razer, Shade, Knox, Lucky, Cash, Rider, Viper, and Train himself would kill anyone in a heartbeat who tried to expose that secret.

Cash and Shade had found the spot when they had searched for Gavin after he had gone missing. Afraid he could have been lost or hurt, they had searched the entire mountainside, finding the two huge moss covered rocks that the men had to squeeze through to come out on the other side and into a large plain surrounded by rocks on three sides and the mountain at its back. The men had come to the conclusion that it must have been a crater that had been filled with time.

"Did you hear what Jonas said?" he asked.

"No. They went to Hammer's SUV and stayed there for almost an hour. When she came out, she went to her car and left. Hammer and Jonas came in to eat lunch, but they acted like everything was okay."

"Thank you for telling me."

Peyton looked like she wanted to say something else, yet she couldn't make up her mind.

"I know you've only met me one time, but I keep my word. You can trust me," Train assured her.

"I hope so. I won't be the only one hurt if you break your word to me." She straightened her shoulders like she was bolstering her courage. Then she walked to one of two closets in the room.

He didn't move, intuitively knowing she didn't want him to see what was inside as she slid the closet door open. However, he couldn't help seeing more shelves of tiny sculptures.

She pulled one from a shelf, bringing it back to the worktable and setting it down next to the one of Killyama.

As Train stared down at the man's face, it took him a minute of admiring the piece before he actually began to realize the face was familiar to him. He tried to place who it belonged to, but he couldn't.

"Who is this?"

"Maybe this will help." Peyton went back to the closet. "Rae doesn't let me keep anything of his around. She doesn't want to see it." She reached up to the top shelf, taking down a scrapbook, before coming back to the table and shoving her drawings to the side.

Opening the book, Train was floored at the image staring back at him.

"Major Timothy Cooper," Peyton said.

"I know who he is...He was in the SEALs. I never served with him, but anyone who's a SEAL knows of him. He's the one who inspired hundreds of men to join the Navy. He's won medals that are almost impossible to win."

"He's Rae's father." She flipped the next page over. It showed the major holding a crying baby as Peyton looked lovingly at the man who showed no pride or affection for the tiny infant he held. "I met him when I was sixteen. I had gone to stay with my aunt and uncle when my mother was killed in a car accident.

"I was jogging one day when a man tried to drag me off the path. Timothy stopped him. He helped me home and stayed with me until my aunt could come home." She ran a graceful hand over the picture; love in every brush of her fingers. "I became infatuated with him. I saw him several times when I went out jogging, and he would stop to talk to me. He would walk me home"—she looked up from the picture, blushing—"and I invited him inside.

"I didn't know he was still married then. Truthfully, I was so in love with him I don't think it would have mattered, anyway. He told me he was separated from his wife. Then, when he was selected to become one of the president's pilots, he admitted he was getting back together with her, that the president wouldn't allow any unmarried men on his team. That's what he told me."

Peyton had been a sixteen-year-old who had been taken advantage of by a man Train and others had respected. If the gossip had gotten out, his career would have been destroyed.

"I still remember that day. I'm ashamed to admit I begged him not to leave me. I told him I was pregnant and didn't know what

I would do. My aunt and uncle didn't know about our affair. They didn't want me there, much less help me raise a baby." She flipped over another page.

"He bought the trailer and the land to put it on. Timothy promised, when he could, we would be able to see us more. He was worried about anyone finding out. I didn't care, as long as I didn't lose him. I was willing to do anything he wanted.

"When he came to Jamestown, I thought we could go places and do things together, but Timothy was always worried about someone finding out, especially when Rae grew older and started calling him daddy. He would smack her hand every time she did and make her call him Timothy."

She lifted her lashes. "You can't hate me any more than I hate myself. I can't justify to myself why I let that happen. I had no friends or family by then—my aunt and uncle had died from cancer. I was so afraid Timothy would turn his back on me and Rae that I tolerated things I never would have done now that I'm older.

"Other than when he smacked her hand, he never touched her in anger...or affection. Rae adored him. She would stare out the window when I told her he was coming and wait until he got here. As she grew older, his visits came fewer and fewer.

"One day, when Rae was in school, Hammer and Jonas came with Timothy. He told me he wouldn't be coming back anymore, and Hammer and Jonas would help us move into a small apartment. I broke down. I didn't want to leave my home.

"The next day, Hammer and Jonas told me that Timothy had changed his mind, and we could stay. After that, we saw Timothy even less—maybe twice a year—while Hammer or Jonas were here every other weekend."

She flicked through page after page filled with pictures of Rae as a young girl. "She was an outstanding student. She would show Timothy her grades when he came, doing everything she could to make him proud. It was never enough. When she was little, she even told Timothy she wanted to go into the military like him when she grew up. He talked her out of it, saying she didn't have what it took to be a soldier.

"She was in sixth grade when the school band was asked to the inauguration. She kept saying the new president wouldn't care if Timothy was married. She kept believing that we would be a family. I tried to tell her it wasn't going to happen, but she just kept telling me, 'You just have to believe, Mama. I do.'

"When she came home from that band trip, the little girl who had left came back a young woman I didn't know." Suddenly, sobs tore from her lips. She pressed a hand to her mouth from crying aloud again. Train put an arm around her shoulder as Peyton gathered herself to continue. "She never told me what happened. Jonas did—they were there also. He said the students had filed in line to shake the president's hand, and Timothy was standing where they had to pass him. When Rae tried to take his arm and talk to him, he moved away as if he had never seen her before."

"The bastard is lucky he's dead." Train's harsh voice had Peyton crying harder.

"You want to know the sickest part? I didn't tell him to go take a flying leap the next time he came. We just pretended it didn't happen. Except, Killyama would find a friend or go to Hammer's to stay the night or whole day when he came, and she wouldn't come back until he left.

"The day he was killed by his wife, she laughed. She laughed so long and hard that Hammer had to take her to emergency room. They said it was hysteria. They had to give her a sedative to calm her down."

"I remembered when he was killed," Train said. "It made all the papers. He was coming home from a mission, and his wife was sitting on the steps when he came through the door. She shot him six times."

"Yes." Peyton nodded. "Killyama…By then she was grown, and they hadn't talked in years. I didn't handle it well. Even though I didn't spend much time with him, I missed him so badly that I'm ashamed to admit I turned to drugs. By the time Killyama found out, I was an addict and kept using them every chance I had. I refused to stop, sneaking out to get some during the middle of the night. She even took my car away so she would have to take me everywhere. When she was gone, I would walk to somewhere the dealers would meet me.

"One night I slipped out then came back to bed to pass out, Hammer, Jonas, and Killyama carried me out of my home and checked me into a rehab center. When I tried to leave, she told me it was the drugs or her. She told me that I had chosen Timothy over her and asked if I was going to choose drugs over her, too. I've been clean ever since."

"Can I ask you a question?" Train handed her a tissue from the desk.

She shakily wiped her tears away. "There isn't much I haven't told you."

"Why does she mail presents so I don't know who they're coming from? Why won't she just give them to me herself?"

Peyton's tear-filled eyes met his. "When she was a little girl and Timothy came by, she would draw him pictures he would never take with him. As she grew older, she would save her money to buy him things. The last time I remember her giving a present, she had bought him a watch. He left it sitting on the table in the kitchen when he left. Usually, I would hide the gifts so she wouldn't get her feelings hurt, but I didn't see it sitting there when we went outside to say good-bye. He was getting in the car when she saw he wasn't wearing it, so she said she would go get it for him. He left as she was coming out the door."

Peyton flipped the scrapbook closed before carrying it back to the closet. Then she opened the second closet. Taking out a small box, she then lovingly packed Killyama's statue with bubble wrap before putting it inside. Placing the lid on, she handed it to him.

"Remember, you gave me you word not to tell anyone."

"Her father is dead; why would it make a difference if anyone found out now? She made sure no one can discover who he is."

"Rae doesn't want his other children to be hurt because of Timothy's past."

Train shook his head in disgust. "That's why he didn't want her to go into the military. He was afraid she would run into her brother and sister."

"Yes." Peyton paused, then told Train, "If Rae took the key, she had a good reason. I don't know what it was, but if she knew it would cost her you, she would never have done it unless it was important. I'm not saying she isn't sneaky—the Lord knows that's why I gave her that silly nickname. What I am saying is that the woman on that sculpture wouldn't want you hurt."

"I agree. That's the one thing I do know now, thanks to you. I can wait until she's ready to tell me." He gave her a small smile in gratitude. "Can I give you a ride back to your trailer?"

Peyton shook her head. "No. I think I'm going to work for a while. I'm used to walking back and forth between the two."

"If you're sure." He looked around the place before saying, "You should get some security. No one is close—"

"Jonas did. I turned the alarm off when we came in."

"You put a lot of trust in a man you're just getting to know."

"Not really." She shrugged. "Killyama would have never introduced you to me if she didn't trust you. My daughter is a good judge of character. Much better than her mother."

"I think you did just fine. You raised a woman you can be proud off. A woman I hope to marry."

"Good luck with that." She smiled warmly.

Train started laughing. "I'm going to need a lot of luck. Fortunately, luck is on my side."

CHAPTER THIRTY-THREE

The grim-faced men entered the vacant building one at a time. It had been vacant for years before T.A.'s new boyfriend rented it for her. She had told him that she wanted it for her bookkeeping business. The numbnut must have taken too many tackles to have believed that story, but it had worked.

"Tracker is here. We're ready," Jonas told Killyama. "Hammer will finish loading up the equipment after you make the call."

"I will. I want to talk to you first." Killyama's hands had been clenched so tightly she had left marks on her palms. She had been standing apart from the men as they checked their guns. "We're wasting time, I know. I just…I need you to promise me something first. When we get there, I know one of you will want to be with me. Not tonight. Tonight, Train comes first."

"No way in hell! I'm sticking with you," Jonas argued heatedly as Hammer came over.

"I'm going to do what needs to be done, and then get the hell out of there. We've planned this for two weeks now. I know what I'm supposed to do. If Train gets hurt, though…If I know you both are with him, I know he'll come out alive."

Hammer's jaw clenched. "In and out, just like we planned."

"Yes." Killyama gave one curt nod. "Jonas?"

He nodded reluctantly. "Fine," he growled. "But I'm checking your equipment myself."

"Good." She briefly squeezed their arms before she took the cell phone from Hammer. "Let's get this show on the road."

❧ ❧

"You want to play a game of pool?" Rider asked Train as he passed through the club room after dinner.

"No thanks. I'm just going to go to my room and watch the news." Train started to pass Rider, but then felt one of the women jump on his back.

"That's all you ever do anymore. Come on; stay down here for a while." A pair of breasts rubbed against his back. "I want to play spin the bottle. Moon and Crash said they'll play."

"You don't need me, Stori. Some other time." *Like when Killyama is here*, Train thought to himself.

He was helping Stori off his back when he felt his cell phone vibrating. Looking down, he felt the sting of disappointment that it wasn't Killyama. Every day of the last two weeks he had hoped she would call to return the numerous messages he had left her.

"Hey, Stud, what's up?"

"What are you doing tonight?"

"Nothing. Why?"

"I just finished your bike. I wanted to see if you wanted to take it out and break it in." Stud's enthusiastic voice sounded like he expected Train to be just as excited.

"I'll come pick it up tomorrow. It's been a long day." The enjoyment of looking forward to the bike was gone.

"Come on; give a brother a break. I've been cooped up with four kids, and a wife who is mad at me because I forgot to start dinner. I rode it to the clubhouse. The brothers are sick with envy."

"Is Killyama going to be there?" Train asked. The tracker he had placed on her phone showed she was home.

"No. I think she's at home tonight."

"All right. Give me thirty minutes." Maybe he could use his new bike as an excuse for stopping by her apartment to show it to her, something to break the ice. He had already promised himself another week of waiting, then he had planned to take matters into his own hands.

"Ask Shade if he wants to come with you. He's been wanting me to make one for him, too. I've already sketched it out for him."

"If you rode my new bike to the Destructors' clubhouse, how are you going to get home?"

"I keep a spare bike behind the club. Don't forget your trailer, or you could let Shade ride bitch," Stud joked.

"I'm not even going to tell him you said that. The brother has no sense of humor. Give me an extra five to hook up the trailer, and we'll be on our way."

Train disconnected Stud's call then dialed Shade's number. He went to the hall closet, pulling out his jacket as members began moving the furniture so they could play their game.

"Stud just called," he said when Shade answered. "My bike is ready for pick up. He wants us to come over to Jamestown to break it in. You in?"

"No, I'm giving John his bath."

"That's fine. I'll tell Stud. He said he has the sketch of the bike you decided to buy—"

"Wait." Train could hear Shade turning off the water. "Stud said I wanted to buy one of his bikes?"

"Yes. Did he get it wrong?"

"No. It's just been a while since I asked him. When are you leaving?"

"I'm getting ready to hook the trailer up now. Five minutes give you enough time?"

"Give me ten. I need to get John dried off and dressed for bed."

"Sounds good." Train hung up, seeing that Moon had spun the bottle and it had landed on Sasha.

"You sure you don't want to play?" Sasha had already lost her top and bra. "Moon dared me to give him a blowjob."

"How's that a dare?"

"He dared me to do it hanging off the bar."

Moon was already helping her onto the bar.

Shaking his head at their antics, he told them, "I'll see you guys later. I'm going to ride my new bike."

The men didn't pay any attention to his leaving, too intent on Sasha.

Stori had Crash lift her up onto the bar, too, so she could see if she could do it.

Either he was going to have to get Killyama back soon, or he was going to have to stop watching the brothers play until he could.

He had finished hooking the trailer up when Shade appeared out of the darkness.

"Jesus, you scared the shit out of me!" Train grasped his chest. "Where the hell did you come from? I didn't see you come out of the club or down the pathway."

"I needed to get my bag out of the factory." Shade tossed his special ops bag in the back seat of the truck. "Help me get my bike on the trailer. I'll ride in the truck with you." From the warning glint in Shade's eyes, Train didn't ask any questions, just helped him roll his bike onto the trailer.

When they were inside and driving out of the parking lot, Train was about to ask Shade what he needed his bag for, when Shade stopped him, shaking his head.

Train gripped the steering wheel tighter, becoming worried about what they were heading into.

Shade turned up the radio and took a pen out of the glovebox. Train couldn't see what he was writing in the dark, and Shade didn't attempt to give him the note until they had stopped at a red light in town.

Train took the note from him, reading it.

I didn't ask Stud about buying a bike.

He crumpled it in his hand, giving it back to Shade.

When the light turned red, he floored the gas pedal, the note sending a sense of urgency through his bloodstream. He didn't know why Shade didn't want to talk, but he never questioned what he was thinking. It was obvious Stud was sending a private warning, needing Shade to come.

Stud didn't know that Shade was in the same special forces unit as Train, but Hammer and Jonas did. Anytime there was a mission, silence was mandatory. They each had a special phone they carried all the time. Neither him or Shade had heard from their unit commander, which was Hammer until the next round of recruitment when he was done for good. It could only mean one thing: a special mission that Hammer had instigated himself. That was the only thing that made sense.

He turned into the Destructors' parking lot, maneuvering the truck and trailer past the rows of bikes. At the back of the club, he saw Stud waiting on his bike.

As soon as Shade and Train got out, Stud tossed Train the keys to his new bike.

"Let's get Shade's bike off the trailer. Hammer is waiting."

With three of them helping unload Shade's bike, it only took minutes. Then Shade pulled out his black duffle bag, sliding the strap through his arms.

When Shade would have gotten on his bike, Stud stopped him.

"Take mine. I'm going to ride yours."

Shade wasn't happy, but he switched bikes without arguing.

As they got to the end of the parking lot, Stud motioned for them to stop.

"Give me your phones. All of them." Stud held his hand out.

Shade and Train looked at each other. They were putting their lives in Stud's hands, willing to follow where he led them, yet now he wanted them to give him their only way of communicating to The Last Riders?

"Hurry! We've got to go, or they'll leave without you," Stud warned.

Train had gotten to know Stud since he had started seeing Killyama, and he had started to respect the man almost as much as Viper. Therefore, both of them handed Stud their four phones, watching as he put them in his jacket pockets.

"When we get there, I'll point out the building, but I'm not stopping. The door will be open. May God be with you, brothers." Stud revved his engine, peeling out.

Train and Shade followed him closely, wondering what the hell they were going into.

They were a couple of miles from the club when Stud pointed toward a large building as he kept going, while Train and Shade slowed down, turning into the parking lot.

Train's adrenaline started pumping when he recognized a few of the cars. Hammer's, Tracker's, and O'Neil's, all members of their elite team, showed it was a high-level mission.

Shade met his eyes before he went through the door. Then Train really knew how bad it was when he saw the number of men getting into their gear.

"Train and Shade are here." Hammer's yell had all the men stopping.

"Did someone die and we don't know?" Train muttered to Shade, feeling a chill travel the length of his spine at the look the men were giving them.

Shade shrugged off his duffel bag. "I have a bad feeling about this one. I have since you told me what Stud said."

They went to a large table where plans were laid out.

"I've scheduled ten minutes to explain what's going on. You being late has taken three of them, so let's get started. Gather around!" Hammer shouted out.

Train watched as the men left what they had been doing to gather around them. When a woman stood up that he hadn't seen sitting at the back of the building, his control slipped, his anger coming out.

"Why in the fuck is Killyama here?"

Train had to put up with her chasing felons across two states, he damn sure wasn't going to put up with her going on a mission when they were loaded up with enough artillery to take out a small country.

ℝ ℞

Killyama felt Train's dark eyes drilling holes into her as she walked over to the command table. She loved him, so she would bear his hatred for her until this mission was over. Then she would get out of his life. Because...what he was about to hear was going to hurt him enough.

She could tell that both Shade and Train expected her to give him a jab at what he had said. Instead, she went to stand quietly next to Hammer.

"Killyama is here because she is part of this team. She's been given a job to do, just like I'm going to give you, yours. Jonas, cue up the video." He met both Shade's and Train's eyes. "The other members have already seen this video. Shade, Train, I'm sorry, but this is going to be hard for you to watch. I expect you to get your shit together once we leave this building. We have a job to get done, regardless of how it personally involves us. Understood?"

"Yes, sir," Train and Shade responded in unison.

"Good." He nodded once then continued, "Months ago, Killyama, Jonas, and I arrested a felon. It was a simple take down. Jonas and I kept the computer with every intention of turning it over to the police, but we long ago figured out some of the best ways of catching other felons is to find what they have on their computer. Is it legal? No, but we did it, anyway. We've never done it this way before, but when Jack Carter said he had friends who would come looking for us, we were concerned about Killyama's safety.

"I know some of you have already said that it jeopardized getting the jumper convicted legally for the crime shown on this tape, but personally, Jonas and I don't give a fuck. And if anyone else who watches this tape still feels that way, you're more than welcome to leave."

None of the men moved.

"Since no one is hitting the door, I'll go on. When Jonas managed to log on to the laptop, we found some sick shit. Jack Carter was involved with the dark web. He had a couple of tapes that turned my stomach, and there isn't much I haven't seen. Jonas was the one who recognized the man we're going to rescue tonight. This brother has been held in a nightmare, and one way or another, it's going to end tonight."

Hammer nodded at Jonas, who hit the play button.

Killyama couldn't watch the tape again. She hadn't even been able to watch through to the end the first time, vomiting in a bag in the backseat of Hammer's car. She kept her eyes on Train's reaction instead, trying desperately to control her own. When his face filled with unbearable agony, he grabbed Shade, who was consumed with his own grief.

"Oh, God, it's Gavin. Tell me that's not Gavin!"

"I can't, brother. It's him."

Train started to reach for the computer. Killyama thought it was because he still couldn't believe his eyes.

"Memphis killed Gavin. He admitted it!" Train yelled. "We tortured the son of a bitch. Why would he admit to something he didn't do?"

"Because he knew he was already a dead man," Hammer stated.

"I'd say that, once Memphis told you what they had done to Gavin when they held him captive, any torture you used on him would have looked like child's play to what you would have done after seeing this." Jonas pulled up another video that was just as sick as the first.

Killyama had been worried that after Train had admitted to the group of men that he and Shade had taken part in torturing Memphis that they would use it against them. However, her worry fell away when she saw the men's faces. If Memphis had still been alive, every man in the building would have killed him.

"You said *they*?" Shade's cold voice brought her attention to him.

"Yes, I knew Memphis had help when Killyama told me that the body dug up behind the Road Demons' clubhouse was identified by DNA. Killyama has lunch with Lily and Beth once a month. When they last went to lunch, she brought up the subject of Gavin, asking them if they knew where the DNA results came from that were used to identify Gavin—"

"Crash sent the DNA sample from the body to the military to cross check it with the records they have on file," Shade answered, cutting Hammer off.

"Yes, Crash used his computer skills to fix the results to make everyone believe the body was Gavin's."

"Turn that tape off before I fucking break it," Shade threatened, teeth clenched.

Jonas shut the computer with a snap.

"Where is he?" Train asked.

"Still with the Road Demons. Crash must have given them a heads up before Viper contacted them, asking permission to search for Gavin's body there. As far as I can tell from Crash's emails, they brought him back to the clubhouse about six months later. Stupid bastard was so cocky that he didn't protect his own shit because, he knew if any of The Last Riders wanted to know anything, they would come to him."

When Train went pale, Killyama looked away, unable to see the look of guilt on both of the men's faces.

"We need to contact Viper. He'll want to be here," Shade spoke up before Hammer could continue.

Jonas tucked the laptop under his arm. "Do you think Gavin is going to want his brother to see him in that shape? They made him a junkie. I think the only reason he's still alive is because the Road Demons are using him as their toy. You think, if Viper goes in there and see what's been done to his brother, there'll be a man left standing? Ohio isn't Treepoint where you have control of the sheriff. Forty or fifty men found dead in a bikers' club will make the news.

"Get Gavin back, and then take your revenge. I'm sure you can come up with something when you're ready. Killyama made it easy for you to keep track of Crash until you want him to know. She put a tracker on his motorcycle. One of mine, not that cheap shit he's been putting on your bikes so he knows every piss The Last Riders take."

"That's why you took Rider's key?" Train asked, though he already knew the answer.

"Yes, and put the port sniffer on his computer when he went to the restroom." She unrepentantly admitted the deception he hadn't caught when she had been by that unforgettable afternoon.

Her nightmares from Kane trying to rape and strangle her had disappeared within days, replaced by nightmare of her relationship with Train ending. They still filled her nights with dread, waking her in the middle of the night to see his accusing eyes staring at her in the darkness.

"As soon as we were able to hack into his computer and found where Gavin is, I called the men in to see the tape. You all will be putting your life and careers on the line. This is not a sanctioned rescue. That's why, when Jonas realized it was him, we didn't turn it over to the authorities. Gavin would have been dead before the police could act. And if we hadn't taken our time, Crash would have had him killed. Jonas and I didn't even tell Killyama until we were sure it was Crash who was posting the videos, and we needed access to his computer to know that for sure.

"We could still go to the cops in Ohio and take the chance that he will still be there, or that one of Road Demons won't put a bullet in Gavin's head to keep him from testifying that he wasn't there willingly. Train, Shade, if this is the way you want to handle it, we'll step down."

"No, I'm in." Train started taking his jacket off to get geared up.

"I was ready to leave five minutes ago. Show us the plan," Shade added.

As the men gathered closer around the table, Killyama held back. She didn't need to listen to Hammer and Jonas go over the plan again. They had gone over it so many times over the last three days that she had every room and doorway in the Road Demons' clubhouse committed to memory.

It was going to take four hours to get there. They had timed it so they would make it to the club in the middle of the night when most of the Road Demons would hopefully be asleep.

Jonas gave the men their wireless headset, reminding them to keep their night vision goggles at the ready.

"Finish suiting up. We're out of here in three minutes. Train, you're taking the lead. Shade, when you take out the Road Demons' lookout, try to get a clean shot. They're going to have a big enough mess to clean up inside the club without having to do the outside."

"Like I give a fuck." Shade's piercing blue eyes had Killyama taking a step back.

She was used to seeing him with Lily. The man she was looking at now was not that man. The man she was staring at now wasn't afraid of death. He wasn't afraid of anything.

"Load up," Hammer ordered.

She let the men go out the door first. Then, as she moved out, she saw that Train was waiting for her.

Speeding up, she tried to squeeze between two men so she could avoid the confrontation. She should have known better.

He took her arm, pulling her to his side. "Go ahead, Ghost, Bandit."

She had no intention of struggling in front of the men, but as soon as the door closed, she jerked her arm free.

"Dude, next time you lay a hand on me, you better be wearing that armor on your dick."

His grave expression didn't alter at her threat.

"We don't have time now, but when we get back, we're going to settle things between us."

"What's there to settle? We're done, remember?" She gave him the peace sign. "Peace out." She opened the door, hoping it would hit him.

"At least you didn't flip me off again. That's as good a start as any." Sliding on his wireless headset, he raised his brow when she started to let him have it.

Afraid the men would hear, she bit back what she had been about to say and climbed into the back of Hammer's SUV where Jonas threw her a searching look over his shoulder.

"It's a go. Let's bring our brother home," Hammer gave the order.

Killyama watched as Train pulled out in the lead with Shade beside him. The other men in the unit followed on their motorcycles, traveling in pairs until the plan would change once they rescued Gavin. Then the men would switch to groups of four and split in different directions.

They had to let the men stop for gas twice. Hammer had planned every detail of the drive, and so far, everything had gone off without a hitch.

As they got closer to their destination, Killyama's hand went to her gun holstered at her waist. Hammer and Jonas had made her go to the target range once a week when she had decided she wanted to work with them bounty hunting. She had never been so grateful for the enterprise they had instilled in her.

She calmed her breathing the way Hammer had taught her to when she heard Hammer tell everyone, "Lights off" as the Road Demons' compound came into view.

Killyama held on to the hand rest when Hammer swerved right, braking the SUV to a standstill.

"Go, go."

Killyama, with her night vision goggles on, jumped out of the SUV, pulling her gun out of its holster in the same motion. She didn't hear the sound of bullets, but she knew Shade had hit his target.

"Lookout one, down. Lookout two, down. Breacher, up."

Killyama moved from behind Hammer as he stormed the club, getting behind Jonas as they waited for Hammer to smash the door open with his favorite toy.

He rammed the door with his entry ram, smashing it open.

"Phase one, complete. Phase two, take over."

She made sure she didn't focus on the sound of the bullets filling the air, concentrating instead on Hammer's voice coming from her headset.

Hugging the wall, they went past three rooms before turning a right into another hallway.

"Breacher, up."

She made herself breathe steadily. They were getting close to Gavin.

As soon as Hammer breached the bedroom door, two men took guard to keep anyone who wasn't on their team from entering. Then Hammer and Ghost went to the bedroom closet, where Ghost used a small torch that had the padlock dropping to the floor in a second.

"Phase three, complete."

Shade went down the basement steps first, Hammer following with his MP5/10 held steady in his hand. Then Ghost went down, and then Train.

Killyama prayed for the next order.

"Retriever, up."

She stayed behind Jonas as they made their way down the wooden steps, forcing back the bile at what she saw.

A dog would have been treated better than Gavin had been. He was filthy and stank in the dank room. He was a man who was so strung out he was trying to fight his way out of Shade's and Train's arms.

"Move away, Train, Shade. Let Killyama take him." No emotion could be heard from Hammer. It wasn't time for that. They needed Gavin calm until they could get him out.

The men let Gavin struggle away from them. He lost his balance and fell back down onto the bed they had lifted him from.

Killyama moved over to him, keeping her voice sweet and cajoling as she gently patted his face to keep his focus on her. "Come with me, Gavin. I have something to make you feel better."

His wild-eyed stare switched from the men to her as she took his arm, helping him to place it over her shoulder. Lifting him, she then led him toward the steps.

"That's right. Just a few more," she cooed calmly as they took each step slowly.

He docilely followed her directions as Train and Shade led them out of the club.

Jonas was in front of them as they neared the hallway. They had to pass a door that had already been opened and cleared. However, as they passed it now, it swung fully open and a biker started shooting at them.

Killyama pushed Gavin into the wall, not releasing him as she pointed her gun at the biker, firing several shots into him.

As soon as he started falling to the ground, she was moving again, determined Gavin wasn't going to die in this hellhole.

Once outside, she filled her lungs with fresh air as Train opened the SUV's back door then ran to get on his bike where Shade was already starting his.

She shoved Gavin inside, jumping in and closing the door as a hail of bullets came down from the upper story of the clubhouse.

Hammer and Jonas got in just as quickly, Hammer yelling, "Phase four, complete! Hostage is secured. Fall out now! Go, go!" as he drove away from the clubhouse.

Killyama kept Gavin on the floor, lying on top of him as she listened to Train's instructions on the headset.

"They're coming from our back, Hammer. Ghost, you lead the way."

Killyama turned to see Train slow to take Ghost's position, watching as Train's headlight moved to the rear window.

"Bank left!" Train ordered.

She jerked her head back down when she heard a bullet hit the back of the SUV.

"Son of a bitch hit my car," Hammer growled into the headset.

"Bank right!" Train ordered.

"Take that southpaw out, or I will," Hammer ordered when another bullet hit the left side of the SUV.

"Get ready to bank left…Now!"

At Train's order, Killyama lifted her head again, despite Jonas telling her to stay down. She was unable to stop from watching, fearing Train would get shot trying to keep the three bikers from following.

When Hammer made the hard right, Train followed. His bike was so low he was riding the curve sideways. The hand that was controlling the bike had to be scraping the pavement as Train lifted his gun, hitting two of the three bikers and sending them speeding into a parked car on the street.

"Two down; one to go."

"I hope the one that will be spitting glass out of his mouth in the ER was the southpaw," Hammer groused.

"Bank left."

This time, she held on as Hammer made a hard left, nearly screaming as she feared the SUV would flip over.

When Gavin's own yell filled the car, Killyama tried to soothe him, murmuring softly to him and forgetting her headset was still on. Staring into his wild eyes with the night vision goggles now off, she tried to think of anything that would calm him.

"We have you, Gavin. You're safe now." She pushed back his greasy hair, telling him, "You know, you're better looking than your brother Viper. I bet the women fought over you. Viper's married and now has a baby girl since you were taken from him. He's missed you every day. All of The Last Riders have. You just need to hang on a little longer until we can get you to a place where you'll be safe. Can you do that for me?"

"Who…Who are you?" Gavin's voice came out in a way that sounded like he didn't know how to use it freely anymore.

"I'm Rae."

"Take me back to my room. If they catch me, they'll hurt you."

"Sweetness, no one is stupid enough to mess with me. You'll never go back to that room again—Viper will see to that. When he gets finished with the Road Demons, their club won't even be standing." She didn't make the promise lightly. If Viper didn't, she would.

She raised up slightly to reach for the baby wipes. Taking one, she used it wipe the dirt and grime off his face. "That feel better?"

She dropped the baby wipe when she saw his eyes start to roll.

"Gavin! Listen to me! Don't you quit now. I'm still here. I'm not going to leave you, so you better not leave me!"

"W-Why? No one else came for me. No one." His gravelly voice held a pain unlike anything she had ever heard before; a pain so deep and raw that only very few people on this earth could ever understand.

Killyama did something she didn't even know she was capable of. She cried.

"No one knew. They thought you were dead. They all did. Viper and Ton still don't know you're alive. They wouldn't have left you there if they had known. Not one day, not for one second. Sweetness, you weren't left behind or forgotten."

"Viper was mad at me. He…They all left me to die. Crash told me it was Viper's punishment."

"Crash lied. Viper would have killed everyone in there if he had known. There isn't a man in the club who wouldn't lay down their life for you." Killyama rested her head against his shoulder, letting herself cry silently for the broken man lying under her. "Did you see

Train and Shade? I should have taken a box of Kleenex inside with me, they were crying so hard."

"They weren't there—"

"Yes, they were. They were the ones crying in the corner." She reached for another baby wipe to dry her face. "I was the only one not crying."

"You're crying now."

"That's because you stink." She smiled in the dark before she felt Gavin trying to get out from under her. "Don't move; you're my Kleenex."

"I'm sorry. They wouldn't let me shower unless—"

She put her hand over his mouth, her tears falling harder. "You smell like a survivor, Gavin. Take a deep breath. You're free. You're free."

She couldn't hold back her sobs when he started crying, too. They tore through his chest.

"I...gave up."

"You didn't give up. You survived. You did what any good soldier would do. You did what you had to do to live. Don't you dare talk about stinking or giving up, or I'll kick your ass when we get out of this car!"

"Killyama!" Hammer's voice came through the headset.

"What?"

"You can get up."

"Okay."

Realizing the headset was still on, she took it off as she climbed up onto the seat. Then she reached down to help Gavin sit beside her. He started heaving.

"Here, I have a barf bag. Hammer's driving makes me puke, too." She handed him a bag that was tucked into the back pocket of the passenger seat.

He didn't vomit, but it was close.

Killyama pushed a button to lower the window.

"I thought I didn't stink," Gavin remarked when he saw what she was doing.

"I did that to give *you* some fresh air."

Laying his head back, he turned to stare at her. "You're lying."

"A little." She took his hand in the dark.

Hammer lowered his own window. "Good to see you, Reaper."

Gavin didn't answer. He couldn't. His head had fallen to the side, resting on her shoulder.

"Reaper?" Jonas turned around in his seat to check on him.

"He passed out. Keep driving. The sooner we get to the Destructors' clubhouse, the sooner we can take care of him. Stud will have sent someone for Dr. Price. He'll be there by the time we get there."

She didn't try to move Gavin away from her, putting her arm around him so he could lie more comfortably.

He was still asleep when Hammer brought the SUV to a stop at the back door of the Destructors' clubhouse.

Hammer and Jonas were getting out when Train opened the back door.

"He's unconscious." Killyama scooted out of the SUV so Train could reach inside, pulling Gavin out in his tight grip.

Hammer and Jonas stood on either side of her as they watched Train and Shade carry the brother who had been lost to them for so many years. The two Last Riders deserved to be the ones to bring an end to Gavin's journey home.

CHAPTER
THIRTY-FOUR

Train came out of the bedroom that Stud had given Gavin with Shade on his heels as Dr. Price immediately started checking Gavin's condition and giving him an examination.

"Did you talk to Viper?"

"No," Shade answered. "I called Knox. All the brothers are on their way. I didn't tell them why. It's going to hit them hard. I didn't want them wrecking while trying to get here."

Train saw Stud approaching from the clubroom and told him, "Viper and the brothers are on their way. As soon as the doctor gives the okay, we'll get out of your hair."

"Take your time. I closed the club to the Destructors tonight. You can lock the door when you leave."

Stud's compassion tightened the bond Train was starting to form between him and the Destructors.

"Has Killyama left yet?"

"No. Hammer and Jonas left, but I told her I would give her a ride home."

"I'd appreciate it if you and her stayed." Train looked away from Stud. "She keeps Gavin calm when he gets agitated."

"I'll tell Killyama. If you need anything else, just let me know."

"Thanks, Stud, I will."

Stud nodded then headed back to the clubroom.

When the doctor didn't come out after a while, Train and Shade left their post in the hallway and went to wait in the clubroom where they found Killyama and Stud sitting by the bar.

They were about to sit down at a table when Viper and The Last Riders came in.

Train and Shade shared a strained look as Viper stopped in front of them, Crash by his side.

"You couldn't wait to get back to our club to…" Viper's words trailed off when he caught sight of their expressions. He looked around the empty room. "What's wrong?"

Train's eyes met Crash's. "You want me to tell Viper, or will you?"

"I don't know what you're…" Crash paled, seeing his and Shade's condemning gazes.

Train lost it, and all the feelings he had been holding in erupted. Lashing out, he struck, planting his fist into Crash's lying mouth.

Knox tried to pull him back, but Train jerked out of his hold, knocking Crash into Razer and Lucky.

"What in the fuck!" Viper reached out to stop him, but Shade held him back.

"He deserves more than what Train's giving him."

Shade's cold voice had Train wanting to kill Crash with his bare hands, his instincts screaming at him to beat him until there was nothing left, but it wasn't his call to make. That wasn't the way The Last Riders handled their justice. Before he completely forgot that and dealt with the piece of shit himself, he stepped back.

"I called you brother…Every man here has. We put our lives in your hands countless times"—Train hit his chest with his fist—"and the whole time you were betraying us! You will never hear brother out of my lips again. I'm going to be the first one to spit on your grave when we get done burying you."

Knox and Lucky each took one of Crash's arms, holding him in place at Train's words.

Sickened at the sight of him, Train turned to Viper. "Gavin is alive," he choked out, the emotional upheaval of rescuing Gavin and having seen the one responsible for the years of torture of a man he considered a brother had him disclosing the reason for his fury. "Gavin's alive," Train repeated, seeing the men's stunned faces.

Viper's face twisted in grief. "No, he's not."

"He's alive. I wouldn't lie to you about this. Your brother—our brother—is alive."

Viper's face filled with anguish as he looked around the empty room, as if searching for Gavin. It was when his gaze skimmed over Killyama's heartbreaking expression that he believed what Train was telling him.

"Where is he?" Viper shouted. "Gavin! You got two seconds to tell me where the fuck he is or I'll fucking kill you."

It was hard to see the man who held every man, woman, and child belonging to The Last Riders' fate on his shoulders be told that the brother he had believed to be dead for seven years was still breathing.

"Brother, move or I'll move you myself."

"Viper, listen to us first. Then we'll take you to him."

Train stepped aside, letting Shade explain Crash's deceit. Every word that came out of Shade's mouth was like a slap to the face. They had all been in warfare and lost men in front of them, but nothing equated to what Train was seeing now as Shade described the hell that Gavin had lived through. All of the men were shell-shocked.

Before Shade was even done talking, Train was holding Viper back. Then Rider tried to go by him, his face tortured beyond belief. Stud managed to hold Rider back with Cash's help. After that was mayhem as all the men were either fighting to get into the hallway, or fighting to hold the others back.

"Shut the fuck up!" Killyama shouted. She was standing on her chair, facing the men and staring them down. "I'm telling you now, the brother you care so much about can't handle this shit. Do you want to hurt him more than what's been done to him already?" Not waiting for a response, she told them, "Go outside and walk it off, or beat the hell out each other—I don't care. But the first one who tries to go into his room without a smile plastered on their face, I'll fucking taze your ass!"

Viper broke free from Train's restraining hold. Train was afraid Viper would go after Killyama, even though Shade had told him it was because of Killyama, Hammer, and Jonas that Gavin had even been rescued.

Viper didn't go for Killyama, though. No, he went for Crash. Knox and Lucky barely had enough time to step out of the way before Viper had him by the throat.

"You stared me in the face when you told me Gavin was missing. You fucking cried when you carried that phony casket to the cemetery, telling me how fucking sorry you were that Gavin was dead." Viper's rage had him throwing Crash against the wall where the helpless man sank to the floor.

"Memphis told me he would kill me if I didn't help him."

Viper picked him up by his T-shirt, punching him in stomach so he didn't have enough breath to continue his lies.

"Memphis has been dead for five. Fucking. Years!" Viper screamed.

"And I was the one who helped you find the evidence to take him out, but then those fuckers put my head on the chopping block. It was me or Gavin..." Crash started to cry, knowing he had betrayed the men who called him family. "I didn't want to die."

Viper spoke so low that the menace poured from his words. "When I get done with you, even the Devil won't recognize you, *you get me?*" Viper hit Crash so hard the man fell back down to the floor, unconscious. Then Viper picked up one of the chairs, raising it over his head.

"Viper, this isn't the place." Knox caught his arm

"*God dammit to Hell*!" Viper cried out, throwing the chair against the wall where Crash had just stood.

Consumed with fury and pain, Viper went berserk, throwing chairs and tables until the room looked like a cyclone had hit it. He threw the biggest table, muscles straining as he lifted it. Then a chair went sailing over the bar, shattering the bottles into smithereens. One lone bottle of whiskey still clung to the shelf, its contents dripping to the floor.

Viper doubled over, hands on thighs, and Train had to blink back his tears as Viper gave a howl of pain that filled the clubroom. When he finally managed to stand erect, Train could see a cut on his cheek where a piece of shattered glass must have cut him.

Killyama strode around the bar, glass crunching under her boots. Taking a bar rag, she handed it to Viper.

He stared at it blankly for a second before taking it, wiping the blood from his cheek.

"Where is he?" Viper finally asked, tossing the rag onto the bar before he turned to stare at Train and Shade.

"I'll take you to him." Train nodded toward the hallway.

Viper stepped around the mess he had created, following Train down the hallway. At the door, Train knocked, and Dr. Price immediately opened it, looking out at the grim-faced men who filled the hallway.

"I've sedated him. Stud warned me what to expect, so I already set up the IV. Viper, I need to get him to the hospital to seek the best way to treat him. I can only give you a few minutes before I call the ambulance."

Viper nodded as Dr. Price moved away, letting him enter. Train and Shade followed him inside the small room where Gavin was lying on the bed, eyes closed.

Viper fell to his knees by his brother's side, tears streaking down his cheeks as he stared at him. Carefully making sure he didn't touch the IV, he pulled his younger brother into his arms.

"Gavin...Baby brother." Viper's hoarse voice had The Last Riders fighting back their own tears. "What have they done to you?"

Gavin's lashes rose, amber eyes staring uncomprehendingly up at Viper. He started struggling against his hold.

"Just kill me. I'd rather be dead than go back there."

"He doesn't recognize us." Train came to stand behind Viper, placing a hand on his shoulder.

"Gavin...don't," Viper pleaded when Gavin still tried to get away from his touch. "It's me, Loker."

"Loker, I'm sorry..."

Viper held him tighter. "I'm the one sorry, I didn't know..." His choked voice prevented from getting any further words out.

Train felt Killyama move near him. She gave a brief squeeze to his arm in compassion, aware of how devastated he was at watching Gavin's inability to recognize them.

"I sent Calder to get Winter and Ton when you told Stud that Viper was on his way. They're here."

Train turned to see Winter and Ton in the doorway as The Last Riders moved out of the way, letting them inside. From Ton's ravaged expression, he had only just been told his son was alive.

"Gavin..." He came to the other side of the bed, crouching down next to him. "Gavin!"

"Dad?" Gavin turned in Ton's direction.

Viper stood. Overwhelmed, he held his arms open to Winter, who flew into them, sobbing.

"My brother—"

"I know, Viper, I know."

Winter and Viper watched as the missing part of their family became whole again.

Crying, Ton pulled Gavin toward him. He stiffened, but let his father hold him.

"Don't let them take me back!" he cried.

"I won't, son." Ton rocked the man like he was a child.

Gavin didn't respond. He couldn't. He had passed out.

"Viper, the ambulance is here," Dr. Price interrupted as he helped Gavin lie back down. "You and Ton can ride in the ambulance with him."

They returned to the clubroom to let the EMT have enough room to get the stretcher inside. The broken furniture had been removed to a corner of the room by the brothers who were looking as anxious as Ton and Viper.

Winter held Viper's hand as they watched the EMTs wheel the gurney down the hallway.

When the men parted, Train could see shock and horror on their faces as they silently watched the gurney being wheeled by. The man who had left their clubhouse one sunny day filled with joy and excitement about going to Treepoint had ended up being unrecognizable to them.

Gavin made no movement or sound until he passed Killyama. Then he reached his hand out, making the EMTs stop.

"Any woman who lets me sleep on her shoulder, smelling like I did, deserves a dozen roses."

A grin tugged up at the corner of her lips. "It wasn't so bad once I got the window down."

"Do me a favor?" He waited until Killyama nodded. "There's a girl—Ton has her name. Call her for me. Tell her I'm..." Gavin started shaking but managed to finish asking for his favor. "Tell her where I am, and that I need her."

Killyama lifted her eyes to Train's, and his heart twisted in regret that the woman who Gavin had left behind was no longer waiting.

"Dude, that's one call that would be better coming from Ton. You don't want to make me jealous, do you?" She placed a tender hand on his. "Get some rest and feel better." With that, she stepped away, letting The Last Riders fall in behind him.

The ambulance's lights cast a glow over the parking lot as Gavin was loaded inside.

"What are we going to tell him?" Train asked Shade as they stood, waiting until everyone pulled out. It wasn't the first time the two had stood alone when a mission was over.

The adrenaline was gone, and in its place was a soul-wrenching discovery that the life Gavin had hoped to live was gone. The casket that had buried on that hillside might not be him, but the soul of the man he used to be wouldn't be coming back.

Grief filled Train in a way he hadn't expected, knowing the ambulance carrying the man inside wasn't the one he had shared beer, women, and dreams with. The eyes that had passed by him hadn't shown a flicker of acknowledgment. If that was hitting him hard, he could just imagine what Viper and Ton were going through.

"We'll tell him the truth. Gavin's strong, and Killyama was right; he's a survivor. Those bastards didn't break him. You can't break steel."

"What did you do with Crash?"

"Knox took him back to the clubhouse. We'll keep him alive until Gavin can take his revenge."

"The Reaper will have his revenge. Then The Last Riders can take theirs."

"Crash will be praying The Last Riders will go first."

The shape that Gavin was in, it would be a miracle if he survived the withdrawals.

"He better be careful of what he wishes for, because it just might come true."

CHAPTER
THIRTY-FIVE

"It's kind of small, isn't it?" Fat Louise remarked, closing a kitchen drawer.

"Bitch, it doesn't matter. I cook maybe once or twice a year." Killyama stared around the tiny living room.

"You might decide to. Then what are you going to do?" Fat Louise came around the kitchen counter, her expression showing she liked the living room less than the kitchen.

"Do what I always do—use the microwave."

"Let's move on to the other one," Sex Piston suggested. "Go look in the bathroom. You can't even squeeze in to put your makeup on."

"I'll take the key back to the landlord." She could deal with a small kitchen and living room, but she had to have a nice bathroom. It was her only necessity.

"This is the fourth one today. How many more are we going to look at today?" T.A. asked as she locked the apartment behind them.

"Just one more. If I don't like it, we'll have to come back another day."

"We've made three trips to Knoxville. You sure Hammer wants to move? There has to be better apartments in town than what he's sending you to."

"He wants to move. It's Mama who doesn't. She calls Hammer all the time, asking him to talk me out of it."

"Peyton's ass will be waving good-bye to you before you admit to yourself she isn't moving." Sex Piston put on a large pair of blinged-out sunglasses.

"She'll move."

"Bet she won't."

"What do you wanna bet?" Killyama tilted her head, considering her offer.

"The shoes Lily lent you." The black lens of the sunglasses turned toward her.

"No." Those were her shoes. Lily had finally stopped asking for them back. She had already taken grief from her as payment for not giving them back.

"You don't need them anymore, and I do. Stud gives me a little something extra when I wear them."

She firmly shook her head. "Pick something else."

"Then the beer cozy. That had to be cheap. Stud—"

"No."

"Damn, bitch, nothing else you have is worth betting on."

"I'll bet my bike that Mama will move to Knoxville."

Sex Piston lifted her sunglasses to rest them on her head. "You'd bet your bike, but not a pair of heels or a beer cozy?"

"Sure, why not? I know she will. Think about it while I go take the key back."

The bitches were already in the car when she came back outside. Sex Piston must have decided not to bet her because she didn't mention it again.

They didn't even get out of the car to see the last apartment, driving past without stopping in the sketchy neighborhood. After that one, Killyama decided to take the reins for her apartment search.

"Hammer said it was up and coming."

"Yeah, they come up to see it and run." Crazy Bitch rolled her window down, waving at a homeless man who was carrying a sign asking for work. He was going from car to car at the red light with an empty milk jug, asking for donations. One look at Crazy Bitch brandishing her Taser, he backed off, as Killyama was trying to get her money out of her wallet.

"Stop that. I was going to give him some money so he could eat." Killyama blew the horn to try to get him to come back.

"There's a liquor a store a block back. Just go there and buy him a bottle; save the fucker a trip." Crazy Bitch hung out of the window when he tried to approach them again.

Killyama heard zapping coming from the back seat as Crazy Bitch tried to scare him off again. Then, as the light turned green, she saw the homeless man picking up a rock to throw.

"If he hits my car, you're paying for the window."

"Sucker couldn't hit the side of a barn." Crazy Bitch scooted up until she was hanging over the center console. "Sex Piston, hand me her wallet. She can give me the five dollars I saved her."

"Crazy Bitch, if I pull over, you're riding back to Jamestown in the trunk."

They drove back to Jamestown after stopping for lunch. She dropped Fat Louise and T.A. off first.

Killyama looked at Sex Piston when she received another text messages. Sex Piston had been getting them for the last thirty miles.

"Is Stud texting you so much because we're running late?"

Sex Piston and Crazy Bitch were going to the Destructors' clubhouse, where they planned to hang out for a while. Stud was supposed to have met Sex Piston there twenty minutes ago.

"Stud and Lily," Sex Piston explained. "I promised Rocky's and Star's hand-me-downs for the church store. They're in my car. I was supposed to drop them by this morning, but you were bitching at me for being late to meet you. Stud's mad because he's hungry, and he wants to go out to eat."

Killyama frowned as she parked behind the club. "Why can't you just take them by her house tonight or in the morning?"

"That's what I've been trying to tell her." Sex Piston waved her phone in front of Killyama's face. "Lily said that the mother she had promised the clothes to is supposed to be there in an hour. The lady doesn't have a car, and a friend is bringing her to town to pick up the clothes. Lily says the woman can't be back to town for another week." Sex Piston gave a long suffering sigh. "I'll go inside and tell Stud to go without me. It's our date night."

Crazy Bitch was already shaking her head. "Don't look at me. My ass is already numb from riding in this back seat."

"I'll do it," Killyama offered. "It won't take long. You can get me a to-go order."

"I can do that. What do you want?" She held her hand out for the money.

"Where are you going?"

"Stud promised me the Green's Steak House."

Killyama gave a low whistle. "What'd you do to deserve that?"

"You bitches don't expect me to tell you all my secrets, do you?"

"Hell yes."

"I'll tell you when you get back. So, what do you want?"

Killyama opened her wallet, giving Sex Piston a twenty. "The cheapest steak on the menu."

Sex Piston kept her hand held out. "A twenty couldn't buy you a burger."

Killyama gave her another twenty. "That better include a steak and a baked potato."

Her hand still didn't move. "They charge extra for sour cream."

"I don't need it." She refused to fork over another dime.

"How about the tip? The waitress will add the cost of your meal to our bill."

Killyama reluctantly gave her another five. "If it costs more than that, buy me the burger."

"I'll get the clothes out of my car."

A few minutes later, Killyama left Sex Piston and Crazy Bitch, who were arguing whether or not Crazy Bitch could go with Sex Piston and Stud to dinner.

It was going to be a quick trip to Treepoint. She planned to be in and out. The diner was across the street from the church store, where The Last Riders ate frequently. If Train's bike was there, then Lily was going to be shit out of luck. She had no intention of seeing Train again.

He had tried calling her every day for the last week, so she had blocked his numbers. She had even gone as far as blocking Beth's and Lily's numbers when she had heard Train's voice after answering a call from Beth.

There weren't any motorcycles sitting outside the diner, so she parked in front of the church store and took the clothes out of the trunk.

Lily saw her coming, holding the door open for her.

"I really appreciate you doing this." Lily thanked her as she carried the two large bags to the counter.

"I wasn't doing anything." Killyama looked around the tidy store that Lily kept organized. She took in the sparse racks and shelves. "Looks like business has been too good."

The store had catered to low income members of the attached church. However, Lily and Lucky, who was the pastor, had branched out to offer clothes and gently used household items to the whole town.

"It always does when the seasons change." Lily started pulling the clothes Sex Piston had sent out of the bags. "This is going to help. There's enough here for three or four families who have children this size."

"I'll be right back. I left something in the car." Killyama headed to her car, taking out her wallet. Pulling out her checkbook, she filled out a check then signed it. Going back inside, she gave it to Lily. "You can use this to fill some of those racks."

Lily stared down at the check. "I can't take this—"

"I didn't ask. I'm telling you."

Killyama tried unsuccessfully to dodge her hug.

"Thank you so much, Killyama. I can even use some of this to buy a few backpacks for when school starts back up in the fall."

"Use it for clothes and coats. I'll make the Destructors kick-in for the Back to School Drive in a couple of months. Woman, quit hugging me. Someone coming in will get the wrong impression, like I'm nice or some shit."

"You can't hide good deeds from God."

"Well, I hope he remembers this one when he meets me, and not the other stuff he's going to blast me for when I arrive at the pearly gates. I better get going. Sex Piston is getting me dinner."

"Speaking of good deeds; can you do one more for me, please?"

Her shoulders dropped. It was hard to tell Lily no. Hell, if Killyama had been born with those violet eyes, she would have ruled the world.

"What do you need?" Killyama put her wallet back in her purse.

"I'm waiting for Krista to come pick up the clothes Sex Piston sent, so I can't leave the store. Do you mind going to the diner for me? I need a cup of coffee."

Killyama raised a brow. "What's wrong with the coffee in the pot behind you?"

"It's decaffeinated. It's all Shade lets me drink."

"You ever think of shoving that pot up his ass when he says that to you?"

She shook her head. "That wouldn't be a Christian thing to do."

"Maybe not, but it would be effective."

"I understand." Lily practically pouted. "I've already taken up enough of your time. I can drink the decaffeinated."

"Jeez…I'll get it for you."

Killyama brusquely left the church store, thinking, if one motorcycle was sitting outside, Lily would do without her coffee.

Since it was so close, she didn't drive. Seeing no cars, she walked across the street where she saw Knox dressed in his sheriff uniform coming out of the diner, carrying his coffee cup.

"Hey, Knox," Killyama greeted.

"Didn't you see the crosswalk?"

"What crosswalk?" she joked.

"The one you just walked by." Knox's stern face didn't even crack a smile.

"Yeah, well, I must have missed it. Gotta go."

Knox moved his large body to block her from entering the diner. "You can come back later for what you were in such a hurry to get that you couldn't take the crosswalk. Follow me to the office. I'm going to write you a ticket."

"Dude, I just crossed the street. I didn't rob the fucking bank," she snapped, trying to step around him.

"Go, Killyama. I'm not joking." Knox tried to take her arm, but Killyama jerked back from his reach.

"I seriously don't like to be manhandled." Her temper rose when he tried to reach for her again. "Diamond will k—" Her mouth dropped open when she found herself pinned against the diner's door. Her reflex was to fight him, but seeing the faces of the diners inside staring stopped her. "Asshole, you're going to be working at the factory when I get done suing you."

She felt the handcuffs clipped around her wrists before Knox turned her around to face him.

"You ready to walk to my office now, or am I going to have to carry you?"

Killyama kicked the coffee cup where Knox must have dropped it when he had handcuffed her.

"I guess you'll be carrying me, you—"

"You just added littering with malice to your charges," Knox stated grimly.

"What charges!" she screeched. Killyama forgot she hadn't planned on going with him as she tried to keep up with his angry strides.

"Jay walking, littering with malice—"

"Is that even a charge? I've never heard of that before?"

"...disorderly conduct, resisting arrest," Knox continued at he opened the door to the sheriff's office.

"How can you get me for littering? It was *your* coffee cup."

Knox skirted the counter where a tramp who had to be seventy years old was wearing a bright pink blouse that made her orange complexation stand out so much that Killyama wished she had borrowed Sex Piston's sunglasses.

Killyama expected Knox to sit her down on one of the chairs by a desk, but he kept going toward the back.

She looked back at the tramp. "Call Diamond and tell her that her husband has flipped his lid."

It was when she was locked in a cell that she truly believed he was serious.

"Knox, this isn't funny. At least unlock my handcuffs."

"Turn around."

She turned around, looking over her shoulder as she watched him unlock the handcuffs. "I get a phone call," she snarled.

"I'll get to it when I'm done booking you. Take a seat. It's going to be a while."

"Son of a bitch, when I get out of here, I'll own this fucking town," she yelled as Knox left.

Ranting until she ran out of steam, she then paced back and forth, waiting for Knox to come back and release her.

Surely Lily would become worried when she didn't come back to the church store. Sex Piston would also get worried when she didn't make it back to Jamestown.

Sitting down on the bunk, she stared morosely at the wall facing the cell, seeing wanted posters. Bored, she started reading them.

When the door opened, it took her a second to look. Then, when she saw Train, she started yelling at him before he could take a step into the room.

"Fucking hell! Are you—"

Train went back out the door, closing it.

Not letting up from screaming at him, she called him every cuss word she could think of and even made some up when she couldn't think of anymore.

Frustrated at his lack of response, she finally shut up and sat back down on the bunk. Ten minutes later, when Train came back inside the cell room, she ignored him, continuing to read the wanted posters.

"Look at me."

She pointedly laid down on the bunk, staring up at the ceiling.

Out of the corner of her eye, she saw Train lean against the cell, crossing his arms against his chest.

"I can stand here all night. I'm not leaving until we get everything straightened out between us."

"There's nothing to straighten out." Still refusing to look at him, she started counting ceiling tiles.

"You know there is, and you running away to Knoxville won't solve it."

"I'm not running from you. Why should I run when I can just kick your ass?"

"Because you love me, and you would rather move to Knoxville and uproot your mama than admit it."

"She needs to be uprooted. That tin can she calls a home will blow away with the next big storm coming our way."

"It's her choice to make, not yours. And that's not why you're doing it. You love—"

Jumping off the bunk bed, she screamed at him, "I *do not* love you!"

"You love me so much that it terrifies you." Train turned toward her. "I got the present you sent me yesterday. I put it on my bike. That kick back whip you sent me is black and red—"

"I didn't send you anything," she denied.

"When Stud gives me the go-ahead, I'll have to take it off. You'll have to buy me another one with blue and black colors." Train's sincere eyes stared into hers.

She gasped. "You're leaving The Last Riders?"

He nodded. "I've already told Viper. I can deal with the Destructors. They aren't The Last Riders, and I'll miss them, but I'll miss you more."

"I'm not asking you to give up the club. Why'd you tell Viper you're leaving? Dude, I'm not getting back with you. I told you that when you tried to talk to me after Gavin left for the hospital."

"Maybe not, but at least I'll be able to see you at the Destructors' club. I miss you, Killy."

She started pacing. "I'm not doing this with you. We are not getting back together. I don't even know if I like you."

"You love me."

"No, I do not. This is crazy! You had Knox lock me up just to convince me I feel something I don't." She sat down on the bunk. "Leave, and tell Knox to bring the key. I want out."

"I haven't had sex since the last time we were together. I can't eat. I don't drink anymore. I don't even watch the brothers have sex. I even found some more grey hairs. I owe Rider a hundred dollars because he knew I was thinking about you, and I didn't pay attention to my cards."

"I don't love you." She bit her trembling lip, turning her head so he couldn't see the telltale sign.

"I'm even willing to forget my rule about you lying to me. I'll even let you drive my bike."

"You going to ride bitch?" She turned back to stare at him.

"Yes."

"You had Rider hold me down!" She jumped toward the cells bars.

Train didn't even try to move away, letting her strike at him, seeing the hurt she had felt when he had told Rider to hold her as he searched her pockets and bra reflected in her eyes.

Stopping, she gripped the bars between them until her hands turned white.

"I know, and I'm not sorry. All you had to do was ask me for the key, Killy. That was all you had to do, but you didn't, because you couldn't bring yourself to trust me."

"I was afraid Crash would get suspicious and get the Road Demons to kill Gavin. It had nothing to do with trust. It had to do—"

"You couldn't bring yourself to put your happiness over someone's life. Do you know how rare you are? It's why I love you so much…You fought like a wildcat to protect Winter, Lily…You're a protector; you can't help yourself." Train pried her fingers from the bars, holding them in his hand. "If you had gone in the military, you would have had a uniform filled with medals."

"Timothy didn't want me to," she admitted, watching his reaction. "My mother told you, didn't she?"

"Yes." He squeezed her hand. "She told me everything."

Killyama sighed. "She doesn't want to move."

"I don't want you to, either. Stay, Killy...please."

"If I did like you..." She then added the end of her sentence hurriedly, "And I'm not saying I do. I don't want you leaving The Last Riders. They might not like me, but they love you."

"Babe..." He broke off at her dark look. "Killyama, they love you. We could compromise. Stay one week at The Last Riders' compound, and then we can stay at your apartment the next week. We can take turns."

"I'm not leaving my cat alone for a week."

"There's a large bedroom with its own bathroom where Lucky and Willa lived in until their house was built. It's empty. Viper would let me have that room if I wanted it."

"I could meet up with Sex Piston the week I live with you and drive in to Jamestown to meet up with Hammer and Jonas when I need to?" Killyama asked, hope brimming in her chest.

"Yes."

His fake acceptance had her grinning. "You're not going to bitch about me bounty hunting?"

"No, but when we get married, and you get pregnant, it stops."

"Deal." She turned his hand, shaking it hard.

"Don't think I don't know you accepted that deal because you never plan to marry me and have kids."

"Doesn't matter. A deal's a deal. Now let me out of this hell hole."

Train laughed. "Knox would be offended if he heard you call his cell a hell hole."

"He'll be lucky if I don't sue his ass. I still might when he gives me my purse back, and I get my cell phone. I'm calling Diamond. Fucker said I littered with malice. Number one: it was his cup. Number two: he was the one who dropped it, so he was the one who was littering."

"Killyama, you should have gone into politics."

"I know, right? I might need to go to law school so I can put bastards like him away for good." She pointed at the poster on the wall.

Train stared at the wanted posters, a frown furrowing his forehead. "What's he wanted for?"

"For being ugly."

He laughed. "You ever fuck in a jail cell?"

"No, and I'm not going to tonight. I've got to go—"

"I thought you would want to be with me tonight?" Train tried to kiss her.

"Not tonight. I gave Sex Piston forty-five dollars to buy dinner for me."

Train placed his hand on the door so she couldn't open it.

"Lover, I know you missed me, but I'm hungry, and I've already paid for it."

"Don't be mad. Remember, we just got back together."

Damn, the fucker was cute when he was afraid of her anger.

"It was Sex Piston's idea...how to get you to talk to me," he confessed, searching her eyes to see if she was mad.

"Is King's still open?"

"Yes." His eyes started twinkling.

"I guess you're taking me to dinner. You can buy me that big-ass T-bone steak on his menu. And you're getting back my forty-five dollars from Sex Piston."

"It'd be easier for me to give you the money back myself."

"Lover, if that works for you, that's fine, as long as it ends up in my purse."

ಇಂ ಡ

Train left the bathroom with a towel wrapped about his hips. He would ask Viper in the morning if he could take Shade's old bedroom, looking forward to the large shower that was down there, already anticipating many memorable showers.

He had wanted them to take that shower when they came back from King's, but she hadn't wanted to. Train thought she had wanted time to herself to call her mother who was still staying with Gavin.

Worried about her changing her mind if he left her alone too long, he opened the door to see her sitting on his bed. She was wearing one of his few white T-shirts. It was large on her, but he could still see the long length of her legs. She was brushing her shoulder-length hair.

He loved her curly hair. The dark mahogany gleamed in the glow of the lamp.

When he closed the door, she stopped brushing her hair, holding the brush loosely in her hand. She wrapped her arms around her knees, a swathe of hair covering the curve of her cheek.

"I have a confession to make."

Train moved closer to the bottom of the bed. "What is it?"

"I had already made up my mind to drive to the clubhouse and see you after I left the church store."

"Were you?" Train stared tenderly at the woman he loved more than life.

"Yes. I was going to be all romantic and shit, too."

"Really? I'm sorry I missed that."

Train threw his towel into the hamper in the corner of his bedroom, sitting down on the side of the bed behind her where he brushed her hair away from her face. She rubbed her cheek against the palm of his hand, but still wouldn't turn around to face him.

"Next time we get in a fight, I promise I will let you be the one to make up."

"I have something for you." She shifted slightly, reaching for her purse. "Close your eyes."

Train immediately obeyed, hearing the snap of her purse as she opened it.

"I kept it in my purse, not knowing when I would be able to give it to you."

Train felt her take his hand that had been pressed to her cheek, placing something in his palm. Then, leaning back against his chest, she relaxed.

"You can open your eyes."

Train stared at the black braided wristband. He smoothed his fingers over it, feeling the stiff leather that was also supple and soft. Braided into the wristband was a silver disc. His eyes narrowed, reading the Apache words she had engraved.

He huskily repeated the words his grandfather had taught him. "I love you."

Killyama raised the hand holding the wristband, pretending to squint down at it. "Is that what it says? Damn, I thought it said something else."

Train played along with her. "What was it supposed to say?"

"Mine."

"Put it on for me?" Train held out his wrist so she could tie it on his left wrist.

"You don't want to put it on you right hand?" she asked as she secured it.

"The left one is closer to my heart."

When she finished, he used the same hand to turn her in his arms. Leaning back against the headboard, he lifted her up until she was sitting on his lap, her knees on each side of his hips.

He knew how hard it had been for her to give him the wristband and the words she still wasn't able to say out loud. Subtly, he wanted to give her the control she still felt she needed. Killyama's father had all the control in his relationship with Peyton and his daughter. She had to learn Train's love wasn't based on control, but love and trust. Until she believed that, he would never see his ring on her finger, or a child they made in her arms.

He slipped a hand to the back of her neck to lower her mouth to his, whispering the words written on his wrist. "I love you."

She licked his bottom lip, her hands pressed down on his chest until he scooted down to lie flat on the bed.

"What are you doing tomorrow night?"

She lifted her mouth from his. "I'm hoping I'll be too tired to move from this bed. Why?"

"The club is having a birthday party for Rider."

"Then I guess I'll be here. He promised me the presents he didn't want."

"You're still going to hold him to that?"

"I may have stolen his keys, but I filled the orders before I did, so I did the job. I should get paid for my services." She ran a hand over his tattoo.

"I don't think he's going to look at it the same way."

"That's what I have my big, strong lover for." She pressed kisses along his breastbone, sensually rubbing her breasts against his chest.

Train cupped her ass cheeks as she bent over him. "You want me to convince Rider to honor the agreement you two made?" He smiled smugly when he reached for a condom, but she pulled his hand back.

"I have it covered." She twisted her T-shirt up to her belly as she sank down on his thickening cock.

He watched the euphoric expression on her face. He didn't need words from her when her expression spoke more than words ever could. Her hazel eyes even turned green with the emotions she was feeling.

He wanted to roll her over and pound his dick inside of her. Instead, he parted the lips of her pussy so every stroke of his dick rubbed against her clit.

"Lover, you get better every time I fuck you."

"I aim to please." He grinned suggestively up at her.

Her knees dug into his sides. "Yes, you do," she groaned.

"I have something I bought for you. Reach into my nightstand. There's a small box." Train gritted his teeth, trying not to come.

When Killyama pulled out the box, she set it down on his chest before removing the lid. After staring at it for a moment, she pulled out the fine silver chain, letting it run through her fingers.

"Let me take the shirt off," Train said, and she set the chain down so she could raise her arms up into the air.

Pulling off the shirt, he then picked up the chain, circling it around her waist before fastening it so it rested against her skin. Part of the chain dangled down with an emerald at the end.

"The emerald reminds me of your eyes."

"Dude, you sure you bought this for me? My eyes aren't green."

"They always turn green when I fuck you. It's how I can tell you want me."

"I'll have to remember that." She wiggled on his cock as she set the box on the nightstand.

Train arched under her to get her to do it again.

"Lover, I'm getting the message you want me to get moving."

He brought his hands to her hips, slamming her down on him and seeing the emerald flashing at him. "I was waiting to buy the letters that I will click on to the chain to spell out my name."

Killyama linked her hands with his, using the leverage to raise herself on his cock. "What are you waiting for...?"

Seeing her eyes widen, he turned, rolling over to thrust inside of her so deeply that it had her screaming his name out loud. Immediately, his climax took over at the bright emerald gaze staring back at him.

"I was waiting for you."

CHAPTER THIRTY-SIX

"You all believe in getting the parties started early around here," Killyama joked to Jewell as she came down the steps from upstairs.

"Ember is just the appetizer." She gave Killyama the first truly friendly smile since she started seeing Train. The polite smile was now gone, and so was the usual wariness.

"Where's Train?" She looked around the room at the rapt faces of the men, not seeing him among them.

"He's in the backyard, grilling the steaks. I see the top Sasha let you borrow and my jeans fit."

"Yes." The black Harley tank top had been sung, but the low neckline looked bitching on her, and the low slung jeans made her ass look like a million dollars. Suckers didn't know it, but they wouldn't be getting them back.

The two women walked outside together where Killyama saw Train at the grill with Razer. The other members were standing around, drinking beers and talking.

Nabbing a beer out of the cooler, she strolled up to the grill, handing it to Train.

"Thanks. It's hot as hell next to this grill. King was supposed to do the grilling, but he started talking to Lily and never came back."

"It's hot as Satan's dick out here." Looking toward Lily, she saw her drinking a soda. "I thought Lily didn't drink anything with caffeine in it."

"She doesn't. She must be celebrating because it's Rider's birthday."

"Hmm, so she didn't have anything to do with you getting Knox to arrest me?"

"Lily couldn't lie if she had to." He flipped the steaks, avoiding her knowing gaze.

She shook her head at his lie. They needed to have a long chat about his propensity to lie to her.

"Which bitch is supposed to come out of that cake Willa made for Rider?"

Train and Razer started laughing.

"No one. It's not that big."

Downsizing Rider's cake was another lie she would have to remind him about.

She patted his ass, deciding to give Beth and Lily the pleasure of her company. She needed to get away from the heat of the grill.

She sat down with them at the small table someone had set up. Lily was talking to Beth, blushing scarlet when she saw her.

"Are you mad at me? Do you want your check back? I haven't cashed it yet. Technically, I didn't lie. I really did promise the clothes to Krista."

"I'm not mad at you. I got my man, and I'm going to file a lawsuit with the city. So it's a win, win for me." She casted Knox a retaliatory look. He had gone to stand by the grill as soon as she had left.

"I would think twice about suing him. He is Sex Piston's brother-in-law, and you said you were going to ask Train to make him, his replacement when he said Shade wouldn't." Lily frowned unhappily.

"I changed my mind when he locked me up in his jail. Besides, Train isn't ever going to need a replacement. I'm going to keep that man alive so long he's going to make the record books."

"That's sweet. You must really love him."

"Lily, don't get on my nerves. I'm in a good mood."

"Come on; let's go make our plates before I tell Knox you're threatening me." Lily tugged her up to her feet.

Killyama let Lily and Beth get in line first. Train slid a big T-bone on her plate when it was her turn.

"Save me a place at the picnic table."

Killyama nodded, finding a spot where they could sit. Moon, Rider, Willa, and Lucky were on the other side of her. She waited until Train sat down before starting to eat, letting the talk flow around her.

"You're being quiet."

She finished the bite she was chewing. "I'm enjoying my steak," she complimented him.

"I aim to please." He grinned.

Despite herself, she leaned closer to him, but then straightened when she saw Willa glance at them.

"If she says we make a cute couple, I'm going to puke," she whispered out of the corner of her mouth.

Train squeezed her thigh under the table.

Relaxing, she finished the rest of her meal.

"You ready to cut your cake, Rider?" Willa asked.

"Hell yes."

Sasha and Jewell got up to clear the empty plates, and Beth and Lily joined them. Killyama lifted her plate then started to lift Train's.

"I'll do that." Stori stopped her, taking her plate and Train's before she could get up. "Just stay. We can handle the cleanup."

The other women all nodded.

Hurt, Killyama tried to keep it from showing. Even Lily and Beth hadn't wanted her help.

Feeling ostracized, she remained sitting, watching as Rider went to stand next to his cake. She was confused. At Train's birthday, he had opened his presents before the cake.

When Rider then made no move to cut his cake, Killyama looked around, seeing the whole club had gathered at the back door.

"Aren't we supposed to watch him open his presents first?" she asked Train curiously.

"No. Just wait. We have a surprise."

"I don't have to watch someone strip, do I?"

"No, babe, you don't have to watch anyone strip," he said softly.

"Thanks for my birthday dinner." Rider nodded to Viper who stood up from his seat to stand by the cake.

Killyama, feeling even more confused, watched Rider go stand with the members at the door.

"Today is Rider's birthday," Viper stated, and Killyama turned her attention to him. "But it's also our opportunity to thank someone who accomplished something we couldn't have done. Killyama brought Gavin home."

Viper's expression wrenched her heart. Her and Stud had gone to the hospital a few times to see Gavin, but he had been too bad off to visit. Viper had explained that the withdrawals were so severe that, as soon as he could be stabilized, he would be going to a rehab center that Dr. Price had suggested.

"I will never be able to express my gratitude, or The Last Riders', with words, because they don't exist. It doesn't matter that you belong to the Destructors', because you belong to us, too. Stud and I agreed you're just too much for one club to handle. You not only got all eight votes, you got every man and woman's who is a Last Rider."

The yells and cheers that came from all the members had her covering her face with her hands.

"Gavin said you deserved a dozen roses, and since Gavin can't be here to show you his appreciation for what you did for him, we wanted to make sure you got them."

When Train pulled her hand down, she saw Sasha place a red rose on the picnic table in front of her.

"Thank you, Killyama...for everything."

She moved away, and Jewell placed another one down.

"Thank you." Jewell wiped her tears as she moved away.

One after another, the women laid red roses down in front of her.

After Lily laid her red rose down, she came around the table to lean down to hug her. "Thank you, Killyama."

Beth then followed her sister's example, and it was everything Killyama could do to maintain her composure.

She was relieved when the women stopped passing by her, almost ready to break.

"I'm the birthday boy, so I get to go first." Rider laid a pink rose on the growing pile of red roses. "I bought my first collector Harley motorcycle for myself on my twenty-sixth birthday. I don't want it. It's yours." He laid a keyring down in front of her. "Thank you, Killyama."

Rider's façade as a ladies' man was missing. What she saw instead was heart-felt gratitude. She bit her lip to keep it from trembling.

Shade came next. At first, he didn't speak as he laid down the pink flower. When he did, Killyama placed her hand over Train's on her lap, gripping it tightly.

He laid a pistol case down on the table. "I got this gun from my father for my sixteenth birthday. I was saving it for John. I don't want it anymore. You can have it."

Lucky went next, setting down a Bible, a bottle of tequila, and a pink rose. "My mother bought me this Bible for my fifteenth birthday. I carried it with me every day when I was in the service. I don't want it anymore. The tequila, I got for my last birthday. I don't want it, either. May God bless you, Killyama. Thank you."

She blinked back the tears that were gathering in the corners of her eyes.

Razer went next, laying down another pink rose. "Beth bought me a booklet of gift certificates for a year of meals at King's restaurant. I don't want it anymore. Thank you."

Knox laid down a pink rose and a DVD collection of *Zombie Apocalypse*. "When I saw The Last Riders belt buckle that Train got for his birthday, I wanted one, too, so Diamond ordered one for me. She gave it to me as an early birthday present, and we already watched the DVDs. I really don't want them and the buckle was too small. She's going to buy me another one, so I don't want it anymore. It's yours. And anytime you get tired of bounty hunting, let me know. I'll hire you as a deputy. Thank you."

Cash laid down his pink rose. "My grandfather gave me this fishing pole for my birthday," he said as he looked over the pole still in his hands. "It was the last birthday I was able to celebrate with him. It's yours. I don't want it anymore. Thank you, Killyama."

As Cash walked away, giving the fishing pole one last look where he had laid it in front of her, the tears started slipping down her cheeks.

Viper was next, but Train turned to her. Reaching into his pocket, he pulled out a necklace and placed it around her neck. "My mother wore this necklace every day of her life. She gave it to me for my birthday, the day before I entered the service, so I could keep a part of her while I was overseas. I don't want it anymore. It's yours." The silver cross necklace sat snuggly in the curve of her throat. "Thank you, Killyama."

Viper then laid down three pink roses. "One is from Train, one is from Gavin, and the last one is from me." He looked up at the clubhouse as he told her, "Gavin and I bought this house when he decided this was where he wanted to build the factory. We split the property into different sections, giving some of the members a part of the land surrounding the club. Last year, I bought some land where I built my house."

Viper laid down an envelope. "It's not my birthday, but I asked Winter for her permission if I could gift it to you. She agreed. It's on the other side of my house. We had planned to give it to Aisha when she grew up, but I've change my mind. We don't want it anymore. It's yours. I hope someday you and Train will build your home there."

He continued, starting to look choked up, "It's because of you that Winter and our daughter won't have just my memories and photographs of Gavin. He'll be here with us. Thank you, Killyama." Viper's voice broke. "Thank you."

He strode away to where Winter was waiting with her arms open. Killyama had to look away when he buried his face in her hair.

She stared down at the massive pile of roses and gifts, whispering, "They don't hate me."

"No, they don't hate you. They love you."

"I won't go that far," she scoffed, unsuccessfully trying to relieve the emotional atmosphere. "But at least I don't have to worry about them cutting my brake lines. I can't keep these presents, though." She cried harder. "Well, except for the tequila...and maybe Shade's gun. John wouldn't have liked it, anyway. He's like Lily."

"Killyama, you don't have to give them back. We gave them to you to show you how much it means to us that we have Gavin back."

She used a napkin to wipe her tears away. "If you're sure, I can use the fishing pole when I go fishing with you and the guys."

Train's smile slipped. "The bothers don't let women go with us on our fishing trips, but you and I can go."

"Or the women can go on our own fishing trip, and you can stay behind."

"Okay, I think the men can live with that."

Mollified, she pushed the DVR collection to the side. "I can re-gift that to Sex Piston. Her birthday is next month."

Willa brought them both a slice of the cake. "I made extra this time. The top three layers are for you to share with the Destructors. I'll pack them up for you before I go to bed. They'll be in the refrigerator for when you leave tomorrow."

"Thank you, Willa."

She smiled, leaving to pass the cake out to the others.

Train helped her pack the flowers and the presents inside the kitchen. They found a couple of small vases, but they had to put a few in large glasses. The loud music from clubroom had the flowers shaking on their stems.

"I asked Viper if we could have Shade's old room, and he said yes. You want me to take you downstairs to show you?"

"Yes. I hope the bed is bigger than the one in your room."

"You're not going to have worry about that." Train grinned, going to a door on the other side of the table.

They were about to go down the steps when Moon came in from the backyard.

"Train, you busy?"

"Depends on what you need?"

"I need some help packing Rider's cake inside."

Train turned toward Killyama. "Go ahead downstairs. I'll be right behind you. Have a look around."

She went down the steps, seeing a stripper pole when she was halfway down. Crossing her arms as she stalked toward it, she walked around it. Then, putting out a hand, she tried to shake it.

"Fuckers, the gazebo outside is about to fall down, but a cannon wouldn't budge that pole."

She took deep breaths, trying to regulate her breathing the way Hammer had taught her. How many bitches' asses had Train watched twirl on it? Little Miss Innocent Lily and Beth hadn't mentioned it was there. Still waters run tit deep in this den.

She looked around, thinking how the exercise equipment would come in handy to work off all the weight she was going to gain at King's restaurant. Then she saw the door Train mentioned. Going through it, she opened the first door she came to, seeing a Jacuzzi.

"Now we're talking." The basement was made for Sex Piston. The bitch was going to have a fit when she told her about it.

Going back into the hallway, she found a bathroom. Taking advantage of the opportunity, she used it and washed her hands, surprised Train hadn't called out to her by now. She had told him that cake was big. Men always had to find out the hard way. Probably had to get more than two men to help.

The door at the end of the hallway was open. Her eyes widened when she saw the large room wasn't empty. Rider's muscular body was over Sasha's as he fucked her.

She turned to leave and walked into Train's chest.

"I'm sorry it took so long. You were right about the cake." Her man's eyes took in what was happening behind her back. "Sorry, Rider, I didn't know you were down here."

"The door was open. Stay if you want to."

Sasha's moans had Killyama giving Train a shove toward the door.

"Don't you want to watch?" He tried to look over his shoulder, but Killyama gave him a harder shove. She knew that glint in Train's brown eyes intimately.

"No. The only one who is going to get pounded into the mattress tonight is me." Slamming the door behind them, she put her hands on her hips, blocking him from opening the door again. "Dude, you're going to buy me a new mattress before I move into that room."

"You're joking, right? We always put clean sheets on the beds when we're done. Do you know how much mattresses cost?"

"Do you want to know what it's going to cost you if you don't?"

CHAPTER THIRTY-SEVEN

"You need any help?" Killyama swung her legs as she sat on kitchen counter, watching Ember and Sasha finish loading the dinner dishes into the dishwasher.

"No, there wasn't much to do. Most of the men ate out tonight." Ember carried two large containers of food to the refrigerator. "Usually the club is full when she makes her casserole."

Killyama shrugged. "You can't give men too much of a good thing." Especially after she had given all the wives the recipe so they could make it for their husbands anytime they wanted it. During the last two months, she had noticed how the men could barely stomach it anymore.

Jumping off the counter, she left the kitchen, seeing Train and Rider were still playing pool. Moon was sitting at the bar, drinking a beer as he watched the two men play.

Killyama was pouring herself a shot of tequila when the two women came out of the kitchen.

"I'm going to go wash my hair," Sasha told the men as she passed through the clubroom.

Ember entwined her arms around Moon's neck. "I want to dance."

Moon turned the music on louder then flipped the main lights off, leaving the lamps on in the room.

"I win!" Rider crowed, lifting his pool stick in the air.

Train laughed. "It only took three games to win one."

"Who's counting?" Rider said as they put their pool sticks down.

"I am," Train quipped, taking a seat at the bar.

Killyama gave him a beer as Rider sat down, lifting a brow when she didn't give him one.

"I'm not a fucking bar maid. Get your own beer."

Rider came around the counter to get his beer while Killyama finished her shot of tequila.

"Rider and I are finished playing. You want to dance some before we go to bed?"

"It's what I've been waiting for."

Train stood up, holding his arms open. "I'm yours for the rest of the night."

"Guess I'll join Sasha in the shower after I finish my beer," Rider commented, opening his beer.

Killyama grabbed Train by his belt buckle, leading him toward the dance floor. "You're mine all the time. Remember that." Slipping her arms around his shoulders, they danced to the music.

By this point, Moon was holding Ember's ass as she ground herself on his leg.

As she relaxed against Train, his cock hardened behind his jeans. He brought his hands to her back, sliding them under her tan and black crop top jacket.

As he rubbed her back, she pressed against his chest, teasing Train's cock with her pelvis during their sultry steps. She could see the desire growing in his eyes.

They tried to outdo the other by using their bodies to torment each other. The sucker thought he could beat her by sliding his thigh between hers, rubbing it against her pussy, which did feel good as the seam of her blue jeans rode her clit with each step.

Wanting more, she slid her hands under his T-shirt as he turned his head to kiss her. She went from want to need as his tongue traced her lips before dipping inside her mouth.

Train reached between them, lowering the zipper of her jacket. She didn't make him stop as he parted the jacket that was still held together by the bottom of the zipper.

Out of the corner of her eye, she saw Moon and Ember had stopped moving, and he had her pinned against the wall with her top down. Moon's back was to them, and Ember had better things on her mind besides the sight of Killyama's tits.

Train flicked one of Killyama's nipples with his tongue, lowering his lips to take the slight sting away. Her senses were swamped with the desire to fuck him senseless.

"You want to go upstairs?" Train asked before he took her other nipple between his teeth.

"In a minute," she muttered, sinking her fingers into his hair to lift his mouth back to hers. He tasted like a storm that was about sweep through her body. "We should have gone to your room five minutes ago."

An arm slid around her waist. With Train's hands on her breast, she tensed.

Rider's desire-thickened voice muttered in her ear, "Just dance. Pretend I'm not here."

Feeling Rider's body at her back and Train's at her front made her feel surrounded. She was honest enough to admit to herself that it felt exciting, and it wasn't the first time two men had tried to dance with her at the same time. Usually she would make one step off, but she didn't tonight.

Train's eyes lit on Rider's hand as it rested on her waistband. Tilting her breasts higher, he clamped his teeth around her nipple.

Killyama felt the jolt of pleasure like a streak of lightning from her nipple to her clit. If Rider had unsnapped her jeans, it might have led to a spark of insanity, but he didn't. He did slide his hand into her jeans, cupping her pussy as they danced. He didn't move his fingers, though, letting their swaying footsteps move them for him.

Her head dropped to Train's shoulder. She bit him through his T-shirt, trying to stop herself from moaning.

"You want me stop?" Rider's hard voice enticed her to arch her hips backward so she could feel her ass against his dick.

"No," she whimpered.

He slid one finger through her pussy, parting the lips so he could play with her clit as Train switched to her other breast. The loud music and the two men had her feeling as if she were being tossed between storms.

She felt herself being turned sideways, and then Train lifted her onto the pool table. Rider shoved the pool stick out of the way, his other hand never leaving her pussy, or giving her the opportunity to ride out the storm.

The storm built when his finger slid inside of her. She grabbed Train's T-shirt, holding on to keep herself from getting lost. When he reached down to unbuckle his jeans and pull out his cock, she didn't think; she just reacted immediately to the sight of the thick cock she wanted.

Train scooted higher so she could reach his cock with her mouth. Letting the head part her lips, she allowed him to dip it into her mouth. Then he pulled back before dipping in again, teasing her like Rider's fingers were doing.

When she felt a mouth brush over her shaking belly, she knew it was Rider's. His tongue investigated the curve of her belly button, playing with her belly piercing. Then she felt his mouth move away before she heard him unzip his jeans.

She raised her head to see Rider move closer as he finger-fucked her, sliding his cock along her waist. Then Train used her hair to turn her attention back to him as he plunged his dick deeper into her mouth.

Lightning streaked through her pussy as she arched into Rider's hand, letting them take control and giving herself over to the two men.

When she felt Rider's cock jerking against her belly, the carnality had her reaching down to grab his cock, giving him the relief he needed. Meanwhile, she continued to suck Train's dick harder as Rider's fingers gave her a storm-crashing climax.

"Dammit, I'm coming," Train moaned, holding her head steady as he angled her so he could reach her throat.

Killyama let him slip out of her mouth when his head went down to the green felt of the pool table.

She awkwardly saw Rider had removed his hand from her jeans and had taken off his T-shirt to wipe her belly off.

"Fuck." Killyama sat up on the table, zipping her top closed as she looked around. "Thank freaking God. When did Moon and Ember leave?"

The men shook their heads, unable to answer her question. They also hadn't made a move to zip themselves back up.

"Zip your pants up. Anyone could come in here," she snapped, getting off the table.

Train gave her a cautious look, as if she was going to rip him to shreds. Rider didn't look as worried, but he took a few steps away, waiting for her reaction.

"I'm going to take a shower and go to bed. I have to meet Hammer at eight." She started toward the kitchen.

"That's all you're going to say?" Train stared at Rider who didn't look as if he believed it, either.

"I'm not a fucking bitch." She glared at them, seeing they didn't believe her. "I'm not going to cry over spilt milk."

The two men relaxed.

Going to the door, she punched it open with her fist. "I just get even."

ONE YEAR LATER

"Open the freaking door, Shade!" Killyama blasted Shade with a heated glare that had no effect on him at all.

"No. You might as well go back to the bridal room."

"I'm just going across the street to get a cup of coffee." Frustrated, she tried to squeeze past him again. If she didn't have that ridiculously tight wedding gown on that Sex Piston had talked her into, she would have jammed a knee into his nuts.

As she huffily turned to go back to the room she had just sneaked out of, Shade said, "The next time you tell them you have to take a piss, tell one of them they better come to watch, or I will."

"Asshole, I don't know what Lily really sees in you…besides those tattoos." She went into the room that had six angry bridesmaids staring at her furiously.

"Bitch, have you lost your fu—freaking mind?" Sex Piston waved her bouquet at her, causing flower petals to drop to the floor.

"I told Train I wanted to postpone this wedding." Killyama blew a tendril of hair out of her eyes that Sex Piston had taken two hours to style.

"You told him this morning when you were getting ready to leave for the church," Lily reminded her.

"You already cancelled it twice. Look at it as third time's the charm." Fat Louise's chipper voice had her wanting to take off her garter and strangle her.

"I look at it this way…I said I'd marry him. I didn't say when." She clenched her jaw. "He suckered me into doing it. Kept telling me how beautiful I was every time I held one of you bitches babies."

The door opened, tempting her to take off on a run. They couldn't have all the doors covered. Most of the people should be sitting in the pews by now.

"It's time for us to take our places."

Her mother's watery eyes had her sighing. She was going to have to go through with it.

Her mother took her hand, giving her a tearful glance. "I've never been prouder of you, Rae. You look beautiful. I love you."

"I love you, too, Mama."

Her pumping heart started racing as her friends filed out of the room.

As she went through the doorway, she took a sidelong look at the door Shade was standing in front of. He waved at her.

Turning the corner, she flipped him off before stopping where the wedding planner had directed her to.

When Hammer and Jonas each took one of her arms, she blinked back the tears that were brimming in her eyes.

Hammer didn't look at her as the planner gave last minute instructions, telling her, "If I could have picked any man in this world for you, Jonas and I both would have picked Train. I served two tours with him and worked with him on countless missions. Train doesn't know when to quit, and even if he thought it would cost him his life, he wouldn't leave anyone behind. He's not your father. Train is the hero you've always needed in your life."

She squeezed their arms tightly, hearing the wedding march begin to play. "I've always had two heroes in my corner." Reaching up, she kissed Hammer on his cheek. "I love you, Hammer." Then, turning to Jonas, she kissed him on his cheek, too. "I love you, Jonas."

She smiled when they reached into their pockets for their handkerchiefs.

"Come on; quit be sissies. It's our turn."

ଚ୦ ଓଃ

Train fidgeted with his tie as he waited for Killyama to come through the church entrance. His fears wouldn't be at rest until he saw her. Getting her here had taken patience…a lot of patience, and determination, humor, empathy, and love. Not only from him, but from all of The Last Riders. They were his family and had helped convince the woman he loved that he was worthy of risking her heart for.

When he finally saw her, he watched as Killyama's hesitation left her face with every step she took to him. Then she stopped at the end of the aisle with Hammer and Jonas by her side.

"Who gives this woman in matrimony?" Lucky's clear voice could be heard throughout the packed church.

"We do," Hammer and Jonas both answered. Then Hammer turned toward Killyama and lifted her veil before kissing her cheek. Turning, she then let Jonas kiss her other cheek.

Train held his hand out for them to place her hand in his. Then he shook their hands before turning to Killyama.

She mumbled something he couldn't hear as they moved to face Lucky.

"What did you say?" Train's heart had stopped beating, panicked that she was going to tell him she couldn't go through with the wedding.

"I said," she whispered slightly louder, "I love you."

Epilogue One

Killyama swam naked through the water, her focus on the man sitting naked on the boulder near the shore.

Treading water, she flipped her wet hair back over her shoulders. "Why aren't you coming back in?"

"I was just sitting here thinking."

"You can't swim and think at the same time?" she teased.

Train stared down at her. "Not when I'm thinking about you. You take a man's whole attention when he's trying to figure you out."

"Tell me. Maybe I can help you." She leaned her head back in the water to keep her hair from getting frizzy.

"I was wondering two things."

"Damn, don't you think you should have done this thinking before you married me?" She frowned when she saw his serious face, her heart beating hard. Then she relaxed, knowing Train wasn't regretting marrying her. Otherwise, he wouldn't have done it in the first place.

"Why did you want to stay in Treepoint for our honeymoon? It was nice of Rachel and Cash to let us stay in their cabin for a week, but I offered to take you anywhere you wanted to go, even France."

"I didn't need to go anywhere. Everything I want is here."

She saw her answer had made him happy when his frown lightened.

"I thought it was because you didn't want me to fly us so far."

"You thought I was afraid of flying to France with you? I have flown with you before."

"Not far, and not where I thought you would want to go."

"See what thinking gets you? Come back in the water," she coaxed.

"Why didn't you go in the military? And don't say your father talked you out of it. I know you wouldn't let anyone talk you out of what you really want to do."

She treaded water closer to the boulder. "Come swim—"

"Tell me."

Her playful attitude dropped. "You're not coming in until you find out, are you?"

"No."

"My mother tell you about the trip I took to D.C.?"

"Yes."

"I never told her that I saw my father that day. He saw me and pretended he didn't know me. When we went back to the hotel, he called me and told me to never come near him in public again. He made me promise to stay away from him...and my brother and sister. They were there with them, and so was his wife.

"I believed that Timothy, Mama, and I were going to be a family. When I realized that wasn't ever going to come true, I made the promise. I was afraid that, if I went into the military, I would see them. My sister joined the Army, and my brother joined the Navy. I would break that promise if I went in, too."

"You could have joined the Marines."

She shook her head at Train's fury for her father's callousness. "Hammer and Jonas would have had heart attacks if I had. It was all good, anyway. I'm happy right where I am. Ultimately, I didn't join because I didn't want to leave Mama and the bitches."

Train dived into the water, swimming toward her. "So you weren't afraid of flying over an ocean with me?"

"No." She wound her arms around his neck.

"Don't forget your promise to me that you would quit bounty hunting when we got married."

She brushed the side of his jaw with her lips. "Not until I get pregnant, and that's not going to be anytime soon."

Train slipped his hand around her waist and down to the tattoo on her lower back. She had tattooed *Train*, with an arrow underneath and one single word that had given him hope when he had kept asking her to marry him. One word that also gave him hope that one day they would have a family.

Believe.

൭ ൬

"Afternoon, Commander Medina. You sent for me?"

"Come in, Captain." Train stared critically at the captain who wanted to make the team to follow in his father's footsteps. "Close the door."

The soldier followed the order without hesitation, standing at attention until Train told him to have a seat.

"I requested for you to speak to me." Train immediately brought up the reason for the captain's visit to his office.

"Permission to speak freely, sir."

Train didn't miss that stubborn jaw, nor the hazel eyes staring back at him as he nodded for the captain to continue.

"I received my invitation to join the squad this morning."

Train gave him a nod. "Congratulations. You will be an asset to the team."

"If you believe that, then why wasn't your score on my evaluation?"

Train leaned back in his chair. "It doesn't matter what my score was. The lowest is always dropped. Your lowest score was a ninety-six. You made the team regardless of me withholding my score."

"Commander, the team works as a cohesive unit. For that to happen, I would like to know if there is a problem between you and me before I decide to accept the invitation."

Train's mouth curled in humor. "There is no problem. You want my score?"

"Yes, sir, I do."

"Very well." Train opened his drawer to take out a flash drive. "To be a member of the unit, each member must be able to perform a variety of duties. That's why becoming a member is so difficult. You have exhibited this skill flawlessly. Actually better than my expectations." Train set the flash drive down on the desk.

The captain started to pick it up, but Train stopped him.

"You already made the unit. You can leave now and be content that you have fulfilled you and your father's dreams. You want my score, though, then solve the equations. The information on that drive was hard to find. I had it encrypted. It will take someone who wants to get into it to be able to read it."

"So, even if I can't solve the equations, I'm still on the team?"

"Yes."

The captain gave him a bewildered look. "I don't understand."

"Let me make it simple. When I give my word of honor, I keep it, but I'm breaking it for you. I hope you make it worth it. Good afternoon, Captain Cooper."

The captain stood up, and Train watched as he picked up the flash drive then left, closing the door softly behind him.

"I wish that was one trait Killyama had inherited."

∞ ∞

"Did you enjoy dinner?" Train asked as he parked.

"It was so good that I'm thinking of changing my name to Mrs. T.," Killyama joked as she got off his motorcycle.

"I never knew it was possible to be jealous of a T-bone."

"Lover, you don't have anything to be jealous of." She used his leather jacket to pull him close for a passionate kiss. "Especially when you taste like A1."

Laughing, they broke apart when headlight beams hit them as a car pulled into the parking lot.

"Who's that?" Killyama asked.

Train narrowed his eyes as the occupants got out of the car.

As the man and woman approached, Train put his arm over Killyama's shoulders.

"Commander Medina," both of them addressed him as they came to a stop.

"This is my wife...Rae," Train introduced her as Killyama remained quiet, staring up at him curiously.

"It's a pleasure to meet you," the man said as he and the woman held out their hands for her to shake.

After Killyama took their hands, she turned toward Train. "I'll go and let you—"

"Stay." Train's arm tightened around her. "Captain, Sergeant, I see you solved the equation."

"Yes, sir. You couldn't give me my score because the unit has a failsafe. No two family members, related by blood, are permitted on the team."

He felt his wife beginning to tremble under his arm.

"The equation was: you could remain silent about being related to your sister and protect your father's reputation, or you could get to know her." Train turned to look at his wife, waiting for her reaction. "Rae, this is Timothy Cooper the Second, and Marilyn Cooper-Smythe. They are your brother and sister."

Killyama practically buried her face in his jacket, achingly aware she felt inferior to them because of the feelings her father had ingrained in her from birth.

"Sir, no respect, but I'd rather have my sister than a position on your team," her brother spoke resolutely. "Marilyn and I both would like to get to know Rae, if we may?" His eyes searched Killyama's.

Killyama straightened, her courage never far away, even when she was overwhelmed. "Are you always going to talk like that?"

Train couldn't help smiling. "Rae, everyone calls him Boomerang, and your sister, Alice."

"Like Alice on the *Brady Bunch*?" She gave her sister a look filled with pity. "I'd kick anyone's ass who called me that."

Her sister shook her head, her hand loosening that had been gripped tightly on her brother's arm, her own nervousness apparent. "No, like Alice Cooper."

Killyama nodded in appreciation. "Hell, I could deal with that."

Her siblings laughed.

"Do you have one?" her brother asked.

"Uh…" She threw Train a dirty look when he couldn't stop laughing at her embarrassed expression. "Just call me Mrs. T."

Epilogue Two

Nine Years Later

"I didn't do it! You did!" Ela shouted at her younger sister.

"Don't blame me! I told you I couldn't reach it!" Bina yelled back, her eyes welling with tears as she bent down next to the shattered glass.

Killyama stood in the doorway, watching as her two daughters argued over who had broken the vase on her desk.

"Don't touch it. I'll pick it up." She stopped Bina before she could cut herself.

The two girls began crying when they saw her.

"I didn't do it, Mama." Ela shot her sister a furious look.

"Mama, I told her she wasn't supposed to be in here." Bina ran to her, wrapping her arms around her mother's thigh.

"You both know you're not supposed to be in here without my permission," she scolded them. "Don't move. I'll be right back."

Killyama went to the kitchen pantry, grabbing the broom and dustpan before hurrying back, afraid one her girls would cut themselves.

"Ela, I told you not to move. I'll clean it." She briskly swept up the mess, throwing it into the trash can beside her desk.

The sight of the roses in the trash can set the girls off in tears again.

Sighing, she figured she could mop the rest of the mess up after she dealt with her daughters.

She sat down in the leather chair behind her desk. "Come here." She held her arms open.

The girls clambered up onto her lap.

"I'm sorry, Mama." Ela patted her baby bump as if the unborn baby was upset, too.

"Me, too." Bina laid her head on her shoulder, lifting dark, soulful eyes to her. "Are you going to tell Papa?"

"No, you two are. We've told you over and over again that you're not allowed to play in here."

"I needed some paper. I used all of mine," Ela confessed.

"Then you should have asked. You knew I was busy with lunch and snuck in here, Ela."

Killyama's calm reaction started the tears flowing again, Ela's tiny shoulder shaking with her sobs. "I'm sorry."

"I can either trust you or start locking my door again. Can I trust you, Ela?"

"Yes, Mama. I won't do it anymore. I promise."

"I do, too." Bina wanted to make sure she wasn't left out if her sister managed to get out of trouble.

"Okay, I'm going to trust you both. Now go eat your lunch; it's getting cold. I made your favorite." She gave them each a big hug as they slipped off her lap.

"Save me some!" Killyama shouted out as she heard them running down the hallway.

She sat back in her chair, smiling lovingly at the sounds of their chatter.

"I told you it was going to be okay," Ela boasted.

"Papa doesn't know yet. He's going to make us sit in time-out," Bina reminded her.

Killyama used her boot to swivel her chair as they started conspiring on how to get out of Train's punishment.

"I told you to wait another year before taking that lock off," she reproved the painting that stared back at her.

Shoving her hands in her back pocket to keep from touching it, the sight of her husband never failed to impress her. It was her mother's talent in Train's portrait that had convinced Killyama to accept his marriage proposal. Killyama had known her mother could see into the soul of who she was painting, and she had definitely captured Train's. His love for her was evident with each brush stroke.

When she was working on a particular case, she could stare up at his portrait and ground herself again. Whatever horror that humanity was capable of, it was filled with love, too.

"I see the girls have been busy." Train's soft voice had her turning toward him.

"Dude, how many times do I have to tell you not to sneak up on me? You want me to give birth in my office?" she snapped.

Train gave her a smug smile, coming toward her to wrap her up in his arms. "You're only mad because I caught you staring at my picture again."

"You're lucky it's your picture hanging there." She sniffed indignantly, trying to pull away. "If Rider's bike hadn't broken down the day he was supposed to give me a ride, there would have been a different picture hanging there."

Train burst out laughing. "There wasn't a chance in hell of that happening," he boosted, gathering her closer.

"You don't think I could have made Rider love me?" She snapped her fingers in front of his face. "It would have been a piece of cake."

Train linked his fingers with hers. "Babe, I don't doubt you could have made Rider love you...if you had been given the chance. Why do you think his bike was messed up?"

Killyama narrowed her eyes on her husband's unrepentant face. "You sabotaged Rider's bike?"

"Yes. There wasn't any way I was letting Rider have first dibs on you."

She leaned up, kissing him. "Sneaky men make me hot."

"Papa!" Their daughters came running into the room, lifting their arms to be held.

Train lifted them up, kissing each of their cheeks. "What have you hellions been up to? I was only gone ten minutes."

"I *love* you, Papa." Ela turned his face toward her.

"I *love* you more." Bina made him turn to face her.

Killyama rolled her eyes toward the ceiling.

"Let's go let your papa eat his lunch. You can tell him how much you both love him when you're telling him about my broken vase."

Train set the girls back down on their feet. "You two go ahead. We're coming."

Their little shoulders drooped as they obeyed their father's order.

"I told you that boys are less trouble."

"Lover, don't blame me. I'm trying!" She pointed at her belly. "If this one isn't a boy, you're shit out of luck."

"It's a boy," Train declared confidently, bending down to place a kiss on her stomach.

She ran her fingers lovingly through his hair, whispering, "From your lips to God's ear."

༄ ༅

Sometime in the future...

The sound of the party taking place outside of the club was muted when he shut the door behind him. Going to the refrigerator, he pulled out another six-pack of beer, setting it down on the counter. Taking one out, he opened the bottle, his eyes catching the portrait hanging on the wall.

The large picture showed the founding members of The Last Riders. His eyes caught on the dark-eyed, somber man with the chain hanging down the side of his leg. He felt the same chain brush the side of his own leg when he turned toward the door.

"What's taking so long, Clash?" a sultry voice asked. "Brick is looking for you."

"Nothing." Clash turned back to the picture, tilting his beer bottle in salute before taking a drink then grabbing the six-pack to leave. "I'm coming."